To Alison

CIVIL GUARD

u... ...ed something
to... ...ve...

DIARMID MACARTHUR

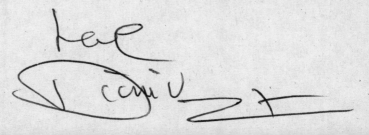

Copyright

SPARSILE
BOOKS

To my girls, with love.

Justice and the law, ladies and gentlemen, justice and the law.

A curious couple. You would be forgiven for expecting monogamy, a mutually exclusive relationship.

You might even suppose that, essentially, they are one and the same thing. The Law. The Scales of Justice. However, let me quote the good Mr Bumble, in Oliver Twist: 'But if the law supposes that...the law is *a* ass, *a* idiot!'

Well, that's pretty plain, eh? I'm sure you've all heard that expression before—"the law is *a* ass'. Then, on a more light-hearted note—and don't worry, I won't sing—there's our friend, WS Gilbert, librettist for Mr Sullivan's 'Iolanthe':

> 'The Law is the true embodiment
> Of everything that is excellent
> It has no kind of fault or flaw...'

I shall refrain from quoting the last line; I am not the law. But no fault or flaw? Do we really believe that The Law is excellent? That Law *is* Justice and vice versa? Let me conclude by quoting Johnson, a somewhat more reliable commentator:

> 'A lawyer has no business with
> the justice or injustice of the
> cause which he undertakes...'

Do we ask a prospective client if he is guilty or innocent? Or do we simply examine and consider the case on its legal merit alone? These are the questions that you will have to face in your career, in particular should you choose to go down the route of criminal law. Innocent or guilty? Does it really matter or is it simply a question of what we refer to as 'due process', the legal requirement that the state must, at all times, respect all legal rights owed to a person?

So there we have it, ladies and gentlemen, I rest my case; but before I leave you to retire and draw your own conclusions, I will sum up; in eight words, rather than my customary eight thousand.

Justice and the Law...two *entirely* different creatures...

RETRIBUTION I
Friday 17th October.

'You're making a huge fuckin' mistake. D'you know who I am, ya pricks?' I'll hunt you down, find out where you cunts live. I'll find your fuckin' family an' I'll hurt every fuckin' one o' them. D'you hear me?'

'I'm fuckin' warnin' you, let me go now an' I might be lenient—'

The blow caught Rik Shearer off guard, knocking him to the floor before he could finish the sentence. Still silent, his two captors tore a strip from a roll of duct tape, placing it securely over his mouth, although Shearer continued his remonstrations. He glared up at them, as if attempting to memorise the few features that he could see under their black balaclavas. His hands were tied securely behind his back, his ankles bound firmly together. One of the captors produced a Stanley knife and, none too carefully, started to cut away Shearer's clothes.

'Mmm...mmmph....bmmmph...'

He was naked now, lying on the concrete and shivering with cold, shivering with nerves, his bravado long since evaporated. He continued to stare at his powerfully built and black-clad captors as they made their preparations. A thick rope had been slung over one of the girders that spanned the abandoned industrial unit and Shearer was hauled to his feet, his bare toes scraping painfully along the rough concrete as they dragged him across the floor. The rope was attached to his hands, still secured behind his back. The men started to haul on it; slowly, excruciatingly, his arms rose behind him as his torso slumped forward. Behind the duct tape, Rik Shearer started to scream in agony, tears running down his cheeks as the pain intensified. It felt as if his shoulders were detaching from his body.

One of the captors held the rope, Shearer scrabbling with his bleeding toes for some form of support, some relief… the second captor walked over to a table, picked up a large square of cardboard and walked back towards the captive. It bore neat, black printing that Rik Shearer couldn't read; not that he cared…

The sign—for sign it was—was hung carefully around his neck by the attached string. The captor stood back, removed his mobile phone, took a photo then checked the image:

A blond, clean-shaven man, of indeterminate age.

A hard, lined face with a scar on his left cheek, just below his eye.

Naked, with an expression of agony on his face.

A cardboard placard, hung round his neck, which read

'Richard Shearer.
#1.
Who's next?'

He was about six feet off the ground now, eyes closed, concentrating all his efforts on keeping as still as possible to prevent further pain, further damage. The duct tape had been removed from his mouth; Rik Shearer moaned softly; he was beyond screaming, beyond threats.

His captors were moving something towards him; it sounded large and heavy and he forced himself to open his eyes.

'Oh dear fuckin' Christ, oh please, no…'

Chapter 1

Bruce Redpath walked over to the large bay window, took a deep breath and exhaled slowly as he gazed out at the view.

The blue-grey expanse of the mighty River Clyde was flecked with small white breakers, whipped up by the chill west wind that was blowing up the Estuary. The tide was out, revealing dark, oily seaweed-clad rocks among which herring gulls foraged, in a rather desultory manner, for shellfish. Maybe they were weary of human leftovers, he mused.

He turned and looked upriver, where a watery sun was shining on the distant houses of Upper Greenock, giving a false impression of warmth. However, a blustery eighteen holes round Greenock Golf club that morning had confirmed that autumn was well under way. A glance downriver, across to the Gareloch, showed an accumulation of dark, stormy clouds; rain was never far away from the tail o' the bank.

He consulted his watch. Four forty-five. Was it too early for a drink? Probably; he'd wait another hour, then pour himself a glass of fifteen-year-old Glenlivet malt and order his customary Saturday night takeaway. Lamb Rogan Josh with boiled rice, a Peshwari Naan, two papadums.

Bruce Redpath was a creature of habit, although not necessarily by choice. As he turned away from the window, the words of an old Drifters song came into his head, as they were wont to do most weekends.

'Another Saturday night and I ain't got nobody...'

He allowed himself a rueful smile; it certainly wasn't for want of effort on the part of Mel Connor, wife of his friend and golfing partner Rob. It seemed that every time he was invited to their house she managed to roster yet another single, eligible female friend to 'make up the numbers' as she euphemistically put it. The last occasion had been particularly tedious, ending with yet another round of the inevitable and awkward half-assurances of a follow-up call. With arched eyebrows and a rather haughty tone, Mel had actually suggested that, in future, she might invite a suitable male partner. Responding with his best 'courtroom' face (and much to Mel's surprise) Bruce had concurred and was awaiting his next invite with considerable interest.

As he walked across the spacious lounge, he caught a glimpse of himself in the large, gilt-framed mirror that hung above the fireplace; one of those unexpected glimpses, 'to see oursel's as others see us', as the Bard had once said. His sandy-brown hair was thick but greying; he was just above average height, with keen blue eyes set in a clean-shaven and kindly face, an asset when dealing with distressed female clients. A reasonable physique for his age. So why was he still alone?

He walked on; best not to dwell on it.

Five-forty-five; curry ordered and on the way, Star Wars Episode Seven lined up on the DVD. First of the evening—but not the last; certainly not the last...

As long as he limited himself to one beer with his curry, Bruce seldom suffered from a hangover, despite having quaffed a quarter-bottle of his preferred malt whisky. He woke on Sunday morning at eight-thirty, stretched and turned on his side, experiencing that same, momentary pang of surprise that he was alone. That same, brief, stomach-lurching sense of emptiness...

He sat up quickly, dispelling the thoughts that occasionally sneaked up and assailed his psyche; he had long since learned to compartmentalise these thoughts, albeit with some rather expensive liquid assistance. After all, what was money for? He decided to go downstairs for a luxurious coffee, a couple of slices of toast and the Sunday papers. His eldest daughter and her family weren't coming over until the afternoon, he could shave and shower later. Despite the rain that was lashing, wind-driven, against the double-glazing of the window, the house was warm and cosy. Bruce enjoyed his Sunday morning routine.

He sat in the comfortable, winged armchair, his back to the same bay window, and took a sip of coffee. He preferred a cafetiere—he had no time for those trifling, fiddly little pods that yielded about a half-cup of coffee. No, at least three mugs, accompanied by chilled single cream, were needed to see him through the first half of his preferred Sunday newspaper. He took a bite of his toast, ignoring the crumbs that tumbled down the front of his rather worn silk dressing gown.

He concentrated on the headlines; a bit of a 'no news' day, he thought. Some political shenanigans, some dire economic warnings, the usual health scares relating to some everyday commodity.

He started on his second mug of coffee and turned the page, where a secondary headline caught his eye.

'Glasgow criminal
brutally murdered'

He swallowed a mouthful of the delicious brown liquid and read on as he slowly munched his toast. Maybe he'd have another slice.

'The body of Richard 'Rik' Shearer was found yesterday in an abandoned warehouse in the south side of the city. The police are treating the case as murder. Shearer, sometimes known as 'Grandpa Rik', had been the subject of a number of high-profile police enquiries and, although never successfully convicted, he was suspected of being

the ringleader of a vicious Glasgow crime syndicate. A number of years ago, he received a 'not proven' verdict following his trial for the murder of thirty-year-old Shelley Moore, an employee in one of his tanning salons.

Although they are not releasing full details, Detective Chief Superintendent Norah Jarvis indicated that Shearer had been 'brutally and inhumanely tortured' prior to his death. She went on to say, 'Despite the fact that Richard Shearer was known to the police and had been the subject of a number of criminal investigations, he has now become a victim and the full force of the law will be used to bring his killers to justice. We cannot, of course, rule out the possibility that this is an act of retribution by a criminal rival, but the public can rest assured that the investigation will be conducted with our usual diligence. Our first priority, as always, is to ensure the ongoing safety of the general, law-abiding public and we will not tolerate anyone who decides to take the law into their own hands.'

Anyone with information relating to this crime should contact Detective Inspector Sorensen at...'

Bruce rubbed the stubble on his chin thoughtfully as he wondered briefly if DI Sorensen was a descendant of the famous Eric, a past player at Greenock Morton Football Club. He also realised that the name of Rik Shearer was vaguely familiar. He would enquire on Monday.

He sat back in his chair and considered the article; although troubling, it wasn't necessarily surprising, as the criminal fraternity had a habit of meting out their own justice. That justice was usually brutal, more often than not fatal but, fortunately, it didn't occur too often and, generally, they managed to keep it among themselves. He shook his head, a rather mournful expression on his face, an expression he often used when stating his client's case. Sometimes he despaired of the human race; they seemed to be distinguished by a dreadful propensity for inflicting pain and suffering upon one another. He closed his eyes, letting his guard drop for a moment...

Then he dozed off.

Nine-fifteen—an early night was in order, maybe a bath. He had been worn out that afternoon by his three-year-old, and much adored, granddaughter Amy. His daughter, Coral, and her surveyor husband Dan, had seemed to welcome the respite. At one point, they had actually fallen asleep on the couch while Bruce and Amy had made paper aeroplanes and dropped them over the top banister, watching them descend haphazardly and decidedly un-aerodynamically to the hallway below. Then, with only a slight pang of guilt, he had treated her to not one but two tubes of Smarties; he briefly wondered if he really wasn't a very good 'Grampa Boos' but the smile on Amy's chocolate-covered face had told its own story.

As he lay in the large, cast-iron tub, submerged to his neck in hot, soapy water, an unbidden thought entered his mind. He tried to compartmentalise it but, somehow, it refused to be subdued. It persisted, it fought back, like toothache.

What had been the nature of Rik Shearer's 'brutal and inhumane' torture?

Detective Chief Superintendent Norah Jarvis could have furnished Bruce with the information he sought; although she hadn't personally visited the crime scene, the report had caused her to lose sleep. Fortunately for Bruce, his imagination could never have visualised the grim and brutal reality of Rik Shearer's execution.

Bruce pulled out the plug and stood up, dripping water. He dried himself off and headed for bed, allowing himself a small whisky as a nightcap.

Just the one.

Probably.

◆◆◆◆◆◆◆◆◆◆◆◆◆◆◆◆◆

Blytheswood Square, Glasgow. There had been a time when it had held the somewhat unenviable reputation as being the haunt of 'ladies of the night' but, fortunately, those days were well in the past. Nowadays, the grand Victorian buildings surrounding the small, city-centre gardens consisted mostly of offices and restaurants.

At one end, the grandeur of Glasgow's former RAC club had been transformed into a boutique hotel. The taxi stopped at the opposite end and Bruce Redpath stepped out, nodding to the driver, who smiled back. The fare would be added to the account and a suitably large tip would be donated at Christmas time. He closed the cab door and climbed up the worn but spotless stone steps to the offices of Redpath, Fox, Carnegie.

It was eight-forty on a damp Monday morning and the lights were already on, office activity already under way. He turned the brass doorknob, pushed open the heavy outer door and entered the vestibule; a further glass door led into the reception area and this, too, he pushed open, to be greeted by the head receptionist, Rayna Aherne, who looked up from the desk and smiled.

His heart lifted. Rayna was Irish, married with five children and, in the eighteen-plus years that she had worked for the Firm, he had never known her to be anything other than irrepressibly cheerful. This was more than could be said for the rather sullen-looking young man seated next to her, currently engaged in a phone conversation with what sounded like an irate client. Although speaking in a polite and educated voice, his expression clearly indicated he'd rather be elsewhere. Bed, probably, Bruce imagined.

'Good mornin', Mr Redpath.'

'Morning, Mrs Aherne.'

In the course of those eighteen years, she had only ever called him Bruce on four occasions. Once when she had been exceedingly drunk. On the other three occasions, when some instinct, maternal or otherwise, had told her that it was the appropriate form of address.

'Good weekend?'

'Oh, pretty quiet, a round of golf on Saturday morning, then...'

'... a lamb Rogan Josh?'

He laughed.

'You know me too well, Mrs Aherne. But the highlight was a visit from Amy yesterday.'

Rayna's face lit up; she adored kids. 'Ah, and how is the wee darlin'?'

As always, her soft brogue came to the fore when discussing children. Or dogs; cats; grandparents... But Bruce knew that, as soon as she lifted a phone, she would have one of the most polite, distinct voices he could ask for from a receptionist. She was often mistaken for being from Canada or New Zealand, and equally often complimented on her telephone manners. He had sometimes wondered what her admirers would make of her at the office Christmas night out.

'She's an absolute joy, I must bring her up to meet you sometime, you'd love her.'

Rayna's eyes went all misty at this proposition. 'Any time, Mr Redpath, I'd be delighted to meet the wee sweetheart. Anyway, Mr Fox is already in the meeting room. I'll wait until Mrs Carnegie and Mr Caira arrive, then I'll arrange for your coffee.'

Bruce smiled. 'Thanks, Mrs Aherne.'

He turned to leave; it was a good start to the week.

The door to the meeting room burst open and an attractive if slightly harassed-looking woman entered. Simon Fox glanced surreptitiously at his watch then looked up at her, raising an eyebrow.

'Oh, don't bloody start, Simon, it was a nightmare getting in this morning. Bloody train stopped just outside of Central. God knows what was wrong...morning Bruce, morning Peter.'

Simon Fox favoured solicitor Olivia Carnegie with a wide grin as the others returned her greeting.

'Oh, sit down, Liv, and have a coffee. Don't want the week to get off to a bad start. It's only fifteen minutes, after all!'

Olivia Carnegie attempted to glare at Simon but, as always, his broad, beaming smile was impossible to resist. With a shake of her head, her scowl faded to her own, rather reluctant, smile as she placed her tan leather briefcase on the polished table and sat on the high-backed tweed-upholstered chair. Bruce watched as she ran her fingers through her short, perfectly-styled ash-blonde hair; in fact, almost everything about Olivia was perfect and he occasionally wondered if she felt, somehow, that she always had to be the best-dressed, the most successful—a woman in a man's world, perhaps? She had no need; with an expensive private education in the capital city and a first-class honours degree from St. Andrew's university, Olivia Carnegie was as good a lawyer as any man Bruce had encountered. He lifted the cafetiere that sat on a silver tray, then poured a small amount of cream into the white china cup.

'Thanks Bruce; God, I needed this,' she said as she took a sip.

'Children, children,' interjected Bruce. 'Behave! I've got a meeting at ten. Right, what's on today's agenda?'

Bruce Redpath smiled; he loved this part of his week, the first hour of each Monday being given over to a partners' meeting; Simon Fox, until recently a criminal defence lawyer extraordinaire, had taken silk the previous year and was now a QC; Peter Caira, a talented corporate lawyer and Olivia Carnegie, a specialist in property law. Olivia could speed-read a fifty-page lease in about ten minutes and find half a dozen faults that others would miss in the course of a couple of hours.

Bruce and Simon had studied law together at Glasgow University and, although their backgrounds were somewhat diverse, they had become close friends, finally setting up in business together. Redpath Fox. Back then it had been a room above a Chinese takeaway in Glasgow's Duke Street but their fortunes had changed. These days the firm boasted a fine suite of offices in a rather grand Victorian building in the now-prestigious Blytheswood Square. Olivia Carnegie had joined some twelve years ago and, despite both she and Simon being in seemingly-happy marriages, Bruce had the sneaking suspicion that there may have been at least one liaison between the two partners. He didn't ask; as a highly sought-after divorce attorney, he felt it best to let them sort it out themselves, as long as it didn't get in the way of the business of Redpath Fox Carnegie! Peter Caira had joined them a few years back, when the need for a corporate specialist had arisen. He was a quiet, self-effacing man with a shiny bald head and dark, round spectacles; however, when it came to his corporate legal talents, the best description Bruce could ever come up with was 'shit-hot'. He smiled at the thought; it was a suitably allegory as, all things considered, despite the banter and the bickering, the four partners got on like a house on fire!

The meeting was nearly over, the final item on the agenda having been the sullen young man at the reception desk; Torquil Carnegie. His mother, Olivia, had held great aspirations for him to follow in her footsteps but, having achieved considerably less than the required grades in his sixth year, he had now departed from his expensive private school and was assisting Rayna Aherne at the front desk. Bruce felt that Torquil was more of a hindrance but, as always, Rayna never complained, simply stating that 'he'll come all right in the end—they always do!' The decision was made to retain him for the moment until a parental decision was made on his future.

The meeting over, Olivia and Peter departed; \as Bruce stood up, he looked over at Simon.

'Em, did you read that article in the papers about that criminal being murdered?'

Simon shook his head disinterestedly.

'Didn't get a chance to look at the papers yesterday.'

'It was just that the name seemed familiar. Rik Shearer. I had the feeling that he may have been a client.'

Simon finished packing his briefcase and looked up.

'Shearer? Hm, rings a bell...may have defended him a few years back; why do you ask?'

'Oh, no reason, it just seemed a bit...well, grisly, I suppose. The police were quoted as saying he was brutally and inhumanely tortured first.'

Simon sniffed.

'Well, that's the criminal classes for you. Still, as long as they keep it among themselves...speaking of which, I need to dash, the Flint trial's coming up and I need to straighten a few things out with my client. Be prepared, as the Boy Scouts say.'

Bruce gave a wry smile. A request for Simon Fox was usually considered a clear indication of guilt and, according to the media, Suzannah Flint, although undoubtedly a particularly wicked woman, was already deemed guilty of the murder of a young Glasgow prostitute. Trial by the Press, he thought to himself. Simon, who was now pulling on his expensive woollen coat, would have his work cut out for him. As he picked up his briefcase, he smiled; what Bruce always thought of as the Cheshire Cat grin.

'Not entirely sure where my fee's coming from. I suspect Ms Flint has a rich boyfriend tucked away somewhere. She's not saying who he is, however...listen, what's the interest in this Shearer fellow anyway?'

'Oh, nothing in particular, it was more the 'brutal torture' bit...' Simon winked at his friend as he opened the door.

'You've got a terrible penchant for the macabre, Bruce, I really think you should have specialised in criminal law. It'd have been right down your street. 'Bye.'

<hr />

Helen Street, Govan; the vast pre-fabricated warehouse proclaimed itself to be the headquarters of Hooley Transport, a fact confirmed by numerous powerful tractor units parked outside. Painted in green and white, with 'Hooley' in black letters, they were accompanied by an array of trailers, some flatbed, some curtain-sided, parked in rows awaiting their next consignments.

Just inside the warehouse, another Monday morning partners' meeting was about to take place, albeit in considerably less salubrious surroundings. The participants, in the drab, dingy office, were equally less salubrious. Seated in a decrepit leather armchair was the man, known in the circles he frequented, as 'The Lawyer'. Paul Maguire had, indeed, been a solicitor until a series of financial misappropriations had resulted in his disbarment. He sucked greedily on a cigarette, his gaunt, grey cheeks hollowing as the smoke filled his lungs. He wore a suit and tie, last remnants of his former career, but closer inspection would reveal the shabbiness of his attire. He squinted through a cloud of cigarette smoke at the man seated opposite him; his employer, he supposed, the term 'friend' implying a questionable level of mutual affection.

David Doyle lit his own cigarette, puffing out a cloud of tobacco smoke as he snapped the lid of his Zippo shut and placed the shiny silver lighter back in his pocket. Son-in-law of Frank Hooley and managing director of Hooley Transport, Doyle was a grizzled, hard-looking man in his late forties. He had been born and brought up in Glasgow's East End, where his former classmates included a number of career criminals.

Doyle spoke, his voice deep, guttural.

'Where the fuck is Pig? Ah told him tae be here fur half-nine.'

Maguire shrugged. 'Not a clue, Davie. Maybe he's forgotten.'

'Fuckin' better no' have...aye-aye, here we go...'

Despite the near-certainty that the visitor would be HGV driver John Piggottt, Doyle surreptitiously reached below the top of the battered wooden desk. Many years ago, he had watched a film in which a private detective had a shotgun installed below his desk. Given his own line of work, Doyle had considered it prudent to do the same. The gun was extremely well concealed and few knew of its existence, but Paul Maguire was one; he slid his chair sideways...just in case.

The figure that entered the room appeared to have stepped out of a fifties movie. Thick dark hair slicked back in a quiff, a checked shirt stretched tightly across a broad chest, skinny jeans and cowboy boots. He even had a red scarf knotted around his throat. There may have been a time when John 'Pig' Piggott would have been considered handsome; now he just looked ever so slightly ridiculous, although woe betide anyone who cast aspersions on his self-perceived allure. He sat down on the vacant chair, took out a tobacco tin and removed a pre-prepared roll-up.

'Mornin' Boss, Paul. Sorry Ah'm late, traffic wis a fuckin' nightmare the day.'

'Aye, well, let's get started,' replied Doyle. 'Got a nice wee job fur ye, Pig. France this time.'

Piggottt pulled a face as he lit his roll-up, the end paper igniting briefly in a tiny flame.

'France? Fuck sake, Boss. Whit am Ah pickin' up—bloody frogs?'

Doyle and Maguire exchanged a sly look.

'Naw, onions.'

'Onions? Yer fuckin' jokin, man!'

Doyle shook his head and gave an evil smile.

'Onions is good, Pig. You ever smelt a container full o' onions? Pure stinkin', which is exactly whit we need tae cover the smell o' the *real* cargo...'

The details of Piggottt's forthcoming trip were discussed with a level of precision and detail of which even Bruce Redpath would have approved. Forty-five minutes later, Piggottt left the smoke-filled office, closing the door behind him. As they listened to his departing footsteps, Maguire lit a fresh cigarette.

'You hear about Rik Shearer?'

Doyle nodded. 'Aye. Deserved whit he got, evil bastard that he wis. Sounded nasty though—any ideas who wis behind it?'

Maguire shook his head. 'That's what worries me. If it's who I think it might be, well...'

An uneasy silence hung between them for a moment, as acrid and unpleasant as the thick blue smoke.

Chapter 2

Wednesday 22nd October

It was Wednesday evening when Bruce received the call, having just finished a pepperoni pizza with a token gesture of side salad. He muted the television and took a sip of his Glenlivet.

'Mel, how are you?'

'Oh, fine, thanks. Busy as always, you know what kids are like. What are you up to?'

'Just finished dinner and about to catch the news. You?'

'Oh, just finished the kids' homework and about to have a glass of wine. Rob's still at work.'

Rob Connor was a detective chief inspector, based in the concrete carbuncle that posed as Greenock's police station. Bruce had the feeling that, for reasons that were quite beyond him, it had recently become a listed building!

'Ah yes, the protector of all that trust in thee!'

Mel laughed. 'Don't you quote common prayers to me, Bruce Redpath...oh, for goodness sake, Ailie, I'm on the phone to Uncle Bruce...Bruce, can you excuse me for a minute, apparently there's an enormous spider on the stairs...'

'Of course...'

Mel and Rob Connor had been late starters in the family business; Ailie and Fraser were ten and seven respectively and, as another friend had once put it, behaved 'like a busy airport without air traffic control'. Bruce smiled; for him, those days were past, fortunately. Or unfortunately, maybe; sometimes he missed them.

Mel returned.

'Spider rescue apparatus deployed, crisis averted. What are they like?'

'I remember it well, and wee Amy's exactly the same, but I wouldn't change it for the world.'

'Me neither. Listen, I just wondered if you were free for dinner at ours this Saturday...?'

He was; of course he was. He didn't bother to ask if Mel was inviting a guest.

He finished the call and took another sip of his whisky. Saturday nights at the Connors' were always entertaining, despite Mel's attempts to marry him off to a suitable partner. He had attended Greenock Academy with Rob and the couple were his oldest, closest friends. He smiled; he supposed he couldn't really blame them for trying!

The television news came on, the music both familiar and strangely comforting, unchanging and dependable in the fickle world of broadcasting. The attractive lady presenter spoke and, in an instant, he was alert, listening.

'Police in Carlisle are investigating the brutal murder of two known criminals, William Bannon and Vincent Scullion. The bodies of the two men were found in a disused industrial unit on the outskirts of Carlisle earlier this evening. Initial reports suggest that the bodies had been badly mutilated, possibly before they were killed. At their trial, in Glasgow last year, Bannon and Scullion were acquitted of murder when the case against them collapsed.'

The camera moved to a close-up of the presenter, her expression suitably serious.

'Their deaths follow the death, in Glasgow last weekend, of Richard Shearer, a suspected member of the city's criminal fraternity. Shearer had been on trial several years ago for murder but escaped conviction when a verdict of 'not proven' was returned. The police have indicated that Shearer may also have been tortured before he died...'

Bruce listened until the report finished then turned off the television. The police weren't saying that the crimes were necessarily linked, but they were keeping an open mind. They also hinted at some kind of underworld vendetta although, as always, they were a bit vague. Bruce frowned; he felt that, as was always the case, there was a lot more to this story than the police, or the press, were telling.

He sat back in his chair and swallowed the last of the whisky; there was something about these cases that seemed to fascinate him. Maybe Simon Fox was correct; did he really have an unhealthy love of the gruesome and the macabre? Was it too late to ditch the rancour of the divorce courts and turn to the brutalities of crime? And, if so, that would present him with an even bigger dilemma; criminal defence or the Fiscal's office? He sighed and stood up; he was probably too old to change now anyway. He headed to the kitchen; he'd have another small whisky before bed.

Just the one...

Katya Meta glared sullenly at the back of her father's large, bullish head as he ran his massive hand over the close-cropped, greying hair. At the base of his skull, large rolls of flesh sat next to the collar of his well-ironed shirt; yet another of the many household chores she was expected to carry out in the absence of her mother. She wasn't an attractive girl, she knew that. She had inherited her mother's looks—peasant looks, as her father frequently referred to them. She wasn't tall either and, at best, her figure could be described as dumpy. She desperately wanted to leave home but where could she go? She had no job, no money of her own, despite the lavish lifestyle afforded by her father's many diverse and secretive business interests.

Katya Meta was a very unhappy young woman.

'Kat, get me another coffee; and make sure it's hot this time, with three sugars. Here, take this cup.'

She walked round and lifted the empty cup from the table.

'Okay, Papa.'

It paid to be nice to him. More to the point, it didn't pay *not* to be nice to him.

'Good girl,' he said, patting her ample rear. She hated it when he touched her like that; she hated it when he came into her room sometimes, in the middle of the night...

She screwed up her eyes, blocking out the images, and stumped hurriedly off to the kitchen. There had been something on the news that had caught his attention, some report about murders, about criminals. She hadn't paid much heed but she knew that his interest was aroused. She recognised the evil, scheming look in his dark eyes; he was planning something.

If only her mother were here, but she had disappeared mysteriously just before they had sneaked into the United Kingdom, the land of promise, the land of opportunity. So Papa had said, but he lied. Having no choice, she had come with him and, now, here she found herself, in Scotland somewhere, in a house too large for them, in the middle of nowhere, surrounded by a high security fence, imprisoned with her brute of a father.

In hell, as far as Katya Meta was concerned.

As the kettle came to the boil, she spooned the coffee and the requested three sugars into the cup. As she put the sugar bowl on the worktop, it slipped out of her hand and smashed on the floor, scattering sugar and shards of white porcelain across the tiles.

'Shit,' she mumbled. 'Shit, shit, shit...'

'What in the name of fuck are you doing? Can't you even make a cup of coffee without breaking something, you clumsy lump?'

She could feel tears welling up in her small eyes.

'Coming, Papa, I'll clear it up after.'

She poured the boiling water into the cup, filling it about a third full, then leaned over and spat into it.

At seven-thirty prompt, Bruce stepped out of the taxi and walked up to the Connors' front door. As modern houses went, it was a reasonably attractive building but the properties were homogeneous, crammed together in serried ranks and each with the obligatory two cars parked in too-small driveways. He remembered walking along the narrow country road as a boy, holding hands with his mum who, for obvious reasons, had called it the 'three farms road'. It wound high up behind what had then been the small, parochial village of Inverkip, now just a crowded dormitory town for nearby Greenock. Although the character of the little hamlet had long since been lost, the Connors seemed happy enough in their five-bedroomed detached executive villa.

He struggled to reach the doorbell as, in his arms, he clutched a bottle of a malt whisky (curiously named 'The Gauldrons'), a bottle of decent Chardonnay, a large selection box from a rather nice local chocolatier and a beautiful, hand-tied bunch of flowers from his local florist. Mel deserved far better than a supermarket bouquet. The children weren't forgotten either, with two bags of goodies hooked over his arm. Circumstances dictated that the invitation was seldom reciprocated, hence the generosity of his gifts. Finally, he pressed the little illuminated button and heard the corresponding distant chime. Usually, he simply had to wait for a few moments until either Bruce or Mel opened the door; tonight, however, he heard voices.

'I'll get it...'

'No, it's fine, Rob, I'm there...'

'No, it's okay...'

Footsteps; slightly faster than normal, almost as if a race were taking place.

'Hi Bruce...oh my, they're just gorgeous.'

Mel took the flowers, stood on her tiptoes and kissed Bruce on the cheek, her curly blonde hair brushing against him. As always, she smelled delicious and was dressed simply, elegantly and beautifully. Rob, who was looking at them from the lounge doorway with a rather odd expression on his face, was a lucky man, Bruce thought. He hoped that Rob appreciated her.

'Come in, come in, Bruce darling. It's *so* lovely to see you,' Mel gushed. She smiled sweetly up at him as she took his free hand. Something was definitely afoot.

Aleksander Krasniki came to, forcing his eyes open and shaking his head in an attempt to clear his mind. He had no idea what had happened, where he was; all he could tell was that his body

28

was, somehow, immobilised. He managed to lower his head and look downwards.

Krasniki ate too much and he drank too much; despite daily, rigorous weight-training sessions, over the course of the last few years his once imposing physique now sported a large pot belly, massive thighs and a hefty backside. His six-foot frame carried it reasonably well, except when he was naked, which he now realised that he was at present. The dark hairs of his body stood up straight in the cold of the room. Why he was naked, he had no idea, but he had greater matters of discomfort to occupy his thoughts.

His hands were raised above his head and tied to a metal bar which was, in turn, suspended from what appeared to be a pulley, attached to an overhead girder. His legs were spread wide, his feet securely attached to a weighted barbell; a brief glance down would have shown him the figure '25' etched into the black metal discs, a combined weight of fifty kilogrammes, plus twenty for the bar. However, his spectacles had been removed and everything in the brightly-lit room was a blur.

He could, however, make out that his captors wore black, their features concealed beneath black balaclavas. One of them approached, carrying a large piece of cardboard with a string attached. As the captor tried to place it round Krasniki's neck, the latter moved his head rapidly from side to side and spat, his saliva flecking the black of the other man's balaclava. Although his English was good, Krasniki spoke with a strong Eastern European accent.

'Pig. You will die for this. Slowly. You will scream for your mother...'

The man ignored him, deftly placed the sign round the captive's neck and stepped back. Removing his mobile phone from his pocket, he proceeded to take several photographs as Krasniki continued to rant, sometimes in English, sometimes in his own tongue. The second captor lifted an object from a table, walking up behind the naked, screaming prisoner. He placed the object against Krasniki's genitals, securing it with several strong luggage ties. It felt cold, hard.

The first captor walked over to a hand-cranked winch and turned it slightly, the ratchet clicking as the rope tightened. Krasniki felt his arms being pulled tighter; the man turned the handle again; it felt as if his arms and legs were being pulled out of their sockets as the seventy kilogrammes of the barbell added itself to his body weight. Another turn; a louder scream. Another; he knew he was going to die...

His captors walked away, opening the door and switching out the bright, overhead lights with a resounding click. As his captors exited, Krasniki was vaguely aware of a softer click, as if something else had been switched on. As the door finally closed, leaving him alone, in excruciating agony and in total darkness, the cold metal object started to turn warm.

'Mel, this tiramisu is absolutely delicious. Em, is there more, by any chance...?'

Mel stood up and smiled.

'The best compliment you can pay a cook, Bruce, is to ask for more. And, yes, of course there is. What about you, Fin—could you manage another slice?'

'Oh, go on then!' replied Finlay Whyte, patting his flat stomach. 'The damage is done now anyway!'

He winked across at Bruce, who smiled back.

Mel Connor had well and truly called his bluff.

Finlay, or 'Fin' was Mel's 'second cousin', an athletic, blond and handsome man in his early fifties, although he appeared a good ten years younger. He was from Edinburgh, with a soft, educated accent that hinted at private schooling, and was staying with Mel and Rob for the weekend. Although neither effeminate nor camp, somehow Bruce knew that he was gay. He wondered if Fin knew of Mel's match-making intentions; maybe he was in on the joke!

The seconds of tiramisu arrived and were devoured with gusto; it truly was delicious. The group sat for a few more minutes, chatting in a relaxed and familiar manner, when a call came from upstairs. Mel made an apologetic face as she and Rob stood up.

'Sorry, guys, bath-time beckons. We shouldn't be too long, we'll get them jammied up and they can come down and say goodnight. Once they're in bed, I'll get the coffee on.'

Rob and Mel left to attend to their parental duties, leaving the two guests alone. Previously, this had been a ploy to allow Bruce the opportunity to 'bond' with the latest 'prospect'. The two men chatted amiably and easily for a few more minutes, Fin asking if Bruce had any kids.

'Yes, two daughters, all grown up, and a granddaughter, Amy, she's the light of my life.'

'As she should be, of course,' replied Fin.

There was a pause, then Fin looked across at Bruce, holding his gaze. He gave a somewhat wistful smile which Bruce found rather appealing.

'You're not, are you?'

Bruce shook his head very slightly.

'No, I'm not, sorry.'

Fin sighed. 'That's a pity.'

'Yes, it is rather.'

Fin raised an eyebrow. 'What do you mean by that, exactly?'

'Well, this has been one of the most enjoyable evenings I've had at Mel and Rob's. You are, by far, the most engaging and entertaining 'prospect' that Mel has come up with and, let me tell you, there have been a good number. So, if I ever change my mind, or my proclivity, you'll definitely be my first call.'

Above the squealing and splashing of bath-time, Mel and Rob heard a bellow of laughter from below. Mel turned to her husband, water dripping from her face.

'You don't think...?'

'Don't be silly. Bruce isn't...'

More laughter; voices raised in animated conversation.

'...bloody hell.'

Mel had departed to make the coffee and, despite the unwritten rule, Bruce couldn't let the opportunity pass, having discovered that Finlay Whyte was a pathologist at Edinburgh's Western General Hospital. He was reasonably certain that this fact hadn't influenced his attitude towards the man. No, he genuinely liked him.

'Fin, I hesitate to ask, but have you heard anything about these murders that have been occurring—you know, these criminals...'

'Hey, Bruce, come on, we don't talk shop...'

'It's not really 'shop', Rob, I just wondered if Fin had heard...em, well, what actually had happened to the victims.'

'They were bloody killed, that's what happened.'

'I know that, but it said that they were—'

'Mate, what's the fascination with all the gory details?'

'It's not a fascination...'

Fin was watching the exchange with a wry smile on his full lips. The conversation ceased suddenly as Mel arrived with a tray bearing a large cafetiere, four Dunoon china mugs and a plate of homemade fudge. She gave Bruce a mock angry look.

'Don't you *dare* quiz poor Fin and get him to divulge sensitive information, Bruce Redpath. Anyway, he's here for a rest, not to talk about his work.'

'I'm not—'

'You were—I heard you.

'It's fine, Mel,' interjected Fin. 'And, in answer to your question, Bruce, I'm afraid it's all well outwith our locale, so I've had nothing to do with any of the post-mortems.'

Bruce looked very slightly disappointed.

'Oh; well, never mind.'

'There was one thing, though. I'd heard that they all had a sign round their necks, with...I think it was something like 'number one, who's next?''

Rob let out a sigh. He disliked bringing the dark side of his work home with him.

'Listen guys, come on...'

'Sorry, Rob, I'm just curious.'

'I know you bloody are. And, if it'll shut you up, I'd heard that too, it's as if they're bein' picked off and numbered, one by one.'

'Do you think it's a vendetta of some sort then?'

Rob shook his head.

'Like Fin, I'm not directly involved, but I'm not sure, the word on the ground is that there's someone new in town and they're flexin' their muscles.'

Mel banged the plate of fudge down on the table.

'Enough, boys. No more nasty work talk. Shove some of that in your mouths, maybe it'll sweeten what comes out.'

Bruce's taxi arrived at one a.m., the evening having flown by. He said his farewells to Rob and Fin, promising to have lunch with the latter next time he was in Edinburgh, struggling to keep a straight face at the look Rob and Mel exchanged. Mel escorted him to the door.

'Don't be a rogue, Bruce. He's a really nice guy.'

'He's absolutely lovely, and I *will* have lunch with him next time I'm in the capital. It's been the best evening I've had with you by far, haven't had so much fun since...'

A dark look swept briefly over his face and, instinctively, Mel pulled him into her arms and held him close, reaching up and gently stroking the back of his head.

'Oh Bruce, Bruce.'

She kissed his cheek as the taxi driver revved his engine slightly. As she gave him a final squeeze, he could feel her tears on his face.

'Thanks, Mel, don't know what I'd do without you—both of you. Love you.'

'Love you too Bruce Redpath. You take care.'

Bruce woke late, with only the slightest trace of woolly-headedness. He lay on his back, thinking about the previous evening, in particular just how much he had enjoyed the company of Finlay Whyte. For a few moments, he considered the possibility that his previously unquestioned sexuality was now open to debate. More out of curiosity rather than anything else, his hand strayed slowly down his pyjama shorts as he thought about the handsome pathologist; a minute or so later, he removed it with a wry smile. He wasn't—well, not yet, at any rate.

He looked at the clock, realising with some alarm that it was after ten-thirty, that he hadn't yet had his coffee and his customary read of the morning papers and that his family were due to arrive for lunch at two o'clock. He jumped out of bed and reached for his electric shaver; there was a roast to put on, after all!

Well-fed and watered, the family had finally departed; the dishes were in the dishwasher, the kitchen was cleared and the empty house still echoed to the happy sound of Amy's laughter. He sat down in his armchair and smiled; he was lucky to have two such loving, supportive daughters, a reasonably decent son-in-law, an intelligent and funny 'significant other', not to mention the little miracle that was his granddaughter. He turned on the television, muting the sound until the news came on as he sipped his well-deserved whisky.

It was the turn of the man with the ties.

'Good evening. Police in Edinburgh are investigating the death, believed to be murder, of another suspected criminal. Forty-six year old Aleksander Krasniki, of Eastern European origin but living in the city, was found in an abandoned workshop in Leith. Details of his death have not yet been released but, once more, it is understood that the victim had been tortured before he was killed.'

As the camera moved to close-up, Bruce leaned closer to the screen.

'Several years ago, Krasniki was tried for the rape and murder of sixteen-year-old Serena Swinburne, of Haddington. Krasniki was accused of breaking into the family home, believing it to be empty as the family were on holiday. Miss Swinburne had been at a friend's party but decided to come home and it was alleged that she disturbed Krasniki, who subsequently assaulted, raped and murdered her. It was then alleged that he set fire to the house in an attempt to cover his crime. However, as Mr Swinburne owned an expensive art collection, the presumed target of the attempted theft, a state-of--the-art sprinkler system had been installed, which doused the flames.

'The case against Krasniki was dismissed by the judge due to inconsistencies in the police reports and failure to properly caution the witness, who claimed that he hadn't understood the nature of the charges due to language differences. Miss Swinburne's mother, Theresa, committed suicide several months after the case collapsed.'

Bruce switched off the television and sat back in his chair, frowning and wishing he hadn't switched on the bloody news in the first place. Absent-mindedly, he stroked his chin; was this yet another gang-related killing? And, if so, why were these murders fascinating him? Was there something pathologically wrong with him that he was so attracted by an unspoken violence that was only hinted at? He didn't think so; no, there was some other reason that, as yet, he couldn't quite put his finger on. But was Simon possibly correct? Should he consider criminal law instead of the sordid dreariness of divorce?

There were too many questions that he couldn't, or daren't answer. He drained the glass of whisky and was about to refill it from the conveniently placed bottle when he had what he considered to be an epiphany.

It suddenly dawned on him that was troubling him most about these cases was the fact that The Law was being circumvented somehow, by persons unknown. Bruce lived for The Law; the solidity, the history, the procedure, due process. He hated it being flouted or abused and had often been accused of being 'OCD' (a phrase he disliked intensely) about his beloved 'due process'. He didn't see this as a flaw, in any way, shape or form. Due process must always be followed. Always.

Now, it appeared that the criminal fraternity was completely disregarding The Law Of The Land, taking it in to their own hands and applying their own, brutal version of capital punishment. It was troubling Bruce.

Actually, it was infuriating him.

He re-filled his glass and contemplated what he could do about it. The answer, unfortunately, was very little.

The woman switched off the television and drew angrily on her strong Turkish cigarette before grinding it out in the near-full ashtray. She was attractive in her own way; long black, naturally-curled hair, dark unfathomable eyes. Full lips, surrounded by the beginnings of the characteristic smoker's wrinkles. She was slim where Aleks had been overweight. Aleks; the young brother who had travelled to London with her, whom she had protected since their parents had been killed. He had come to Scotland with her when the situation in London had become too dangerous. He was a stupid boy sometimes, especially where women were concerned. No self-control, that was Aleks' trouble.

And now he was gone. There had been no visit from the police; her presence in Scotland had, as far as she knew, remained undetected, a situation that she had worked extremely hard to maintain. Even when Aleks had got into trouble, when he had killed that stupid rich cow, she had remained in the background, out of sight, under the parapet. But now she had failed him, that cute little boy with the cheeky grin, the muscles, the roving eye and the restless penis. He was gone forever.

She fought back the tears, saving them for when the time was right; for now, there was a job to be done. She stood up and crossed to one of two central heating radiators installed below the large bay window that looked out over the Firth of Tay. One was just a normal fixture, currently blasting out heat against the cold of the night outside. But even Aleks, who had been a frequent visitor, hadn't known the secret of the other radiator, identical in appearance and fittings to the first. She grasped the two valves at the top, unscrewed them then withdrew a long metal rod. Carefully, she removed the front panel to reveal a well-crafted interior, with four narrow shelves fitted in to the body of the dummy radiator. These were filled with carefully-wrapped and counted bundles of banknotes, to the value of three hundred thousand pounds. Two pistols and a quantity of boxed ammunition. Several passports; two genuine, four counterfeit. She looked briefly at her brother's passport, placing her finger gently on his sombre, brooding image before placing it carefully, reverently almost, back on the shelf. A bundle of packaged documents, including some treasured family photographs. Two small, carefully shrink-wrapped packages of high-grade heroin plus a few packets of cocaine.

On the bottom shelf were four cheap, pay-as-you-go mobile phones, untraceable and each with only one number programmed.

Burner phones, each kept charged by small charge packs. She reached for one and lifted it out, switching it on and accessing the single number as she lit a fresh cigarette. Rain lashed viciously against the window but she paid no attention. When her call was answered, she spoke quickly, and without emotion, in her own language. She terminated the call, stared out of the window and drew deeply on her cigarette, the warmth of the smoke in her lungs comforting her, reminding her of home.

Loosely translated, the final few sentences of the call were:

'Can you find who did this? Find who killed my little brother. Please?'

'And do you wish me to have them killed?'

'No, bring them to me; alive.'

Agni Krasniki had lost her brother. Someone, as yet unidentified, had gained a powerful, dangerous and vicious enemy.

Dzhokhar Meta lifted a heavy crystal glass, swallowed the last half-inch of premium vodka and grinned. He had had his eye on Agni Krasniki for some time now. She was an attractive woman, sexy and slim but with good broad hips. Long legs that could easily wrap themselves around his massive, powerful torso...

He laughed out loud; he was getting ahead of himself. No, it was best to wait, to savour the moment when it came. Which it undoubtedly would. Once he had delivered the goods, Agni would very much be in his debt. He trusted nobody, that was the safest way, of course. But he was in a very powerful position now, he was in his prime and he had his reputation to consider, after all. Dzhokhar Meta needed someone by his side, someone as passionate as him; someone as ruthless.

He reached for the bottle, emptying it into his glass. He frowned; there wasn't enough to satisfy his thirst.

'Kat, Bring me another bottle of vodka, the one in the fridge. And for fuck sake be careful.'

'Yes, Papa,' came the surly voice from the adjacent room.

Meta let out a long sigh. He'd have to do something about Katya, especially if his plans for Agni Krasniki came to fruition. He didn't want his fat, ugly daughter hanging about when there was better, more tender meat on offer. He'd make some enquiries, offer a dowry, maybe. He'd soon find someone to take her off his hands if the price was right. He sat back and drained the clear, fiery liquid as he considered his options, laid his plans. One thing was for sure, Aleks Krasniki had been nothing more than a stupid boy and had deserved everything that had come his way.

Chapter 3

Monday 27th October

The customary Monday morning partners' meeting had concluded; Peter Caira had left promptly for an appointment with a client, leaving Bruce, Simon and Olivia finishing their final cups of coffee. Bruce placed the china cup back on his saucer.

'I see there's been another murder.' he stated, to neither partner in particular.

'Mm—sorry, what's that, Bruce?' responded Simon, who was busy texting. Olivia Carnegie looked up from her own phone.

'Oh, I saw that too—some foreign guy this time. God, it sounds pretty brutal, by all accounts. Still, at least they're managing to keep it among themselves.'

Simon put his phone in his pocket.

'Yes, that's exactly what I said to Bruce last week.'

'It's just not right, though.'

Simon and Olivia looked at their partner curiously. Simon gave a slightly patronising smile.

'Well, *of course* it's not, Bruce, murder never is...'

'That's not what I mean, though. Someone's taking the law into their own hands and, once we go down the route of turning a blind eye as the criminal classes take the law into their own hands, then humanity is on a very slippery slope.'

It was Olivia's turn to smile.

'Oh, come on, you're being a bit melodramatic! I mean, it's all pretty horrible but we've seen this kind of thing before. Take the Krays in London back in the sixties, they were a right nasty bunch. Then there were the ice-cream wars up here, back in...well, the eighties, I think, it was before my time! But it's all the same thing, really—they bump each other off until a new pecking order is established. If they take out a few bad guys on the way...'

She shrugged '...well, is that such a bad thing?'

Bruce looked at her, aghast. 'I can't believe you're taking that attitude, Olivia!'

'I'm not taking an "'attitude',"' she snapped back at him, emphasising the word by italicising it with her fingers. 'I'm just saying. Yes, of course it's wrong, but these people never abide by the law anyway, they have their own set of rules. If they apply those rules to the ordinary people then by all means go after them with the full might of the law. But if they administer justice to one another, they don't hurt any innocent bystander along the way, let them get on with it, I say. Consider it a cull of the criminal contingent.'

She smiled at her alliteration and stood up, leaving Bruce staring at her with a look akin to anguish on his face. Once she had left the room, Simon lifted his briefcase, got to his feet and gave Bruce a conspiratorial grin.

'Don't take her too seriously. You know what she can be like once she gets a bee in her bonnet! Anyway, she *does* have a point,

I suppose, although if the bad guys start killing each other off, I could end up redundant! Right, must dash, got a meeting at eleven.'

Bruce sat in the leather chair, staring across at a calendar displaying a spectacular snow-capped mountain view while failing to notice that the page was for the previous month. The truth was he couldn't decide which partner's attitude had shocked him the most.

David Doyle wasn't expecting visitors; as the door burst open, his hand moved rapidly to the trigger of the concealed shotgun, relaxing as the haggard features of Paul Maguire appeared, cigarette between thin, bloodless lips. His expression was bleak as he sat down.

'Whit is it, Paul, ye look like ye've seen a fuckin' ghost.'

Maguire took the cigarette out of his mouth and exhaled, although little smoke seemed to escape from his lungs.

'Pig's been lifted.'

The silence was intense. Doyle stared at the ex-lawyer, then spoke softly, although with undisguised malice.

'Fuck. Stupid...fuckin'...bastard!'

He punctuated the words by banging his clenched fist on the desk.

'Wait—Holy Christ, he didn'ae call you, did he?'

'He did, but don't panic, it was on one of my burners. It's well away, don't worry. Untraceable.'

Doyle stood up and began to pace back and forth across the small office. He pulled out a pack of cigarettes and lit one with his Zippo.

'Fuck, FUCK! How in the name o' fuck did the stupid cunt get himself lifted?'

Maguire remained calm; he had been a good lawyer, many years ago.

'He didn't have time to say; he'd just been pulled over on the A2, just outside Dover, flashing lights, three cop cars. Must've been a tip-off...'

Doyle turned angrily. 'Aye, well God fuckin' help them if Ah get ma hands on them.'

'Take it easy, Davie. We've got a plan in place for this, remember?'

Doyle sat back down, shoulders slumped, his expression having changed from anger to worry. He flicked ash from his cigarette on to the floor.

'Aye, an' it fuckin' better work.'

Paul Maguire smiled, revealing nicotine- stained teeth. He pulled out another cheap, pay-as-you-go burner phone.

'It will, Davie, it will. Leave it to me—we'll be as clean as the proverbial whistle.'

◆◆◆◆◆◆◆◆◆◆◆◆◆◆

It was one of life's little pleasures; leftover roast beef, re-heated Yorkshire puddings, roast potatoes and mashed turnip. But then there was the gravy, thick, concentrated, rich and beefy...all washed down with half a bottle of Shiraz!

The dishes were in the dishwasher, the kitchen was tidy; Bruce topped up his wine glass and sat down with a golfing magazine, looking enviously at the sun-drenched venues featured in that month's issue. He sipped his wine, placed the glass on the table, closed his eyes and fell asleep.

The rain battering against the window woke him. He had no clue as to how long he'd been sleeping; the autumn was proving to be a near-continuous series of Atlantic storms. He glanced at his watch, discovering that it was a minute after nine. He fumbled for the remote then switched on the television; it was a different lady, attractively dressed in smart trousers and a black blouse. She had long auburn hair and he felt a sudden contraction in his stomach as he became aware of the resemblance...he narrowed his eyes slightly, concentrating on what the newsreader was saying.

'...on the A2 north of Dover. The lorry, owned by Glasgow-based company Hooley Transport and apparently containing a shipment of onions from France, was stopped after police received a tip-off. Six foreign nationals, believed to be Vietnamese, were found inside and were taken to hospital, where one, an infant, sadly died later this afternoon. Two remain in a critical condition, suffering from severe malnutrition and dehydration. The driver, fifty-six-year-old John Piggottt, from Glasgow, has been remanded in custody. We're now going live to Duncan Kerr, our Scotland correspondent, who is outside the offices of Hooley Transport. Duncan, what can you tell us about this company?'

Kerr's familiar, lived-in face appeared on the screen, nodding throughout the customary four-second delay. An array of police cars and flashing lights formed a fitting backdrop.

'Well, as you can see, there is still a considerable police presence at the premises of Hooley Transport in Glasgow's Govan. Company spokesman, Paul Maguire, earlier stated that they are 'horrified and shocked' that this has happened and deny any knowledge of the alleged people-trafficking. No arrests have been made at Hooley Transport, although the police are still searching the premises. However, I'm led to believe that the police have also searched Piggottt's house in the north of the city. Chief Superintendent Norah Jarvis gave a statement earlier this evening saying that 'significant evidence and documentation' had been recovered from Piggott's home and that there *was* a possibility that he was acting without the knowledge of his employers. No doubt company directors Frank Hooley, David and Maria Doyle and Paul Maguire are hoping that this proves to be the case.'

'Thank you, Duncan...'

Bruce switched off the television; it seemed that each day brought fresh news of the evils of society and the thought of an innocent and helpless infant dying in such horrific circumstances made him sick to his stomach. At least there had been no additional gangland murders...well, he assumed not, but he couldn't quite bring himself to turn the television back on. He stood up and returned to the kitchen; he needed another glass of wine after that horror story!

'See, I told you not to worry.'

'They're no' fuckin' away yet.'

Maguire shrugged his narrow shoulders. 'So? They'll not find a single thing here, trust me. The boys planted all the stuff in Pig's house, they've got nothing on us.'

Davie Doyle looked far from convinced although, acting on Maguire's advice, the concealed shotgun had been hastily removed earlier that day and surreptitiously thrown into the nearby River Clyde.

'Aye, but whit if the bastard talks, turns...whit is it, 'Queen's evidence'. Never trusted the fucker, dressin' like a fuckin' cowboy...'

Maguire lit a cigarette and exhaled a vague, blueish haze. He leaned forward and lowered his voice to a gravelly whisper.

'Pig's not going to say a word. Not a single—fucking—word! Don't you worry, we'll take care o' it.'

He winked menacingly and tapped the side of his nose as he sucked greedily on his cigarette, drawing the smoke into his lungs. Davie Doyle smiled for the first time that evening.

'Yer a fuckin' marvel, Paul, a fuckin' marvel!'

Maguire returned the smile. 'Amn't I just, Davie.'

A large dose of Gaviscon had done little to relieve Bruce Redpath's dyspepsia the following morning as he sat on the Glasgow-bound train. He hadn't slept well, despite having finished the entire bottle of wine. Or maybe because...he didn't care to analyse it.

What was the world coming to? His life had been spent upholding the letter of the law. It was the rock, the foundation of his career, his success. Now, that rock was being eroded by persons unknown, presumably from the worst of the criminal classes, intent on taking the law into their own hands in some detestable gangland power struggle. At least, that was what the police seemed to suspect. Then there was the shocking news about those poor illegal immigrants. He gave a shudder; the thought of that family, presumably having spent their meagre life savings, huddled in the back of a cold, inhospitable lorry, starving, thirsty, a young child dying in their arms...it didn't bear thinking about.

And yet, he couldn't stop himself...

'Good morning Mrs Aherne...are you all right?'

Rayna Aherne snuffled and nodded.

'Yer, Mr Redpath...I take it you saw the news...?'

He didn't need to ask to what news she was referring.

'Yes, I'm afraid I did; shocking.'

A tear ran down her cheek. 'Oh, the very thought of that poor wee thing, dyin' in the back of that lorry.'

Bruce stepped over and patted her hand. 'I know, Mrs Aherne, it's just awful.'

She looked up at him, her expression pleading. 'Please tell me that whoever did this won't get off, Mr Redpath. I mean, surely to God they'll be found guilty?'

'I sincerely hope so, Mrs Aherne, I sincerely hope so.'

He also fervently hoped that his partner, Simon Fox, wouldn't be asked to defend.

It had been an extremely busy week and Bruce was relieved that it was Friday morning; divorce seemed to be on the rise but, despite the obvious financial benefits for Redpath Fox Carnegie, Bruce couldn't help but despair of the apparent lack of marital perseverance that seemed to be all-too-prevalent these days.

His mood hadn't improved by the time he reached the office, fifteen minutes late. The roads in Glasgow seemed to be in a permanent state of disrepair, with numerous roadworks and closures causing delays and frayed tempers among those forced to negotiate the seemingly labyrinthine streets. He had an appointment at nine-thirty, a new client hell-bent on ensuring that his allegedly unfaithful wife received the bare minimum in the divorce settlement. Bruce recognised the man for what he was; a misogynistic, miserly boor. The poor woman was probably better off without him but as he was paying Redpath Fox Carnegie a handsome fee, Bruce had no choice but to put his personal feelings aside. He sighed wearily; he wouldn't have been too disappointed if the wife's solicitor managed to dredge up some dirt on his client that might make for a fairer settlement. He thanked the cabbie, ran up the steps and entered the office. Rayna Aherne wasn't in her seat; instead, he was greeted by the rather surly countenance of Torquil Carnegie, who appeared to be chewing gum. Bruce strode over to the desk, his hackles rising.

'Torquil, would you mind not chewing gum at the desk—it isn't an image that we like to project.'

The young man glared up at him. 'It's nicotine gum. My mum said it was all right.'

Bruce struggled to maintain his composure; he didn't want a row with Olivia but he wasn't prepared to allow this kind of behaviour from a youth who was only there under sufferance.

'Well, I'm telling you it's *not* all right, Torquil. Spit it out—now.'

Torquil Carnegie gave an insolent sneer, pursed his lips and spat the chewing gum across the desk and on to the carpeted floor, just as Rayna Aherne came out of the kitchen, carrying two steaming mugs. Her eyes widened in astonishment.

'Pick that up immediately!' barked Bruce, his temper snapping.

'Pick it up yourself—you told me to spit it out.'

'Last warning—pick it up, Torquil...'

'Fuck off.'

Carnegie junior stood up, defiantly raising his middle finger before grabbing his jacket from the coat rack. He stormed out, leaving Rayna Aherne and Bruce Redpath staring in astonishment as the door slammed behind him. Rayna turned back and smiled.

'Coffee, Mr Redpath?'

The day was finally over; he had managed to avoid an all-out confrontation with Olivia Carnegie but he knew that she wasn't exactly delighted about the incident involving her son. Bruce considered that this was probably because she now hadn't a clue what to do with the truculent, wayward youth. At least she had been able to keep an eye on him at the office, but now—well, Bruce knew that the boy had dabbled in illicit drugs on more than one occasion. Unsupervised during the day, he didn't care to dwell on what Torquil Carnegie might get up to!

He exited the black cab at Glasgow's Central Station, thanked Gary, his driver, and made his way into the concourse. A newspaper vendor, an endangered species nowadays, was plying his trade just inside the entrance. Bruce didn't usually bother with the Evening Times, but the headline immediately caught his eye.

> 'People-trafficking
> suspect found dead'

He crossed over and bought a copy of the paper, pausing to read the leading headline.

'Glasgow man, John Piggottt,
being held by police in
connection with the six
immigrants found in his
lorry, one of whom, a toddler,
later died, was found hanged
in his cell this afternoon
and was pronounced dead.
An investigation is now
underway as to how...'

The words started to blur in front of him. The newspaper vendor was peering at him over the top of his disreputable reading specs.

'Y'awright, sir?'

'Wh...what?'

'Ah said, y'awright? Look like ye've jist seen a ghost...'

'Oh, yes...yes, I'm fine, just a bit light headed for a moment there, thanks.'

He walked slowly away, grasping the newspaper. What the hell was the world coming to?

Chapter 4

Saturday 2nd November

Bruce opened the bedroom curtains and let out a groan of dismay; yet again, there was no way that his regular four-ball would be golfing that Saturday morning. It was shaping up to be a long, bleak winter. He padded downstairs, switched on the kettle, popped two slices of bread in the toaster then turned on the wall-mounted television in the kitchen. The morning news had just started.

'...surely be asking questions as to how Piggottt was able to hang himself?'

'Absolutely, Tom. I mean, something like this should never have happened. Prisoners are always searched to ensure that there's nothing they can use to harm themselves. They'll be looking very closely at whoever had access to the prisoner...'

The voices droned on as he prepared his coffee and buttered his toast. He sat down on a kitchen stool, tuning back in to the depressing conversation.

'...that there's any relation to the spate of what seem to be revenge killings in the north of the country?'

'Well, of course, that question has to be asked, Tom; after all, Piggottt *was* from Glasgow so there might be a connection. The police are remaining tight-lipped but I don't think they'll be ruling anything out at this stage...'

He picked up the remote and switched the set off just as two baseball-cap-adorned youths appeared behind the reporter and started making obscene gestures. He gave a wry smile; at least it didn't just happen in the west of Scotland! He sat for a few minutes, finishing his toast, then he stood up, lifted the cafetiere and mug and made his way through to the living room. The sky remained dark and foreboding, matching his mood perfectly. He sat down on his favourite chair and stared moodily out at the turbulent waters of the Clyde as he tried to figure out why these brutal, violent cases were bothering him so much. Was it really just the fact that his beloved Law was being usurped? He wasn't entirely certain but there was a faint nagging doubt, buried somewhere deep in the recesses of his brain, that there was another, more personal, reason.

He had fallen asleep again and he experienced a brief twinge of worry; was there something wrong with him? Maybe he should consult his GP, he might have low blood pressure; or diabetes, maybe; an under-active thyroid perhaps? He shook his head; this wouldn't do, he needed something to occupy him—well, apart from work, golf and his granddaughter. 'The devil makes work for idle hands' was what...

He shook his head as if clearing his thoughts. Simon had repeatedly told Bruce that he needed a hobby, something to fill his spare time, especially during the long winter months. He stood up with a sigh; he had a plan, maybe not what Simon had envisaged (his partner had actually suggested a model railway, although Bruce wasn't entirely sure whether he was being flippant) but it was something that should occupy both his mind and his time, for the rest of the morning at least. He yawned, got out of the chair and headed for the small study that faced the large and rather unkempt rear garden. He sat down and fired up his laptop.

It was the deep rumble from his stomach that made him look at the corner of the computer screen and he was astonished to see that it was 1.43 p.m. He leaned back in the leather office chair and stretched; there was shopping to be done and he had received a rather last-minute dinner invite from Rob, his friend having assured him that it would just be the three of them plus the kids. Mel had apparently given up trying to 'fix him up' with a suitable partner for the time being (she had probably run out of eligible candidates, Bruce mused). He smiled; it was probably just as well that they didn't realise how much he had enjoyed the company of his last would-be partner, bluff or not!

He hadn't really had much of an idea what he was looking for at first; a connection, maybe, a pattern. Although it was a task normally now delegated in the office, Bruce still had a pretty good knowledge of the internet, a useful asset when trying to unearth the past on behalf of a client. He knew how to access old newspaper databases, he was beginning to find his way around social media and he often managed to resurrect long-forgotten titbits, liaisons, police investigations and the like. A number of pages in the notepad next to the computer were now filled with his neat handwriting, each with a heading. As he picked it up and started to read, he absent-mindedly rubbed his chin as he realised that he hadn't yet shaved.

Richard 'Rik' Shearer
Billy 'the Bandit' Bannon
Vincent Scullion, 'Skully'
Aleksander 'Aleks' Krasniki

Four brutal murders in the space of a few weeks.
Four known criminals.

John Piggottt, 'Pig'
Died in custody. Suspicious circumstances?

Although he didn't know the full details, the deaths all appeared to be preceded by considerable violence. Except for the last, John Piggottt, who had hanged himself while in police custody. He turned the page and continued to read his notes.

Richard 'Rik' Shearer.
Resident of Glasgow (Clarkston)
Age at time of death—47
Several convictions in his teens and mid-twenties for grievous bodily harm and common assault. Served two prison sentences. Subsequently kept out of trouble and apparently worked his way up the criminal hierarchy, latterly known among same as 'Grandpa Rik'. Built up a chain of tanning salons across the Central Belt, suspected of money laundering and drug distribution but never

charged in connection with either. Known as a vicious and violent thug, he was eventually charged with the murder of Shelley Moore, a thirty-year-old woman who was manageress of several tanning salons in the East End of Glasgow. It was thought that Shearer had had an affair with Moore but, after they split up, he believed that she had been stealing from him (never proven). Shearer allegedly assaulted Moore in one of the salons, raped her, tied her up and left her in an ultraviolet tanning booth, the door jammed shut. It was several days before she was found, having suffered severe burns. Cause of death was undetermined but considered to probably be due to a combination of dehydration, shock, loss of blood and UV burns. Shearer was arrested and brought to trial six years ago. The original trial was abandoned after family members of two of the jury were assaulted, presumed to be in an attempt to influence the verdict. At the re-trial, Shearer received the uniquely Scottish verdict of 'Not Proven'. There was conjecture that the second jury had been 'informed' of the original assaults and were afraid of returning a guilty verdict. This, too, was never proved.

Bruce let out a long sigh as he read the final part.

Solicitor for the defence was Simon Fox.

He would maybe check the case notes on Monday but, by all accounts, it had been a masterful piece of work by Simon, his partner. Bruce knew he couldn't have it both ways; his own personal mantra being 'due process,' at the end of the day Simon was only ensuring that the accused received a fair trial, a trial that would stand scrutiny. He knew only too well that, in the days of capital punishment, defendants had been hanged on a guilty verdict that was later overturned. The outcome of a criminal trial had to be beyond reproach, but with people like Shearer, an evil career criminal...

He shook his head. No, it didn't matter. The law had to be seen to be correct and not based on opinion or belief. The verdict had to be 'guilty beyond reasonable doubt' and obviously, in Shearer's case, there *must* have been reasonable doubt. Or were the jury simply afraid? He frowned; he hoped not! He read on.

Bannon and Scullion, both from Glasgow's Maryhill, allegedly ran a large protection racket and money laundering operation. One business owner involved in the scheme, a jeweller called Andrew Goldstein, having decided to terminate the arrangement, had threatened to report them to the police. Bannon and Scullion had paid him a visit, seemingly in an attempt to dissuade him from this course of action. When he refused, in what was assumed to be a warning to anyone else so inclined, they had cut off his hands, leaving him to bleed to death. He was found in his jeweller's shop by his teenage daughter.

Each defendant provided the other with a seemingly unshakeable alibi and they were acquitted. The defence Counsel for Scullion had been Duncan Frobisher (now deceased). Counsel for Bannon had been Carol Veitch.

Veitch had been in the year above Bruce at University. He had had a very brief, drunken dalliance with her at a student party, before...

He might give Carol a call and see what she remembered about the case, although it was over three years ago. She was a busy defence Counsel based near Glasgow's High Court, no doubt having seen many of the worst of Glasgow's hoodlums pass through the books of Carol Veitch. His eyes moved to the next page.

Aleksander Krasniki.

Bruce shook his head slowly; the details of this case had distressed him the most, as Krasniki's victim had been an innocent sixteen year old girl. By all accounts the man was clearly a predatory monster (there had been previous, unproven allegations) and thoroughly deserved to be convicted, but his defence attorney, Arshid Maan had argued that his client had misunderstood the charges. Maan claimed that Krasniki hadn't been provided with an interpreter (despite having been a British resident for fifteen years, apparently he couldn't understand what was being said) and that the arresting officers hadn't correctly read him his rights (it was strange that Krasniki had managed to understand that much). The judge had been forced to dismiss the case on this technicality and Krasniki had walked free.

Bruce placed the notepad back on the desk and put his hands behind his head. The murder of Krasniki was different; he didn't appear to be a member of a criminal gang as such, he seemed to be more an opportunistic thief, yet he had been punished in a similar manner to the others. Why was that? Was there something about the victim that the police hadn't discovered, or hadn't made public? Maybe he could ask Rob if he had heard anything on the police grapevine; when Mel was absent, of course.

The case of the last victim, John Piggottt, was a perplexing one and Bruce wasn't sure that it was connected at all. That the man was guilty of people-trafficking clearly seemed to be beyond any reasonable doubt and he would most likely have faced a charge of manslaughter, in addition to charges of people-trafficking. But someone had obviously 'got to him' while he was being held awaiting his hearing and, no doubt, the police would be making every attempt to find out who that was. Somehow, he didn't seem to fit the pattern of the others. Bruce was about to close his computer; he couldn't find any connection between the victims, Krasniki didn't appear to be a member of any crime syndicate and Piggottt had hanged himself in jail. Still, at least it had passed the morning—and the early afternoon. He moved the mouse then stopped, the arrow hovering on 'close all programs.'

What about Piggottt's employers?

Piggott's employers were currently ensconced in a booth in The Carthorse, a dark and dingy Glasgow south-side watering hole. The majority of the clientele were watching Celtic playing Aberdeen on the large flat-screen television, leaving Davie Doyle and Paul Maguire in relative peace to chat as they finished their third pint of the afternoon. Maguire drained his glass and stood up.

'I'm going outside for a fag.'

Doyle also got to his feet.

'Ah'll join ye, fuckin' rubbish that we cann'ae huv a smoke wi' oor pint.'

A few minutes later, cigarettes lit, the two were standing under the door canopy, off which the rainwater was pouring on to the pavement and splashing against their legs.

'Fuckin' shite this,' exclaimed Doyle, as he drew angrily on his cigarette.

'I know. Way of the world, I'm afraid.' He paused, inhaling deeply. 'I take it you've not heard anything?'

Doyle shook his head, a grim smile playing on his lips.

'Naw, an' Ah hope tae fuck we don't. Cost us a bloody fortune tae sort Pig...'

Paul Maguire looked around furtively, replying in a half-whisper.

'Ssh...yes, but it was worth it. I told you it'd be taken care of—I wasn't sure we could have trusted the bastard to keep his mouth shut, in which case we'd all have been fucked. No, it was a good investment...'

Doyle threw his cigarette-end into a puddle, where it fizzled briefly.

'Ye're right, we couldn'ae. Nope, Ah think we're in the clear, thank fuck.'

Doyle lit a second cigarette and Maguire followed suit. They stood smoking in silence for a few minutes, listening to the incessant pattering of the rain, then Maguire asked.

'You heard from Suzi?'

The question seemed innocent enough but it took David Doyle by surprise. Rather naively, he had assumed that his affair with Suzi Flint wasn't common knowledge. However, Paul Maguire made it his business to know as much as possible about his so-called employer. David Doyle coughed and spat the phlegm into the puddle.

'Em...naw, Ah telt her no' tae get in touch, even if she could. Last thing Ah fuckin' need is Maria findin' oot. If she telt her auld man...'

Maguire nodded sagely. Even though he was ageing, Frank Hooley was a massive slab of half-Scottish, half-Irish manhood who still regularly attended the gym, his ham-like fists connected to bulging biceps and triceps.

'Indeed, Davie.'

'An' that fuckin' brief better come up wi' the goods—costin' me a fuckin' fortune.'

'I told you, he's the best you're going to get; she's in with a fighting chance.'

Doyle threw his half-smoked cigarette into the same puddle.

'Fuckin' hope so. Huvn'ae had ma hole fur weeks—come on, let's get back inside. Ah'm bloody freezin', time fur a wee hauf...then Ah'm headin' home.'

He turned and put his arm round Maguire's scrawny shoulders.

'Christ, Ah'm that desperate Ah might even try an' talk Maria int'ae a wee bit o' rest an' recreation, if ye know whit Ah mean...?'

Doyle winked suggestively and Paul Maguire leered back. His morals were as non-existent as Davie Doyle's and he neither approved nor disapproved of his co-director's long-standing affair. However, he wouldn't like to be in Doyle's shoes if Frank Hooley ever found out. The man had been known as a right hard bastard in his day and, tough as Davie Doyle may be, Maguire certainly wouldn't back his friend in a bare-knuckle contest with old man Hooley

The two men turned and opened the door, the sectarian chanting of the football fans, the smell of beer and perspiring humanity washing over them in a unique and rather unsavoury Glasgow balm. Neither man noticed the dark four-by-four that had been parked a few hundred yards further along the road as it started its engine and drove slowly away.

Bruce finally closed down the laptop and, rather stiffly, stood up. It was after four and he still hadn't showered or shaved. He stretched and rubbed his aching neck; his investigations had certainly occupied his time on this dismally wet Saturday.

He hadn't been able to glean much information about Hooley Transport, the company that had employed John Piggottt as a driver. The company report showed that there were four directors, Frank Hooley, David Doyle, Maria Doyle and Paul Maguire; the name of the latter rang a faint bell with Bruce, although he couldn't quite figure out why. There had been a few scrapes over the last few years, mostly traffic violations involving lorries or drivers, but none of the directors had a criminal record as far as he could determine. He took a deep breath and exhaled slowly. Although he still wasn't entirely sure why he was so fascinated (or was he obsessed? No, of course not...) by these murders, his curiosity was now well and truly aroused. After all, due process hadn't been observed...

And that would never do.

As he closed the door to the study, he had an idea; there might be someone who could help him with his rather unorthodox enquiries. He took out his phone, scrolled through his contacts until he came to the one he was looking for, then pressed the dial button. It was worth a try.

'All right Bruce...?'

Rob peered closely at his friend as he entered the warm, homely environment of the Connor household.

'...you growin' a beard, mate?'

Bruce rubbed his chin in some surprise. 'Em, no, I forgot to shave, that's all.'

Rob chuckled. 'Ah, standards slippin', bad sign that—listen, come on through.'

'No surprises tonight, then?'

Rob threw back his head and let out a loud guffaw. 'Hah! No, I think Mel's learned her lesson, at least for the...'

'And what lesson might that be, Robin Connor?'

'Mel—how are you?'

Bruce embraced the soft, feminine form that was Mel Connor, lingering for a moment as if drawing comfort from her. She seemed to sense his need and held him tighter, her hand rubbing the back of his head gently. She knew...after a few seconds, she drew away.

'*You're* a bit bristly tonight, Bruce Redpath!' she said, smiling as she stroked his cheek. 'Anyway, you two away through and grab a drink, dinner'll be about forty-five minutes. G and T for me, dearest.'

Mel withdrew to the kitchen on a waft of Dior and the two friends were soon seated in the comfortable leather chairs in the lounge, Rob sipping beer from the bottle, Bruce sipping a large malt from a crystal tumbler.

'Aah! Islay?'

Rob nodded. 'The farm distillery, Kilchoman. You like it?'

'Love it.'

He took another sip. 'Em...Rob...?'

His friend looked across with a slight frown on his brow.

'If it's work-related, then no—I though we had an agreement?'

'It's not really, well, not anything that involves you or me, specifically.'

Rob took a swig of beer and sighed. 'It's not about these gang-related murders again, is it?'

Bruce nodded. 'Well, I was doing a bit of research today and—'

'Bruce, you're a superb divorce lawyer and, in the highly unlikely event that I ever need one, you'll be my first port of call; well, if Mel doesn't grab you first! But, with all respect, leave the detective work to us detectives. What's the fascination with all this anyway?'

'To be honest, I don't exactly know. I've always been drawn to the macabre, I suppose, and this is certainly all that, with those hints at extreme violence. But the other thing is that I just can't abide people taking the law into their own hands, it infuriates me.'

He drained the glass. 'I don't know if I've ever told you, but the reason I decided to read law in the first place was because, from an early age, I had a great sense of right and wrong, of justice, I suppose, instilled into me. I remember watching some old cowboy films when I was a youngster—can't remember what they were now—but the baddies usually got their come-uppance at the end of a Colt .45 or a rope slung over the nearest tree. Of course, I thought this was great and I used to ask my dad why we couldn't just go out and shoot the baddies. He explained all about law, justice, the right to a fair trial. Said that was why it was called the 'Wild West', that it was a lawless society.'

'Aye, your dad was a solicitor too, wasn't he?'

Bruce gave a wry smile.

'Yes, I've probably told you all this before; he ended up as Procurator Fiscal in Paisley. He was a contemporary of the legendary Joe Renaldi.'

'God, he got a few bad characters off the hook in his time.'

'He did, and although my old man was the fiscal, he really respected Renaldi; apparently the man was a real charmer out of court. You see, my dad had an absolute belief in the fairness of the system, due process, as he called it. So, even if you were certain that someone was guilty, it had to be proved beyond reasonable doubt. All Renaldi was doing was demonstrating that there *was* reasonable doubt and that a conviction would be unsafe.'

He paused and took another sip of whisky.

'There was an old professor who lectured us at the Uni; he was always reciting quotes about the law. Some were just nonsense but there was one, accredited to Johnson, I think, that stuck in my mind "A lawyer has no business with the justice or injustice of the cause which he undertakes."'

Rob slugged his beer. 'Very profound! But I suppose, from your point of view, it makes sense. For you, it's all about adherin' to the law rather than the right or wrong of the participants and their actions. Not from ours though; there's nothin' worse than seeing a crook whom you know to be as guilty as sin walk free just because of a technicality. Makes me sick to the stomach sometimes.'

There was a brief, rather awkward silence.

'Em...to quote someone else, "the law is an ass!"'

Bruce smiled; he wasn't going to correct his friend. Although the grammar was technically correct, it rendered the quotation slightly inaccurate. It wasn't '*an*', it was '*a*'!

'Indeed. Anyway, remember that my dad started working back in the days of capital punishment—there was no way back from being hanged, after all.'

'No, I suppose not.'

'So, as I said, it was drummed in to me from an early age that justice must be done...and be seen to be done. So, when I see so-called justice being carried out by, well, God knows who...'

'The cops involved are pretty certain it's a power struggle, from what I can gather, although no-one's quite sure where that power lies. There's talk of some new player...'

His voice tailed off and Bruce raised a questioning eyebrow.

'What?'

'Oh, nothin', really—well, nothin' I can put my finger on. But there's a vague undercurrent among the senior officers... Bruce, I shouldn't really be tellin' you this...'

A voice emanated from the dining room.

'Bruce, Rob, children, dinner's going out in five so, if you need the toilet, now's the time. Rob, can you get me another G and T please, sweetheart?'

Rob stood up hastily but Bruce followed and caught his friend's shoulder before they exited the room.

'What, Rob? What were you going to say?'

Rob Connor looked down at the floor as he spoke, his tone low and uneasy.

'Well, this goes no further, but I get the impression...well, there's a feeling that, as long as the general public aren't involved, we should just let them get on with it. Saves us the bother of catchin' them, tryin' them, then watchin' them walk free thanks to some smart-ass QC...sorry Bruce, all respect to Simon, of course, but you know what I mean. We know that all these victims were guilty as hell, they just managed to slip off the hook for one reason or another.'

Bruce was aghast. 'But that's...I mean...how do *you* feel about it?'

Mel's face appeared round the doorway, her expression severe.

'If you two are talking shop, then you're not getting any pudding.'

Bruce managed a smile. 'Ah, but what's *for* pudding, Mel?'

Chapter 5

Monday 4th November

Rayna Aherne possessed one of the most honest, open countenances that Bruce had ever encountered. It was always a joy to be greeted by her ready smile, particularly on such a sleet-swept Monday morning. Today, however, she wore an expression somewhere between mild amusement and slight irritation. He closed the glass inner door and strode along to the reception desk.

'Good morning, Mrs Aherne—everything okay?'

She smiled up at him; she would make the kind of witness that a solicitor either loved or loathed, depending whether she was for the prosecution or the defence. The jury would adore her, they would believe every word she uttered, they would empathise, sympathise, fantasise...

'Oh yes, Mr Redpath, just fine—'

She was interrupted as the door leading to the office behind opened and a figure came out, carefully clutching a steaming mug. Freshly trimmed hair, a white shirt and a simple, striped tie, Torquil Carnegie looked across at Bruce and his face immediately started to redden. He placed the cup carefully down in front of Rayna.

'Thanks, Torquil.'

'Em, you're welcome, Mrs Aherne...um...Mr Redpath, may I have a word...in private, please?'

Bruce avoided the mischievous glint in Rayna's eye.

'Very well, Torquil, give me a few minutes, then come through to my office.'

Bruce glared up at the distinctly nervous young man; he had decided to keep him standing for the time being.

'Well? You wanted a word with me, Torquil?'

With what was obviously a great effort of will, Torquil Carnegie made eye contact. Bruce was mildly impressed; a proper apology was a difficult thing to accomplish.

'Em...look, Mr Redpath, I'm really, really sorry, right? I mean, I was bang out of order the other day...'

He cast his eyes down for a moment, then looked back up.

'I'm, like, totally ashamed of my behaviour. Totally!'

'Are you, Torquil? Really? Or has your mother put you up to this...oh, for God's sake, have a seat before you fall over.'

The nervous young man sat down with a sigh of relief.

'Thanks. Well, yes, she did, but I really felt like shit...oh, soz, I felt awful after I walked out. You see, things have pretty much gone tits-up...oh soz again, well...'

Bruce stifled a smile; the young man's vocabulary was rather amusing.

' ...let's just say my life hasn't quite gone according to plan recently.'

He leaned forward, an earnest look on his clean-shaven face.

'Look, Mr Redpath, I'd like to start again, clean slate and all that. Please! I know I didn't make it to Uni, I know I've been a disappointment to my mum and dad but maybe I could become a para-legal or something, I don't know...'

He looked appealingly at Bruce; he was very like his mother sometimes. Bruce steepled his fingers and frowned.

'Hmm, I have to say it *was* pretty shocking behaviour. But it takes a lot of courage to come back and apologise, Torquil, and I admire and respect that. Very well, but you're on your last warning.'

'I realise that, Mr Redpath. I won't let you, or my mum, down again. You have my word.'

Torquil leaned further across the desk and proffered his hand; Bruce took it, finding the young man's grip firm and resolute. Maybe there was hope for him yet.

'If there's anything I can do, you know, maybe a bit more... well, legal, I suppose.'

'Rather than helping Mrs Aherne at the reception desk, you mean?'

The young man nodded enthusiastically. 'Well, as a matter of fact, there is. I'll need to check with Mr Fox, of course, but...'

'Isn't Mr Fox in Court this week?'

Bruce had completely forgotten that Suzannah Flint's murder trial had started that morning. He also realised that he was late for the weekly partners' meeting. He stood up.

'Oh, yes, you're right. Okay, I suppose it doesn't really matter. Tell me, Torquil, have you ever been down to the basement?'

◆◆◆◆◆◆◆◆◆◆◆◆◆◆

Bruce leaned back in his chair and let out a long sigh; the afternoon meeting with his latest client, had been particularly tedious. As was often the case, the allegations she made about her estranged husband were both exaggerated and unsubstantiated. If truth be told, he felt extremely sorry for the husband, who had left his shrewish wife for his office cleaner. With assurances that he would, of course, do his very best for her, he had finally closed the door on the malicious and malcontent sixty-year-old, wondering if it really was too late for a change of direction, or even a change of career! His rather bleak thoughts were disturbed by a knock at the door; he checked his desk, ensuring that there was nothing of a sensitive nature visible.

'Come in.'

The door opened; a rather dusty and slightly dishevelled Torquil Carnegie entered, carrying a large file in his hands and with an uncharacteristic grin on his youthful, and usually sullen, face. He certainly seemed to be making an effort, Bruce thought.

'I see you've been busy, Torquil.'

'Yeah, Mr Redpath. I found the case notes—eventually—and I've had a good look through them.'

He placed the folder on the table, but remained standing.

'Have a seat...right, what have you managed to find out?'

Torquil sat down and opened the file, taking a sheet of paper from the top.

'Well, I've made some notes. So, this Rik Shearer dude, seems he was a real nasty son-of-a...em, well, he wasn't a particularly nice guy.'

'No, well, I'd already gathered that much.'

'So, this woman that he was supposed to have murdered, Shelley Moore. I've done a bit of digging on her...'

'Digging? Exactly what kind of digging?'

'Oh, just on-line, Facebook, Instagram, that kind of thing. It's awesome what you can pick up if you know how. Find out where they went to school, track down their friends, they often refer to the anniversary of the death. It's a bit like the people who leave flowers and football scarves beside the road where there was a crash. Pretty morbid, if you ask me, but you can learn quite a lot just by looking at the comments.'

'But the poor girl's been dead for a number of years—hasn't the trail...well, gone cold, for want of a better term?'

Torquil grinned. 'Thing is, Mr Redpath, you'd be surprised how many people still have a presence, even after they're dead. I mean, you lose a daughter, a husband, the last thing you think about is stopping their Facebook account. Especially when older folk are involved, sometimes they don't even know the person was on f-b in the first place. I mean, say your wife died suddenly, would you know where to start? Anyway...Mr Redpath, are you okay?'

'What? Oh, yes, sorry, I'm fine. So, I take it you've found something?'

'Well, I've found out a bit about Shelley Moore's family.'

He consulted the rather untidy scrawl on the page he was holding.

'So, she was from Kirkintilloch, had her own flat in the town. Her mum and dad were still alive at the time, although I think they're both dead now. Probably the shock didn't do them much good...'

Torquil possessed the callousness of youth, Bruce realised. Not a bad characteristic if you're going to start raking through the detritus of a historic murder case, he supposed. Torquil was speaking again.

'...had a brother and a sister. The sister's married, lives in East Kilbride, as far as I can gather. The brother was in the army, came out five years ago. Can't find any trace of him at all, it's odd...'

Bruce felt a faint tingle on the back of his neck.

'The army? Any idea which regiment?'

'Yes, he was in the Royal Marines. Sergeant Andy Moore. Seemed to have a pretty distinguished record. He served in Europe and Afghanistan, he appears to have done a bit of undercover work. He was good at languages, apparently.'

'How did you manage to find all that out?'

'Oh, as I said, just a bit of digging.'

'And is anyone going to *know* that you've been digging, Torquil?'

The young man shook his head.

'It's pretty much all in the public domain. You just need to know where to look. Anyway, this dude, Andy Moore. Can't find any trace of him, no online presence, no friends, his sister doesn't have him on any of her accounts...'

The young man paused and looked up.

'...here, are you thinking that he maybe had something to do with Shearer's death?'

'I'm not sure what to think, Torquil. Even if he is involved, if he was getting revenge for his sister's murder, he'd have no reason to kill the others...'

Torquil raised an eyebrow. 'Mr Redpath, can I ask...why are you investigating these murders? I mean, surely it's a job for the police?'

Bruce took a deep breath and exhaled slowly; it was a question he had repeatedly been asking himself.

'Torquil, you've done a very good job here and I think it's only fair to be honest with you. This is all completely unofficial and, you're quite correct, it *is* a job for the police. You see...'

Was there any point in explaining his stance on the law, on 'due process'? Probably not.

'...I just can't abide people taking the law into their own hands. These killings, well they're all pretty brutal, for a start. Granted, all the victims have been particularly wicked people themselves, but it's still not right to kill them out of hand.'

'Why not? I mean—'

Bruce slapped his hand on the desk angrily, causing the young man to jump.

'NO! It's just wrong and it's the first step to an anarchic, lawless society. Next thing you'll have groups of local vigilantes hanging people they suspect of crimes from the nearest lamp-post! That's what our legal system is there for, to bring people like that to justice.'

Torquil smiled. 'But surely justice and the law are different things.'

As Bruce sat on the crowded train home that evening, he reflected on just how much Torquil Carnegie had surprised him. At the end of the previous week, he had all but given up on the arrogant, 'entitled' young man, but now...? He smiled.

It seemed that Bruce Redpath had enlisted a willing assistant in his quest to discover who was responsible for the murders of Messrs Shearer, Bannon, Scullion and Krasniki; and, of course, why.

And that comment about 'justice and the law?' Bruce was sure he had heard it before somewhere, although he couldn't quite identify where...

The week passed quickly, a seemingly endless procession of dis-
illusioned spouses beating a path to the doors of Redpath Fox,
Carnegie. In an attempt to catch up on his paperwork, he had
stayed late on Friday evening, but now Bruce exited the train and
made his was wearily up the same worn, stone steps of Greenock
West station. The six carriages had disgorged the usual array of
week-weary travellers and he was relieved to finally arrive outside
to a crisp, clear early-winter's night. He crossed to the pre-booked
private hire car and got in.

'Hame, Mr Redpath?'

'Yes please, Hana—oh, could you stop at the off-licence round
the corner?'

He saw the female driver smile in the rear-view mirror.

'Sure thing, Mr Redpath. Been a tough auld week?'

'Just the usual, really. The trouble with being a divorce lawyer is
that you tend to see the worst of humanity.'

She laughed. 'Hah! Ye want tae try bein' a female taxi driver in
Greenock at wan o'clock on a Sunday mornin'!'

He smiled back; Hana was probably right. And, if truth be told,
the week hadn't been too hard. The usual procession of clients, a
mix of male, female, young and old. All with their own particular
set of gripes and grudges, all wanting and expecting a better
settlement than they were probably entitled to. And, sadly, all
fallen out of love with the person of their dreams.

Torquil Carnegie had continued to surprise Bruce. The young
man seemed to have taken a genuine interest in the brutal killings
and had managed to unearth a few more facts, none of which
indicated a connection between the victims, unfortunately.
Bruce had attempted to contact QC Carol Veitch to see if she
remembered anything of note regarding the trial of William
Bannon but she hadn't returned his call. She was a successful and
busy Counsel and probably had much more important matters

to occupy her rather expensive time! Arshid Maan, Krasniki's solicitor, had moved abroad, having retired early on the proceeds of a highly successful career. He shook his head slightly in the darkness of the cab. He knew he should really let it drop; it was becoming an obsession and, anyway, there had been no further reported killings that week. Maybe the balance of power had been restored after all.

Half an hour later, he was home and soon there was a ribeye steak sizzling nicely in the pan, the oven chips were browning, the peas were in the microwave. He uncorked the bottle of Cabernet and poured a glass, savouring the first mouthful. He wouldn't have too much, though. The weather forecast was good for Saturday and he was looking forward to his first game of golf for weeks, Rob having texted to say that the other two members of the four-ball were available. He was very slightly disappointed that there was no invitation to spend Saturday night in the Connor household, but there was a limit as to how much he could impose himself upon their hospitality. He smiled; he was extremely fond of Rob and Mel—maybe he should ask them over sometime—after all, he entertained his own family fairly regularly. Which reminded him, his older daughter, Coral, had asked him over for lunch on Sunday, which would make a pleasant change. The only problem was that he would have to drive and he'd be unable to enjoy a glass of wine with his lunch. Still, he'd be home by seven, he could have a wee whisky, then a bath. He took another hefty slug of the tart, full-bodied wine, then topped up his glass. The oven was beeping and the steak was ready.

It had been a thoroughly enjoyable weekend. On Saturday, he and Rob had won their golf match, after which he had spent a pleasant afternoon in the clubhouse with a harmless, if slightly raucous, crowd of fellow golfers. The highlight, of course, had been the Sunday afternoon spent in the company of Amy, his granddaughter; and her parents, of course.

He looked at his watch; there was just time to pour himself a whisky before switching on the television for the nine o'clock news. The killings had slipped well down from the headlines and, thankfully, there had been no fresh atrocities. He breathed a very faint sigh of relief; it seemed to be over, he could relax. Before he retired for the evening, he might have one final look at the cases, see if there was anything he had missed linking the victims. Then he could put it all away, hopefully for good.

He'd maybe have one more wee whisky as a nightcap.

Just the one.

The Monday morning train clanked tediously across the massive girders of the Clyde bridge, stopping and starting for no apparent reason. Bruce had been dozing fitfully but now, as they slid into Glasgow Central's platform twelve, he reached down and lifted his briefcase from between his legs in preparation for the usual inane race towards the ticket barriers; as if a few seconds made any difference.

Soon he was in the taxi, heading to the office. For some reason he had slept through his alarm that morning and his customary schedule had been severely disrupted; he had barely had time to shave far less eat breakfast of listen to the morning news.

He had promised himself that he would drop his unofficial enquiries into the brutal series of murders. It was a promise he had fully intended to keep but, after dozing in his chair for almost an hour, he had been wide awake and had decided to have another quick look over his findings.

And another small whisky.

He let out a slight groan of despair, his driver catching his eye in the rear-view mirror.

'You okay, Mr Redpath? Hope you're no' sickenin' for somethin'!'

'No, I'm fine, Gary, just didn't sleep that well last night.'

Gary smiled and winked at Bruce's reflection; he had smelt the stale whisky fumes from his passenger's breath...

'Bruce, are you okay? You seem a bit distracted this morning.'

Bruce turned towards Olivia Carnegie, dragging his thoughts back to the Partner's meeting.

'What...oh, I'm sorry, I was just...'

The door opened and Simon Fox entered, the wide, Cheshire-cat grin on his face.

'Morning all!'

There was an expectant pause, then Peter Caira stood up and extended his hand.

'Very well done, Simon. Another feather in your cap.'

'Thank you kindly. Yes, I have to say it *was* a challenge but we got there in the end, rather more quickly than I might have expected too!'

The others offered their congratulations. It had been late on Friday afternoon that an unexpected verdict of 'Not Guilty' had been returned in the trial, for murder, of Suzannah Flint. Following some careful direction by the Judge, the jury had returned after only fifty minutes with a unanimous verdict. Simon sat down.

'Mind you, she's a right nasty bitch, is Ms Flint. Condescended to give me a peck on the cheek, shook my hand and thanked me for my help before being whisked off by some weaselly-looking chap...'

'Paul Maguire,' interjected Peter Caira. 'Used to be a solicitor but he got struck of for fiddling the books.'

Simon looked quizzically at his partner.

'Really? And how do you happen to know that?'

Peter smiled.

'I saw them on the BBC news when they came out of court and I recognised him. He was at Uni at the same time as me. Clever bugger but always a bit shifty, if you know what I mean. I wasn't the least bit surprised when he went off the tracks.'

'Hm,' replied Simon. 'Wouldn't have put Ms Flint with that wee runt, mind you, she'd eat him alive.'

Peter grinned.

'I'm not sure that she *is* with him, Simon. Paul Maguire is one of the directors of Hooley Transport and I had some dealings with them a few years back when they were expanding their operation down in Govan. As far as I could see, his only interests are smoking, drinking and money. I don't know if you remember but, a few weeks back, one of their drivers got arrested for people-trafficking then conveniently hanged himself while he was in custody.'

Bruce was aware of the blood thumping in his temples and his mouth felt dry as he spoke.

'Em, so what's the connection between Hooley Transport and the Flint woman, Peter, do you know?'

Simon spoke before his colleague could answer.

'Mind you, that might explain where my fee is coming from. If Flint *is* associated with Hooley transport, maybe they're putting up the money.'

Bruce sensed that the moment had passed as Simon opened his briefcase, continuing in a somewhat disinterested tone.

'Is there still actually a Hooley involved in the business, I wonder?'

'Frank,' replied Bruce. 'His daughter, Maria, is married to David Doyle, they're both directors.'

Simon's head snapped back up. 'Bruce, how the hell do you know that...oh wait, don't tell me; is it something to do with these bloody murders?'

Bruce sighed and nodded. 'Well, actually...'

Olivia looked at him with a sympathetic expression; she was very fond of Bruce but her tone was somewhat harsh.

'Bruce, you really need to drop it, it's obviously not doing you any good. I mean, why, in God's name, are you still digging about in the affairs of the criminal underworld...'

'...and in my old case notes too, apparently,' interjected Simon. Olivia looked across at him in surprise.

'What?

Simon turned towards her. 'Yes, after enlisting the help of your son and heir! Sent the poor lad down to the basement to dig out the case notes from the trial of one Richard Shearer. Bruce, I'm worried—'

'Well, you needn't be. I'm perfectly fine, if you want to know, so let's just leave it at that. Anyway, Olivia, you were saying...'

The meeting had ended and Bruce had rushed off to meet a client, for whom he was insufficiently prepared due to his late arrival. Simon finished his text, placing his phone in his pocket as Olivia rose to leave.

'Hang on a minute, Liv.'

As if expecting his request, she sat back down.

'Is he all right, do you think?'

She frowned. 'I don't know. I really don't know. I thought...'

She paused, as if not wanting to put her thoughts into words, but Simon finished the sentence for her.

'...you thought he smelled of drink. Yes, so did I. God, I hope he's not turning into a bloody alcoholic. Remember a while back, he had a bit of a problem...'

Olivia snapped back at him. '...and no bloody wonder, after...'

She stopped mid-sentence. Simon Fox stared at her.

'What?'

'Oh Christ, Simon, it's ten years. Ten years next month...'

He dropped his head into his hands. 'Oh God, so it is....'

Bruce found it hard to concentrate on what his client was telling him, although he had a fleeting thought that, if she had expected tea and sympathy, she had come on the wrong day. He knew that Olivia and Simon would be discussing him; Simon was usually the first to leave and he had hesitated on the pretext of reading a phone message. If he was being honest, he didn't blame them. His behaviour had been rather bizarre recently and he still wasn't exactly sure why. Was it just his obsession (no, it wasn't an obsession, it was just a rather unhealthy interest) in these cases? Or was there something else—he still couldn't quite put his finger on the vague niggle deep in his cranium.

His client finally departed, with Bruce giving assurances that he would do his very best. He ran his fingers through his hair, realising that it felt very slightly greasy. He had meant to wash it that morning but, as he had overslept, he hadn't even bothered showering. He lifted the corner of his jacket and sniffed, making a face as the sour aroma of unwashed sweat assailed his nostrils. What the hell was wrong with him—and why had he overslept in the first place? He shook his head, knowing the answer; because he had sat up until well after two in the morning, looking over those bloody cases.

Obsessed? No, of course he wasn't. But he had thought it best to check, just in the off-chance he had missed anything...

He picked up the phone and asked Torquil to come to his office. The young man was there in seconds.

'Yes, Mr Redpath...oh, are you okay?'

No, he bloody well wasn't!

'Yes, I'm fine...listen, Torquil, I take it there's been no fresh, em... cases overnight?'

Torquil smiled knowingly. 'Nada, Mr Redpath. I've been keeping my eyes on the news and social media but there's been nothing.'

Bruce let out a sigh.

'Good, good. Look, I've been having a think and a chat with the Partners, I'm not sure if there's any point in carrying on with this...'

He looked up at the young man's face, which had immediately taken on an expression of dismay. Bruce suddenly realised that what Torquil Carnegie needed most was a project. An idea popped into his head.

'...but the thing is, I'm working on a divorce case at present and I'd like your help. Now, first and foremost, what I'm going to tell you is all highly confidential and does not go any further than this office. Not even to your mother—understood?'

Torquil grinned. 'Sure thing, Boss!'

Bruce felt that the 'Boss' epithet should irritate him; instead, he rather liked it!

'Okay.'

He handed Torquil a folder.

'I want you to see what you can find out about a man by the name of Aiden Goff; and you may as well do a bit of digging on his wife, Pam. She's my client but it's always best to know what her dirty little secrets are.'

As he explained about the case, Bruce realised that he'd normally have entrusted this in its entirety to a private investigator by the name of Calum, or Cal, Gibson. He'd see how Torquil got on first and maybe save the Firm a bit of money.

As the grinning Torquil Carnegie left the office, Bruce also remembered that he'd called Gibson a week or so ago but the detective hadn't yet got back to him. He frowned; it wasn't like Gibson not to follow up on a request. Presumably there was nothing to report...his train of thought was broken as Torquil's head popped back round the office door.

'Em...can I get you a coffee, Boss?'

'Oh, yes, thanks, that would be most welcome.'

The boy was full of surprises, he mused and, as Torquil Carnegie departed once more, Bruce Redpath smiled—for the first time that day.

Chapter 6

Bruce had had a busy week and a particularly busy Friday morning. He was in his office, drinking a coffee as he prepared for yet another particularly acrimonious divorce hearing, due to start on the following Monday. As he studiously leafed through his case notes, there was a knock at his door.

'Come in.'

Olivia Carnegie popped her head round the door and smiled. 'Busy?'

He sighed; of course he was. Marriage most certainly wasn't for life these days.

'Never too busy for you, Olivia, come on in. What can I do for you?'

She was holding a folded newspaper, which she handed to him.

'Thought you might be interested in this.'

He took it and looked at it; it was that day's copy of a well-known and well-respected Edinburgh newspaper..

'I was over in the capital this morning, bought it to read on the train.'

She pointed to an article, with the heading:

'Bonnar's Byte
by Miriam Bonnar'

Bruce looked up at Olivia. 'Miriam Bonnar? Who's she, when she's at home?'

Olivia laughed; she had a lovely, musical laugh, Bruce thought.

'You've never heard of Miriam, Edinburgh's resident conspiracy theorist? I'll leave you to have a read, Bruce—oh, but don't, for

God's sake, tell Simon I gave you it, he'll just think I'm encouraging you! Catch you later.'

'Thanks,' he called as she left, trailing a waft of expensive perfume in her wake. He needed a bit of light relief from 'Rahmani vs. Rahmani' so he sat back and started to read the article.

....you heard it here first, folks...

And another one bytes the dust (apologies, Freddie). That makes four—to date! Shearer, Bannon, Scullion, Krasniki. All bad men (am I allowed to say that?) All brutally murdered (well, apparently, although our friends in the police aren't saying much). So what's going on? Is this just some vicious gangland vendetta, a violent power-play? I thought so, until Aleksander Krasniki became victim number four. The others? Well, they all had form, but what they all had in common was that, over the past few years, they had each been tried but not convicted.

Rik Shearer—'weel-kent' Glasgow hoodlum, apparently not averse to employing the old-fashioned art of razor slashing in his youth. Owner of a chain of tanning salons, inside which his ex-lover, Shelley Moore, met a particularly violent and unpleasant end. After a re-trial, Shearer's case was deemed to be 'not proven' amidst claims of both witness and jury intimidation.

Billy Bannon and Vincent Scullion, another pair of Glasgow 'ne'er-do-weels'.

Double trouble, extortionists and money-
launderers supreme. When one of their
so-called 'clients' refused to play ball, they
cut off his hands and left him to bleed to
death. Somehow they, too, slipped off the
hook when the case collapsed amidst more
hints of jury and witness intimidation—
oh, and not to mention giving each
other a seemingly watertight alibi!

These three victims were believed to still
be active in the criminal underworld
and, by implication, potential
targets in a possible 'turf war.'

But then came victim number four.

Aleksander Krasniki, who had been tried
for the rape and brutal murder of sixteen
year-old Serena Swinburne. However,
apparently the poor man didn't understand
the charges and the Judge was forced
to dismiss the case... Krasniki wasn't a
known member of any criminal gang; evil
and wicked he may have been but, by all
accounts, he wasn't an 'organised' crook.

So why kill him? Why indeed?
I have a theory—but then, dear reader,
you knew I would, didn't you?
I suspect that persons unknown are targeting
some of the nastier members of society,
especially those who have managed, one way
or another, to walk away from a trial. I think

*that there are people out there, people who
know that the law has failed and that justice
has not been done, who are watching out for
Good by ridding us of the Bad and the Ugly,
where the Law has not been able to do so.
And, if that is the case, I, for one, applaud
them. How often have we seen the worst of
society walk away from a collapsed trial; a
'Not proven' or 'Not guilty' verdict, free to
offend again? As someone once said, 'The law
is an ass' and sometimes it most definitely is.
So, whoever you may be, I suspect that you
are operating outside the normal parameters
of our moral and legal society but, let's face
it, so are the scum that you are taking down.
Good on you—it's about time someone
took a stand. I'm going to christen you...*

'The Civil Guard'

Bruce finished the article but continued to stare at the page, the words beginning to swim. He couldn't believe what this woman was saying in print, that it was even remotely acceptable for anyone to take the law into their own hands, especially in such a brutal manner. That was the road to anarchy. Yet this Miriam Bonnar, whoever the hell she was, had been given prime column-space in one of Scotland's oldest and most-respected newspapers, praising her so-called 'Civil Guard'. He read it again, his hands shaking slightly with a combination of rage and indignation. He would write to the editor...

Suddenly, he placed the folded paper down on his desk. While Miriam Bonnar's opinion on justice was entirely abhorrent to him, her theory had struck a chord somewhere deep within him. What if these murders *weren't* actually acts of criminal retribution?

What if persons unknown, maybe not with a specific criminal background, *had* formed an organisation to administer their own warped ideas of justice upon those acquitted of crimes, of which they may actually have been guilty.

What if 'The Civil Guard' actually existed?

Bruce could feel beads of perspiration break out on his forehead. That notion was worse than that of a gangland feud.

Much worse.

But what had surprised him most was that both he and Torquil Carnegie had completely overlooked the simple answer, the obvious connection between the killings.

All four men had been tried for their crimes.

And all four men had walked free.

'You okay, Bruce?' asked Rob Shearer as, on Saturday morning, they stood on the first tee of Greenock Golf club, waiting for the game in front to move up the fairway. 'You're lookin' a bit peaky.'

'Peaky? What's that supposed to mean?'

Rob Connor smiled at his friend. 'Listen, mate, never forget that I'm a detective! Somethin's botherin' you.'

'There's nothing bothering me, Rob, I'm absolutely fine.'

Rob held his hands up. 'Okay, okay, I was just sayin'...'

He leaned towards his friend, dropping his voice to a whisper.

'...but, strictly between you an' me, I strongly suspect that if, by any remote chance, you'd been stopped and breathalysed this mornin', you'd have been lucky if you'd got away with it.'

Bruce felt his face redden and his temper rise.

'Now, hang on a minute—'

His friend straightened up and smiled, but there was a hint of steel in it.

'I'm just sayin', as your friend. Look, I've known you since we were twelve, I'd hate to see you in trouble, that's all. Right, that's us ready to tee off, let's see if we can take the money again this week.'

It was the persistent ringing of his mobile that woke him up. Despite he and Rob winning their four-ball, Bruce had arrived home feeling both irritated and slightly guilty; if truth be told, Rob was most probably correct. He had realised that he had had a good bit more to drink on the Friday night than he had intended to. Something *was* bothering him, he just couldn't put his finger on what it might be.

The mobile stopped ringing then started again as he dug it out from the side of the chair.

'Rob.'

'Bruce, sorry, did I disturb you?'

'No, it's fine, I was just having a wee nap.'

'Listen, mate, I'm sorry, I realised that I was a bit harsh with you earlier...'

'No. you were right, and I'm a bloody idiot. I *did* have a few too many last night and I probably shouldn't have driven.'

'For God's sake, I'd have come and got you—I mean, it's not as if you haven't driven me home in the past...'

Five minutes later, Bruce had an invitation to an impromptu dinner at the Connor household. He smiled as he ended the call; Mel's dinners were seldom impromptu.

'How is he?'

Rob Connor shook his head as he put his phone back in his pocket.

'Honestly don't know. I mean, we've made our peace and he admits he wasn't fit to drive.'

'Stupid idiot! How would *that* work, as a lawyer?'

'I don't know; not well, I'd imagine. I'm sure there's something else botherin' him though...'

Mel raised her eyebrows and tilted her head as she gazed at her husband..

'Of course there bloody is!'

Rob's mouth opened in surprise. 'Oh shit!'

'Exactly. Ten years, Rob. Ten fucking years...'

Her eyes started to fill with tears as Rob's strong arms enfolded her. He gritted his teeth, feeling the long-buried anger surge through his veins as his wife sobbed quietly into his shoulder

Sunday. Of course, it had to be a Sunday.

He was an enormous man; obese, undoubtedly, probably about six-feet-three in height. A presence to be reckoned with in his day, imposing and authoritative. A man who once commanded respect..

At the moment, he was lying on his back, spread-eagled and tied securely to an ancient and solid wooden table.

He was naked.

The corpulent, white mass of his aged body sagged in all the wrong places, spreading grotesquely across the scored surface of the table. The skin was mostly hairless, with distinct varicose veins in his rather spindly legs. A cardboard placard lay on his chest, secured by duct tape. He was mumbling incessantly as two dark-clad figures, balaclavas covering their features, went about their business. He was in a building with rough stone walls; it was surprisingly warm, although the naked man was shivering, from fear mostly. He could see a flickering red glow on the dirty, corrugated-iron ceiling of the dimly-lit room. He could feel a vague warmth on his left-hand side but he couldn't bring himself to turn towards it, to determine the source of the heat. There was a faint hissing sound breaking the silence.

He was terrified.

One of the two masked men bent down and rummaged in a bag, lifting out a peculiar implement. It resembled a pair of heavy-duty fire tongs, the kind that once hung on the companion sets in the days of coal fires. The dull surface of the metal was relieved by engraved medieval-style script. He moved towards the naked man, opening and shutting the handle with his leather-gloved hand. As he did so, the implement made a sharp 'snicking' sound. The naked man averted his eyes as he continued to mumble, but his captor moved the implement to follow his gaze. He recognised it, of course. An ancient artefact, symbolic of the atrocities once carried out in the name of religion, a relic of the Spanish Inquisition. Dear God, surely not...?

'Oh dearest merciful God, spare me, pardon my sins...'

His captor turned away and took a few steps in the direction of the warmth. The naked man could resist no longer; he turned his head in time to see the dark-clad man place the implement into what looked like a small, gas-powered forge, its charcoals glowing a bright orange. He attempted to raise his voice slightly

'Holy Mary, Mother of God, bless me, for I have sinned....'

It came out as a hoarse whisper; his throat was dry, his heart rate elevated, beads of perspiration rose on his wrinkled brow. It was partly fear, he knew, but it was partly the side-effects of the two little blue pills he had been forced to swallow an hour or so earlier.

Two...

He stared at the ceiling and closed his eyes as he continued to mumble; sometimes in English, sometimes in Latin.

One of the captors placed his latex-gloved hand on the naked man's upper thigh and started to stroke it gently.

'Pater noster, qui est in caelis...'

The hand moved slowly, irrevocably upwards to his flaccid appendage, encircling, coaxing...within a few minutes, the combination of a double-dose of Viagra coupled with the skilled, sensual massaging by the captor, elicited the desired effect. Despite his resistance, his fear, he was now engorged.

The naked man closed his eyes, his prayers turning to pleading as the other captor walked towards the little forge and removed the glowing implement.

Chapter 7

The post usually arrived late morning in rural West Lothian but, on this cold, misty Wednesday, it was one-thirty before Dzhokhar Meta crossed to the window, alert (as always) to the sound of a vehicle outside. He watched the red van perform an awkward three point turn before it disappeared back down the badly rutted road, the postman having deposited the mail in the metal letterbox adjacent to the heavy security gate that guarded the short driveway to his house. The unclassified road led to a long-disused quarry; one way in, one way out, just as Meta liked it. The house had originally been occupied by the quarry manager and had been in a poor condition when Meta and his daughter moved in, but large sums of money had been spent making it comfortable and, more importantly, secure.

Meta was a man who took no chances; a domestic letterbox could always provide an opportunity for unwanted packages; dangerous packages. He opened the front door, looked briefly about then walked down to the box. Opening the little hatch carefully, he took the few letters out and looked at them. An electricity bill. A flyer from his local hardware store. A plain, slightly bulky brown envelope, his name and address neatly printed on a white label. He considered it carefully, then took the three items of mail into the house.

Once he was in the kitchen, he placed the brown envelope in the sink. He donned a pair of plastic DIY goggles and a pair of thick gardening gloves then, keeping it at arm's length, he carefully slit the envelope open with a knife.

Nothing happened; it was safe.

He took off the protective equipment, lifted the envelope out of the sink and looked inside. It contained a small bundle of photographs which he regarded quizzically before pulling them out. He lifted a pair of off-the-shelf reading spectacles from the worktop and looked at the prints, his frown deepening as the colour drained from his face.

Each of the first five showed the image of a naked man, securely and cruelly bound and wearing an expression of terror, of agony, or a combination of both. Each wore a cardboard placard on which was written their name, a number preceded by a hash-tag, followed by the legend 'Who's next?'

Meta had seen worse; the images were brutal and graphic, but he was a brutal man by nature.

It was the sixth image that bothered him most.

A simple cardboard placard, on which was printed: 'Dzhokhar Meta. Are you next?'

Meta sat for a few minutes, scrutinising the images. He rubbed his coarse, stubbled chin as his eyes narrowed; he would have to be vigilant. Maybe it was time to bring in some trusted associates, just in case. There was little that Dzhokhar Meta feared, but he didn't want his photograph being added to those clutched in his ham-like fist, especially when their expressions spoke of untold horrors.

He placed the graphic images on the table and reached for his mobile.

Having spent Wednesday morning in the dreary confines of a courtroom, Bruce decided to have lunch in his favourite Glasgow delicatessen, conveniently located only a block away from the offices of Redpath, Fox, Carnegie. Although the small eatery was busy, he had managed to procure a table for one, tucked in a nook under the stairs. A radio was playing softly in the background, barely audible above the hum of conversation and the clatter of dishes.

He had taken the first bite of his Tuscan sausage and mozzarella ciabatta when the one o'clock news came on.

'A murder investigation is under way following the discovery this morning of the body of disgraced ex-Bishop Brendan Devenney, who was tried several years ago on a number of charges of sexual assault against young men. One of the alleged victims committed suicide during the trial and a verdict of not guilty was eventually returned, but it is understood that the Catholic Church brought pressure to bear on Devenney, who resigned shortly afterwards.

'Devenney's body was found in a disused farm building near Duns, in the Scottish Borders but police have not yet said how he died. However, in a short statement, they have indicated that he was brutally assaulted before he was killed and that they are not ruling out a link to the recent spate of murders in which the victims were similarly assaulted prior to their deaths...'

The announcer's voice droned on as Bruce sat, staring unseeingly at the underside of the stairway. Leaving his mostly- uneaten lunch on the plate, he reached for his jacket and briefcase and stood up. At the counter, the proprietor gave him a concerned look.

'Was your lunch okay, Mr Redpath—you've hardly touched it?'

'What? Oh, yes, yes, it was fine, Marco, just need to get back to the office, that's all.'

He presented his card for payment.

'A bit of divine retribution there, don't you think?' asked Marco, as he took payment for the uneaten food. Bruce stared at him.

'What?'

'On the news—didn't you hear it? The murder of that ex-Bishop. I mean, you know, with my background, I'm a born and bred Catholic, but that man, a disgrace to the Priesthood...'

Marco Matonti pulled a face. 'He got off, didn't he?'

Bruce could feel his head start to spin.

'Em, yes, I think so.'

'Aye, it said so on the radio. One of the poor buggers that he interfered with took his own life and he bloody got off with it. Bastard—sorry, Mr Redpath.'

Bruce took a ten pound note out of his pocket and placed it on the counter. Marco gave him an odd look.

'You've just paid by card, Mr Redpath.' He grinned. 'Unless you're being particularly generous today?'

Bruce flushed slightly. 'Em, oh, yes, just put it in the box.'

'Cheers, Mr Redpath.'

Bruce turned to leave, but Marco had a parting shot.

'Anyway, he deserves all he got, if you ask me...good on them, whoever's taking all these scumballs out...'

Bruce was sitting at his desk with his head in his hands when there was a knock at his office door. He rubbed his face, trying to focus his attention.

'Come in.'

Torquil Carnegie's head materialised around the side of the door.

'All right, Boss?'

'Em, yes, Torquil, come in.'

The young man entered, once again looking very slightly dishevelled and dusty. He was clutching a folder and Bruce presumed that he had paid another visit to the archives in the basement. He forced himself to appear enthusiastic.

'You've been busy, I see—what's this?

Torquil smiled as he placed the folder in front of Bruce, He read the rather grubby label that was stuck to the front.

> Bishop Brendan Devenney.
> Defending Solicitor Simon Fox.
> Case Notes.

Bruce stared at the words.

'Are you all right, Mr Redpath?'

Bruce looked up at the young man, unsure whether to be angry or grateful.

'Why did you look this out?'

'I heard the news at lunchtime and I figured that this guy's death might be another of those retribution murders...'

Bruce started at Torquil's choice of adjective; it was the second time he had heard 'retribution' used in the space of an hour.

'...so I had a wee dig about and it turned out that it was Mr Fox who defended him.'

Bruce let out a long sigh.

'I see. That was very perceptive of you.'

'Cheers; thing is, like all the others, it's a fair bet the dude was guilty but walked. You know, Boss, I'm beginning to suspect that all this shit isn't gang related and that someone's going after all these people who've got away with murder...'

Torquil sniggered at his own joke.

'...literally!'

Bruce presumed that Torquil hadn't read the article by Miriam Bonnar.

'Yes, well, you're not the first person to suggest that.'

He opened the bottom drawer of his desk and took out the copy of the newspaper that Olivia had given him, handing it to Torquil. The young man read it and placed it back on the table.

'Shit...soz...that's a kinda interesting theory, pretty much what I was thinking! Who's Miriam Bonnar anyway?'

'Ask your mother—she seems to think that Ms Bonnar is Edinburgh's very own conspiracy theorist.'

Torquil frowned. 'Hm, I'm not so sure, she might actually have a point. Listen, Chief, let me have a look at these notes and see if I can dig up anything relevant.'

He stood up to leave.

'Oh, and by the way, Mrs Aherne's away home...can I get you a coffee?'

'Em, yes please; oh, and...'

Torquil Carnegie paused half way through the door.

'...can we just stick with 'Boss' please, rather than 'Chief'?'

<hr>

Dzhokhar Meta turned off the television, having watched the evening news, then lifted his glass; it was empty. He shouted.

'Kat. Bring me the vodka, the bottle in the fridge.'

A few minutes later, his daughter appeared with the bottle of chilled vodka. There was an unusual expression on her pasty features and he suspected the reason. Apart from himself and his daughter, the house was now occupied by three of Meta's henchmen; tough, hard men, their allegiance to Meta unquestioned. One of them, a swarthy individual with a bad squint, had seemed, for some unfathomable reason, to have taken a liking to his daughter. He smiled; that would suit him just fine. As Katya handed him he chilled bottle, he grasped her hand and leered up at her.

'What were you up to in the kitchen?'

She looked away, trying to free her hand.

'Nothing, Papa. Just talking to Janik.'

'Janik, eh? Good, about time you had a man. Off you go.'

He patted her ample rear as she turned away, oblivious to the look of disgust that passed over her heavy features. He filled his glass and took a mouthful. The news bulletin had put a name to the last of the photographic images that he had received; an ex Bishop, accused of sexual offences against young boys. Served the bastard right, though Meta, entirely unaware of the irony. His thoughts turned to Agni Krasniki and, suddenly, a vague idea started to form in his calculating mind. Maybe he was going about things the wrong way; maybe there was an opportunity here. A grin spread across his coarse features as he swallowed more vodka.

Dzhokhar Meta had the beginnings of a plan.

As the Friday evening train screeched to a rather jerky stop in Greenock West station, Bruce remembered that he had run out of whisky. As he entered the cab, he realised that, once again, it was Hana, one of his regular drivers, who was behind the wheel. He felt a pang of embarrassment; last time she had driven him home on a Friday, he had asked her to stop at the off-licence. He did a quick calculation—was it one week, two...no, definitely two, that was okay. She needn't know about the bottle he had bought the previous weekend in the supermarket.

'Evening, Hana.'

'Evenin' Mr Redpath. Hame?'

'Em, yes, but if you could just...'

'...stop at the off-licence. Aye, nae problem, Mr R...'

He ignored the slight frown that he saw Hana give as she glanced at him in the rear-view mirror. It was only a bottle of whisky, for God's sake...

He heated up a pizza; he hadn't felt much like cooking after the week he'd had. The death of Devenney had shocked him deeply, having concluded that the killings were over. However, something was troubling him more; Simon had come into his office that afternoon in a rather indignant frame of mind.

'Bruce, what the hell's going on?'

Bruce looked up at his friend.

'Sorry? What do you mean?'

'I've just found out that Olivia's boy took another of my old case files out of the basement. A certain ex-Bishop by the name of Devenney. Did you sanction this?'

Bruce could feel his hackles rising.

'As a matter of fact I didn't. Torquil acted on his own initiative. He'd heard the news about Devenney's murder, he did a bit of research and he discovered that you'd defended the man.'

'Yes, I did. A rather unsavoury character, to say the least, but it was my job to ensure a fair trial, as you are only too well aware. I'd like to know why you think it's acceptable for young Carnegie to go rummaging about in confidential case files.'

'Simon, he's doing research for me—'

'Yes, on bloody divorce cases, not on closed murder trials!'

Simon sat down across from Bruce and lowered his voice as he leaned across the desk.

'Listen to me, Bruce. I've asked you nicely, now I'm telling you. You need to drop this bloody unofficial investigation into these killings. It's affecting your health; and your...'

He stopped mid-sentence as Bruce glared across at him, a shocked expression on his face.

'What? What were you going to say?'

Simon Fox shook his head. 'Nothing. Never mind.'

'No! It's too late—you were going to say it was affecting my work, weren't you?'

Simon sat back, his expression stony. 'Bruce, take a look at yourself. You've been late a couple of times recently—you've *never* been late in all the time that I've known you! Both Liv and I have noticed a smell of drink.'

'That's utter nonsense, Simon. I have never—I repeat, *never*—had anything to drink during working hours!'

'I'm not saying you have, but you've come in to work a couple of times *smelling* of drink, which leads me to conclude you've had a skinfull the night before.'

Bruce was angry now and raised his voice. 'And what the hell gives you the right to question what I do when I'm in my own home?'

Simon leaned forward again.

'Oh, for Christ's sake, don't get all high and mighty with me. If you come in here stinking of whisky, if you can't stop your hands from shaking, then we need to ask some rather serious questions.'

Bruce had been holding a document and immediately dropped his hands on to the desk. He was speechless; Simon lowered his voice again, favouring Bruce with a half-smile.

'Listen, my friend, please, for your own sake, drop this. You're putting yourself under terrible pressure for no reason that I can see. Leave it be. Look, away home and get an early night. The forecast looks half-decent for tomorrow, you should get out for a game of golf. Don't do any more of your bloody amateur investigations—and don't take refuge in a bloody bottle either. Talk to someone; me, Liv, Peter, to bloody Rayna Aherne, she's always had a soft spot for you. Talk to your friend Rob, he seems a decent sort...for a cop!'

He stood up and headed for the door.

'But you can't go on like this, Bruce Redpath. Get a grip, my friend. Get a bloody grip.'

Bruce had eaten the pizza too fast and was already suffering from indigestion. He had opened a bottle of beer but it sat, still half-full, on the table in front of him as he stared morosely at nothing in particular. It had been an awful week but the worst part, by far, had been his row with Simon. Since the very first days of Redpath Fox, he couldn't remember ever having had an argument with his co-founder and the day's heated exchange had left him sad and bruised. He *wasn't* drinking too much; sure, he enjoyed a whisky occasionally, who didn't? But he was in control....wasn't he?

Angrily he stood up, lifting his plate and depositing the pizza crusts in the bin. The bottle of Highland Park, which had been on special offer, stood unopened and inviting on the worktop. He'd leave it a bit, maybe have a small one as a nightcap, otherwise he'd never sleep...

Paul Maguire lay naked on top of his bed, propped up on his pillows and with a glass of brandy on the bedside table. A dim sidelight illuminated the rather untidy room, hazy with tobacco smoke, and a laptop sat astride his scrawny white thighs. His mobile buzzed but he barely noticed, immersed as he was in the images on the screen...it buzzed again; and again. Finally, with a string of oaths, he picked it up and looked at the caller display; anyway, the moment had passed—for now! He slid his sweaty thumb across the screen to answer the call, noting that it was nearly two in the morning. How time flew...

'Davie. Everything okay?'

The voice on the other end sounded breathless, panicky.

'Naw, it's no fuckin' okay. Suzi's disappeared.'

Maguire frowned. 'What exactly d'you mean 'disappeared'?'

Doyle sounded barely in control of himself.

'Ah mean she's fuckin' no' here. She messaged me yesterday but Ah wis goin' over tae bloody Frank's hoose wi' Maria an' Ah couldn'ae get oot o' it...fuck sake...'

'Davie, Davie, calm down, what the hell's going on?'

'She got sent these photies. Photies o' all those guys that were killed. They were naked an' everythin', looked like they were bein' tortured or somethin', she said. Fuck sake, it scared the shit oot o' her, Ah've never heard her soundin' so feart...'

Maguire felt a frisson of unease run up his spine.

'Listen, calm down...'

'...but it wis the last photie that really freaked her. It wis a picture o' a bit o' cardboard, a sign, like. Some cunt had written on it 'Suzannah Flint—are you next?''

The frisson turned to a full-blown shudder. Paul Maguire had heard some troubling rumours over the last few days but this was the cold, hard evidence that he had dreaded. He took a deep breath.

'Davie, what makes you think she's disappeared? Maybe she's just baled out, gone to stay with a relative or something, after all the carry-on with the trial.'

'Fuck sake, Paul, Ah'm at her hoose noo. When Ah arrived, the front door wis open, the lights were on, but there's nae sign o' her. Her mobile's lyin' in the kitchen, she never goes naewhere withoot her fuckin' mobile...'

'Maybe there was an emergency.'

David Doyle was nearly screaming down the phone now.

'Her fuckin' motor's still in the drive! Ah mean, where the fuck would she go...hang on...there's a car comin', maybe it's a taxi...'

'Davie. DAVIE!'

'Aye, it looks like a—'

There was a sudden crash as if the phone had been dropped and Paul Maguire listened in horror as he heard the sound of a scuffle followed by some muffled oaths. This was followed a few seconds later by the sound of a vehicle driving away at speed.

'DAVIE! Fuck sake...'

Maguire jumped out of bed, all thoughts of adult entertainment now forgotten. He dressed hurriedly and, disregarding the copious amount of brandy he had drunk, lifted his car keys from the hall table. By the time he entered his BMW, he was already on the phone to some of his associates, giving them a synopsis of the conversation and summoning help. But, as his car roared along the quiet street, he knew already that he was too late.

Chapter 8

Saturday 22nd November

'Oooh, *lovely* putt Bruce, my lad...'

Bruce Redpath grinned at his friend as the other two players smiled graciously in their defeat. He walked across to the cup and lifted his golf ball out, mentally throwing it to the crowd amidst rapturous cheering and applause!

'Must've been about twenty-five feet, I reckon. A beauty,' continued Rob. 'Right, let's get in, I'm bloody freezin'...good game, lads, thanks.'

They shook hands and headed for the warmth of the clubhouse.

Forty-five minutes later, they were standing outside in the car park. Rob seemed hesitant as he spoke.

'Em...everythin' okay, Bruce?'

Bruce frowned. 'Why the hell does everyone keep asking me that? Yes, I'm absolutely fine, thanks. Really!'

'Good, good...'

'Listen, Rob, I was thinking...'

Rob Connor smiled. 'Oh-oh, never a good sign...'

Bruce laughed.

'No, seriously, it's been ages since I had the two of you over for something to eat. You'd said that the kids were staying with Mel's folks this weekend, why don't the two of you come over tomorrow afternoon, we'll have an early dinner.'

Rob looked surprised and very slightly uneasy.

'Em, are you sure, Bruce, wouldn't want to put you to any trouble?'

'It'd be no trouble; after all, I often have one or other of the girls over, sometimes both. No, it'd be lovely to return the invite, although I warn you, the food may not be up to Mel's usual high gastronomic standards...'

Rob leaned forward and spoke in a conspiratorial tone. 'You couldn't see your way to makin' mince 'n' tatties, could you?'

Bruce arrived home, already planning the following day's menu. It was high time that Rob and Mel visited, it had been a long time since...

He entered the kitchen and experienced a brief pang of guilt as he saw the empty bottle of Highland Park. He had drunk one glass the previous evening, then poured the remainder down the sink. It really *was* time to change!

Mel and Rob Connor were spending Saturday evening in the time-honoured fashion of couples suddenly finding themselves alone, the kids safe at a grandparents house.

Sound asleep in front of the television.

Bruce was in his kitchen, a lone bottle of beer beside him, busy preparing a cheesecake.

Paul Maguire was watching football on the television when his phone rang. He picked up the handset; he had been half-expecting the call.

'Maria.'

'Paul, where in the name of fuck is Davie?'

'Davie? Is he not at home?'

The venom in Maria Doyle's voice was unmissable; he knew that she seriously disliked him.

'You know perfectly well he isn't. He's with that fuckin' tart Flint, isn't he?'

'Who?'

'Oh, don't come the fucking innocent with me, Paul Maguire. I've known about his sordid little affair for years and I was hopin' that the bitch was goin' away for a long time. Would've done too, if it hadn't been for that smarmy prick Simon Fox. Bastard—all lawyers are bastards, mind you. I don't know how the hell she afforded his fee...'

Despite his disbarment, Maguire knew that the insult included him. He also knew perfectly well how Suzi Flint had afforded the fee...

'Aye, well...'

'Anyway, I saw you waitin' for her outside the court; let's face it, you're hardly her type, you wee prick—'

Paul Maguire snapped back. 'Give it a fucking rest! I'm not going to sit here and listen to your fucking insults—'

'Then tell me where the fuck my husband is.'

He paused for a moment; she'd find out soon enough. He let his breath out slowly and reached for his cigarettes.

'Maria, I haven't a fucking clue. I wish I did...'

David Doyle and Suzannah Flint woke to find themselves in pitch blackness, naked and shivering. Unseen, Doyle sat up and shook his head, as if trying to clear it; he knew he had been drugged and he was struggling to cope with the events of the last twenty-four hours. It seemed like a nightmare. Suzi Flint whimpered as she reached out, her hands groping for him in the darkness. Her nasal, south coast drawl was subdued and terrified.

'D-David, D-David, where are you...?'

'Ah'm here, pet, it's awright...'

As he spoke the words, he realised that things were very far from 'awright'. He reached out in the direction of the voice and grasped her hand, pulling her towards him; suddenly, he realised that there was something around his neck. A piece of string, it felt like, with a square of cardboard attached. Suzi Flint was shaking almost uncontrollably, from cold, from fear. He reached towards her; she, too, had the adornment and Doyle yanked at it, causing her to let out a small yelp of pain as the string cut into her bare neck. He wrenched his own placard off and pulled her into his arms. Her skin felt like ice and she started to sob uncontrollably, her tears warm on his cold, naked shoulder. He held her closer.

'Wh-what's h-h-happened, David? Wh-where are we?'

'Fuck knows, Suzi. Listen, you curl up on the floor, try tae stay warm, Ah'll hae a look aboot...'

He stopped mid-sentence. It wasn't going to be a look, was it? Releasing the chittering woman, he crawled around on his hands and knees, his fingertips exploring. The floor was of rough wood and he felt a splinter pierce the palm of his hand.

'Fuck,' he mumbled.

'Wh-what? What is it?'

'Nothin'. Just got a fuckin' skelf in ma haun. Hang oan...'

His hand moved forwards then came up against a wall and he reached up, exploring. Metal, corrugated...he knew now exactly where they were; well, what they were imprisoned in, at least. He stood up and made his way along the wall until he came to another, running at right angles. He stopped.

'We're in a fuckin' container. Fuckin' bastard...'

He banged on the metal with the palm of his hand, wincing as he drove the splinter deeper into his flesh.

'Fuckin' let us out. Help! HELP!'

Nothing. His cry resonated off the walls and Suzi Flint started to wail in desperation. He stopped banging, realising that his efforts were futile.

'Haud on, Suzi, haud on, let's see if there's anythin'...'

His hands groped further along the metal until he came to the door which, with all the strength he could muster, he tried to move. As expected, it was as solid and unyielding as the surrounding walls; there was no way out. He gave up, his heart sinking, then he shuffled across until he came to the opposite side of the container before heading back down.

'Fuck! Ya bastard!'

'D-David, wh-what is it? Where are you?'

He could hear Suzi Flint's teeth chattering loudly in the silence of the container. He tried to sound optimistic as he replied but he had a vague suspicion what he had tripped over.

'It's awright, ma foot hit somethin'...hang oan...'

He reached down and felt for the object. Large, square, heavy... he located a handle, he lifted the container, hearing the sloshing of the liquid, identifying the smell...

'Fuck,' he mumbled inaudibly.

He placed the jerry-can back on the floor and walked around it, but his foot connected with something else, something softer. He bent down once more and groped in the blackness. It felt like a sack...his fingers came into contact with a small object placed on the top, an object that seemed familiar...lifting it, he knew exactly what it was. Taking a few steps away from the petrol, he flicked his thumb and the cheap disposable lighter sprang to life, its tiny flame flickering on the dark metal of the container. Suzannah Flint was shivering violently, her slim body curled foetus-like on the rough wooden floor as she sobbed pitifully. Beside her were the two pieces of cardboard. He peered at the writing, although he already suspected what it said.

Suzannah Flint
#6
Who's next?

He didn't need to turn over the second placard; he was undoubtedly number seven.

A few feet away sat a green, ten-litre jerry-can, containing petrol; nearly full, judging by its weight. Beside it was a sack of onions.

Onions.

A locked container, a sack of onions, ten litres of petrol...and a lighter.

David Doyle was faced with a very difficult choice.

'Did you *really* make that cheesecake, Bruce?' asked Mel, her tone sceptical as she arched an eyebrow.

'Yes, honestly. Last night. Baked it in the oven and everything.'

Mel Connor reached forward and cut herself another slice.

'My, you're a dark horse, Bruce Redpath. After all these years, it seems that I've got competition.'

She placed a large forkful of the delicious lemon cheesecake into her mouth. Bruce filled her wineglass and she nodded her thanks.

'Mmm. Ith...delich...uth...'

Rob shook his head as crumbs splattered across the table.

'An' you're the one who's always tellin' the kids not to talk with their mouths full.'

She gave him a mock glare as she swallowed the dessert.

'Yes, but it's 'do as I say, not as I do' — isn't that right, Bruce?'

He laughed. The afternoon was going much better than he could have imagined. No intrusive memories...

Bang...just like that. Mel noticed and smiled, reaching across and taking his hand.

'It's been a really lovely day. Just great—hasn't it Rob?'

'Sure has. Don't know how you're no' like the side of a house, mate, if you cook like that all the time!'

'I don't—most of the time it's leftovers, pizza, curry...'

'God, that's even worse,' laughed Mel, draining her wine glass and jerking her thumb in her husband's direction. 'And I can't believe that you actually made this bugger mince and potatoes.'

Bruce grinned as he slid the bottle towards her. 'Don't forget the doughballs; anyway, it *was* a special request...help yourself, Mel—Rob, another coffee?'

'Aye, that'd be great...holy shit!'

'What?' exclaimed Bruce and Mel in unison.

'Have you looked outside recently?'

They turned and looked out of the dining-room window, where large white snowflakes were swirling in a near-blizzard, Rob stood up and crossed over, gazing out into the garden.

'It's bloody lyin' too—Mel, we'd best be making a move if we've to pick up the kids...aw shit, what now...?'

His phone was ringing and he swiped the screen, exiting the room.

'DCI Connor...yes...'

Mel and Bruce chatted easily for a few minutes, then Rob returned, a serious expression on his face.

'Bruce, I'm really sorry, mate, I've been called to an incident... Mel, you'll need to phone your folks, see if they can get you...'

'Listen, I can pick up the kids and take Mel home. It'd be a pleasure,' interjected Bruce. Rob gave him a questioning stare.

'Em, are you sure you're...well, okay?

Bruce smiled. 'You didn't notice, then?

Mel turned and looked at her husband.

'I did, Rob. Our Bruce hasn't touched a drop all day!'

Bruce slept well that night; after collecting Ailie and Fraser from their grandparents, he had driven the family back to Inverkip. Although the main roads had been cleared, the hill road behind the little village was white and treacherous but, eventually, he deposited them safely outside their door and made his way home.

He didn't even have a nightcap; as sleep engulfed him, he smiled to himself. It was a very good start.

There had been more snow throughout Monday and the trains were running late. It had been a dreary, depressing day at the office and Bruce was half-asleep, vaguely aware that the train had just passed through Port Glasgow. He was weary, but there was something else.

Torquil Carnegie was off for the week, having been invited on a last-minute skiing trip to Austria with some family friends. Bruce was decidedly envious but, to his great surprise, he also realised that he missed the youth; his cheeky smile, his odd 'modern' vocabulary, the 'Boss' epithet...

He wasn't alone; by all accounts. Rayna Aherne felt the same.

'Ah, you see, I told you he was a good lad, Mr Redpath. Just needed a bit of guidance, is all. He's become very fond of you, you know. Did him the world of good, that talkin'-to you gave him.'

'Yes, he *has* come on, Mrs Aherne, and he's been a great help...'

His eyes jerked open again as his phone pinged. He dug the handset out of his coat pocket; the message was from Mel.

> *Fab afternoon yesterday, Brucie,*
> *we really enjoyed ourselves*
> *and thanks for the lift home.*
> *xx. Just a heads up, Rob doing*
> *a press interview for BBC, on*
> *@ nine. My hubby's famous*
> *at last! Much love, Mxx.*

Bruce smiled; he adored Mel Connor, she had been his rock when...

Almost instantly, his eyes closed again.

Bruce had been lucky not to miss his station, only waking as the doors to the carriage slid open. Finally back home, he sat back in his chair and switched on the television, watching fifteen minutes of drivel before the news came on. Finally, the familiar opening sequence ran; it was the turn of the 'tie-guy' again. Bruce turned up the volume.

'Good evening. Police are investigating what they suspect was an attempted double murder in the west of Scotland town of Greenock yesterday, believed to be linked to the recent spate of so-called retribution killings over the last few weeks.'

The camera panned closer; it was a particularly nice tie tonight, Bruce noticed.

'We're now going live to Greenock, where our correspondent Duncan Kerr is at the scene. Duncan, what can you tell us about this incident?'

The screen flicked to the familiar face of Kerr, the presenter suitably clad in a puffy red jacket and a woolly hat. He was standing next to what looked like a snow-covered bridge parapet, nodding sagely as he listened to his introduction.

'Good evening. Well, at the moment we know the identities of the two intended victims to be David Doyle and Suzannah Flint. Doyle is a director of Hooley Transport, one of whose lorries was involved in a recent, and fatal, people smuggling incident. The other, Suzannah, or Suzi, Flint, was found not guilty at Glasgow's High Court last week, where she had been on trial for the brutal murder of a young prostitute. Apparently they disappeared from the Glasgow area some time on Saturday evening.'

'I understand that the Police are saying this is an attempted murder; can you tell us more about that?'

'Well, I don't have the full details as yet but my understanding is that the two had been locked inside a disused shipping container at the back...'

As he spoke, Kerr turned and pointed behind him; two large cranes were just discernible in the distance, the entire scene harshly illuminated by tall lighting towers. He turned to face the camera once more.

'...of this loading yard, at Princes Pier. Apparently some local children had entered the yard under the pretext of having a snowball fight when they heard banging coming from one of the containers. They reported this to their parents, who called the police. Had they not done so, it's likely that Doyle and Flint would not have been found for some time. They are currently being treated for hypothermia in Inverclyde Royal Infirmary and, as far as I am aware, police have been unable to interview them at this stage. I've also been informed that one of them is in a life-threatening condition, but that's all the information I have at present.'

'Thank you, Duncan.'

Duncan Kerr nodded as the camera returned to the newsroom.

'Earlier today, Detective Chief Inspector Robin Connor, who is leading the investigation, gave us this interview.'

Despite the gravity of the report, Bruce couldn't help smiling. Rob appeared on-screen, looking surprisingly relaxed, despite the snow that had been falling, flecking his short, dark hair and his green Barbour jacket. The voice of Duncan Kerr spoke off-camera.

'DCI Connor, what can you tell us about this incident?'

'Well, first of all, Doyle and Flint are clearly very lucky to be alive, although I understand that one of them is in a critical condition. And had it not been for these children, it's likely that they would have died of hypothermia, or worse.'

'Worse? Would you care to elaborate, DCI Connor?'

Rob hesitated only very slightly, his expression sombre.

'Em, no, I'll leave you to draw your own conclusions.'

Kerr contrived to sound very slightly put out.

'I see—my understanding was that they had been provided with the wherewithal for self-immolation—can you confirm this?'

'No comment, sorry...'

Bruce gaped at the screen in horror as Rob continued.

'...but I can say that there are similarities to the other brutal murders that have been carried out recently, which is why we believe that they may be connected.'

'And am I correct in saying that both the victims, or intended victims, were known to the police?'

Rob nodded again, his dark brows knitted in a frown.

'We *are* working on that basis; however, as my colleague in Glasgow has commented previously, we are takin' these crimes very seriously indeed, despite the suspected background of the victims. We cannot, and will not, allow persons unknown to take the law in to their own hands.'

'Naturally, of course not. Tell me, Chief Inspector, I believe that the couple were found naked...'

'No further comment. Thank you very much.'

Back to the studio. A short pause.

'In a surprise move in Parliament today, the Chancellor announced...'

Bruce couldn't care less what the Chancellor had announced. He switched off the television, reflecting that Rob had come across as confident, professional and relaxed; Mel would be proud of him. But the news was troubling, to say the least. Another two attempted murders; or would they have been classed as suicides, a desperate, brief and agonizing alternative to hypothermia and starvation? His stomach was churning and he could feel the blood pulsing in his temples as he stood up, heading for the kitchen. As he entered, he heard his phone vibrating on the worktop. He picked it up, looked at the caller display in some surprise, then swiped the screen.

'Cal—I thought you'd forgotten all about me.'

'Good evening, Mr Redpath. No, no, I hadn't forgotten...just saw your friend, DCI Connor, on the television; I thought he acquitted himself well.'

'Yes, so did I. It's very troubling, though, I thought that we'd seen an end to all this.'

'Yes, as did I, to be honest, Mr R, and that was why I hadn't called. Basically, I had nothing to tell you. Nobody I spoke to knows what the hell is going on...'

Bruce waited, sensing that Cal Gibson had something more to say.

'...but that's changed now, for sure.'

'In what way?'

'Well, I was out at the weekend, just having my usual 'wee sniff aboot among the riff-raff,' as you might say. Here and there, listening, learning...managed to get round a few nefarious haunts. 'Major Strasser has been shot, round up the usual suspects' and all that jazz.'

Bruce shook his head; he was familiar with Gibson's verbal procrastination, interspersed with his rather arcane quotations. He suspected that "Major Strasser' was probably from a film but he wasn't going to rise to the bait and ask.

'Any joy?'

He sensed the slight disappointment in Gibson's tone. 'Well, it seems that, after the rather unpleasant demise of the former Cardinal...'

'Bishop, I think he was, actually.'

He immediately regretted the interruption. There was a long pause.

'All the same, as far as I'm concerned, Mr R. 'The jackdaw sat on the Cardinal's chair.'

Bruce hadn't a clue where this one had come from. Did Gibson sit up at night reading the *Oxford Dictionary of Quotations*? Finally, the private investigator continued, in a rather huffy tone.

'Anyway, it seems that a number of prominent members of the criminal fraternity received some rather unpleasant and troubling photographs in the mail this week.'

Gibson had Bruce's full attention now. 'Really? What kind of photographs?'

'Photographs of all the victims—well, up to and including the Card...Bishop. 'All naked to the hangman's noose'...'

Bruce gritted his teeth; it was becoming irritating.

'...and all in circumstances of considerable discomfort, shall we say? But there was also a sixth photo included in the set, Mr R. A sixth.'

Bruce tried his best not to *sound* irritated.

'And what was that, Cal?'

'Well, I am reliably informed that each of the victims had a sign around their necks; name rank and number, if you get my drift.'

'Em...I'm not sure I do.'

Gibson let out a long sigh, as if Bruce was being deliberately obtuse. 'Their name, the chronological number of their death, followed by the sixty-million-dollar question.'

This time it was Bruce who sighed, somewhat impatiently.

'And what *was* the six...the question?'

Cal Gibson gave an evil chuckle. 'Simple, Mr R, simple. 'Who's next?' Then the sixth photo simply had the name of the recipient, followed by the question 'Are *you* next'. Really set the cat among the proverbial pigeons, that one.'

Bruce remained silent, digesting this rather shocking information. So the criminal fraternity *were* being targeted, one by one; or by two, if Doyle and Flint were the latest potential victims.

'I see. I don't suppose you have ideas as to who's behind these killings?'

'None. There's talk that it's some new kid on the block, out to prove himself to be the hardest bastard in the land. But no-one seems to have the faintest idea who that may be, although there's talk that he—or she, for that matter—isn't from around these parts, if you understand my meaning.'

Bruce did; it was well-enough known that there had been an influx of Eastern European criminals over the last few year, out to make a name—and a reputation—for themselves. Gibson paused.

'If you don't mind me asking, Mr R, what's your interest in all this? I mean, a job's a job, especially when you're paying, but it's usually divorce cases you have me investigating. I'd be leaving it to the police, if I were you...or are you thinking of following in Mr Fox's footsteps? As they say, 'The fox knows many things'.'

Bruce had the feeling that this might be a Greek quotation, but again he didn't ask.

'No, Cal, I have no intention of taking up criminal law. Actually, it's just a passing interest—'

Was it? It was an interest Gibson obviously didn't share—the investigator interrupted.

'But I'll tell you this...'

Bruce didn't respond; he knew better than to interrupt.

'...there's a lot of very bad people out there who won't be sleeping at all well these nights, Mr R. 'Don't wait for the last judgement, it happens every day!' If you know what I mean.'

Bruce Redpath tried very hard not to let out a groan.

He finished the call and leaned against the worktop. Although Gibson's news was troubling, indicating that there might well be more killings to come, he knew that both Rob and Simon were right—he should drop the matter and let the police deal with it. Even Cal Gibson seemed to be questioning his motives, but the mantra his father had drummed into him played over and over in his mind.

'Due process, Bruce. Justice must be done and be *seen* to be done. The law applies to everyone—never forget that. Our whole society depends on that fundamental fact. No-one is above the law.'

As he tried to shake the jumble of thoughts out of his head, he looked up at the kitchen clock; five to ten.

He'd just have one small whisky before he went to bed...

Then he gave a wry smile. No, he wouldn't—he had poured it all down the sink.

Chapter 9

Tuesday 25th November

Paul Maguire and Frank Hooley shared a dislike of one another. Hooley didn't trust Maguire, believing him to be both cunning and self-serving, but he had tolerated him as a director of Hooley Transport for the undoubted legal and financial acumen that he brought to the table, not to mention the controlling influence he managed to exert on his similarly-disliked son-in-law, David Doyle. Maguire, on the other hand, considered Hooley to be little more than an ignorant and aggressive thug, a man likely to lash out with his massive fists first and to ask questions later. Hooley was currently sitting in Davie Doyle's customary chair, puffing out clouds of smoke from a small, noxious cigar. He was running his hand along the lower edge of the battered desk.

'Whit the fuck happened tae the bottom o' the desk, eh? Been forcin' open drawers?'

Maguire bit back a sarcastic response.

'Davie had a shotgun fitted under the desk...just in case. I told him to get rid of it when Pig got arrested. I knew the police would be calling.'

Hooley threw back his head and gave an evil cackle. 'Hah! Jist like the bugger, playin' at big-time crooks, eh. An' aw' this shite aboot bein' him bein' kidnapped. Whit the fuck's that aw aboot, eh?'

Paul Maguire shook his head. 'Frank, it's just like I told Maria. Paul was over at...'

'...at his fuckin' tart's hoose. Aye, Ah know.'

'...yes, well, she'd disappeared too, in case you hadn't noticed.'

Frank Hooley leaned across the battered desk and blew a stream of cigar smoke into Maguire's face.

'Aye, funny that, she gets aff wi' murder, next thing the two o' them fuckin' disappear. Then they turn up in a fuckin' container doon in Greenock. Whit the fuck has Davie Doyle been up tae, Maguire? Who's fuckin' cage has the wee bastard been rattlin', that's whit Ah want tae know?'

He leaned back again, clasping his hands over his ample stomach, cigar clenched between his teeth.

'It'll be on account o' that wee hoor, Flint, She's probably got some fancy man who's mightily pissed off at the baith o' them. Hell fuckin' mend him—lucky he's still in the fuckin' hospital, jist wait till Ah get ma fuckin' hands roon the wee turd's throat.'

He took a final puff on his cigar before grinding the butt out in an overflowing ashtray.

'Aye, funny, right enough...'

Maguire didn't think it was funny at all, having realised that he was wasting his time. Neither Frank Hooley nor his daughter, Maria, believed a word of what he had told them, choosing to think that Doyle and Flint had simple absconded together. And how had they ended up in a container? Although he hadn't spoken to Doyle yet, Maguire had a pretty good idea and it had nothing whatsoever to do with a cuckolded admirer of Suzi Flint.

No, he knew that they were alive simply on account of pure luck, nothing else. Another day and...well, he didn't like to think what would have happened. Hooley and his hard-faced bitch of a daughter could think what the hell they liked; it wasn't his job to convince them. He would be absolutely fine; Frank Hooley was correct in one respect, Maguire *was* cunning and self-serving... the big bastard was talking again.

'...and Ah'm back in charge noo, so you'd better watch yer step, Paul Maguire. Ah've got ma beady eye on you.'

Maguire stood up and calmly walked out of the office. This conversation was terminated—for good.

Half an hour later, Maguire was propping up the bar in The Vaults, a somewhat dilapidated south-side hostelry under the approaches to Glasgow Central station, a fact confirmed by the near-constant rumble of trains as they passed across the adjacent over-bridge. At this hour on a Tuesday afternoon, there was little custom; just a few old worthies, a couple of students obviously out to experience a traditional Glasgow 'working' men's pub' and, next to him at the bar, a character known to him simply as Shug.

Maguire was only acquainted with the scruffy, nondescript man from drinking in The Vaults; he wasn't the type of person with whom he would normally choose to socialise but, in the past, Shug had been the occasional provider of information that had proved useful. Now that Maguire was 'between jobs' (as he chose to think of his current situation) it might be worth putting out a few feelers. He had explained his disagreement with Frank Hooley and bought Shug a whisky. The man rubbed his coarse, grey stubble and let out a loud belch.

'So whit the fuck happened tae Davie Doyle, d'you think? Ah heard he ran aff wi' that burd o' his—mind you, Ah saw her comin' oot the court, nice lookin' bit o' stuff.'

Maguire shrugged; should he tell Shug? He came to a decision and related the events of the previous Sunday night.

Shug shook his head, a suitably sombre look on his pasty features.

'Fuck sake, Mr Maguire, that's pure hellish, that is. Ah mean, Ah heard aboot them gettin' found oan the news but, obviously, Ah didn'ae know about them bein' kidnapped...fuck sake, man! An' ye've nae idea who it wis whit took them?'

Maguire shook his head.

'None, and I've not had a chance to speak to Davie yet. He's still in hospital down in Greenock and the police are waiting to have a go at him—as is his father-in-law, it seems. But I doubt very much he'll say anything to them, though. Davie Doyle is no fan of Scotland's finest.'

He took a sip of his own whisky, relishing the fiery burn as it slipped over his throat.

'No, I think he'll be wanting to find out for himself—and take his own form of revenge. Anyway, I'd best be going. Listen, Shug, you've got my number, I'm in the market...if you know what I mean?'

Shug grinned and gave Maguire a knowing wink.

'Aye, Ah know. If Ah hear o' anyone wantin' a bit o' advice, Ah'll pit them your way.'

Maguire drained his glass, nodded then turned and strode out of the pub, pulling his cigarettes out as he went. Shug waited for a few more minutes then zipped up his greasy wax jacket and walked slowly towards the door, leaving his own whisky un-drunk on the counter. He pulled out his phone, the latest, most expensive offering from Apple, and checked his messages. One of the old worthies sitting nearby called across to him.

'Here, mister, are ye no' wantin' that whisky?'

Shug turned towards the old man and smiled.

'No, I'm not, I'm driving. Help yourself, my friend. "Freedom and whisky gang the-gither" after all.'

The old man looked at him as if he was speaking Greek. The man known as Shug shook his head sadly and sighed, carefully placing his phone back in his pocket before removing the keys of his Range Rover, presently parked up a secluded side-street a few blocks away, from the other pocket of the decrepit jacket.

'It's bloody Burns, you ignorant old bugger,' he mumbled, as he pushed the door open and stepped outside and in to the cold, sleety Glasgow afternoon.

◆◆◆◆◆◆◆

As Bruce's taxi wended its way through the Tuesday evening rush-hour, he leaned his head back on the seat. It had been another busy day and, the following morning, he was due to travel to Edinburgh to meet a client. Despite his best efforts to hold the meeting in his own office, the client was, apparently, unable to travel to Glasgow and Bruce had finally relented; the man could well afford the additional expenses. The only bright spot of the day was lunch with Finlay Whyte although, when Bruce had phoned the previous evening, the pathologist had told him that he already had a lunch engagement.

'Listen Fin, it's fine, I'll catch you another time.'

'Don't be silly, Bruce, it's not what you'd call an official lunch and you'll be more than welcome. Anyway, you'll probably get on like a house on fire. Her name's Paula Noone.'

Bruce was unconvinced. 'Do you work with her?'

Finlay chuckled. 'Well, you could say that, she's a Detective Chief Superintendent...'

The morning meeting was over and Bruce was in a taxi, heading up Edinburgh's grey, but dry, Leith Walk. He had spent the last hour and a half in a spacious, modern waterside office in Leith, listening to the usual complaints while admiring the view across to the Fife coast. His client's wife didn't understand him, she was too busy with the house, the kids and her own career to have sex. Surely he couldn't be expected to remain celibate, he was a normal, healthy man, after all. It wasn't his fault, his secretary had come on to him...

Bruce had met the secretary upon his arrival. Dark, dangerous eyes, dark hair, dark stockings (no doubt about that—she had managed to flash an inch of thigh when she had bent over to retrieve a pen, although it most certainly wasn't for Bruce's benefit).

Bruce had asked about the alleged other women and his client had given him a leering look and a wink. Well, if it was on offer, what could he be expected to do? After all, his wife didn't understand him, she was too busy...

Blah, blah, blah...

He would add on an extra two hours for lunch; after all he had to eat.

'Bruce, how are you?'

Finlay smiled and shook his hand warmly as an attractive, if rather gaunt, woman stood up. Bruce's impression was one of near-exhaustion and he immediately felt a pang of empathy for her.

'This is Paula—Paula Noone. Paula, my very good friend, Bruce Redpath.'

Bruce was slightly surprised at the introduction; he had only met Finlay once and, apart from the previous evening, he hadn't spoken to him since that somewhat surprising dinner at Mel and Rob's. He had obviously made a good impression.

'I'm very pleased to meet you, Bruce, I've heard a lot about you from Fin. You're a divorce lawyer, I believe?'

'Yes, for my sins.'

'And do you enjoy the work?'

What was the point in lying? 'No, Paula, I bloody hate it, if truth be told.'

It had been an excellent lunch and excellent company. Finlay had been as charming as Bruce remembered and Paula Noone had proved to be an intelligent and witty (if rather cynical) companion. With some difficulty, Bruce had resisted the temptation to discuss the murders but Finlay had obviously sensed his propriety. As the deserts arrived, the pathologist turned to Paula.

'Oh, by the way, Bruce here has shown a considerable interest in these so-called 'retribution killings'.'

It was said in a casual, throw-away manner, but the change in Paula Noone was dramatic. Her mouth closed, her eyes narrowed and she sat back in her chair, folding her arms across her chest.

'I'd rather not discuss work, if you don't mind, Finlay. This *is* supposed to be a social occasion, after all.'

The two men exchanged a quick glance, Bruce noticing the slight embarrassment on Finlay's face. He smiled, hoping to diffuse the surprisingly awkward atmosphere that had materialised so suddenly.

'Oh, it's not *that* much of an interest, it's really only because my partner, Simon Fox, defended a couple of the victims.'

He lifted a spoonful of his tiramisu, a poor substitute for Mel's.

'Actually, we've got a young man working in our office—he didn't make the grade to study law—and he's taken a bit of an interest, keeps him out of mischief. You know what these young people are like, they've got a morbid fascination for the gruesome and the macabre.'

He looked down at his plate, realising that the description fitted himself every bit as much as it did Torquil Carnegie. Paula Noone leaned forward and toyed with her apple and pear crumble.

'I see. Look, I'm sorry, I don't really get a chance to socialise much, what with the pressures of the job...I don't really like talking shop, if you know what I mean.'

'I completely understand. I wouldn't like to be asked for advice on a divorce in the middle of my tiramisu...be worse if it was a banana split, mind you...'

It was a feeble joke but the ice was broken; Paula smiled, Finlay gave Bruce a brief wink of thanks and the conversation moved on. But it had been an odd reaction, mused Bruce, scraping his plate. Detective Chief Superintendent Noone had become very defensive, very quickly.

'So what do you think *that* was all about, Bruce?'

He shook his head. 'I honestly haven't a clue, Fin. She just clammed up completely. In my experience, that usually means we touched a nerve.'

'Hm, my thoughts exactly. I don't even think she's been involved in any of the investigations—no, wait, the Krasniki murder, she might have been...oh, here she comes...'

Paula Noone returned to the table, carrying her coat. Finlay stood up and reached inside his jacket.

'Right folks, this is on me.'

There was the customary mild altercation over who was settling the bill but Finlay was insistent. As they left the restaurant, he casually sidled up to Bruce. 'You can pick up the tab next time I'm over in Glasgow.'

'Absolutely, it'll be a pleasure.'

Finlay White had smiled at him. 'I know it will...'

The train was passing through the northern suburbs of Glasgow when Bruce's phone pinged with a BBC newsflash. He read the brief statement.

> *Breaking news.*
> *Suzannah Flint, the woman found locked*
> *in a shipping container in Greenock*
> *on Sunday night, has died in hospital.*
> *Police are now treating her death as*
> *murder and are linking it with the other*
> *five so-called 'retribution killings'.*

Six.

So far...

Cal Gibson had been correct in his assertion, but how many more? Not only that, how many more who had been defended by Simon Fox? Bruce closed his eyes as the train roared into the tunnel and started its descent towards Glasgow Queen Street station. He needed a drink; badly!

Simon had been out of the office on Thursday and Friday; for some reason, Bruce was thankful as he wanted to avoid any discussion about Suzi Flint. Well, if he was being truthful, he wanted to avoid a repetition of the previous Friday's scenario with his old friend. He was still hurt at the way Simon had spoken to him, whether he deserved it or not.

The Friday evening traffic was the usual gridlock and he arrived at Central Station just as his usual train pulled away; the next wasn't for half an hour—maybe he had time for a quick drink... as he headed for the bar, his phone rang and he took it out; it was Rob Connor.

'Rob! How are you?'

Rob let out a long sigh. 'Long story. Listen, Mel's heading over to her folks' house tonight with the kids. I don't suppose you're free for a drink?'

'Em, yes, that'd be fine, I've nothing on. I'm running a bit late, missed the bloody train. What time are you talking?'

'About eight?'

'Yes, I should manage that, I'll grab a fish supper once I'm in Greenock. Where d'you fancy?'

'Dunno, Bruce. Em, what about the Bay Bar?'

Bruce laughed. 'God, that's a blast from the past! Right, The Bay it is, eight o'clock. See you then. Em...Rob?'

'What?'

'Is everything okay?

'I'll tell you when I see you. Cheers.'

He decided against the drink and headed for the platform instead. It wasn't like Rob to suggest going to a pub and he had the feeling that DCI Connor had something on his mind. He took out his phone, scrolling to the news item on Suzannah Flint's death; it provided little more detail but as he read Rob's name in relation to the case, he assumed that to be the cause of his friend's worries.

As he put his phone away, he smiled. What was it his father used to say? Oh yes:

> Never assume—it makes an
> 'ass' out of 'u' and 'me'

Chapter 10

Friday 28th November

Bruce Redpath and the small pub, aptly named The Bay went back a long way. He had had his first legal drink in the tucked-away little establishment that backed on to Gourock's Cardwell Bay, longer ago than he cared to remember. He smiled; he had also had his first 'illegal' drink here, a couple of years before, in the days when beer was cheap and landlords more tolerant. The bar had a front and rear door, ideal for the occasional times that the police came calling, searching for underage drinkers. At the time it had seemed daring and dangerous but, in retrospect, he realised that if the police had been serious about making any arrests, they'd have placed officers at *both* doors.

It was only about a mile from his house and he'd walked, relishing the exercise on this cold, crisp winter's evening. Cardwell Road, the main thoroughfare through Gourock, was still busy as he pushed open the swing door and entered. He hadn't been in for a number of years but the cosy, low-ceilinged room looked exactly as he remembered, only considerably quieter and with clean, smoke-free air. Ed Sheeran was playing softly in the background, a couple of gaming machines winked invitingly on the far wall and at least two customers had the company of their dogs. The age-old excuse for a quick pint while walking their canine friend was obviously still valid!

Rob Connor was sitting at a table in a small alcove, nursing a pint of heavy and with a second sitting opposite him. Bruce sat down across from his friend.

'Evening Rob—I take it that's for me?'

Rob looked up with a desultory smile. 'Aye—cheers, Bruce. Thanks for comin' along.'

They each took a draught of their beer. Bruce wiped the foam from his top lip and placed the glass back on the table.

'Well, I have to say it's nice to come down here again—it fair brings back memories, doesn't it?'

Rob nodded but didn't speak. Bruce was concerned—it wasn't at all like his friend.

'So what's bothering you? Must be serious to invite me out to a pub for a drink.'

Rob looked across at Bruce, his face set in a frown. He opened his mouth to speak, then looked about, rather furtively, Bruce thought.

'It's these bloody cases. These so-called 'retribution killings'.'

Bruce nodded as he took another mouthful of beer. 'Yes, I though it might be; and the press *do* like a strap-line, don't they? They're having a field-day with all this. But that's not what's bothering you, is it?'

There was another pause.

'No, it's not. See, the thing is...'

Bruce waited again.

'...well, in a nutshell, I've been kind of 'warned off'.'

Bruce stared at his friend for a moment, not liking the sound of what he was hearing. His immediate thoughts were for Mel, Ailie and Fraser. If anything happened to them...he took a deep breath.

'You mean you've been threatened? Good God, Rob, but surely—'

Rob shook his head. 'No, not threatened. Like I said, warned off—told to scale back the investigation.'

He looked around again. 'Basically, quietly 'advised' to let them get on with it. If they want to go around killin' each other then, apparently, that's okay.'

Bruce opened and shut his mouth, like a fish out of water. 'But...but...'

'Aye, 'but' indeed. But it's *not* fuckin' okay, Bruce, is it? You know that, I know that, but I'm quietly bein' told not to try too hard, to let the case slip away. Which is bad enough, of course, until...'

'Until the next one?'

Rob nodded. 'Aye.'

'And you think there'll be a next one, don't you?'

Rob sat up, grasping his beer glass. 'Of course there bloody will, Bruce, I'm certain of it.'

He lowered his voice and leaned across the table. Bruce wondered if he'd started drinking early, his eyes had a peculiar glazed expression. Maybe it was just stress.

'You see, you probably won't know this, but they all had signs, signs around their necks, with their names written, markin' them off, one-two-three...'

Rob had obviously forgotten having mentioned this to Bruce a few weeks ago; he numbered the words off on his fingers as he spoke.

'...then—'Who's next after that? Doyle and Flint; they were numbers six and seven. There'll be more, you bloody wait an' see.'

Bruce expressed surprise; he didn't mention his conversation with Cal Gibson.

'Really? God, that's awful. So where's this coming from? I mean, from just how high up are you hearing this instruction?'

Rob shook his head. 'The Chief Super, she had a quiet word today. Very pleasant, all strictly 'off the record' of course. Just said that the 'powers-that-be' wanted to concentrate resources on cases that involved the protection of the public rather than the protection of those wishing to harm the public—her words, not mine. You know as well as I do that we're pretty seriously understaffed.'

Bruce nodded in agreement. 'And by the 'powers-that-be', exactly who does she mean?'

Rob shook his head and gave a shrug. 'Don't really know for sure. Divisional Commander, maybe, for all I know it could even be the even the Chief bloody Constable. But it certainly looks like someone considerably further up the chain wants us to step back our investigations. And it doesn't sit comfortably with me. Not one fuckin' bit.'

It didn't sit comfortably with Bruce either; in fact, he could feel his temper rising at the very thought of the course of justice being perverted in the near-certainty that further killings would take place. It went against everything he represented, against his faith and belief in the legal system. He finished the dregs of his pint and stood up; he needed another drink. Rob looked up and nodded, lifting his own empty glass.

'Same again, if you're buyin'. Wouldn't mind a wee hauf to go with it...'

Bruce made his way over to the bar, vaguely aware of a draught as the door opened. A woman walked in front of him and he waited a moment, allowing her to pass but, as he stepped forward, he stumbled over a small, black spaniel that the woman was trailing behind her on a lead. The dog let out a yelp and the woman turned. Bruce immediately bent down; he liked dogs.

'Hey, wee fellow, I'm sorry...'

The dog licked his hand and looked at him with dark, appealing eyes. He patted its soft, woolly coat as the woman spoke.

'I'm so sorry, I should have probably lifted him. Are you okay?'

He stood up, the dog nuzzling his leg affectionately.

'Oh, I'm fine, thanks, I was more worried about him. What's his name?

'Oh, he's called Bruce...'

Bruce Redpath stared at her in astonishment.

'...after Robert the Bruce.'

He continued to stare.

'Em, are you okay?'

'What? Oh, yes, yes, I'm fine. It's just that *my* name's Bruce!'

The woman put her hand to her mouth, letting out a small giggle; Bruce experienced a curious, long-forgotten flip of his stomach.

'Oh my, that *is* a coincidence...but I hope you don't mind my dog being called after you?'

He smiled. 'Don't be silly, why should I? Anyway, it's a great name for a dog!'

'It's a great name for a man, too...oh, I'm sorry again, that sounded rather forward...'

She removed her glove and extended a graceful, slender hand.

'...but, as both you and my dog have already been introduced, I'm Joanna—Joanna Hume.'

His stomach gave another flip. She was very attractive in an understated way. No make-up, dark hazel eyes framed by auburn hair flecked with silver. Full lips, currently parted in a very appealing smile.

'Bruce—of course—Bruce Redpath.'

'Hello Bruce Redpath—it's nice to meet you.'

She gave the faintest suggestion of a wink and Bruce could feel his face redden very slightly. He was aware of the barman hovering.

'Em, can I get you a drink, Joanna?'

'Well, I was about to offer to buy you one, seeing as I nearly tripped you up!'

'Oh, no, please...anyway, I'm with my friend over there...'

He looked across—the table was empty.

'Oh! I think he's maybe gone to the toilet.'

'So it's a 'he' then. That's a relief.'

Was she flirting with him?

'But, if you *really* don't mind, it's a gin and slimline tonic. Oh,...'

'What?'

'Em...gosh, this is rather rude, but could I maybe have a packet of peanuts as well, please? I do like a wee savoury snack with a G and T.'

Bruce didn't think it rude at all; in fact, he liked her forthright manner. He liked her dog and he realised that, within a very short space of time, he also rather liked Joanna Hume.

'Of course you can—actually, you've put me in the notion, I'll have a packet too.'

He ordered the gin, two pints, two double Glenmorangies and two packets of peanuts. Joanna smiled at him.

'A whisky man. Good for you, I always think I should give it a try but I'm never quite sure what to order. Maybe I just need someone to guide me a bit.'

No, he wasn't mistaken, she was definitely flirting with him. Or was she just being friendly? It had been such a long time...the drinks arrived and she raised her glass.

'Cheers, Bruce. Very nice to make your acquaintance.'

'Nice to meet you too, Joanna.'

She raised her glass and took a sip of her drink. He lifted his whisky and did likewise, taking a large mouthful. Canine Bruce, sensing that he was being ignored, gave a whine and pawed at Bruce's leg; he bent down and tickled the little dog behind its ears for a few moments, then stood back up as Joanna put her glass back on the bar; very close to the tray containing his own drinks, he noticed.

'Ahh. So, Bruce, do you come here often?'

She burst out laughing again and he joined her.

'Oh God, that has to be the corniest line ever! Actually it was a genuine question—you see, I just moved to Gourock a few weeks ago and this would appear to be my 'local'. The fact that it's dog-friendly makes it ideal, but I always feel a bit self-conscious walking into a bar on my own, if you know what I mean.'

'Yes, I do. And in answer to your question, no, I don't really come here at all, although I live just about a mile away. I started my drinking career here, though, many years ago!'

'Really...'

She turned her head for a moment towards the table and Bruce did likewise. Rob was staring across at them, a grin spreading across his rather careworn features. At least that was an improvement, Bruce thought.

'...it looks like your friend's returned.'

Bruce sighed. 'Yes, I'd better get back over, I suppose.'

He turned round to the bar and lifted the drinks, carefully balancing the tray containing the four glasses. Joanna Hume smiled at him again.

'Em, maybe we'll bump into each other again?'

Before he could stop himself, the words were out of his mouth. What the hell...

'Let's not make it 'maybe'. Life's too bloody short. By any chance would you be walking canine Bruce next Friday, say about eight?'

Her smile widened—it seemed to light up the room.

'I'm away next week, Bruce, I'm visiting my sister down south, but I'll be back the following week, so I'll make a point of being here; along with canine Bruce, of course... now, go and speak to your friend before he gets cramp in his face. Don't forget your peanuts, by the way.'

She could have put them on the tray but, instead, she lifted the packet and placed it under his pinky; her hand rested on the back of his for a brief moment, warm, soft...he smiled at her and walked away; as he did so, she gave him that same, small, hint of a wink. This time his stomach did a somersault.

Joanna had left after that one gin, Bruce the dog whining to get back out and resume his walk. She gave him a shy little flutter of a wave with her fingers as she left.

Rob had given him a brief third degree about his new acquaintance before continuing with his own rather bleak narrative, although he had little fresh to add. Without going into much detail, he revealed that David Doyle had not really provided any useful information, maintaining that he had no idea who their captors were or why he and Flint had been abducted—other than with the obvious intention of being killed. Suzi Flint hadn't been questioned at all, having never regained consciousness.

'But I'm certain the bugger's hidin' somethin'. My worry is that, havin' survived, he's liable to be seekin' revenge, especially since Flint, his fancy bit, died. We could end up with a full-scale gangland feud if we're not careful.'

'And I take it you've voiced this theory?' asked Bruce, his thoughts straying elsewhere. He was feeling decidedly light-headed, and, although he hadn't had a great deal to drink, he had rather lost interest in the conversation. He experienced a brief pang of guilt—there had been many times in the past when his friend had listened to his own angst-laden ramblings—but it had been ages since he had felt this...well, he wasn't entirely sure what he felt but it was a bloody good feeling. Finally, he decided to call it a night.

'Listen, Rob, it's been a pretty hectic week and I'm really tired, so I'm going to head off. When's Mel coming for you?'

Rob looked at his watch. 'She'll be here in about fifteen minutes, unless she stays bletherin' to her mum. You're sure you don't want a lift?'

'No, I'll be fine walking. Could do with a bit of fresh air anyway.'

At the back of his mind was the vague notion that Joanna Hume might be taking another walk with the canine Bruce.

'Listen, I don't know what the forecast for the golf is for tomorrow...'

Rob shook his head, a slightly sour expression on his face.

'Forget it, mate, I'm still workin' to tie this bloody case up at the moment. Need to get the reports all done, the boss wants them on Monday. Like I said, I've been pretty much told to wrap it up and leave it be. Load of shite, if you ask me.'

Bruce didn't; he felt he needed to get away. They said their farewells and he exited The Bay, aware of Rob heading to the bar for a final drink. Funny how the tables can turn so quickly, he mused.

The night was chill, a cold north wind blowing across from the snow-capped hills of the lower highlands, just across the Clyde. The lights of distant Craigendorran and Helensburgh twinkled merrily as he walked along past Battery Park, past the modern flats built on the site of the old torpedo factory, before turning left into The Esplanade. His head was spinning; the fresh air was playing its usual tricks and, as he passed the entrance to the Royal West Sailing and Boating club, he stopped for a moment, leaning both hands on the railings. He felt as if he might pass out; he hadn't drunk *that* much, surely? Maybe he had food poisoning. He took a few deep breaths, trying to stay calm; his house was less than half a mile away, after all. He was vaguely aware of a car drawing in to the side of the road; he heard a door open then, after a few seconds, a voice asked.

'Excuse me, are you okay?'

He tried to speak but his mouth was dry, he was struggling to form the words. The figure moved closer, silhouetted dark against the streetlight, and looked at his face. Bruce was aware of a slight chuckle.

'Know the feeling, mate. One too many, eh? Or two, by the looks of it. Have you got far to go?'

Bruce still couldn't speak; his head was spinning badly now but he managed to shake it as he tried to point in the general direction of home. As he removed his hand from the railings, his knees started to buckle and he felt a strong pair of arms reach under his armpits, supporting him.

'Here, steady on, mate. God, you're in a right state. Listen let's get you in the car and I'll drop you at your house—if you can tell me where it is. That's it, just lean on me, you're nearly there...'

He sat down; the car was warm and comfortable...

The man seemed kind, caring...

Blackness enfolded him.

Chapter 11

Friday 28th November

He felt dreadful.

His head was pounding mercilessly and waves of nausea swept over him. There seemed to be something over his head, he couldn't see and he was having difficulty breathing. He lifted his hands but, immediately, a firm grip around his wrists prevented him. He tried to stand up but the same firm pressure on his shoulders prevented from doing so. He slumped back—he hadn't the energy to struggle.

From what he could feel, Bruce surmised that he was sitting on a solid chair, presumably with a hood, a sack of some sort, over his head. Had he been abducted– and, if so, by whom... and why?

He also supposed that he had been drugged and he realised that all he could do was to wait and see what happened; but his heart was pounding and he still felt as if he was struggling to breathe. He was aware of a rising sense of panic; he had always been mildly claustrophobic.

Without warning, the sack was pulled from his head; he blinked in the sudden brightness for a few seconds until his eyes became accustomed to the level of light. A brief glance around showed that he was in a large, windowless space with a vaulted, whitewashed ceiling, illuminated by a number of upward-facing spotlights. Somehow he felt that he was underground; there was a faint, earthy smell. A basement, a wine cellar, maybe? Several solid wooden doors led off the room, all firmly closed. He risked a further look to either side; there was no wine visible but, standing slightly to his rear, one on each side, were two black-clad figures. Tall and menacing, their hands were clasped in front of them as they stared straight ahead through the holes in what looked like balaclava hoods; ski masks, probably. He looked to his front once more, registering the details as best he could.

A long table faced him, almost like a banqueting table; solid, the wood appearing old somehow...there was no banquet, however. Eight figures sat behind the table, each dressed in black, each wearing a similar hood with two holes for the eyes and one for the mouth. It was impossible to tell their age or gender. He stared at them as the eight pairs of eyes regarded him; expressionless, unreadable, menacing...

Finally, one of the figures spoke. At first Bruce couldn't tell which one it was, until the figure lifted up a piece of paper that had lain in front of them.

'Good evening, Mr Redpath. First of all, I must apologise profusely for the inconvenience. It was never our intention to have to bring you here in this manner and, other than some minor discomfort, I hope you have not been harmed in any way.'

It was a cultured, but aged, male voice, one that had undoubtedly been very powerful in its day and, although very slightly querulous, it still commanded attention. He wasn't sure if it was a question or a statement, so he opted for the latter and remained silent. The speaker paused for a few seconds; maybe it *had* been a question.

'Now, I am sure that you have a number of questions. Before we begin, however, I will ask a few of my own.'

The speaker's voice was also sonorous and mesmerising. Bruce felt that, in other circumstances, the man would probably be charming, offering him a brandy, a cigar maybe...but these were most certainly not other circumstances. Again, he remained silent, staring as impassively as he could manage at what he now considered to be his interrogator.

'So, you are Mister Bruce Kiloran Redpath, aged fifty-two, residing at The Esplanade, Greenock? Is that correct?'

As this was a direct question he decided that he should probably answer it. His voice sounded thin in comparison to that of the other man.

'Yes.'

'And you are a partner in the Glasgow law firm, Redpath, Fox, Carnegie?'

'Yes.'

'And you were married to Dorothy Anne Redpath, nee Carmichael, sadly deceased?'

He could feel the sudden rush of blood to his head. He tried desperately to pull the shutters down, to close the door but, in the face of such a direct question, he was helpless. He hesitated; when finally he spoke, his voice was hoarse, breaking.

'Yes, but you have no right—'

'Thank you, Mr Redpath, let us just stick to answering the questions at the moment, if you please.'

Despite his distress, his rising panic, Bruce began to suspect that the man was, or had been, a lawyer; the mode of questioning certainly seemed to indicate it.

'You have two children, Mr Redpath, Felicity, aged twenty-two, and Coral, aged twenty-six?'

He swallowed, trying to compose himself; how did this man know all about him, about his family, about...?

With a considerable struggle, he finally managed to force shut the imagined door in his mind.

'Yes.'

'Neither of whom live with you anymore?'

He shook his head. 'No.'

His interrogator sat back in his chair, placed the paper on the table and clasped his hands; he looked relaxed.

'Mr Redpath, have you any idea why you are here?'

Bruce had thought of little else since he had regained consciousness. Surely none of his own clients' spouses would have taken such vindictive action? Could it be something to do with Simon, the family of a defendant's victim, perhaps? Suddenly, a tiny flash of realisation began to form in his brain. He shook his head—surely not...?

'No.'

Somehow, Bruce could sense that the man was smiling beneath the mask. There was a ripple of movement among the other hooded figures, some of whom now turned towards Bruce's interrogator.

'Oh come, Mr Redpath, surely you have been wondering why you have been drugged, abducted, hooded and brought before us? No theories, no ideas? You're a clever man, Mr Redpath, and an excellent solicitor. You also seem remarkably calm for someone in your position.'

Bruce felt anything but calm; he was sweating, his pulse was elevated, he felt as if he was on the verge of outright panic. Composing himself, he waited a moment, choosing his words carefully, formulating his sentences with precision. He tried to imagine that he was in a courtroom, addressing a jury, a judge...he was safe there. He cleared his throat and tried to swallow, realising that he was parched.

'May I have some water please?'

The interrogator nodded and one of the hooded figures behind him approached, handing Bruce a crystal tumbler before pouring water into it from a plastic bottle. Bruce drained the glass and handed it back.

'Thank you.'

He took a deep breath. 'In my position, as you put it, there is nothing that I can do. I appear to be entirely at your mercy, having been drugged, abducted and hooded—your words, not mine—then brought here and held entirely against my will. There is no point in becoming hysterical. I have no doubt that you will do what you plan to do with me, one way or another, and I do not intend to give you the satisfaction of witnessing any loss of self-control on my part.'

It had taken every ounce of Bruce Redpath's self-control to utter these words as calmly as he had done, however. There was a pause.

'I am impressed, Mr Redpath, indeed I am; and, of course, I would have thought that, by now, you would be only too well aware of whom you are in company with and why you are here, although not of what will happen to you. Let me put you straight on that point.'

He paused again, for effect. Bruce continued to stare at him as the spark of realisation fanned to a flame of certainty.

'We do not intend to physically harm you. We have brought you here for one reason and for one reason only.'

This time the pause indicated that the man was waiting for a response. He decided to comply.

'And what, may I ask, is that reason?'

'Quite simply, to plead our side of the case, Mr Redpath.'

The sentence confirmed Bruce's suspicion that he was talking to a fellow legal professional; at least that put them on an equal footing—up to a point.

'I see. And what case might that be?'

The man let out a snort of impatience. 'Please do not be pedantic, Mr Redpath. I am quite sure that, by now, you know who, or what, we are—well, other than our personal identities, of course— and I know for a fact that you are familiar with what we have done and what we are capable of doing. What I want you to know, to understand, is why.'

Bruce was aware of his heart-rate settling and his temper rising; he fought to control it.

'I see. You want to explain to me why you have kidnapped and tortured to death a number of reasonably high-profile criminals, a rapist and a paedophile. Is that correct?'

'If you choose to put it like that then, yes, that is correct. But, of course, it is not quite as simple as that, is it?'

'As I see it, murder is murder, no matter who the victim.'

'You are quite correct. Murder is murder and, as such, it should be punished. Severely. There are many who argue for the return of capital punishment—'

'I am not one of them.'

'That's as may be, Mr Redpath. Nonetheless, there *is* a strong case for execution. An eye for an eye—'

'Nonsense! That makes the executioner every bit as guilty as the executed.'

'Does it?'

'Of course it does.'

'But what if murder goes unpunished, if the murderer remains free to continue with his relentless quest for death and destruction? What then?'

'He will be brought to justice eventually. There is no place for vigilantes in a civilised society.'

'Vigilantes? Is that what you believe us to be?'

'What else would you call it? The lynch mob? You are as bad as them, if not worse.'

Bruce was becoming angry now, his emotion overriding his fear. His adversary seemed to sense this and didn't respond immediately. When finally he spoke, his voice was softer, more gentle.

'Mr Redpath, let us put this argument aside for the moment.'

Bruce remained silent; he felt the hooded figure's eyes boring into him.

'I am aware that you lost your wife almost exactly ten years ago. For that I am truly sorry, perhaps more than you realise...would you care to explain how she died?'

Bruce felt his heart-rate rise again as he fought to block out the memories, the images he had struggled to contain for...

Ten years! No, it couldn't be...was it really ten years?

Bruce shook his head and mumbled, 'I get the impression you already know.'

'Yes, you are correct, of course, and I will also leave that tragic matter aside for the present. In which case, let me put this to you.'

He paused again for effect, then stood up once more. He was a tall man, with a slight stoop. An imposing figure, nonetheless, 'You see, my associates and I...'

He swept his arms around him, including the other seven hitherto silent members of what Bruce was now starting to regard as 'The Jury'

'...we are people of considerable influence and of considerable wealth. That, however, is not our common bond. Indeed, our bond is one of a much more personal and tragic nature for we, too, have all lost a loved one. Not to cancer or to disease, nor to any other medical condition. Not to what a coroner might refer to as 'Death by Misadventure'. No, instead, we have all lost a loved one due to a much more unnatural cause. I am referring, of course, to criminal activity. Illegal substances, for example; and, sadly, to that most violent of endings, murder. On occasion preceded by some brutal act, be it assault, rape...'

He let the sentence hang for a moment, then swept his arm round, once again including the other hooded figures.

'So, Mr Redpath, each and every one of us here has lost a family member, a close friend, through criminal activity of some sort. Drug overdose, or a related cause such as suicide, murder, rape. Of course, I include you in our unfortunate and tragic company.'

He stopped and let out a long sigh. 'There is no specific cure for this, just as there is no specific, all-encompassing cure for cancer, for heart disease or the like, but we are attempting to treat the problem. Just as medical research strives to kill the cancerous cells, we strive to kill the malignancy at the heart of organised crime. The so called 'crime barons', those violent, sociopathic, psychopathic individuals at the root of all this evil. These vile destroyers of innocent lives, innocent families...the suppliers, the dealers, the importers, the rapists, the murderers...we wish to send out a clear message to all these people. You will be held accountable for your actions. You will be punished, without mercy.'

His voice was rising to a crescendo and, despite his anger, Bruce was almost spellbound; the man was a natural orator. He continued, his tone dropping slightly.

'But the root of the whole problem is, I am very much afraid to say, our flawed legal system.'

Bruce had heard enough. Once again, he tried to stand up and this time he was unhampered. He shouted at the anonymous man, seemingly taking him by surprise.

'That's complete and utter nonsense! We have one of the finest legal systems in the world! You're a bloody lawyer, of that I have no doubt; how can you possibly think that your course of action is acceptable?'

'Simply because the law, that which you so vigorously defend, has failed on the occasions of those that we have already dealt with. Shearer, Bannon, Scullion, Krasniki, Devenney and Flint. We were unfortunate with Doyle, although I believe that he will suffer now, just as we have done. But our message is clear. There is now a force higher than the law...'

'NO! There can be *no* force higher than the law—you are nothing more than vigilantes, no better that those—'

'ENOUGH, Mr Redpath. You are wrong!'

'No, YOU are wrong—'

'Sit down, please.'

Bruce felt himself being pushed back in to the chair. He dropped back down, shaking his head. The man continued, his voice becoming more conversational.

'You see, we are not that different, you and I. Society wishes to conquer diseases like cancer, diseases that kill thousands every year, destroying lives, families. Yet it is a naturally-occurring phenomenon that we are only just beginning to understand. We, on the other hand, wish to conquer organised crime, that dreadful malignancy that...'

He paused again and looked at those sitting next to him.

'...that took our loved ones. We understand it, we have the wherewithal to stop it and yet our legal system has failed to do so. All through legal technicalities, simple errors made by our overworked police force, by intimidation and of course, by the employment of a clever—and expensive—defending Counsel. Can't you see our point of view?'

Bruce thought about this for a moment. Could he, in a way...?

'No. Absolutely not. That is why the law exists, that is its purpose. To an extent I might understand the sentiment but, as soon as you set yourselves above the law, then you are lost.'

'That is not the case, Mr Redpath.'

'It is—of course it is! If you set yourselves up as Judge—as you appear have done—and jury, then where do you stop? It's the same moral dilemma as euthanasia. First of all, it's just for those who wish to end their lives, those who are suffering from dreadful terminal diseases. But what's next? Kill everyone over ninety—or over eighty...seventy-five? And as for you—what's next? Maybe it starts with murderers, with rapists. But then, what if someone is knocked down and killed by a drunk driver—is it acceptable to kill them? There might be mitigating circumstances, the defendant's point of view—what about that? Once you cross that line, then the line becomes fluid. The more times you cross it, the more fluid it becomes. It should—it must—*never* be crossed.'

He was angry, angrier than he had felt for a very long time. Who the hell did this man—this man of the law, undoubtedly—think he was, self-appointing himself and his wealthy friends as captors, judge, jury and executioners? He drew himself up as fully as the hands on his shoulders would allow.

'You are wrong, sir. And, just as you put it to me, I put it to you, you *know* you are wrong.'

The Judge placed his clenched fists on the table and leaned towards him; despite the mask, there was menace in the gesture.

'Then, Mr Redpath, we will have to agree to disagree. Before we do, however, I would like to ask one of my friends to speak.'

He turned to his left; the request was obviously anticipated. As he sat down again, one of the other masked figures stood up, staring intently at Bruce through the eye-holes of the ski mask. A slight figure, almost frail, bent over as if in constant pain.

'Bruce.'

It was a woman's voice, soft, emotional, sad.

'I am going to tell you a story, a truly dreadful story. I know that you have suffered your own tragedy, for which I am extremely sorry, but I hope that your own experience may give you some insight into what I am about to recount ...'

Bruce had the feeling that the woman was fighting back tears.

'I had a friend—we had known each other since school, we had shared the usual ups and downs of life, including my own very messy divorce and subsequent breakdown...'

She paused, catching her breath. 'She and her husband had a wonderful life. They had a successful business, they were prosperous, they were happy—I have to admit that, given my own disastrous marriage, I was, at times, highly envious. But they worked hard, they were honest and I could never grudge them either their success or their happiness. They had two beautiful daughters, both of whom excelled at school and who were making their own way in life. The eldest daughter had left home and was embarking upon a successful career when, tragically, she contracted cancer. Over a period of two years she had both breasts removed, then part of her intestine, resulting in her requiring a stoma. Gruelling chemo and radiotherapy ensued, alas, to no avail; she died, surrounded by her adoring family. My friend and her husband were, understandably, devastated; sadly their younger daughter, who had recently split from her partner, seemed even more so. She had worshipped her sister, she had confided in her and, now, that adored big sister, her best friend, had been taken...'

She stopped; Bruce could hear the emotion in her voice.

'I won't bore you with the details. I did my utmost to support them as a family but, sadly, I still had my own, somewhat more trivial issues, to deal with. Suffice to say, on the pretext of helping to relieve her grief, someone introduced her to cocaine, then crack, then heroin. She became a shadow of her former self. Her parents tried everything, rehab., counselling; finally, everyone believed that she was clean, but she wasn't. She turned to the streets to make enough money to feed her habit without anyone knowing....'

She started to sob, almost uncontrollably; the figure next to her pulled her down on to her seat and comforted her. After a minute or so she continued, her voice unsteady.

'A few years ago, she was found dead, in an old industrial unit in...'

She managed to stop herself before identifying the location.

'...she had been abducted and brutally sexually assaulted. The pathologist isolated five different types of DNA from the semen found...'

She started to cry again. 'She had been gang-raped, strangled then ignominiously dumped, naked, in a shit-hole...'

The woman broke down completely and Bruce couldn't help but feel sorrow and abject pity for her and for the family involved. It was, indeed, a tragic tale. As she continued to sob, the Judge stood up once more, taking up the narrative.

'So, an innocent girl robbed of her sister by cancer. An innocent family, not only robbed but traumatised, destroyed even, by the impact of drugs. Sadly, that wasn't an end to the story. There was an extensive investigation and the supply chain was discovered, as were the rapists; it transpired that one of them was the poor, unfortunate girl's 'dealer'. The police were thorough, they were passionate about bringing the girl's killers to justice. And they did, only to have the case thrown out on a technicality. The perpetrators are still walking free, still dealing but, rest assured, they are on our list.'

The Judge took a deep breath then sighed. 'Alas, it proved to be too much for my friend's husband, a good, honest man whom I, too, was proud to call my friend. After the case was thrown out, he took his own life. This completely innocent woman has now lost her entire family group. One to cancer, one to drugs, and their ultimate effect, and one to the wrongs of our legal system.'

He paused, peering at Bruce through his mask. He sat down.

'Let me give you some insight as to what we do here, Mr Redpath. You see, we—'

'I know perfectly well what you do here. You seek out those whom you perceive to have evaded justice, as you see it. Then you mete out your own form of justice—vile and brutal, it would seem—the justice of a lawless society—'

'No.' The man banged his fist on the table. 'If you will do me the courtesy of listening for a few minutes—'

'And why the hell should I? I am here against my will and I have no interest in what you do, other than to prevent it.'

The interrogator let out a long sigh. 'Then I rest my case. I had hoped to persuade you to join us, Mr Redpath. You have an excellent legal mind, you are a fair man, you believe in justice and, sadly, you possess the qualification...'

Bruce shouted back at the man. 'Join you! God forbid! I believe in due process, in the law—the law of our country, not in the justice of a bloody kangaroo court—'

He was interrupted by a fresh bout of sobbing from the woman who had spoken. Despite his situation, he was genuinely moved by her grief and he turned towards her.

'Em, excuse me...'

The masked woman looked up.

'Look, I'm so, so sorry for your friend's loss and for the grief it has undoubtedly caused you. I cannot begin to imagine how awful that must be...'

The hunched, still-sobbing figure responded with a nod of her head.

'But I am afraid I just cannot agree with your point of view. You are still setting yourself above the law—'

The interrogator interrupted once more, emphasising his points by banging his fist on the table once more, punctuating his words.

'A-law-that-has-repeatedly-failed! Don't you see—it has failed this family, it has failed countless other people, criminals walk free and continue their vile trade.'

'But it must be up to the police to ensure that their case is watertight—'

'Yes, yes, due process, I know. But you and I also know that these people are the scum of the earth. We know for certain that they are guilty. Yet, because of some mistake, some minor procedural error made by a policeman in the heat of the moment while acting under extreme pressure, some clever barrister sets them free! And for a hefty fee—ask yourself, Bruce, how much does your partner, Simon Fox, gain when he successfully defends the likes of Rik Shearer? Or a debauched paedophile like Brendan Devenney? A brutal killer like Suzannah Flint, who killed a young prostitute by throwing boiling fat over her before pushing her down a flight of stairs? Then there was Doyle, her partner. We believe that he was behind the recent people-smuggling incident, in which an infant died, were you aware of that fact?'

He paused and took a breath. 'So, I ask you, Mr Redpath, do you believe for one moment that these people were innocent—'

'But we are not *saying* whether they were innocent or guilty!' shouted Bruce. 'We are only saying that due process hadn't been achieved. We cannot convict unless we are beyond reasonable doubt, you know that! Once we discard that, we are lost! You can't bring back someone you've convicted and hanged if you discover later that you've made a mistake! That's why capital punishment was abolished in Britain.'

'But, in cases such as these, you and I can be in no *doubt* that the likes of Shearer was a career criminal, the lowest of the low. Devoid of morals, devoid of principles, entirely dishonest and self-serving. The man was undoubtedly as guilty as sin, as were the others. They deserved everything that they received and you know it. And, of course it sends a very clear message to the greater criminal fraternity; hence our brutal methods, which you have already questioned. These people walk in daily fear of execution by their so-called associates. A stabbing here, a drive-by shooting there...it is part of the fabric of their life, a known and accepted risk. But when they see what *we* are capable of, the manner in which they are likely to meet their end...well...'

He shrugged. 'If, by doing what we do, we save one life, prevent one rape, remove one supply chain of heroin, then surely we will have accomplished *something*, will we not?'

'Look, I totally agree with your description of Shearer, the man was an absolute beast. But, until he is...was...properly convicted, you are entirely wrong to act as you did. The fundamental precept of our system of justice is 'innocent until proven guilty.' And what about habeas corpus? Shearer was tried and the law failed. Yes, he may well have walked free on that occasion but he would most likely have been convicted eventually.'

'Most likely? Do you think that's good enough, because I don't. Do you think that 'most likely be convicted eventually' offers *any* sense of justice, of closure, to the families of his, and his criminal associates', victims? And how many more people would have to die before then, may I ask?'

'...um...well, I don't know...'

'Of course you don't. And what if it was one of your own daughters?'

Bruce felt a chill run down his spine.

'But they don't take drugs...'

'Nor did this poor unfortunate girl until tragedy befell the family. You do not know what awaits around the corner, Mr Redpath, and you cannot foresee what may happen. What if that vile rapist, Krasniki, had accosted one of your beloved girls in some dark alley up in Glasgow? The man was an animal, completely devoid of morals, out to satisfy his own warped sexual needs. And let me assure you, if those such as Krasniki, Shearer, Doyle and the rest of that vile bunch see an opportunity, they will seize it and take full advantage of it, purely for their own satisfaction or gain. We are determined to prevent that, whatever the cost.'

Bruce almost screamed with anger, with frustration.'Then you have lost your moral compass! You have lost...you have lost your soul! God help you.'

'God? Ha, let us not even start down that road...anyway, enough. I have said my piece, you have said yours...'

The man paused again, looking to those seated to his right and left. He appeared to be considering some complex legal problem.

'...but if we cannot convince you by simple reason, then I am left with no alternative. You will see how we operate at first hand, Mr Redpath.'

He turned towards one of the men standing behind Bruce and commanded.

'Bring in the prisoner.'

Chapter 12

Friday 28th November.

'Bastards. Fuckin' bastards...'

Paul Maguire reckoned it was about the tenth time David Doyle had uttered those words. Doyle had been released from Inverclyde Royal Hospital that afternoon and, having discovered that he had been summarily evicted from the marital home, it had fallen to Maguire to collect his friend and offer him accommodation. Temporarily, it was to be hoped; Maguire was most protective of his solitude and valued his privacy far too much to consider having a long-term lodger. Still, needs must; after all, Davie Doyle had offered him sanctuary and employment when his own life had descended into chaos.

Maguire regarded his ranting friend across the dining-room table. He had known Doyle for more years than he cared to remember, first as a client then, latterly, as a business associate. Doyle was shrewd, street-wise and savvy, he was hard and he was unprincipled. He was a crook.

What he lacked most was imagination.

Maguire had listened to Doyle's story with an initial sense of disbelief but also with a growing unease. He was certain now that Doyle's narrative wasn't fabricated; quite frankly, the man wasn't capable. However, it still sounded like a work of fiction—of horror, in fact. Who the hell *were* these people?

'Paul? Are ye fuckin' listenin' tae me?'

He tried to look sympathetic, a characteristic somewhat alien to him; neither was he particularly good at dealing with bereavement.

'Aye, of course I am; I know, it's awful, poor Suzi—listen you need to eat something...'

Doyle looked up at his friend with a glazed expression.

'Ah'm no' fuckin' hungry.'

He slugged back the last of his blended whisky and reached for the near-empty bottle. Maguire looked on; he had another half-dozen bottles of a distinctly better-quality spirit safely stashed away but he didn't intend to let Davie know that.

'You'll end up with a bloody ulcer if you keep drinking on an empty stomach. At least have a sandwich—or I could heat up a pizza.'

Doyle drained the bottle into his glass and stared into it, shaking his head.

'Whoever the fuck these bastards are, they're dead meat. We need tae find oot who wis responsible...'

Maguire took out his cigarettes and offered one to Doyle.

'Might not be so easy. Whoever it was, they're organised, professional and, as you've found out, absolutely bloody brutal.'

'Aye, don't fuckin' remind me.'

To Maguire's astonishment, two tears ran down Doyle's grey, unshaven cheeks. Glasgow born and bred, he felt decidedly uneasy in the presence of a tearful grown man; with the exceptional circumstance of the defeat of one's football team, of course. Doyle rambled on.

'Poor wee Suzi. She wis so fuckin' cold, Paul, like ice, she wis. Ah tried, Ah tried tae keep her warm but she jist kind o'...'

He snorted loudly, as if sniffing back his emotion..

'...she jist faded away—wan minute she wis kind o' mumblin' like, then she jist stapped. Poor wee Suzi...'

Suddenly, he banged the table with his fist. Maguire jumped.

'Bastards, fuckin'...'

He looked across at his friend; Maguire had witnessed David Doyle in many moods but he had never before seen such a look of anger, of pure hatred, on the hard man's face. The tears were past.

'How the fuck are we goin' tae find oot who's behind this?'

Maguire didn't know, but he wasn't going to tell Doyle that. He stood up.

'Davie, I'm going to get us some food and, while it's heating up, I'll make a few calls, get a few feelers out.'

Doyle raised the glass of whisky and gulped it back.

'Cheers. Fuck knows whit Ah'd dae withoot ye.'

Fuck knows indeed, thought Maguire, as he exited the cramped, smoky dining room.

Paul Maguire had eaten no dinner himself, having been occupied collecting his friend from the hospital in Greenock. They had driven to the Doyle family home where, on that wet and miserable afternoon, Maria Doyle had deposited two suitcases, containing what she considered to be the sum total of Doyle's clothes and possessions, on the pavement.

Both case-lids had been wide open.

With nowhere for Doyle to go, Maguire had been left with no option but to take him back to his first-floor tenement flat in Glasgow's Pollokshields; at least he had a couple of spare bedrooms. As he put the two frozen pepperoni pizzas in the oven, he wondered if it had been a wise move. Doyle seemed to have taken possession of the dining room as 'campaign revenge' headquarters. The sooner he made some headway towards finding out who was responsible for Doyle's and Flint's abduction, the sooner he could return to his bachelor ways, his personal pleasures. He closed the oven door then opened one of the adjacent cupboards, a disorganised collection of tins and jars. He rummaged about, selecting a large tin of grapefruit, then removed it from the cupboard. A quick twist and the false can opened, revealing three cheap, pay-as-you-go burner phones. He selected one, switched it on and, when it had booted up, he scrolled through the numbers.

Fifteen minutes later, the pizzas were ready and the messages delivered; he didn't necessarily expect any immediate replies but he left a few succinct enquiries with a few select individuals. Job done.

Maguire had never been a particular fan of Suzannah Flint, but he and Davie Doyle went back a long way. To an extent, he 'owed' Doyle, but that was by no means his prime motivation.

No, Paul Maguire was much more concerned that he, too, might find himself on the 'who's next' list...

<hr />

One of the masked men standing behind Bruce Redpath had walked over to the nearest door. After unlocking it, the man disappeared for a few minutes before returning with a hooded figure, hands tied in front of him and feet tethered together by a short piece of rope that caused him to shuffle along like an old man. He was dressed in grey designer joggers and a hoodie, with bright yellow trainers on his feet. His guard dragged a chair across, placing it about eight feet away from where Bruce was seated, then pushed the man roughly down into it. The hooded figure mumbled incoherently and tried to stand, but his captor grabbed him by the collar of his hoodie and held him in place.

The man who had interrogated Bruce stood up,

'Unmask the prisoner, please.'

The guard pulled the hood off, revealing a young man, blinking in the light just as Bruce had done. He looked right and left, his eyes resting on Bruce for a moment, and Bruce could detect the fear in them. He had a round, babyish face with dyed-blond hair, shaved at the sides and long on top. Had he been asked, Bruce would have described him as what his daughters referred to as a 'ned'. He continued his incoherent mumbling; he had a strip of silver duct tape across his mouth.

'Take off the tape,' commanded the interrogator.

The guard reached down and ripped off the silver strip with a loud rasping sound. The young man let out a yelp.

'Ya fuckin' prick—that wis sair. Jist wait till ma bro' hears about this, you're aw' in deep fuckin' shit—'

'Be quiet please!' roared the interrogator. The young man stopped for a moment, then resumed his tirade.

'An' who the fuck're you, ya wanker? Fuckin' let me go or—'

Without warning, the guard raised his hand and slapped the young man heavily on the side of his head.

'Oww—fuckin'...'

He tried again to get out of the chair but the guard grabbed him roughly around the throat and forced him back down. The interrogator spoke again.

'This is your last warning. Be quiet or I'll have the duct tape put back on. Maybe over your nose as well, see how you like that.'

Bruce could contain himself no longer. He, too, tried to stand, but his own guard prevented the movement. He cried out.

'Stop it! You have no right to do this, whatever you think this man's done. You are not the law!'

He screamed the last five words and the Judge looked over at him.

'In here, Mr Redpath, we are, I can assure you. Now, I am going to ask you to be quiet also. I do not want to have to threaten *you* with duct tape.'

'I thought you said you were not going to physically harm me?'

'I did, but that does not necessarily include physically silencing you. Please, Mr Redpath, do not force my hand.'

Bruce decided that it was pointless arguing. The Judge looked back at the young man, silent now in the face of the threat; Bruce could see his eyes dart back and forth, as if evaluating his chances of escape. These were pretty much nil, Bruce thought. The Judge spoke again.

'Good. Now, I am going to ask you some questions and I expect an answer. Do I make myself clear?'

'Away an' fuck yersel,' was the response. The guard slapped the side of the man's head again, harder this time.

'Aaaah, ya fucker...'

'SILENCE!' yelled the Judge There was; absolute, this time.

'Your name is Darren Fitzpatrick Beagan?'

The blood rushed to Bruce's head; he recognised the name instantly, although he hadn't actually recognised the young man.

'I asked you a question. Your name is Darren Fitzpatrick Beagan—is that correct?'

The man mumbled.

'What?'

'Aye. Ah fuckin' said 'aye'.'

'Do not be insolent.'

The Judge read out Beagan's address, receiving another grunted 'aye' in response.

'And you are acquainted with a man by the name of Christopher Tilstock, usually known as 'Kristoff'?'

He was. Bruce already knew that he was. The man nodded his assent.

The Judge walked along to the end of the table then stepped out in front of it, towards the figure. He stopped about six feet away, looking down at Beagan, who cowered away. The interrogator turned towards Bruce and pointed at him.

'Do you know who this man is, Beagan?'

The man turned and looked at Bruce for a moment

'Huvn'ae a fuckin' clue.'

'Really? Are you sure. Look again, Mr Beagan. Look closely. Are you sure you don't recognise him?'

Beagan looked and shook his head.

'Naw.'

'Very well. I will tell you who he is...'

Bruce wanted to raise his hands to his ears, to block out what he was about to hear, but he seemed to be frozen, paralysed. The Judge continued, his voice booming, filling the space of the room.

'This is Mr Bruce Redpath, Mr Beagan. He is a lawyer, and an exceptionally good one. He is also a family man—or rather was...'

Beagan turned towards Bruce once more, a look of realisation spreading across his face; or was it panic, perhaps?

'It was ten years ago, ten years next week, that you, Mr Beagan, robbed Mr Redpath of his happiness. You were racing in a vehicle that you had stolen earlier that evening. You had been drinking and you had 'done' a line of cocaine, had you not?'

There was no reply; Beagan was staring, open-mouthed, up at the interrogator. He, too, seemed paralysed, such was the effect of the man's voice.

'You were racing against your friend 'Kristoff' Tilstock, driving at nearly eighty miles an hour on the A761, the back road from Port Glasgow to Kilmacolm. You came round a bend on the wrong side of the road and crashed into the vehicle being driven by Mr Redpath's wife, Dorothy, who was returning from visiting her elderly aunt in Kilmacolm. Following the crash, Mrs Redpath's vehicle left the road and turned on its side.'

Bruce thought that he was about to vomit as the man continued.

'The car went on fire, Mr Beagan, did it not? Mrs Redpath was trapped inside. You stopped and got out, you went over, then you got into Mr Tilstock's car and left the scene.'

Bruce tried desperately to close the door, to push the memories, the horrors, back inside, but the Judge's words were relentless.

'Mrs Redpath was still alive, trapped in the burning vehicle. Mr Redpath was at home, looking after his two teenage daughters, while you left his wife to die.'

'Ah never...Ah got aff wi' it. You cann'ae...'

'YES WE CAN, Beagan. In here, we can do whatever we like. You could have chosen to do the right thing, to save her life. You and Tilstock could easily have got her out of the vehicle. In Tilstock's original statement, later refuted, he claims that it was a small fire initially. She could easily have been saved, Mr Beagan but, instead, you ran off, leaving her to her fate. Like a coward, Mr Beagan. You saved your own skin at the expense of the life of an innocent woman. And you did not 'get off with it'. The case was dismissed because your brother, William, or 'Billy' intimidated Mr Tilstock and his family.'

'That's fuckin' shite, Billy never...aaahhh'

The guard had administered another slap to the side of Beagan's head but Bruce only heard, he didn't see; his eyes were screwed tight shut as he re-lived the horror of that night, the police car at the door, the useless words of sympathy...the interrogator was talking again.

'As I was saying, you intimidated them until they changed their story. Mr Tilstock's own car was set on fire outside the family home. His father was assaulted outside a pub, left with brain damage. The perpetrators were never caught but it was common knowledge that the beating was administered by your 'heroic' big brother and local hard man, Billy Beagan, and his friends.'

The Judge started to pace across the stone-flagged floor, his slow footsteps somehow ominous.

'The case collapsed, Mr Beagan. Tilstock refused to testify against you and, eventually, you were left facing only charges of stealing a vehicle and of driving recklessly while under the influence of drink and drugs. Meanwhile, Mr Redpath was left with no wife, no mother for his girls...and no justice...'

He turned towards Beagan again and roared.

'NO JUSTICE, Mr Beagan.'

Silence.

Bruce wanted to scream, he craved anything but that dreadful, empty silence that allowed the memories to flood his brain, overwhelming his senses...

The Judge at the trial had been apologetic and quite obviously furious at the collapse of the case. The Connors had sat with Bruce, one on either side, Mel squeezing his hand as Beagan was found guilty of the lesser charges.

As Beagan was led away from the dock, grinning at his friends present in the courtroom, he had turned towards Bruce, curling his fingers and moving them up and down as he mouthed 'wanker' at him. The policeman had pushed the prisoner forward, turning and mouthing 'sorry' to Bruce, but it was too late. Mel and Rob

Connor had led him from the courtroom, bereft, hopeless and on the verge of a nervous breakdown.

Now, he felt he was in the same place again. The interrogator was pacing once more, hands clasped behind his back.

'So, Mr Beagan, you served your sentence, you got out early for 'good behaviour' and here we are.'

'You cann'ae, Ah fuckin' got aff wi' it...'

The Judge turned.

'Yes, in a way I suppose you *did*, Mr Beagan, I suppose you did. That was then. But tonight you find yourself in a very different courtroom.'

He walked back across to Beagan, staring down at the cowering young man.

'You see, Mr Beagan, there is a big difference between justice and the law. Tonight, it is *our* law and, believe me, justice *will* be done.'

He turned to face the other seven hooded figures. Each gave a nod. He turned back.

'Guilty, Mr Beagan, We find you guilty.'

Beagan stood up, unhindered this time.

'Get tae fuck, ye're aw' fuckin' deid, wance Billy gets tae hear—'

This time there was a grunt of pain as the guard drove his fist hard into Beagan's midriff. The young man fell to his knees, retching, gasping for breath.

'Take him away.'

The guard dragged Beagan across the flagstones and back to the side room, into which they both disappeared. The interrogator returned to his chair and sat down. He nodded; the guard behind Bruce stepped away and returned with a fresh crystal glass, handing it to Bruce. He took it, raising it to his lips; brandy. He drained the glass, choking as the liquid burned his throat, welcoming the warmth that spread through his body.

There was silence for a few minutes then, eventually, the Judge spoke again, He sounded weary now, his voice was hoarse.

'I am incredibly sorry for what I have put you through tonight, Mr Redpath. I had hoped that my arguments would have won you over but, alas, they did not. I was left with no alternative...now can you see our point of view?'

Bruce didn't look at the man. He shook his head, mumbling.

'Why? Why did you rake all that up again?'

'Because I had to, Mr Redpath, to let you see why we do what we do. Surely you must have hungered for revenge?'

He had; many times, until the psychiatrist had taught him how to repress the anguish, the hatred, the pain...

Close the door; as quickly as you can...shut it all out.

'Beagan is a vile, remorseless and ignorant individual who hovers constantly on the verges of criminality. He has been in trouble since, although he has never repeated the actions of that night, thankfully. He will never change; sooner or later he will offend again and it may, once more, cost an innocent victim their life. As he said himself, 'he got aff wi' it.' Justice most certainly *wasn't* done, was it, Mr Redpath? He 'got aff wi' it', didn't he?'

Bruce nodded.

'Well, tonight you have the chance to serve justice upon this guilty man, Mr Redpath. Because, despite what happened in court, all those years ago, you *know* him to be guilty. The law failed that day, didn't it. Didn't it, Mr Redpath?'

He nodded. Had he looked up, he would have seen the Judge nodding too. He felt himself being raised gently to his feet and led across the flag-stoned towards the door. Suddenly, the interrogator's words rang out, echoing around the room.

'Fiat justicia ruat caelum! Justice *can* and *will* be done tonight, Bruce Redpath, one way or another. The choice is yours.'

The guard opened the door and led Bruce inside. The room was about twelve feet square, the earthy, damp smell even stronger. In the dim light of an ancient table-lamp, he could see that the floor was of bare earth and, standing at one end, was the first guard. He was tall and powerful-looking, menacing in his black combat trousers, black boots and shirt, his face hidden by the balaclava. Bruce shuddered, filled with revulsion; the man reminded him of images of the nazi blackshirts in the late nineteen-thirties. Beside him was a chair in which Darren Beagan was securely tied, staring at him with a fresh look of terror in his eyes. The guards nodded and left, closing the door behind them. He heard the faint click of a key turning in the lock.

Bruce stared at Beagan for a few moments; it seemed so long ago, somehow. He thought he had got over it but, tonight, the interrogator had scraped away the scab, revealing the deep, unhealed wound below. Did he hate this trembling man, sitting helplessly before him?

He didn't know.

Unexpectedly, Beagan opened his mouth, his voice pleading, like a child.

'Please, Mister, dinn'ae hurt me, Ah didn'ae mean it, Mister, honest. Ah wis feart o' gettin' burnt. Ah didn'ae mean it, please, fur fuck sake...'

Bruce stared at the pathetic, snivelling creature; yes, he *did* hate Beagan.

He turned back towards the door and tried the handle; as he expected, it was locked. In the dim light, he noticed a sheet of paper lying on the ground, raised slightly as if it was concealing something. He bent down and lifted it, squinting at the neat writing,

> You have half an hour.
> You have one shot.
> Choose wisely.

He looked down in horror at the handgun that was lying on the grey, musty earth.

Three-forty-five on a bitterly cold Saturday morning; an electric-powered vehicle accelerated noiselessly along Greenock's Esplanade, unseen and unheard by the sleeping residents. In the doorway of a detached villa, sitting a little way back from the road, the figure that had just been deposited on the doorstep by the vehicle's occupants hauled itself to its feet, fumbling with numb, frozen fingers for the doorkey. After a few minutes, the door opened and the figure disappeared inside, closing the door behind them.

About fifty yards or so along the road, strategically parked in the small pool of semi-darkness between two streetlights, a black four-by-four started its engine and drove slowly past, making sure that Bruce Redpath was safely indoors. A light shone briefly in a downstairs room, before being extinguished.

That was all the reassurance that was needed.

Chapter 13

Saturday 29th November.

He was wakened by a banging that seemed to be emanating from deep within his aching cranium. He opened his eyes, wincing as the bright morning sunshine seared his retinas. Why were the curtains open; and why was he lying face downwards on the living-room sofa, fully clothed? The banging continued and he tried to sit up; his head was spinning and the inside of his mouth felt like sandpaper. How much had he had to drink...?

The banging continued, louder this time. A voice shouted, authoritative, urgent.

'Mr Redpath. Open the door, this is the police.'

The police? Had something happened? His first thought was for his daughters; had some dreadful accident befallen one of them?

Then, with a sudden jolt that sent a shot of adrenaline through his malfunctioning system, he remembered...

He managed to stand up, leaning on the back of the sofa; he was still wearing his outdoor jacket—was that vomit down the front? He stumbled through the hallway as a fresh onslaught of banging sounded.

'Mr Redpath. Last warning, open the—'

Bruce opened the door, screwing up his eyes as daylight flooded into the hallway. Two figures were standing on the doorstep, one female, one male. Behind them, parked on the road, was a red saloon car and a marked police car; there were two uniformed constables standing at the entrance to the driveway. The woman standing before him spoke, briefly holding up her identification.

'Are you Mr Bruce Redpath?'

With considerable effort he managed to respond with a monosyllabic 'Yes.'

'Detective Chief Inspector Mazzoni; this is Detective Sergeant Scott.'

She indicated the tough, stony-faced man standing beside her, his powerful physique clearly visible under his thick navy sweater. Bruce had the impression that he was there in case the need for physical restraint proved to be necessary, a highly unlikely scenario, all things considered.

DCI Mazzoni was speaking again as she moved past him.

'Can we come in, please, we'd like a word with you?'

He didn't seem to have a choice and indicated the door on the right that led to the dining room; he wasn't entirely sure if the living room was in a presentable state. DS Scott closed the door and stood with his back against it as DCI Mazzoni sat down on a dining chair. There was to be no escape, then.

'Sit down, please, Mr Redpath.'

He glanced briefly at the mirror on the facing wall, turning away hurriedly at the sight of the unshaven, grey and dishevelled reflection; he appeared to have aged overnight by about ten years. He half-sat, half-collapsed onto the chair opposite her, leaning his elbows on the table. The glance in the mirror had shown that he looked an absolute mess and he hoped he wouldn't have to explain his appearance. He swallowed in an attempt to lubricate his parched throat.

'Em...is everything okay?'

DCI Mazzoni gave him a scrutinising look.

'You tell me, Mr Redpath.'

Bruce frowned. 'Em, sorry, I don't...look, has something happened—I mean, you don't just turn up at a person's house first thing on a...'

For a moment he struggled to recall the day.

'...em, on a Saturday morning for no reason.'

DCI Mazzoni exchange a brief glance with her colleague.

'First thing, Mr Redpath? I'd hardly call eleven-fifteen first thing.'

Bruce looked at her in astonishment. 'Eleven...I'm sorry, I had no idea...'

The hairs on the back of his neck were starting to tingle and he stopped speaking. Something wasn't right. DCI Mazzoni waited for a few moments before speaking again, her tone more formal.

'Mr Redpath, are you able to account for your movements yesterday evening?'

He opened and closed his mouth several times; he was still struggling to come to terms with what had happened and he certainly wasn't going to share his experiences at this stage.

'Mr Redpath?'

'What?...oh...yes, sorry, well, I had a drink down at The Bay with my friend Rob...'

She looked across at her colleague again. 'That'll be DCI Connor, I presume?'

'Oh, yes, you'll know him, I'd imagine...'

She nodded. 'Of course. Please, carry on.'

'Em, well, then I walked home...'

'What time would this be, Mr Redpath?'

'Um...I'm not exactly sure, Rob's wife was picking him up about ten, I think, so it would be a bit before that, probably.'

'Hm, I see. Did Mr Connor not offer you a lift?'

He suspected that she had already spoken to Rob.

'Yes, but I decided to walk, you see...'

'Why was that, Mr Redpath?'

'I wanted some fresh air, it was a nice night and it's only about a mile from here.'

'I see. Did you meet anyone on your way home?'

'No, no I didn't.'

He paused; he had answered with a lie, averting his eyes as he did so and he knew immediately that it had been a mistake. A few years back he'd taken a short course in neuro-linguistic programming and his action had been a dead-giveaway. Mazzoni stared straight at him.

'You're *quite* sure, Mr Redpath? No-one at all?'

He shook his head. 'No.'

DS Scott spoke for the first time; Bruce turned towards the man, who was standing with his arms folded across his broad chest, a sneering expression on his face.

'An' you came straight home, I suppose?'

'Yes.'

The man nodded, pursing his lips. 'Without seein' anyone?'

'That's what I said.'

'Aye, I know. Just wanted to be certain, that's all.'

156

DS Scott cast a quick glance at his superior, a vague smirk on his lips. DCI Mazzoni took up the questioning once more.

'So did anyone see *you*, Mr Redpath—I mean, is there anyone who can corroborate your story?'

'Em, well, probably not, it was quite late, there weren't many people about...'

Scott spoke again. 'No-one out walkin' their dog, nothin' like that?'

He felt a vague, nauseating lurch in his stomach as he remembered Joanna...he couldn't even recall her second name.

'No—listen, what's all this about?'

The two officers exchanged a long, meaningful glance, then DCI Mazzoni spoke again.

'Mr Redpath, is the name Darren Beagan familiar to you?'

His heart skipped a beat...several beats. 'Darren Beagan?'

'That's what I said, Mr Redpath, Darren Beagan. You know who I'm talking about, don't you?'

His head began to spin but he attempted to retain eye contact as the second lie spilled from his mouth.

'Well...not really...'

DCI Mazzoni gave him that same, scrutinising stare.

'That's not my understanding, Mr Redpath. I think you are *perfectly* well aware of who Mr Beagan is, are you not?'

Before Bruce could respond, DS Scott interjected.

'Thing is, Mr Redpath, Darren Beagan was found murdered last night.'

He could feel an icy blackness creeping upwards from his feet. Beads of perspiration formed on his brow, flashing lights appeared before his eyes and the last thing he was aware of was DCI Mazzoni yelling.

'Christ, Stu, the bugger's going to pass out, catch him...'

Bruce found himself sitting in a bleak, windowless interview room in Greenock's police headquarters, his head resting on his arms as he leaned on a battered metal table that was bolted to the floor. A few laminated sheets of paper were taped to the surface, which he knew to be lists of the formalities to be followed when cautioning or charging a suspect. A plastic cup of coffee sat, untouched, before him as he tried to reconstruct that morning's events, far less those of the previous evening...he felt as if he had just awakened from a particularly bad nightmare.

When he had come to, head pounding and waves of nausea sweeping over him, he had been lying on his dining-room floor. He had a vague recollection of DCI Mazzoni asking if he was okay but he hadn't answered—it had seemed pointless.

He had been cautioned; he had been allowed a brief, accompanied visit to the toilet, where he had retched painfully for a few minutes, although his stomach had been empty. After that, he had been escorted to the marked police vehicle and driven away, with no chance to wash, to shave or to change his soiled clothes. He had stared straight ahead, hoping that none of the neighbours had been watching. It was a vain hope, alas...

Before he had been escorted from the house, he had searched briefly, and in vain, for his mobile phone as there was one person that he desperately needed to talk to.

Simon Fox.

He groaned; what the hell was going on?

His bleak reverie was broken as the door to the room open and he managed to pull himself upright. DCI Mazzoni walked in, accompanied by DS Scott. Mazzoni was carrying a sheaf of papers and a plastic bag. Without uttering a word, they sat down across from him, making a show of consulting their notes. Finally, Mazzoni looked across at him.

'How are you feeling, Mr Redpath?'

He had two choices; a show of bravado or the truth. He opted for the latter.

'Dreadful, if you must know.'

She favoured him with a half-smile that, somehow, didn't transmit itself to her piercing grey eyes.

'Hm, sorry to hear that. Right, let's get on...'

She switched on the video recording equipment and read the formalities in a dreary, but clear, monotone. Time, place, date, those present...despite his particular speciality, Bruce was familiar enough with the procedure. Once she had finished, she looked across at Bruce.

'So, Mr Redpath—may I call you Bruce?'

He nodded; she may as well.

'Bruce, then, have you anything you'd like to say?'

He shook his head. 'No, not until I've consulted with my lawyer.'

Scott sneered; Bruce really didn't like the man.

'Thought you *were* a lawyer, Bruce?'

He could feel his temper rising. 'Of course I am, DS Scott. And, as I'm sure that you are perfectly well aware, I am, in fact, a divorce lawyer. As such, criminal defence isn't my speciality.'

'So you're admittin' that you *are* a criminal, is that what you're sayin' Bruce?' smirked Scott.

Bruce wasn't going to let himself be goaded in this manner, not by an ignorant bully like Scott.

'I think that, if you care to listen to your audio recording, DS Scott, you'll find that the word 'criminal' was simply used as a pronoun and, as such, is unlikely to be admissible as a confession. Don't play silly word games with me, please.'

Scott glared across at Bruce but didn't respond, although DCI Mazzoni attempted to stifle a smile; whether it was at Bruce's expense or the sergeant's, he wasn't entirely sure. The smile disappeared; Mazzoni lifted the sheaf of notes and slid the plastic evidence bag from underneath, holding it up. Bruce's eyes widened.

'Do you recognise this, Bruce?'

He opened his mouth, then closed it again.

'No? Is this your iPhone, by any chance?'

Bruce had briefly searched in all his pockets before leaving the house but there had been no sign of it. He knew that it had been in his jacket when he had left the Bay Bar and, as he had slept in the living room, he couldn't see how it could be elsewhere. He decided not to respond.

'No? Well, as it happens, we're fairly certain that the phone *does* belong to you, Bruce. Why, you might ask? Well, as I'm sure you know, inside the leather cover, along with twenty-five pounds in cash, there is a Bank of Scotland debit card and several business cards with your name on them. So, unless someone stole those cards, I'm going to assume that this *is* your phone. Your fingerprints will confirm this fact, of course.'

She emphasised 'fact' and Bruce felt a chill run down his spine; he had forgotten that they had taken his fingerprints upon arrival at the police station. Mazzoni placed the bagged phone on the desk between them, all three occupants of the room staring at it.

'Can I ask where you found it?' said Bruce, his mouth dry and his voice hoarse. He picked up the coffee, which was stone-cold, and took a drink. Although it was pretty disgusting, he would have drunk anything at this stage.

'You can ask,' said DCI Mazzoni. 'But let me ask *you*, Bruce, where do you *think* we found it?'

He shook his head. 'I...wait, I'm not going to be drawn into this. As I said, I'm not saying anything further until I've spoken to my lawyer. I need you to get in touch with Simon Fox, of Redpath, Fox, Carnegie.'

He glared across at Scott, willing him to respond, but the man remained silent, a bored expression on his face. He had heard it all before, obviously.

'Fine,' said Mazzoni. 'Interview terminated at...'

She consulted her watch and stated the time, switched off the recording and stood up.

'We'll leave you with your thoughts for a wee while, Bruce. But we'll be back, you can rest assured.'

It hadn't been long; he was back in the interview room and, as the door opened, he stood up wearily.

'Simon! Thank God!'

Simon Fox strode into the room, elegant even in jeans, a white pullover and a black leather jacket. The Cheshire Cat grin flashed, albeit briefly, as he extended his hand.

'Bruce...Christ, you look like shit—what the hell have you been up to? God, sit down before you fall over. Hang on...'

He went back to the door and spoke to someone outside. Bruce couldn't make out the words but he could hear the authority in his partner's voice. Well, his Counsel now, he supposed.

'Right, that's sorted. They're bringing us a couple of coffees. Probably be the usual machine crap but it'll be better than nothing.'

Bruce felt a wave of hope wash over him. Simon would sort this out. 'Em, Simon, I hadn't managed to phone you, how did you get here so quickly?'

Simon smiled. 'Your good friend, Robin Connor. He heard you'd been brought in for questioning and he managed to track me down. Decent chap—for a cop.'

He sat down at the table and placed his expensive briefcase on the battered surface, snapping the lid open. He took out a Cross ballpoint pen and a notepad.

'Right, my friend. First of all, have you seen a doctor—the state you're in, anything you've said to them might well be inadmissible.'

Bruce nodded; a rather unsympathetic GP had examined him prior to his interview.

'Yes, she said I just had a hangover but that I was fit to be questioned.'

'Damn! Right, tell me what happened, from the very beginning. And remember, I'm your brief—I need to know absolutely everything. And I mean *everything*, do you understand?'

Bruce nodded; he understood.

'Except, of course, whether you're innocent or guilty,' he added with a grin. 'We'll leave that to the jury!'

Bruce's heart sank. Innocent or guilty of what, exactly? He daren't imagine...

Twenty minutes later, Simon placed his pen on the desk, sat back in his chair and regarded his friend; Bruce was a complete mess. He remained unshaven, his sandy-brown hair was unwashed and sticking out from his head and it also appeared somewhat greyer. He had obviously slept in his clothes and it looked as if he had been sick down the front of his shirt. His eyes were red, his hands were shaking and he stank to high heaven.

Simon had, of course, dealt with many such individuals throughout his career but, to his considerable distress, Bruce was undoubtedly one of the worst. And as to this story of his.

'Well?' asked Bruce.

Simon didn't answer.

'Simon?'

'What?'

'Do you believe me?'

Simon Fox took a deep breath.

'Bruce, I've known you nigh on thirty-five years and I've never known you to lie. Why should I think you're lying now?'

'That wasn't really an answer—do you do believe me?'

Simon leaned forward. 'It's not a question of whether or not I believe you, Bruce. It's whether *they* believe you...'

He jerked his thumb in the direction of the door and leaned back, realising that this was going to be tricky.

'Right. As I said, I've never doubted you and I'm not going to start now. Is there any way whatsoever that you can corroborate your story?'

Bruce shook his head. 'No, of course there isn't.'

'Hm; that *is* a bit of a problem...and I would really like to track down this woman you met, Joanna...?'

'Hume. Joanna Hume. But what bearing could she possibly have on...'

The penny dropped, as did Bruce's lower jaw.

'Oh my God, you think she spiked my drink...of course, that would explain what happened, why I felt so bad when I got outside...'

Simon nodded. 'I'm pretty certain that's what must have happened, which makes the chances of tracking her down remote to the point of impossible. Did you not think it odd that her dog was called Bruce?'

'No, why should I...wait, of course, it was a superb ice-breaker, wasn't it?'

'Obviously! She knew exactly who you were, she gained your attention, she won your trust, it would only take a few seconds to slip some flunitrazepam—rohypnol, to you and me—into your drink. Unfortunately it's probably too late to test for it, especially since you've been so sick...Bruce?'

Bruce Redpath was wearing an expression like a wounded animal. Simon shook his head.

'You liked her, didn't you?'

Bruce nodded.

'That was the whole point, though. Listen, I'm really sorry.'

'Don't be, I was a bloody fool. I mean, why the hell would a woman as attractive as Joanna show any interest—'

'STOP' shouted Simon, slapping his hand on the table. 'The last thing we need is you feeling sorry for yourself on account of some random woman, whose only intention was to drug you in order to facilitate your abduction. And I very much doubt that her name *is* Joanna Hume! Come on, Bruce, catch a grip of yourself. There are plenty of attractive woman out there—from what you've told me, your friends Mel and Rob seem to have paraded a selection for your perusal with unfailing regularity! Anyway, enough of that.'

He consulted his notes. 'Right, here's what's going to happen. We'll get the formal interview over with, let me do most of the talking. Do not—and I repeat, *do not*, mention what happened last night. At present, we're sticking with the fact that you passed out at the end of the Esplanade. Next thing you can remember is finding yourself on the couch, severely hungover and without a clue as to what happened during the intervening hours.'

'But surely I should be telling them the truth—'

'I'm not asking you to lie about what happened, only to omit some of it at this stage. You can always choose to remember later, once we manage to obtain some evidence to confirm your version of events—if we can, that is! Just let me handle it, okay? After all, this is what I do for a living, in case you hadn't noticed.'

He let out a long sigh. 'You see, I'll be brutally honest with you, there is no way on earth that they're going to buy this story of yours without some form of corroboration. What we really need to prove is where you *weren't,* as opposed to where you were.

'But what do you mean, Simon. Where 'wasn't' I, that's so important?

Simon gave his friend a long look. 'You don't know? They haven't said, have they?'

Bruce shook his head.

'Damn. Okay, well...they believe that you were at an abandoned industrial unit near Lynedoch Street, where Beagan's body was found.'

Bruce shook his head in denial. 'But I wasn't there, Simon, of course I bloody wasn't there. Why the hell would they think that I was?'

Simon looked his friend directly in the eye; Bruce held his gaze. 'Because they found your phone about six feet away from the burnt-out car containing Beagan's body. Right, let's get this done...'

Chapter 14

Saturday 29th November.

Paul Maguire got to his feet, pulled up his trousers and flushed the toilet. He hadn't particularly needed to go but it had provided him with a short respite from the rantings of his newly-acquired lodger, David Doyle. The man's fury was now directed equally between the killers of Suzannah Flint, his mistress, and Maria, his wife. Maguire washed his hands, taking his time in drying them, then unlocked the door and walked into the hall. He lifted his phone from the table and scrolled to the two new messages that he had heard arriving, heralded by the honk of 'old car horn' while seated on the lavatory; both were replies to his 'feelers' of the previous evening. The first was from Shug, his acquaintance from The Vaults. The scruffy, ingratiating wee man seemed to have a good nose for sniffing out the dirt but, on this occasion, Maguire was disappointed.

'Soz, nae clue M8. Let u know if I hear nthing.'

Maguire pulled a face; despite the demise of his legal career, he was still an educated man and he detested 'text-speak'. He scrolled to the next message; it was from an acquaintance in Edinburgh, an accountant who had suffered a similar fate to Maguire and had actually spent some time in prison, something which Maguire had avoided by the skin of his teeth. It had been a long shot but he was surprised at the reply.

'Might have something. Heard of a party with similar grievances as DD. Let u know.'

Terse, but at least the words were mostly intact.

He doubted if he'd receive any further replies and he took the phone back into the kitchen, switching it off before returning it to the false grapefruit can and putting it safely back in the cupboard. He was about to leave the kitchen when he paused; reversing his actions, he removed the burner phone once more and switched it back on. You just never knew...

Doyle had been on a call, to his estranged wife judging by the language. Maguire entered the living room, which was fuggy with tobacco smoke, as Doyle threw his phone onto the couch on which he was sprawled. Unkempt, unwashed and, if Maguire was being totally honest, unwanted.

'Fuckin' bitch,' exclaimed Doyle.

'Maria, I take it?'

'Aye. Wants a fuckin' divorce noo, fuckin' cow.'

Maguire bit back a sarcastic response; he recognised Doyle's volatile mood and didn't want to risk provoking the man into violence.

'And how do you feel about that, Davie?'

' Ach, fuckin' let her dae whit she wants. Bit fuckin' late for me, though. Poor wee Suzi...'

Maguire hoped that Davie Doyle wasn't going to break down once more but, instead, the man dragged himself off the settee and stood up.

'Awright if Ah grab a shower? Ah'm fuckin' mingin', man.'

'No problem, you know where it is. Towels are on the radiator.

Doyle gave him a grim smile. 'Hope you huvn'ae stunk the place oot, eh?'

As Doyle left, Paul Maguire flopped on to the couch and lit a cigarette. It was shaping up to be a very long winter.

Agni Krasniki took a deep draw on her cigarette and stared out of the window. The sun was sparkling cheerfully on the distant waters of the river Tay but there was no cheer in her mood. Her heart was cold and, despite his promises, Dzhokhar Meta had, so far, failed to bring her any news of her brother's killer.

The ringing of her phone broke her reverie and she picked it up. Speak of the devil...and the Devil spoke in English.

'Agni, my dear, are you well?'

She exhaled smoke. 'My heart is heavy, Dzhokhar. I miss poor Aleks—he was a stupid big lump of a boy but he was always my little brother. I will not be at peace until I have avenged his murder.'

'I understand. Family is family, after all, especially for those such as us, a long way from our homeland. We should stick together, should we not?'

Agni Krasniki gave a grim smile. She knew only too well that, should Meta succeed in bringing her brother's killer to her, it would be at a price; that price was herself and it was a price she was prepared to pay. She had known worse, after all, and Meta was a powerful and prosperous man who could look after her, take care of her. Anyway, she could close her eyes and bear it with the best of them...

'You are right, dear Dzhokhar, of course. Have you any news?'

She heard the man give a deep-throated chuckle. 'Yes, I may have. I have been given information on the organisation behind these killings—as you will know, there have now been six deaths, including poor Aleks.'

She knew; she had been following the stories on the television, anxious for any snippet of news that might lead to the killers. She fervently hoped that the police didn't get to them first; that would not be justice, in her book.

'There was an article by some stupid woman in an Edinburgh newspaper—did you see it?'

She hadn't; she seldom read newspapers; in fact, she seldom read, her schooling having been less than adequate.

'No, I did not.'

'No matter. This woman has suggested that the killings have been carried out by some group that she referred to as the 'Civil Guard'.'

Krasniki frowned. 'And what the hell is that?'

Meta grunted. 'Huh! Well, she seems to think it is an organisation of some sort that is taking the law into its own hands, punishing criminals who have walked free.'

'And what do *you* think?' she asked, somewhat impatiently.

'I think we will find out soon, if my plan is successful. Do not worry, dear Agni, I think we are close. I will be in touch.'

She ended the call with a feeling somewhere between frustration and elation; as she had done many times before, she sat back in her chair and planned the revenge that she would take on her brother's murderers once they were brought to her, each version more brutal, more sadistic than the last. This time, however, there seemed to be more certainty; more 'when' rather than 'if'.

She was mildly surprised to find that the thoughts of the violent and brutal punishment of Aleksander's killers had aroused her. She stood up and headed to the bedroom, pulled down her tight jeans and her pants then reached into her bedside drawer. She lay down on the bed, the gentle buzzing exciting, tantalising...

God help them when she got her hands on them...

◆◆◆◆◆◆◆◆◆◆◆◆◆

'Well, that wasn't too bad.'

Bruce didn't exactly agree with Simon's assessment of the interview; he now had an idea what the term 'the third degree' meant and it hadn't been at all pleasant. DCI Mazzoni had proved to be an intelligent and cunning detective, asking searching questions and staring at him in a most disconcerting way, as if waiting for him to trip himself up. Fortunately, Simon had fielded a number of these lines of enquiry and had given every bit as good as Bruce had got. DS Scott had interjected occasionally, usually with a degree of sarcasm. Simon had seldom responded, favouring Scott with a look of absolute scorn, as if the officer wasn't worthy of a verbal response. After about an hour, the interview had been concluded with no charges being brought.

'You think? I thought it was a bloody nightmare!'

'Nonsense. For a start, they haven't charged you with anything which, I have to say, I find slightly surprising, given the circumstances.'

The circumstances, and the evidence, had been fairly compelling. Bruce Redpath's phone had been found a few yards away from Darren Beagan's burnt-out car; the young man's charred, unrecognisable corpse had been found, securely bound, inside the boot.

The police had interviewed Beagan's friend, Christopher Tilstock, who had told them that he and Beagan had been driving around the area on the Friday night and had parked on the Esplanade. This, according to Tilstock, was their regular Friday night routine. Sometime after nine-thirty, Tilstock had left to buy their customary Chinese takeaway but, when he returned, both Beagan and his vehicle had disappeared.

Beagan's car had subsequently been reported as being on fire early on the Saturday morning, at an abandoned factory near Greenock's Lynedoch Street. Someone resembling Bruce's description had been seen in the vicinity by a taxi driver, who had noticed the smoke and the flames. The evidence certainly wasn't conclusive but, as Bruce had managed to avoid any mention of his abduction (continuing to claim that he had no recollection of the evening's events after he had left The Bay) DCI Mazzoni and her sergeant seemed to be in no doubt that he was guilty of Beagan's murder. As far as they were concerned, in addition to the circumstantial evidence, he had motive, opportunity and, unfortunately for him, no alibi!

'I would imagine that their reticence is due to the fact that the evidence is still circumstantial and the taxi driver's description is rather vague. However, if they come up with any more concrete evidence...'

Bruce felt close to panic. 'But what on earth could they come up with, Simon? I mean, I wasn't there, I didn't...'

Simon held up his hand. 'Listen, we just need to wait and see. If they can somehow track down CCTV, or any other witnesses who saw you near the locus, then...'

The sentence hung between them for a moment before Bruce spoke.

'But I told you—I bloody told them—I wasn't anywhere *near* the locus. That's the thing—if we tell them the truth, tell them what really happened, then that would surely put me in the clear.'

Simon Fox remained silent.

'Wouldn't it? Please, let's just tell them...'

Simon shook his head, a grave expression on his handsome features. 'They won't bloody believe you, Bruce, honestly. Let's face it, you have motive—of course you have and they'll know it. They'll be only too well aware who Beagan is—was—and of his previous convictions; or lack of them, I suppose. You would appear to have had the opportunity and you can't account for your movements during the period involved, other than your rather fanciful story about being abducted. And, of course, Beagan was parked on the Esplanade within the time-frame of you leaving The Bay.'

He sighed and ran his fingers through his thick hair in a rather exasperated manner. 'And then there's your bloody phone, of course...'

Bruce felt his anger rising. 'It's *not* a bloody fanciful story, it's the truth. Don't you believe me? Someone must have taken my phone, placed it at the crime scene'.

Simon took a deep breath then exhaled slowly. 'But can we prove that? No! Anyway, it seems that the only prints they've found on the phone are yours. So, as I said before, it's not a question of whether I believe you or not, it's—'.

'...yes, it's a question of whether the *police* believe me. I appreciate that, but surely I can just tell them what really happened and see—'

Simon raised his voice. 'No you bloody *can't*! Try telling Mazzoni that you were abducted, taken to some unspecified location where some guy in a mask tells you he's carrying out these vigilante attacks before producing Beagan and offering you the chance to shoot him? And all without a shred of bloody proof—don't be ridiculous! Besides, they have conveniently omitted to tell us whether Beagan was shot or if he burned to death.'

Bruce felt like he'd been slapped across the face, the harsh words stirring the horrific memories once more. But he realised that Simon was probably correct; said like that, his story did sound pretty far-fetched. He dropped his head in despair. Simon started to pack his briefcase, snapping the lid shut.

'Look, I need to head up the road, we're having a dinner party tonight and I need to collect the wine...'

Bruce could have wept; the idea of a simple dinner, in the company of friends, of family, seemed like a world away from his present predicament.

'I'll come back tomorrow and see what's happening. Bruce, you need to rack your brains and try to think if there's anything, anything at all, that you can remember about your abductors, about the place you were kept. We need to find out who took you and where you were. I'll see if I can set the wheels in motion to track down this Hume woman, see if there's any CCTV at...what was the name of the pub?'

'The Bay. It's in Gourock, just past the Battery Park.'

'Right. If I can, I'll have a chat with your friend Rob Connor, although he may feel it would prejudice his own position, being 'one of them'. And I'll give that investigator we use—Gibson, isn't it—a call, see what he can come up with; he usually has an ear to the ground, doesn't he? Look, whatever you do, don't say a bloody word to them, tell them you're not making any further statements without me present.'

He stood up and lifted his briefcase. 'Don't give up, Bruce, they haven't decided to hang you yet.'

They might just have well as done, as far as Bruce Redpath was concerned. As Simon left the interview room, he dropped his head onto his arms and started to weep.

At first Bruce thought that it was the worst night of his life but, on consideration, he realised that it was probably the second-worst; actually, the third-worst...

The worst, by far, had been the night that he had been told of Dorothy's death. As he lay in his hard, uncomfortable bed, locked in the bleak confines of a prison cell, he finally replayed those dreadful moments from ten years ago, when his friend, Rob, had arrived at his door to inform him that his wife had died in a tragic road-traffic accident. It was only later that he had discovered the grim and grisly details of her death.

The next had been the day that Darren Beagan had been found not guilty of manslaughter, instead being found guilty of vehicle theft and driving while under the influence of drink and drugs. He could still remember the mocking smile and Beagan's vile hand gesture as he left the dock. Mel and Rob had ushered him out, trying their best to shield him from the press who were gathered in a baying throng outside the court. They had taken him to their home, at that time an upper-floor villa conversion in Gourock, where Mel's mum had been looking after Bruce's girls and one year-old Fraser Connor.

He had collapsed on the floor, he remembered, Mel's arms folded around him. He had wished he was dead.

Now, as he lay, staring at the peeling paint of the ceiling, he began to wish the same...

He must have fallen asleep at some point. He heard the door opening and a warder entered, his lined face smiling and cheery. He was an older man, with a countenance that spoke of having encountered pretty much every aspect of humanity. He was carrying a tray.

'Mornin'. Sleep okay?'

Bruce sat up on the bed and ran his fingers through his greasy hair. 'Actually, better than I thought, thanks. Managed a few hours, probably.'

'Good for you. Bit scary the first time, so they tell me. Right, here's a bit o' breakfast, get that doon ye and you'll feel a lot better.'

As he left, the man turned and gave Bruce a conspiratorial wink. 'An' if you fancy any more tea, just bang on the door, awright?'

This simple act of human kindness set Bruce off on another bout of uncontrolled (and unashamed) sobbing. After a few minutes, however, he dried his eyes and set to on the rapidly cooling breakfast. Despite everything, he was absolutely ravenous!

He had no way of judging time; lunch had been brought, not particularly appetising but probably better than he might have expected. This was all new to him, after all! He was lying on his back, staring once more at the ceiling when he heard the door being unlocked. A uniformed policeman appeared.

'Mr Redpath, come with me, please.'

Bruce stood up wearily; despite his inactivity, he was exhausted. Stress, presumably...

As he was escorted along the dull corridor, he wondered if he was about to be charged. He was almost beyond caring and he could now understand how false confessions arose. Were the accused just so worn down by the interminable waiting in a bleak, drab cell that they would agree to anything in an effort to move the process forward? The door to the same interview room was opened and he entered, the policeman remaining outside.

'Simon! God. I'm glad to see you!'

Bruce received the benison of Simon Fox's full Cheshire Cat grin. 'And just wait 'til you hear the news...'

'Hang on a minute, Davie, that's my phone.'

'Aye, awright. Might be news, Ah suppose...'

Paul Maguire trotted through to the hallway, glad to have an excuse to absent himself from Doyle's company. He picked up the cheap mobile, thankful that he had retrieved it from the false grapefruit tin, pressed the button to answer it and held it to his ear.

'Is that Paul Maguire?'

The voice was thick with an Eastern European accent and Maguire felt a frisson of fear run down his spine. He had a suspicion who was calling him and he was alarmed that the "burner" number had been so readily obtained. He had heard whispers, rumours, none of which were pleasant.

'Depends who's asking.'

There was a deep, malicious chuckle at the other end. 'Hah! Very good! I assume that you *are* Maguire?'

'As I said, it depends—'

'I am Meta, Dzhokhar Meta. Perhaps you have heard of me?'

Paul Maguire had, indeed, heard of Dzhokhar Meta; he was, in fact, the man that Maguire had suspected of being behind the killings. Why the hell was he phoning? He chose his words carefully.

'Yes, Mr Meta, I have. How can I help you?'

'Let me ask you again. Are you Paul Maguire?'

It was obvious that the man knew.

'Yes, I am.'

'Good. And you are a friend of David Doyle?'

Maguire hesitated. Why was Meta asking this, he wondered.

'Yes.'

'Good. My understanding is that your friend was abducted and placed in a shipping container, along with his woman, Suzannah Flint, who later died. Am I correct?'

Maguire was curious now. 'You are. What's your interest in this, Mr Meta?'

'My interest, Mr Maguire, is that I want to find out who is responsible for these killings. Not for myself, you understand, but for a very good friend of mine who also lost someone, someone very dear to them.'

'And who might that be?

'I am not at liberty to tell you, Mr Maguire. But we share the same desire to find out who is responsible for these barbaric acts...'

From what Paul Maguire knew, Meta was no stranger to barbaric acts himself.

'I see, Mr Meta. So, exactly what can I do for you?'

'I would like to speak to David Doyle. Face to face.'

'What?'

Simon grinned again. 'You see, I knew you'd be pleased!'

'An alibi? What kind of an alibi? And from whom?'

'Well, as I said, it is a pretty tenuous alibi but it's enough and, at the moment, it's your 'get out of jail free' card. All will be revealed later—oh, there *is* a condition attached...'

'A condition? What kind of condition? Simon, what the hell's going on?

'Listen, they've agreed to release you, just leave it at that for the time being. As far as you're concerned, you're out of here.'

A wave of emotion threatened to engulf Bruce Redpath; he could have hugged Simon but he restrained himself. Maybe after a shower, a shave...

'So what happens now?'

'Well, they'll want a final chat with you, of course—you're still a suspect, or a 'person of interest' as they like to put it. You won't be able to travel anywhere without informing them, but that's about it. Half an hour and you'll be free. Right, I'll get them in, get it over with. And remember, not a bloody word about last night or you'll be completely fucked.'

Chapter 15

Sunday 30th November.

Bruce was sitting in the passenger seat of Simon's Porsche, as they sped along Greenock's Dalrymple Street. The world looked the same; somehow, it had felt like an eternity since he had been arrested and it was hard to believe that it had only been a day. He turned to his friend.

'Hang on, am I not going home?'

Simon glanced sideways. 'Don't be bloody silly—the press will be all over you like flies round the proverbial. No, we're going for a coffee first.'

'A coffee? Simon, I don't need a bloody coffee! In case you'd failed to notice, I need a shower, I need a shave and I need a change of clothes, for God's sake.'

'Yes, and all in good time, Bruce. But we've got a commitment to honour first...'

It wouldn't have been Bruce's first choice for a celebratory coffee but it was impersonal and reasonably quiet inside the McDonald's restaurant. Besides, it hardly felt like a celebration! Simon entered first, glancing about to ensure that they hadn't been preceded by anyone hoping to grab a photograph.

'Right, come on...oh, there he is...'

He nodded and headed towards a secluded corner table. The man seated in the chair looked up from his phone and gave a weak smile. At first Bruce didn't recognise him—but that was one of Cal Gibson's greatest assets, the ability to appear anonymous, to blend in with any given situation. The private investigator was dressed in a rather shabby, red North Face jacket, faded leans and climbing boots. A woolly hat sat on the seat beside him and he looked as if he had just stepped off a hillside in the Highlands. Bruce looked from Gibson to Simon.

'What's Cal doing here?'

'Have a seat, Bruce, I'll get the coffee. Fancy a cheeseburger? I'm bloody starving.'

Bruce sat down across from Gibson. 'Cal.'

'Mr Redpath—how the devil are you? "There mark what ills the scholar's life assail...".'

Bruce knew this one; rather reluctantly he finished the quotation. 'Toil, envy, want, the patron, and the jail. Johnson, I believe. What brings you here? Simon said something about an alibi?'

Gibson smiled. 'Got it in one. Yes, Mr R, I provided your alibi.'

Bruce frowned. 'And how, may I ask, did you manage that?

Gibson had the good grace to look slightly abashed. 'Because I saw you being abducted...and I also saw you being returned home.'

Simon returned with three coffees and three cheeseburgers with fries. As he had walked back to the table, for a moment he thought that he might have to drag his friend away from the rather unsavoury character that was Cal Gibson. Bruce was leaning across the table, attempting to pull the private investigator to his feet by his shirt front, in what his mother used to refer to as 'the jumper treatment'. He quickly placed the tray on the table and hissed at his friend..

'Bruce—BRUCE, for fuck sake, don't cause a bloody scene! If they call the police, you'll be back inside before I can finish my bloody burger. Get your arse back on the chair and listen to what he has to say. Sorry, Cal, Bruce is just a bit...'

'It's fine, Mr Fox, don't worry,' replied Gibson, re-arranging his shirt collar. 'Anyway, it's only a shirt and I've probably got spare buttons at home ...'

Simon turned to his friend. 'Bruce, calm down and listen, will you?'

'He bloody *saw* me, Simon. He sat back and watched while I was being abducted.'

'To be fair, Mr R, at that point I didn't *know* you were being abducted. I thought you were just...well, four sheets to the wind, as it were—I assumed the guy knew you and was giving you a lift home. It was only when they drove on past your house that I realised something was amiss.'

'And you still didn't come after me?'

Gibson shrugged. 'What was I to do, Mr R? There were a few of them, I hadn't a clue where they were going...I did go as far up the M8 as Govan then turned back.'

'You could have called the police!'

'And say what? That you were pissed as a fart, that some good Samaritan gave you a lift...'

'...that I was drugged and abducted, for God's sake.. and I could have been bloody murdered!'

'...but, like I said, how the hell was I meant to know any of that? Look, Mr R, I'm really sorry but, well...'

He shrugged again, as if dismissing Bruce's concerns. 'Anyway, I was there when they dropped you off, made sure you were indoors okay. And here we are!'

'Oh, that was bloody kind of you. I don't suppose you thought to get the registration number?'

Simon answered. 'Of course he did, but it was false. It was one of the first things the police checked when Cal spoke to them. Registered to an address in Caerphilly, of all places. No help at all, I'm afraid.'

Gibson shrugged again, smiled and took a bite of his cheeseburger. Simon put his hand on Bruce's arm, sensing that his friend might launch a fresh attack.

'Right, let's all calm down. Cal, tell Bruce why you were following him in the first place.'

Bruce glowered across at Gibson. 'Yes, I'd be very interested to hear the reason!'

Gibson masticated for a moment, then swallowed the mouthful of burger. 'I was being paid to follow you.'

Simon restrained Bruce again.

'Bruce, for fuck sake,' he hissed 'will you stop—the manager's looking over. I'm warning you, if you go back in, that'll be it.'

Bruce relaxed very slightly. 'So why the hell *were* you following me, Gibson? I though *I* was paying *you* to investigate these killings?'

Gibson gave an almost-apologetic smile. 'Yes, that's very true, Mr R. But someone was also paying *me* to keep tabs on *you*. Times are tough, you know, and a man has to eat.'

Bruce was clenching and unclenching his fists. 'You little shit...'

'Now now, Mr R, no need for that.'

'No fucking need? Oh, I think there is very *much* a need. Who the hell was paying you to follow me—and why?'

Gibson looked across at Simon who was devouring his cheeseburger and fries with gusto, obviously amused at the exchange.

'Tell him, Cal. Part of the deal, remember?'

Gibson shrugged. 'Miriam Bonnar.'

Bruce stared at Gibson. 'What? The conspiracy-theorising journalist?'

'The very one.'

'But...but...I mean, why the hell was *she* having me followed?'

Gibson smiled. 'You don't remember her?'

'No, of course I bloody don't, I've never met the woman in my life!'

'Actually, you have; in court—you represented her husband in their rather bitter divorce nigh on eight years ago. Took her to the cleaners, apparently. I have to say, Mr R, Miriam Bonnar—or Miriam Westcott, as you knew her—isn't a fan.'

Bruce was staring morosely out of the windscreen as Simon's Porsche swept eastwards up the A8 towards Langbank, where his daughter, Coral, lived. He mumbled.

'Sorry, Bruce, didn't catch that?'

'I said, do you believe him?'

'Have we any reason not to believe him? First point, he had no need to come forward with his story, he could just as easily have let you remain in custody. Second, he didn't need to tell you that he followed you, even if it wasn't all the way, did he?'

'I suppose not. But all that crap about that Bonnar woman? I mean—'

'A woman scorned, Bruce. I suppose it was only a matter of time before some disgruntled former spouse decided to come after you with the intent of doing something malicious. Like Gibson said, she was just looking to 'dig some dirt' on you for the purpose of revenge; just as bloody well too, or you'd still be in a cell. No, all in all I think he's telling us most of the truth.'

'Most?'

'Oh yes, most. He's definitely holding something back; just remains to be seen what.'

They sped through a roundabout.

'Em, that was the Langbank turn-off.'

His friend gave him a sideways glance. 'I'm well aware of that, but there's a silver Skoda been following us since we came out of McDonalds...no, don't bloody turn round, we don't want them to know we've spotted them!'

'Is it the police?'

Simon shook his head. 'Doubt it, to be honest. No, it'll be the Press; probably tried to have a chat with Gibson too, if I'm any judge.'

Bruce was horrified. 'Oh God, do you think he'll have said anything to them?'

Simon grinned. 'Last I saw of him, he was heading to the toilet; I strongly suspect that it was a rather different character who came back out...right, we'll head up the M8 a wee bit then I'll soon shake these buggers off.'

◆

Once they reached the motorway, Simon gunned the Porsche up to 120mph, leaving the Skoda behind in a cloud of dust. He took the Erskine Bridge turn-off, doubling back before heading along the old A8 through the town of Bishopton. At the end of the village, he turned left onto one of the narrow country byways that criss-crossed Renfrewshire.

'Right, let's hope that's the last we'll see of them; if not, this route will sort them out.'

By the time they arrived at Coral Wilson's house, Bruce felt decidedly queasy, despite the hard suspension of the sports car. Rather unsteadily, he exited the car as Simon glanced about for any sign of reporters

'Good, I'd say we're in the clear; I told you I'd shake them off!'

There was something about Simon's cheery tone that rang slightly false, Bruce thought but, before he could comment, the door to the modern, architect-designed house opened and his daughter ran down the drive; she was already tearful.

'Dad! Oh Dad...'

She threw her arms around him then quickly drew away, her face contorted in distaste as she held him at arms' length.

'God, you smell awful!'

He gave her a rueful smile. 'Sorry, I am an old jailbird, after all...'

She grabbed him again. 'Don't bloody joke about it.'

Dan Wilson came out of the house, their daughter, Amy, carried high up in his arms.

'Grampa Boos, you stay with us?'

'Yes, Amy, it looks like it, my darling.'

She stretched her arms towards him then she, too, recoiled, burying her face in her father's shoulder.

'Grampa smells like poo, Daddy.'

Dan Wilson laughed. 'Ah, Bruce, out of the mouths of babes.'

Bruce was becoming decidedly fed-up with quotations, especially when they were inaccurate.

Simple things; a shower, a shave, fresh clothes and a hot meal. Bruce felt human again. Amy had, reluctantly, allowed herself to be put to bed and the four adults were seated in the Wilson's large, comfortable living room, the wood-burning stove emitting a comfortable blanket of heat. They all clutched a glass of whisky as Bruce finished relating the events of Friday night. Coral was staring into the amber liquid, her eyes brimming with tears; she had only been a teenager when her mum had died. Dan gave her a squeeze, drained his glass and stood up.

'Bloody hell, that's a helluva story. I mean, I'm not saying I don't believe you but...'

'But what, Dan?'

Bruce was fond of his son-in-law but there was a disbelieving tone in the younger man's voice that irritated him. Simon interjected, sensing impending discord.

'Let's not go down that road, Dan. After all, I'm acting on Bruce's behalf and I don't doubt his story for a minute. I'd just like to know what this bugger Gibson's keeping back from us, though...yes, thanks, another would be nice! Look, it's good of you to put me up tonight. Means we can crack on early and discuss... well, things.'

Coral looked alarmed. 'But what is there to discuss? My dad's been released, surely that's it...isn't it? Simon?'

Bruce and Simon were shown to the two guest rooms in Coral and Dan's rather sumptuous home. Dan was damping down the wood-burner as Coral opened the curtains and gazed almost unseeingly for a moment at the spectacular view across the Clyde. He crossed over and put his arms around her.

'You okay, love?'

She shook her head and snuffled as Dan gently stroked her hair.

'I know, Cor, it just brings it all back, doesn't it?'

She started to cry again. 'It was just so horrible. I mean, what happened. Dad was...well, broken, I suppose. Auntie Mel and Uncle Rob were fantastic but they must have been devastated too. Auntie Mel was really close to Mum, they were more like sisters than cousins. And poor Uncle Rob—he was one of the first policeman at the scene, he must have recognised the car...'

She burst into another paroxysm of grief for a few moments, then continued. 'So, Fliss and I stayed with them for a few weeks until Dad...well, he'd started drinking apparently...Uncle Rob told me later...he just couldn't cope. No bloody wonder.'

For the first time, she told Dan about the way Beagan had behaved after being sentenced. Her husband could feel the anger rise inside him as Coral continued. '...but there's no way Dad would have...oh God, I can't even say it...'

The door opened softly behind them and they both turned. Dan smiled but Coral remained gazing out into the darkness.

'Simon! Is everything okay? Can I get you something?'

'No, nothing thanks, I just wanted a chat with you both.'

Dan crossed back over and opened the stove door once more, allowing the remaining heat to escape. Coral finally turned, wiping her eyes as she sat back down.

'What is it?' asked Dan.

Simon Fox pursed his lips for a moment then looked at Coral.

'This is a bit awkward, I'm afraid...were you aware that your father had started drinking again?'

She shook her head as she stared at the glowing embers of the fire. 'Dad's always liked a wee drink...'

'That's not what I mean. There's been a couple of times that he's come in to the office reeking of whisky.'

183

'What? Surely not...'

Simon nodded. 'I'm afraid so.'

He paused, as if struggling for words.

'Em, has your dad spoken to you about these murders at all?'

Dan answered. 'These so-called retribution killings?'

He looked across at his wife but she remained silent, still gazing into the dying fire. Dan continued. 'He's mentioned them once or twice, just in conversation, really. Why do you ask?'

'For some reason he seems to have become obsessed with them. He'd been making unofficial...well, enquiries, let's just say. God knows why, a morbid fascination, I suppose. Then there's this journalist, Miriam Bonnar; apparently she's well-known as a conspiracy-theorist. That's who Gibson was working for; well, in addition to your father, of course. Anyway, she had written a piece about the murders; in it, she claimed that responsibility for the killings lay with some secretive organisation that she termed the 'Civil Guard'. Olivia, one of our partners, had shown your dad the article; I haven't spoken to him about it but, having read it, I wondered if...'

Coral turned and looked across at Simon's rather troubled countenance, her face reddening with anger.

'Are you saying you don't believe my dad, Simon? You think he's making all of this up on the strength of a newspaper article? God-all-bloody-mighty—'

'Cor, calm down, sweetheart,' interjected Dan. 'Simon's not saying that...'

'Then what *is* he saying, exactly?'

The ensuing silence was disturbed only by the distant sound of Bruce Redpath's contented snoring. Eventually Simon shook his head.

'I honestly don't know. The thing is, there isn't a shred of proof to substantiate what he claims happened...'

'But what about that man—Gibson, wasn't it—who said he'd seen my dad being abducted?'

Simon shook his head again. 'Gibson has stated that Bruce was very drunk and that someone helped him into a car. His friend, your Uncle Rob, has confirmed that he was drinking with your dad in The Bay that evening—and it's quite possible that your father had been drinking before that. We haven't been able to trace the woman in the bar and there's no way of proving that she put anything in Bruce's drink, although it's highly likely that it *was* her. Then, according to Gibson's timescale, there's about six hours unaccounted for.'

'But, if that's the case, why did the police release him?' asked Dan.

'Because, at this stage, other than his mobile phone, they don't have enough evidence to hold him—yet! While Gibson's statement implies that Bruce was drunk and, presumably, incapable of carrying out Beagan's murder...'

Coral winced at the word.

'...if they can get hold of any CCTV, if they can find any other witnesses who claim they saw Bruce near the crime locus...'

His voice tailed off and he shrugged. Coral had started crying again but she looked Simon Fox directly in the eye.

'Do you believe my father is innocent?'

Simon took a deep breath. 'Coral, my job is to ensure that the law operates fairly and is above reproach; what your dad refers to as 'due process'.'

'But surely...I mean, is it not your job to get him off?'

She put her hand to her mouth, realising the implication of her comment. Simon gave a weak smile.

'No, Coral, my job is not to 'get him off'. As I'm sure you've just realised, that implies guilt in the first place. If his case goes to trial then it will be my job to ensure that the trial is absolutely fair. I'm sure you'll have heard the expression 'guilty beyond any reasonable doubt'; well, my task, if you like, is to raise that doubt, to question anything that may seem unfair or prejudicial to my client, in this case your father. I will assess all the evidence and examine every possible alternative to the facts that prosecuting counsel may lay out. But it is not in my remit to get a guilty party 'off', as you put it.'

Coral looked aghast. 'Oh my God, you think this could go to trial?'

Simon nodded. 'It might.'

'But...but...surely you've asked, surely my dad's told you he's innocent...it's so unfair, so unjust, after all he's been through!'

Dan crossed over and sat beside his distraught wife, staring at Simon as he stood up and headed towards the door.

'As I said, it's just about making sure that every single letter of the law is followed, and to give your father the best possible chance of avoiding an unfair conviction. You know, an old professor of mine used to quote, 'a lawyer has no business with the justice or injustice of the cause which he undertakes.''

The wind whistled in the eaves of the old quarry house as Dzhokhar Meta lay in bed, gazing at the ceiling. He leaned over to the bedside table and switched off the light, lying in the darkness with his eyes wide open. A lecherous grin spread across his heavy features. The bed was large and half of it was empty but, soon, that would change. He imagined Agni Krasniki lying beside him, warm, naked, agile...he imagined her caress as she turned towards him, grateful and indebted. Finally, he closed his eyes. Tonight he was safe and protected, his henchmen awake and vigilant in the downstairs rooms. Maybe Janek was fucking his daughter; he didn't care.

He was a powerful man who, through the fear that he instilled, commanded respect. He gleaned information, he heard snippets from those wishing to ingratiate themselves with him. But Meta was a cunning beast, also divulging such information as suited his purposes.

As sleep engulfed him, as he lost control of his conscious thoughts, the realisation that he had set a trap, in which he was the bait, flashed briefly through his mind.

Dzhokhar Meta was playing a very dangerous game.

Chapter 16

Monday 1st December.

'Are ye sure this is goin' tae be awright, Paul?'

Paul Maguire didn't reply; he had been asking himself the same question ever since they had left Glasgow. He looked in his rear-view mirror where, in the late-afternoon gloom, two sets of headlights were reflected. He replied with a confidence that he didn't exactly feel.

'Listen, Davie, the boys are right behind us, it'll be fine.'

Doyle cast a glance behind him, as if for reassurance.

'Fuckin' better be; an' you still don't think this bastard's behind these killin's?'

Maguire shook his head, as much to convince himself, if he was being honest.

'I don't. The man's got an ulterior motive somewhere. He seems to want to find out who's responsible as much as we do. Right, I think it must be about here, have a look at the directions.'

They were on a back road near the central Scotland town of Shotts, driving through a heavily wooded area. In the distance, the ubiquitous tall telecommunications towers disappeared into the low, leaden clouds, from which a fine drizzle was falling.

'Says there's a forestry road up tae the left; look, is that it?'

Maguire indicated and turned the car into the narrow, unmetalled road. The headlights in the mirror disappeared for a few moments and Maguire stopped, taking out his phone.

'Right, Chic, you come up the track but keep a couple of hundred yards behind us. Tell Paddy to stay at the end of the road. Keep your eyes open.'

He placed the phone back in his pocket, put the car in gear and set off, driving carefully up the heavily rutted track. After a few minutes, they entered a wide space, presumably for the turning of forestry vehicles. Parked at one side, facing back down the road, were two dark-coloured four-by-fours.

'Looks like this is them.'

'Ah don't like it, Davie. Ah mean, whit if ye're wrong?'

The door to one of the vehicles opened and a tall, powerfully built and shaven-headed man exited, giving them a curt wave of acknowledgement.

'Looks friendly enough,' commented Maguire, trying unsuccessfully to keep his voice light. He wound down the window and the bald man called across, his voice heavily accented.

'Mr Meta is in the back of this vehicle. Can you send Mr Doyle over please? On his own.'

Maguire looked across at his friend, who was now visibly shaking.

'Fuck sake, Paul.'

'Davie, do you want to find the people who tried to kill you? The people responsible for poor Suzi's death. For fuck sake, we're here now, just get it over with, one way or another!'

As the powerful vehicle lurched back down the muddy, rutted track, Dzhokhar Meta turned to the shaven-headed man who was driving, speaking in his native language.

'What do you think?'

The man didn't respond at first, instead looking right and left as he pulled out on to the main road. Seeing the vehicle that was parked at the road-end, he smiled.

'Huh, backup! What do I think? I think that Doyle is a man of limited intelligence and limited imagination. His story is almost beyond belief but I do not believe that he has the ability to make it up.'

The bald man frowned; as Meta's second-in-command, he was used to the feeling of power, of being in control. The idea of some anonymous 'higher authority' didn't sit comfortably with him. He continued. 'But if we do choose to believe him, then we have to decide very carefully what our next move will be. I do not like the sound of this, Dzhokhar. What is your plan?'

Meta gave an evil leer. 'A trap, my friend. With a very appealing bait!'

Bruce spent most of the day sitting in his daughter's lounge, drinking coffee and dozing fitfully. He felt like a caged animal, afraid to venture outside or even to approach the windows in case the press were lurking nearby. He desperately wanted to phone Rob Connor but Simon had warned against that course of action; after all, Rob *was* a policeman. At some point in the afternoon, he realised that it was actually Mel that he really needed to talk to but, given that she was Rob's wife, he daren't even speak to her. He placed his face in his hands and let out a groan. He got to his feet, intending to make yet another cup of coffee, when Coral's house phone rang. He stared at it for a few seconds, unsure as to whether or not he should answer it. The number was unlisted but you just never knew...

As the answering machine cut in, it rang off then, after a few minutes, started again. Bruce crossed over and plucked up the courage to lift the receiver. He didn't say anything, he just listened.

'Hello? Hello, is there anyone there? Bruce, is that you...?'

Mel Connor; he could feel tears welling up in his eyes. 'Mel, Thank God!'

'Oh, Bruce, darling, are you okay?'

He decided to tell the truth. 'No, Mel, I'm very far from being okay...'

It was the sound of a car reversing onto the driveway that finally caused him to terminate the call.

'Mel, I think that's Coral home, I'd better go. Simon said I wasn't to speak to anyone.'

'But I'm not just *anyone*, I'm one of your oldest friends. And I can't understand why Simon didn't just let you tell the truth!'

'He said that the police wouldn't believe me. To be honest, I'm not sure *he* believes me.'

'Did you ask him?'

'No, but he says that guilt or innocence are irrelevant.'

'But that's rubbish, surely? How the hell can being innocent not matter?'

Bruce sighed; now certainly wasn't the time to start a discourse on the merits of due process and all that it entailed. He heard a key in the lock.

'That *is* Coral, Mel. I have to go. Listen, thanks for phoning, I don't know what I'd do without you. Love you, 'bye.'

'Love you too, Bruce, please take care, 'bye.'

He placed the phone back on the cradle as his daughter walked into the lounge.

'Who was that, Dad?'

He hadn't the energy to lie. 'Em...Auntie Mel.'

Coral dropped her bag on the chair and glared at her father.

'What? Dad, Simon said that under no circumstances were you to talk to them! What the hell—'

'No, he said I wasn't to talk to *Rob*—that's different.'

'No it bloody isn't, Dad, and you know it! Auntie Mel is Rob's wife, she's bound to say something to Uncle Rob.'

He stood up and walked across to her. 'And what if he does? Would that be such a bad thing? After all, it's the truth.'

She shook her head in exasperation. 'Is it? Is it really?'

He looked at his daughter in near-shock. 'You don't bloody believe me, do you?'

She turned away. 'I don't know what to believe any more.'

'You bloody what? Jesus Christ, Mel, what the hell were you thinkin'?'

Rob Connor couldn't remember the last time he had lost his temper with his wife but his self-control had evaporated instantly when she had told him of her phone call to Bruce.

'He's our oldest friend, for goodness sake. The poor man's been through hell the last few days, especially given that it's ten years since Dorothy died. He's at his wits' end.'

Rob was pacing back and forth across the kitchen floor.

'I know he is; and I know it must be hard for you too. You and Dorothy were close, I appreciate that.'

He saw the brief flash of pain on her face.

'Look, I'm sorry, love, and I'm sorry for Bruce, but you have to remember that he's also a bloody murder suspect!'

'But he's been released, Rob, surely—'

'Yes, until further evidence comes to light, which it could well do. Look, I hate to say this but it's not looking particularly good for Bruce at the moment. Carla Mazzoni's pulling out all the stops to find some CCTV evidence that shows him near Beagan's car. Once they find that...'

The tears welled up in Mel's eyes, brimming over and running down her soft cheeks. 'Oh no, please, please don't say that, Bruce would never...'

He grabbed her shoulders. 'Look, Mel, yes, we've known Bruce for years but people change, especially after what happened with Dorothy. If he's been harbouring that grudge all this time, if the opportunity presented itself, you don't know *what* he might be capable of.'

She sobbed and fell against him, shaking her head. 'No, no, he'd never kill anyone...he didn't...he told me what really happened...'

The words were out; she could have kicked herself, she had promised Bruce she would say nothing. Rob pushed her away, still grasping her shoulders firmly.

'*What?* What the hell do you mean, 'he told you what really happened'?'

She shook her head.

'Mel, you need to tell me.'

'No, I promised—'

'It's too bloody late for than, Mel Connor. Tell me. NOW!'

Rob Connor was sitting on the edge of the couch, a near-empty crystal tumbler in his hand. He lifted it and drained the dregs of the large whisky that he had poured himself. Mel gave him a plaintive look and he shook his head.

'Fuck!'

'Ssh, the kids might hear.'

'Sorry. But, really...'

'Don't you believe him?'

He looked at his wife; he knew that she was desperate for him to back her up, to believe in their friend and to accept the fantastic tale that he had spun. His immediate reaction had been to tell her that it was utter nonsense but, by his troubled expression, Mel suspected that there was a tiny niggle of doubt at the back of his mind, something he couldn't quite resolve. He let out a long sigh. 'God knows. I mean, quite honestly, it sounds like a load of crap...sorry. But why the hell didn't he tell Mazzoni all this when she questioned him?'

'He said that Simon advised against it.'

'Did he say why?'

She paused for a moment. 'Em...he didn't think they'd believe him.'

He shrugged. 'Well, there you are. It doesn't sound like Simon believes him either, does it?'

He dropped his head and gazed morosely into the empty glass, pursing his lips in thought. Mel raised an eyebrow as she spoke, her voice soft and gentle. 'What, Rob? What is it?'

He frowned as if collating his thoughts and sighed again, twirling the empty glass in his hand. He needed a refill.

'I don't know...probably nothin', but remember when I was investigatin' those two characters that were found down at Princes Pier, locked in the container?'

Mel nodded enthusiastically. 'Yes, and you were told to stand down. What was it—something along the lines of just letting them get on with it as long as it didn't involve innocent members of the public?'

'Well, in not so many words but, yes, I suppose so. At the time I just thought it was the usual, that we were overstretched and if the crooks wanted to take each other out, let them get on with it. But what if...'

He shook his head dismissively. '...no, it just doesn't make any sense.'

'Doesn't it?' responded Mel. 'How many times have you gone off on a rant when one of these people manages to get off on a technicality, or is found not guilty when you know damned fine that they're rotten to the core? How many times have you said that it makes you sick, after all the work, the preparation, then some clever Counsel gets them off the hook. Well, maybe someone finally decided to take a stand; after all, Bruce said that every one of these criminals that's been murdered has been tried but hasn't been convicted.'

'That's not strictly true,' he replied half-heartedly. 'As far as I know, David Doyle never stood trial for anythin' particularly serious, it was only the woman. But...'

His voice tailed off as he continued to stare into his glass.

'Rob... come on, it's me you're talking to.'

He looked up at her, a stab of guilt piercing him. He loved this woman he had always tried to protect her from the harsh realities of his job. With a sigh of resignation, he decided that this occasion would be no different. He stood up.

'Look, love, you know the whole foundation of our legal system; if these men, no matter how bad they were, have been tried and found not guilty, then that's an end to it.'

She grabbed his arm, almost pleadingly. 'Is it? I mean, really? Think back to Beagan's trial, to what it did to poor Bruce when that little shit got off with killing poor Dorothy? I know how I felt, God knows what Bruce must have gone through.'

He dropped back on to the couch, still clutching the empty glass; the need for a refill was now almost overwhelming. They sat in a gloomy silence for a few minutes as their thoughts strayed to the horrors of the trial all those years ago.

'Mel, I agree that it was an awful time but...'

He stood up again, rather more resolutely this time. 'Just let it drop. The whole thing'll just upset you—Christ, it's bloody upset *me!* I wish to God you hadn't spoken to Bruce. Anyway, what's done is done, we can't go back and change it.'

Mel's eyes blazed. 'And that makes it okay? You've changed your tune, Rob Connor—at the time I clearly recall you saying that Beagan should be bloody shot, if I recall.'

'Just let justice and the law run their own course.'

Mel shook her head. 'I'm not sure that justice and the law are necessarily the same thing anymore.'

'Bonnar's Byte'
by Miriam Bonnar

'...you heard it here first, folks...!'

Dear readers, I am delighted to be able to bring you an update to my story last week. Of course, I am unable to share my sources with you; suffice to say that I have utilised my extensive research team to confirm the theory that I propounded and I can tell you this...

My suspicions have been confirmed— the Civil Guard is a reality!

You may have observed that there was another murder last week, that of a vile young thug who, a number of years ago, was tried for the cowardly manslaughter of an innocent woman in a road traffic accident. He ran his victim off the road while he was driving a stolen car, under the influence of both alcohol and drugs. Her car caught fire and the victim burned to death, trapped in her own blazing vehicle.

He could have saved her.

He didn't.

Like the others, he managed to slither out of a guilty verdict and, after serving a brief jail term for lesser charges, he was free to roam the streets once more. Meanwhile, the family of the victim were left to come to terms with their loss and their never-ending grief.

Is the execution of this pathetic excuse for a human being justice? Call me old-fashioned, but

I believe it is. I also believe that the subsequent arrest (on suspicion of said young thug's murder) and release of high-flying divorce solicitor, Bruce Redpath, was simply a ploy by Scotland's Finest, an attempt to 'be seen to be doing the right thing.' An arrest is an arrest, even if it is a 'wrong 'un!'

Now, dear readers, don't get me wrong. I consider people such as Mr Redpath to be just one rung up the ladder from the low-life that inhabit the bottom of the swamp, preying on the tragedy that is divorce, draining the bank-balances of their distraught victims. But I do not believe that Mr Redpath is a killer (except, perhaps, of passion!)

I believe that this is another instance of the Civil Guard at work.

I also believe that Bruce Redpath knows a lot more about the Civil Guard than you or I do. I wonder if he'd care to share his knowledge?

For a fee, undoubtedly...

Miriam Bonnar re-read the piece one final time, a smile of satisfaction on her heavy and rather embittered features. She saved it to her laptop, then to a flash drive before pulling the little blue stick out of the computer and dropping it in the pocket of the checked shirt that stretched tightly across her ample bosom. Finally, she opened her email and attached the completed document to a brief note to her editor. After one last, critical read, she pressed 'send'.

She switched off the computer, drained her gin and stood up; as always, her copy had been submitted in time for the following day's edition. Sure, her editor might have a few objections but she usually got her way. After all, she also knew a thing or two about him.

Chapter 17

Tuesday 2nd September

Paul Maguire hadn't slept well. Apart from missing his hitherto nightly visits to a well-known adult website, the near-continual rasp of Davie Doyle's snoring made any form of quality sleep all but impossible. Maguire had finally resorted to earplugs but he awoke that morning tired, with a pounding headache and he was, as his mother used to put it, crabbit as hell!

He switched on the kettle and waited; sure enough, within minutes Doyle arrived, unshaven, dishevelled and the inevitable fag already clamped between his dry, cracked lips. He looked bloody awful, thought Maguire, with an uncharacteristic pang of sympathy. After all, Doyle *had* lost his...well, Maguire wasn't exactly sure what Flint had been. Lover, mistress? But there was no doubt that Doyle was on a slippery slope of some sort, driven on only by an all-consuming desire for revenge. As he scratched his greasy hair, he spoke in a gravelly, phlegm-ridden voice.

'Gonn'ae make us a tea, Paul, Ah'm fuckin' parched. Ah'll stick on a couple o' slices o' toast.'

Maguire took a second mug from the cupboard and dropped in a tea bag as his friend applied his meagre culinary skills to the bread. He spoke, choosing his words carefully.

'I've been meaning to say, I'm becoming a wee bit worried about you.'

'Me? How? Ah'm fine, just cann'ae wait tae get ma hands on the bastards that did wee Suzi.'

With a grimace, Maguire poured the boiling water into the mugs; it was like listening to a cracked record, repeating over...and over...

'Are you *sure* you're okay? I mean, I know it must be hard for you but you're pinning all your hopes on this guy Meta. He's got his own agenda. I'm not sure what his reasons are but I suspect you don't really enter into the equation.'

Maguire had made a few discreet enquiries into the provenance of Dzhokhar Meta, but the man appeared to operate in the shadows. What he *had* learned was that Meta was brutal, ruthless and operated in an entirely different league from David Doyle. The problem was how to tell his friend.

'I mean, surely if Meta gets hold of whoever was responsible for Suzi's death, that'll be revenge enough?'

Doyle shook his head as he put a thick layer of butter on the toast..

'Naw, Ah want tae see those bastards suffer ma'sel'. Fuck, is the marmalade aw' done?'

Maguire tried to hide both his scepticism and his irritation. Doyle was eating him out of house and home.

'There's a new jar in the cupboard...do you really think that Meta will let you know when, or if, he finds them?'

Doyle shrugged as he lifted the mug of strong, steaming tea and the plate of toast, slopping some of the brown liquid onto the kitchen floor. 'Fuckin' better—he doesn'ae want *me* as an enemy—c'mon let's go an' see whit's oan the telly.'

As Paul Maguire followed his rather malodorous friend through to the lounge (avoiding as best he could the trail of tea drips from Doyle's mug) he shook his head. He was wasting his time; as was Doyle, if he seriously thought that Meta had any intention of keeping him in the loop.

The morning had dragged tediously by; just after midday, Bruce had switched off the television and headed to the kitchen, where Coral had left him a portion of frozen homemade soup. He heated it up then, along with a couple of slices of wholemeal bread, he headed back to the living room.

He had heard nothing from Simon Fox and he almost wished that the police would contact him, even if just to break the tedium. Simon's parting shot had been that he would be in touch as and when anything further happened, so Bruce presumed the old adage that 'no news was good news'. Still, his spirits seemed to have sunk to an all-time low and his constant inactivity had left him with little appetite.

The soup sat in its bowl, half-eaten and cold. He closed his eyes for a few minutes, hoping to block out the feeling of near-despair that seemed to be his constant companion, but he jerked back into wakefulness at the sound of a car entering the gravel driveway. Crossing to the window and surreptitiously peering from behind the heavy curtains, he suddenly felt his spirits rise; the gleaming white Mercedes saloon told him that he was about to receive a visit from Olivia Carnegie. They lifted further when the passenger door opened and Torquil scrambled out, clutching a Marks and Spencers' food bag. Maybe things were not so bad after all...

'Bruce! God, you look pretty rough—are you bearing up okay?'

Olivia brushed her red lips against his stubbly cheek, the waft of perfume briefly overpowering the smell of freshly-baked bread that was emanating from Torquil's food parcel. The young man grinned, nudging his mother with an elbow.

'For God's sake, that's hardly going to cheer him up, is it? Afternoon, Boss, you hanging in there okay?'

Bruce smiled back at the young man's brashness and seemingly irrepressible cheerfulness, realising just how much he had missed the youth. To think that, just a few weeks previously, he had effectively dismissed him. Olivia had the good grace to look very slightly guilty.

'Sorry, Bruce, I suppose that *was* a bit mean. Anyway, no bloody wonder, after what you've been through.'

'Simon's filled you in, I take it?'

She nodded.

'Everything?'

Olivia frowned. 'Well, I suppose. I don't really know. What do *you* mean by 'everything'?'

Bruce had the suspicion that Simon had omitted the minor detail of his abduction. 'Oh, never mind. I suppose The Man likes to keep things close to his chest; always did!. Anyway, come on in—is that for me, Torquil, that's very kind...'

As he took the heavily-laden bag, he noticed the bottle of malt whisky that was lurking inside, tucked under some large packets of crisps. He'd maybe keep that one in his bedroom for his own personal use. Torquil smiled and delved into the back pocket of his skin-tight jeans, the crotch of which seemed to be on a parallel with his knees..

'Oh, and I brought you this, Boss; figured the cops still had yours. It's my old one but it should do the job. I've restored the factory settings and put in all the numbers I could think of from the office. You just need to set it up for your thumb-print and you're good to go. Put a few games on too, in case you get bored!'

Bruce gratefully took the iPhone from Torquil; he could have wept.

They stayed for just over an hour, chatting easily about the every-day running of Redpath, Fox, Carnegie while studiously avoiding any mention of his own case. Rayna Aherne was asking kindly for him; Peter Caira sent his regards.

There was no further mention of Simon Fox.

Bruce opened the bag of premium coffee that had been among the goodies and had prepared a cafetiere, their beverages being accompanied by a selection of delicious sweet treats. It surprised him how something as simple as an afternoon coffee with some friends could lift his spirits but, finally, they were saying their farewells at the door. Olivia suddenly stopped, half way towards the car.

'Oh, I nearly forgot—I though you might be interested in this.'

She removed a sheet of paper from her handbag and handed it to Bruce.

'In today's on-line edition. Looks like you're famous...bye!'

As the powerful saloon roared along the quiet street, Bruce sat down and read the article from that day's newspaper that Olivia had given him.

> *...I also believe that Bruce Redpath knows a lot more about the Civil Guard than you or I do. I wonder if he'd care to share his knowledge? For a fee, undoubtedly...'*

His heart plummeted back down to his borrowed and rather shabby carpet slippers.

A cold, east wind was blowing up the Firth of Forth, bringing with it a chill dampness that spread over the bleak West Lothian countryside in a faint blanket of mist. Dzhokhar Meta stood up and crossed to the window, pulling the heavy curtains aside and looking out onto the impenetrable darkness. Earlier in the day, some sixth sense had told him that the trap might be sprung sometime soon and a text message received about half an hour ago had confirmed his suspicions. His thoughts were interrupted by his daughter's voice, as always a hint of complaint in its tone. The sooner he sold her off the better.

'Papa, I need to take the bin down, they will be collecting it tomorrow.'

He paused for a moment, his heavy brows knitted together in thought, then turned and gave her a rare smile.

'Leave it, Kat, I will do it.'

Katya Meta looked at her father with an expression of near-astonishment; her father seldom did anything to help with the household chores. Come to that, he seldom smiled at her...her face lit up. 'Okay, thank you, Papa.'

She paused at the door, her scowl returning.

'Papa, why are the men not here?'

He turned and leered at her. 'Huh, you're missing Janek, eh? Don't worry, he will be back for you, I'm sure.'

In fact, he was certain; he'd offered the man a hefty sum of cash to take his daughter off his hands, in preparation for welcoming a new woman into his home.

'But why did they go—I thought you were worried?'

He snapped back at her. 'Well I'm not worried now, stupid. Everything's fine, do you understand?'

He stood up, brushing her aside and leaving her glaring at his back. He went into the kitchen and lifted his Barbour jacket from the peg beside the Aga cooker. As he slipped into it, zipping it up, the warmth seeped into his heavy frame. He had the feeling he might be needing it tonight as he opened the back door, triggering one of the security lights. The other had mysteriously stopped working a few days back but he hadn't bothered to have it fixed. After all, he wasn't afraid of the dark...

He grabbed the handle of the wheelie-bin and set off round the house, triggering the lamp at the front. As he walked down the drive, he took the control for the heavy security gate out of his pocket and pressed the button. The gate slid across with a faint hum then, when the opening was about three feet wide, he pressed the button again, stopping it. He walked slowly, deliberately, then passed through the gap, trailing the bin before turning it and placing it at the side of the road. He lifted the lid, as if checking the contents when, suddenly, a four-by-four roared into life, its bright spotlights dazzling him. As it roared towards him, he felt an arm go round his neck. Instinctively, Meta dropped to the ground, swinging round and punching upwards between his assailant's legs; a man, presumably, as there was a grunt of pain. As the figure bent over, clutching his groin, Meta stood up and brought his knee into contact with his attacker's face, the blood warm through his trousers as the man's nose disintegrated. He turned as the vehicle screeched to a halt behind him, too late to react to the arm that was swinging something towards his skull.

Katya Meta watched in horror, frozen to the spot behind a rhododendron bush. She had followed her father, partly because she was afraid to be in the house on her own and partly because she didn't trust him. She suspected that there was an ulterior motive to him performing even this small domestic task and she had slipped on her heavy boots before sneaking across the grass, keeping his solid figure in sight. She hated him at times—well, most of the time—but he was all she had.

There were three men now, their faces concealed by black ski-masks; one had put a bag over her Papa's head and used a piece of plastic to tie his hands behind his back before dragging him towards the vehicle. With some difficulty, they bundled his heavy, inert body into the rear of the vehicle. The third man was on his feet again, blood seeping through his mask from the remains of his nose and dripping on to his hands His associates closed the rear door of the vehicle, then one of them handed a wad of what looked like kitchen roll to the injured man before they clambered into the car and sped away. She managed to make out part of the registration before she turned and stumped as quickly as she could towards the house.

Katya had never been permitted to have a phone; Papa said that it was so that people wouldn't find out where they lived. He had said that there were a lot of bad people who wanted to hurt them and it now seemed that he had been correct. She started to cry; she didn't know anyone, she had little money, she couldn't drive, what was she going to do, alone and frightened? She wiped away the tears, trying to think, then crossed the hallway to the room that Papa used as an office. She pushed the door, letting out a sigh of relief as she realised that it hadn't been locked.

As she entered, the faint, lingering smell of cigars and cologne, underlaid with the acrid smell of her Papa's stale sweat, stopped her in her tracks and she had to fight back the tears once more. She shook her head determinedly then started rummaging through the drawers of his desk. In the bottom one, she found two old mobile phones, one of which seemed to be out of charge. However, the screen on the second lit up as she lifted it, although the battery display told her it had only three percent of charge remaining. She pressed the home button but it asked for the six-digit security code and she started to cry again, having no idea what it was. She pressed it again and again, willing it to work.

Suddenly, the display changed...

Dzhokhar Meta was a careful man but it had never crossed his mind that his daughter might try to use the phone to summon the emergency services.

The powerful four-by-four sped along the deserted country road, heading towards the town of Slamannan. The occupants paid no heed to the two decrepit farm cottages beside the road, surrounded by a clutter of near-derelict outbuildings. Some of the windows were boarded up, the others dark and dirty. There was no sign of life, other than several discreetly-placed infra-red security cameras...

The occupants of the cottages were already seated in two equally-powerful four-by-four vehicles, engines warmed up, weapons checked and ready. As the tail lights of the captors' vehicle disappeared into the gloom, the ramshackle doors were thrown open then, a few seconds later, two vehicles burst on to the road, their tyres screeching as they set off in pursuit.

Chapter 18

Wednesday 3rd December.

'Are you hurt?'

'*No—well, no' really. Bastard smashed my nose, but I'll survive. Had a lot worse.*'

'What about the others?'

'*Haven't a fuckin' clue, sorry. Target wis taken out, though, no choice really, in the end. Think we're at least one man down. There wis a mist, that wis how I managed tae get away, eh.*'

'How the hell did the police find out?'

'*I was goin' tae ask you the same thing.*'

A pause.

'What are you suggesting?'

Another pause.

'*I'm no' really suggestin' anythin'. But, like you say, how the hell did they find out, eh?*'

A deep sigh.

'More to the point, how the hell did Meta's men find out? At least, I'm assuming that's who they were.'

'I'd say so; heard them shoutin' in their native tongue. I'm pretty certain it wis a trap, with Meta as the bait.'

Another pause.

'Hm, you might have a point. They're getting wise then, but I suppose it was only a matter of time. We need to discuss our strategy...right, do you think you can get back here okay?'

'Aye, I'm on my way already. Should be there by the evenin' '

'Good. And if you hear anything else, let me know. You're sure you're okay? You've got money? Don't want you using a card, too easy to trace.'

'Aye, I'm good, thanks. Plenty o' cash for tickets an' the like.'

'Okay, I'll see you later. Take care.'

'You know me. Born survivor, eh!'

'Oh, one more thing...'

'Aye?'

'For God's sake make sure you're not followed...'

Bruce hadn't slept well; while the visit from Olivia and Torquil had lifted his spirits temporarily, Miriam Bonnar's *Byte* had left him seriously concerned and upset. His name was now even more in the public domain and he wondered if the day would bring the inevitable intrusion of the media. He also had a slight hangover; having surreptitiously taken a glass from the kitchen, he had managed to consume about half the bottle of malt whisky that Olivia had brought. His mouth was dry and, dragging himself from the bed, he made his way down to the kitchen, where Coral was tidying before heading to work. Dan had already left, dropping Amy at nursery on the way. It had been deemed 'unfair' to expect Bruce to act as babysitter, but he had the suspicion that his daughter and son-in-law didn't really trust him. Given the way he felt, perhaps they were correct!

'Morning, Dad—sleep okay? You don't look too good.'

He was becoming weary of being told how bad his appearance had become, although a quick glance in the bathroom mirror hadn't filled him with self-confidence. He tried not to get too close to Coral in case she detected the whisky fumes which were, undoubtedly, lingering.

'Dad, I told you, you probably shouldn't watch the news...'

Bruce knew that Coral only had his best interests at heart and didn't want him to hear anything that might upset him. But he was desperate for news of...well, anything, he supposed. The sooner the so-called Civil Guard was tracked down, the sooner he would stop being a 'person of interest'. He called back to her as he sat down in the lounge, a cereal bowl in one hand and a mug of coffee in the other.

'I appreciate your concern, Coral, but I'll be fine. Anyway, I'm yesterday's news now...'

Hopefully, he muttered to himself, as he took the first mouthful of what resembled shredded cardboard. The Wilson household seemed to be on a permanently healthy diet.

He switched on the television, just in time for the early morning headlines, and he lifted his mug, taking a sip; he was beginning to feel human again.

'...large-scale manhunt is under way in East Lothian this morning following what police believe to be a gang-related shoot-out that left three men dead and an armed police officer seriously injured. It is believed that an unknown number of the men involved in the incident escaped on foot and the public are warned not to approach anyone they think might be suspicious but to call nine-nine-nine instead. It is not known how many people were involved but police have made three arrests, two of whom are in hospital with gunshot wounds. They believe that there may have been at least a further two men involved, who they think escaped across open countryside. We're going live now to Duncan Kerr, our Scottish correspondent. Duncan, can you give us an update?'

The obligatory pause as a suitably sombre-faced Kerr nodded his head.

'Well, Peter, as you can see, operations here are being hampered by the thick mist, which has prevented the use of the police helicopter. There are roadblocks on all roads around the Slamannan area and police have extended their search as far north as Falkirk and south towards Whitburn. These men are believed to be armed and extremely dangerous so, as you've already said, the police are urging the public to be vigilant and to report any sightings of suspicious individuals. The suspects are thought to be dressed in black paramilitary style clothes and, as I mentioned, they are believed to be armed.'

'And has there been any indication as to the identities of the victims, Duncan?'

'Well, although it hasn't been confirmed officially, I understand that one of the victims was...'

With a frown of concentration, Kerr consulted a notepad.

'...em...Dzhokhar Meta, a man seemingly known to the police. I also understand that he was found inside one of the vehicles, apparently having been abducted, and had died of gunshot wounds to the head...'

Kerr turned briefly. '...I'm about to be joined by the Assistant Chief Constable of Scotland's police, Amelia Khan.'

The camera panned to a tall, sharp-featured woman; her dark hair was swept back beneath her regulation headgear and she was wearing an even darker expression on her face. She was dressed in full upper body armour over a standard police uniform, the only giveaway to her rank the braiding on her hat.

'Ms Khan, this is a shocking incident, is it not?'

She gave him a look that clearly questioned his need to state the obvious. 'Well, of course it is! The only redeeming circumstance is that it took place in remote countryside; had it happened in a built-up area, the casualty list would most likely have been higher.'

'Indeed. And what can you tell us so far?'

'Little more than you've already stated. An armed police officer has been taken to hospital with serious gunshot wounds, although his condition isn't thought to be life- threatening, thankfully. Three people have died from gunshot wounds and a further two are in hospital, also having sustained gunshot wounds which, although serious, are also not believed to be life-threatening.'

'And I believe that several of those involved in the incident may have escaped?'

She gave him another frosty stare. 'Yes and, as you stated, I would urge members of the public to call the police if they see anyone dressed in black military-style fatigues. '

She turned to face the camera. 'These men are extremely dangerous and we believe them to be armed. If you see anyone answering to their descriptions, or anyone who looks suspicious, it is *imperative* that you phone the police and that you do not approach or challenge them.'

'Do you believe that this incident is gang-related, Ms Khan?'

'I can't comment on that at present. However, I will say that a number of those involved are, or were, known to the police.'

'Is it correct that one of those killed was a suspected crime baron called...'

He consulted his notes, revising his pronunciation slightly.

'em...Dzhokhar Meta?'

'Again, I can't comment until the families of the deceased have been informed.'

'Ms Khan, as I said earlier, this is a truly shocking incident and the public are, naturally, concerned that the level of violence in Scotland's criminal underworld seems to have escalated dramatically over the last few weeks. What are the police doing to combat this up-turn in extreme and brutal violence?'

The look she bestowed upon Duncan Kerr would have withered a lesser man, but he was an old hand at this game.

'Mr Kerr, I can assure you—and the public—that Police Scotland are treating this matter, as well as the recent spate of killings, extremely seriously. We cannot, and will not, allow such violence to take place and we will leave no stone unturned in our search for the perpetrators of last night's atrocity...'

She seemed to be about to continue when Kerr interrupted.

'There are reports that the previous killings were carried out by an unknown agency, styled by one journalist as the Civil Guard. The suggestion is that this group is acting outwith the restraints of the law to serve justice on—'

Amelia Khan looked as if she were about to explode. 'I am well aware of the journalist to whom you are referring and I am rather surprised that you are giving her irresponsible assertions any credence. To the best of our knowledge, no such agency exists. As I have said, this is an ongoing investigation into what we believe to be a dangerously violent 'turf war' and we will not rest until we find those responsible. The notion that there is a so-called 'Civil Guard' meting out their own form of justice is, quite frankly, absurd. Thank you.'

She turned abruptly and walked away as the camera panned back to Duncan Kerr, a very slightly discomfited look on his heavily jowled face.

'Em, thank you, Ms Khan. Anyway, back to you in the studio, Peter..'

'Dad...Dad? Are you okay?'

Bruce was staring at the screen, mug half-way towards his mouth. He turned and looked at his daughter, who had her jacket on in readiness for the daily commute.

'Sorry, Coral, what...?

Agni Krasniki also turned off her television. She lit a fresh cigarette, her dark brows set in a scowl of anger. So that was it; Meta had failed, he had not lived up to the promise he had made and he had died in the attempt. She knew all about men like Meta; she had learned at an early age exactly how to exploit her sexuality to get what she wanted. She had always known what the price would be if Meta had succeeded in bringing her brother's killer to her and it had been a price she had been prepared to pay.

But he had failed.

She exhaled a cloud of smoke; Meta had been her final hope. Now? Well, she would have to rely on her own wits; after all, it certainly wouldn't be the first time.

Agni Krasniki was used to coping on her own.

She would find a way.

Bruce had finally persuaded Coral that he would be fine on his own and, rather reluctantly, she had left for work. Resisting the temptation to retrieve the half-empty bottle of malt, he made himself another coffee, went into the lounge and switched the television back on.

As he had expected, the killings were the main topic of the day, with a variety of so-called experts, retired senior police officers and minor politicians giving their views. However, as he had also expected, there was little further information being given. He toyed with the mobile phone that Torquil had given him; surely these killings were connected with the previous ones in some way and, if that was the case, surely the police might now have someone in custody, someone who might be able to corroborate his story and exonerate him. Finally, he scrolled through the meagre list of contacts and pressed 'call'.

'Bruce. How the devil are you? I was going to call you later today.'

Were you? wondered Bruce.

'Well, I suppose I'm okay, Simon, thanks. I thought I might have heard from you sooner.'

He had tried very hard to keep the reproach from his voice, but there was a fractional pause before Simon Fox replied.

'Oh, well, I said I'd call if there were any further developments and there haven't been, thankfully.'

'Is that a good thing, do you think?'

'Look, obviously the police haven't managed to find any further evidence.'

'They won't, because I didn't kill Beagan.'

He heard his friend let out a sigh.

'Well, let's hope we don't have to prove that.'

'Simon, can I ask you something?'

'Not if it's whether I believe in your innocence. You know the score. My job is to ensure that, in the event that this *does* go to trial, every single procedure has been done by the book, every single piece of evidence can be corroborated and that there is absolutely no room for doubt if...'

The pause hung between them like old-fashioned analogue static.

'If I'm found guilty?'

'Don't put words into my mouth, Bruce Redpath,' said Simon with a chuckle; Bruce knew that his friend was trying to defuse the situation. 'Look, I'll come down and see you tomorrow, we can have a chat; how's that?'

'Yes, that would be nice, Olivia and Torquil were down yesterday.'

'I know, she told me. Said you looked like shit.'

'That was kind of her.'

The conversation continued for a few minutes on a more light-hearted note before Simon had to leave for an appointment. It was only afterwards that Bruce realised they hadn't discussed the latest killings, the whole point of his call in the first place. Still, at least Simon was paying him a visit; that was something to look forward to, along with the remains of the malt whisky that were safely stowed in his wardrobe.

Another bowl of Coral's home-made soup, another news bulletin, another post-prandial nap... Bruce had briefly given further consideration to a glass of whisky, if only to relieve the monotony, but quickly put the thought out of his head. That really *would* be the slippery slope.

He was dozing fitfully when his mobile announced an incoming call; the raucous 'submarine dive-alert', Torquil's choice of ringtone, was both unfamiliar and rather alarming.

With a mumbled oath, he picked up the handset and looked at the screen; the call was from the office and his heart skipped a beat.

'Hello?'

The voice that replied was that of Rayna Aherne. He breathed a long sigh of relief and a smile spread over his face.

'Hello, Mrs Aherne!'

'Oh, Mr Redpath, how lovely to hear your voice, I've been so worried...'

'And I can't tell you how good it is to hear *your* voice.'

They chatted about nothing in particular for a few minutes, the concern in her soft lilt unmistakeable. Finally she stated the reason for her call.

'You see, Mr Redpath, I'd spoken to Mr Fox and he had said it was best to leave you be, but there's been a number of calls from that investigator, Cal Gibson—he says it's most urgent.'

Bruce could tell from Rayna's tone of voice that she had little affection for Gibson. Neither had he, after what had happened!

'Gibson! What the hell does he want?'

'He wouldn't say. He wanted me to give him your number but I refused and I said that I'd phone you. I just told him that it would be up to yourself whether or not you wanted to speak to him.'

Trust Mrs Aherne, he thought, with a wry smile. Bruce still hadn't forgiven the private investigator for allowing him to be abducted without intervening. Still, maybe the man had news. He sighed. 'Oh, I suppose I've nothing better to do—let me check that Torquil's put his number on the phone.'

'I'm sure he will have, he was very thorough. He's fair come on, has the lad!'

Bruce smiled again, more warmly this time; Rayna Aherne had a great capacity for both empathy and forgiveness (Gibson obviously being a rare exception). Sure enough, the private investigator's number was in his list of contacts.

'Yes, you're right, it's there. Okay, I'll give him a call, if only to stop him from pestering you.'

They said their goodbyes, Bruce with considerable reluctance. He missed the perennially cheerful Rayna, not to mention the irrepressible Torquil Carnegie. He scrolled to Gibson's number, his thumb hovering over the call button. Should he?

'Mr Redpath! Good to hear from you, sir. How are you?'

The man's ingratiating tone immediately tempted Bruce to hang up, but he refrained.

'Well, I'm alive and I'm free, I suppose that's something.'

'Ah, 'No injustice is done to someone who wants that thing done', as they say!'

Bruce couldn't help himself; his patience snapped. 'And *who* says that, exactly, Cal?'

There was a pause.

'Well, I'm no' quite sure, Mister Redpath, it's just a quotation...'

'Nulla iniuria est, quae in volentum fiat.'

'Eh? What was that?'

'That's the original quotation. It's Latin. More usually quoted as 'Volenti non fit iniuria', if you want to be pedantic. Anyway, I gather you've been trying to reach me. What was it you wanted?'

The silence this time was considerably longer, to the extent that Bruce wondered if Gibson might have ended the call. Finally, the man spoke, his tone rather frosty.

'Yes, well, I'll come to the point. Miriam Bonnar would like to speak to you.'

That's a surprise, thought Bruce. 'Why?'

'Well, I don't *know* why, Mr Redpath, I suppose you'd have to ask her that.'

Bruce realised that he had offended Gibson and he gave a rather smug smile. Hell mend the man; and thank Heaven for all those dull periods spent in Mr Arbuthnott's latin class in Greenock Academy, learning obscure quotes from Romans such as Domitius Ulpianus...

'Hm. Well, give me her number and I'll have a think about it.'

'So can I tell her that you'll call her?'

'Tell her I might; as I said, I'll think about it.'

With a considerable lack of emotion, Bruce and Gibson said goodbye. As Bruce leaned back on the couch, the smug smile was still on his face. Hopefully Gibson would desist from 'quoting quotations' from now on. The smile faded as he considered whether he should call Miriam Bonnar. The woman was presumably looking for a story and he had an inbuilt mistrust if the press. Still, an afternoon of inactivity stretched before him; at least it would break the monotony!

He was bored; at least, that was his excuse. But he was also curious...he had added Miriam Bonnar's number to his contact list and, with a mug of coffee sitting before him, he pressed the call button. She answered on the second ring.

'Hello. Who is this, please?'

The voice had a distinct Edinburgh tone, deep and rather husky, giving Bruce the impression of a smoker.

'Ms Bonnar? This is Bruce Redpath.'

He heard a sharp intake of breath. 'Well, Mr Redpath, I must say this *is* a surprise! After speaking to Cal, I wasn't exactly expecting you to call me.'

'To be absolutely honest, neither was I.'

'So why did you?' she asked, her tone rather sarcastic. Bruce was asking himself the same question.

'I'm not sure. Curiosity, I suppose.'

'About what?'

'Well, for a start, about why you had Cal Gibson follow me.'

She didn't reply immediately.

'I take it he told you who I am?'

'Well, yes, he mentioned that I'd represented your husband in...'

'...in screwing me to the tune of about two hundred grand! How you could bring yourself to represent that rotten shit that I had the misfortune to be married to is quite beyond me. Did he happen to mention his offshore accounts?'

Bruce couldn't recall the exact details of 'Westcott vs. Westcott' but he had an impression of an overweight, overweening individual who reeked of cigars. He didn't think offshore accounts had been mentioned, however.

'Look, Ms Bonnar, I was just doing my job. Had I been representing you, I would have been equally diligent and I can only act on information given...'

'Whatever. Anyway, as the Proclaimers so famously said, 'It's over an' done wi', it's over an' done wi'...' Water under the bridge.'

Bruce let out a silent groan; another bloody quote! 'In which case, back to my question. Why was Gibson following me?'

Bonnar let out a long sigh. 'Oh, Christ, I don't really know. It was just a whim, a desire for revenge, I suppose. If it's any consolation, he had also been following my ex at one point.'

'At one point? So was I just the latest in a line of targets for you to wreak revenge upon?'

'No, as a matter of fact *he* died of a heart attack last year. Serves the bastard right, he was a fat pig who smoked too much. Had it coming...'

This was pointless, Bruce thought; and it certainly wasn't helping his demeanour.

'Look, Ms Bonnar—'

'Oh, for God's sake, call me Miriam.'

'Very well, Miriam, Gibson said you wanted to speak to me.'

'Yes, well, I'm not sure that you'll have much to say to me now.'

Bruce shook his head. 'Look, I'm assuming you're after an exclusive of some sort. Well, you're not going to get it—'

'Oh, grow up!. This isn't about the column.'

'Really! And you expect me to believe that?'

'That's up to you...'

Her voice lowered slightly, as if she was adopting a conspiratorial tone, Bruce had an image of her casting a furtive glance around to ensure no-one was watching her.

'Listen, by any chance have you heard of Detective Chief Superintendent Noone?'

Bruce was about to exclaim 'What, Paula?' but managed to stop himself in time.

'Em...I think the name's familiar.'

'Well, I can't say too much, but I'm led to believe that she shares my suspicions about this Civil Guard.'

This was news to Bruce. Paula Noone had been extremely reticent about discussing any aspect of the so-called retribution killings.

'And what makes you think that?'

'I really can't say.'

'From what you've written so far, it appears to me that you're very much in favour of their actions.'

She sighed again. 'I know. It's all part of the plan, you see.'

'The plan! Are you telling me that you actually don't *agree* with what they're doing—or what you're saying in your column, for that matter?'

'Of course not! How the hell could you think that I would possibly condone that—well, apart from the purposes of selling copy, that is! Look, I don't know how much you know about my column...'

'I've only read the parts concerning these killings.'

'Yes, well, I daresay you've gathered that I'm known as 'Edinburgh's resident conspiracy theorist?"

'Pretty much.'

She snorted. 'Huh. And do you honestly think that's the kind of journalism I want to be writing?'

'Isn't it?'

'No, of course it bloody isn't! But since you, Bruce Redpath, managed to financially cripple me all those years ago, a girl has to do something to pay the rent and, let's face it, I'm too old and too ugly to work the streets! Hence 'Bonnar's Byte'. It sells copy, it sells papers, it sells downloads. And I bloody hate it!'

There was venom in her tone and he didn't quite know how to respond. 'So what do you want from me? Simon Fox, my Counsel—well, he's actually one of my partners—advised me against telling the police any of this.'

'Yes, Cal told me as much. That's why I wondered if we could get the information that you have...well, 'in the back door', if you like. I could unofficially contact Paula Noone rather than you divulging the details to the officers who arrested you.'

'They didn't actually *arrest* me, Miriam, they just questioned me.'

'You were locked up for a night, weren't you?'

He shuddered; the memory was still raw. She continued, a warmer tone on her voice.

'Look, we've *got* to fight this, I know that—and you know that! We can't have these bloody vigilantes—whoever the hell they are—

taking the law into their own hands. I can get your information to Paula Noone unofficially—I don't even need to divulge my source.'

Her voice lowered even more, she sounded rather sultry, he thought. 'You want to bring these sadistic bastards, who are operating outside the law of the land, to justice, don't you Bruce? Well, I assure you, so do I...'

He leaned his head back against the cushions and let out a long sigh. The conversation with Miriam Bonnar had been exhausting, cathartic and confessional. More to the point, she believed him, which was more than any of his friends or family appeared to do. He rubbed his face, realising that he hadn't shaved. Had he done the right thing?

Yes, he thought that he had. Maybe now something would finally be done about the so-called Civil Guard, before any one else fell victim to their brutal methods.

He stood up and looked at his watch. Four-thirty, just time for a swift one before Coral and Dan arrived home with Amy.

He certainly deserved it.

Name, rank, number...

Name, rank, number...

He had been repeating the mantra since the drenching in ice-cold water that had brought him back to consciousness. At first he had thought that he was drowning but, very quickly, he had realised that this was not the case. Although he was wet and cold, he was definitely not underwater. Instead, he appeared to be suspended painfully by his arms.

And he was naked.

He shook his head, trying to bring his thoughts into focus. Where was he? What had happened? He couldn't remember.

What he *did* know was that his head was pounding and his arms were aching, the ropes that were tied around his wrists were digging deep into his chilled flesh as they suspended the weight of his muscular frame.

He was freezing.

He looked around, trying to get his bearings. Wherever he was, it looked old, near-derelict. Dirty, rough stone walls, a high ceiling with wooden cross-beams; presumably he was suspended from one of those. There were no windows and the dim light seemed to be provided by a few storm lanterns that had been placed on the floor. He guessed that he was in an old farm building of some sort.

Aware of movement behind him, he tried to turn his head. Suddenly he screamed as a blow struck him in the region of his kidneys, sending his body into a spasm of pain, wrenching his shoulder joints in their sockets. Behind him, someone was laughing. They began speaking, softly and with a heavy accent.

'Ha! That as just to show you how helpless you are. But do not worry, my friend, we are not going to beat you to death.'

Somehow, the words failed to reassure him.

Name, rank, number...

Name, rank, number...

His teeth chattered as he mumbled the mantra.

'What? What did you say?' the voice hissed, closer now.

He stopped mumbling, although his teeth continued to chatter. He could smell the other man's sour breath, its warmth like the caress of a lover on his shoulder as he spoke again. Best that he name his captor, his interrogator—or so he had been taught. So far, he had never had to put it into practice but it was worth a try; anything was worth a fucking try.

'Huh...nothing, eh?' Sour-breath laughed. 'That will change, I assure you. We will be using more... effective methods.'

Something was being trundled across the rough concrete floor. He attempted to turn but it was too painful. He also realised that there was something tied securely around his left leg and, looking down, he could see a thick, black cable running across the floor. Where it was attached to him, the insulation had been stripped away, revealing bright copper wire, twisted tightly around his ankle. His stomach started to churn.

Name, rank, number...

Name, rank, number...

Sour-breath spoke again.

'You see, I need you to give me some information, my friend. And you will, I can assure you. Nothing too difficult, a location, a name, maybe. We will see.'

Another two men came into his line of vision, pulling what he recognised as a small portable generator; he had used them in the army, although this one was painted a bright, cheerful yellow. They stopped a few feet away from him and lifted the end of the cable that was attached to his ankle. After a few moments of consideration, they attached it to the machine. Sour-breath, too, was now visible and he recognised the man; he had seen him before, earlier that day. Tall, well-built, with a shaved head, he was wearing thick, rubber-soled boots and had heavy-duty rubber gloves on his hands. His lips were bared in a cruel smile.

'So, the easy way or the hard way, the choice is yours.'

The other two men were turning a handle and, suddenly, the little generator roared into life, the smell of the exhaust reminding him of his first motor bike; comforting, nostalgic...

Sour-breath lifted a pole, to one end of which was tied a soaked sponge. From the other end, a second cable snaked back to the generator, now burbling happily while continuing to issue hazy blue exhaust fumes. The man approached, holding the pole in front of him.

Name, rank, number...

Name, rank, number...

'Now, where will we start...?'

Chapter 19

Thursday 4th December, morning.

Bruce awoke in a sweat; he had dreamt that he was back in a prison cell, calling out for his deceased wife, Dorothy. There had been a gun in his hand, he had killed someone...the sense of tragedy, of loss, was overwhelming.

He sat up suddenly, looking around in a panic. He realised that he was in Coral's spare bedroom, the comforting sounds of the morning routine filtering up from downstairs. His mouth was dry—had he really finished a whole bottle of malt in two days?

He realised that he had. He also realised that it was within the realms of possibility that he really did have a bit of a drink problem. He swore gently, swung his legs out of bed and headed to his personal en-suite—no expense had been spared on Coral's house.

Half an hour later he bade farewell to his son-in-law and to his adored granddaughter. As they headed to the car, Coral gave him a scrutinising look.

'Dad?'

'Yes, dear?'

'Were you drinking last night?'

He averted his eyes; could he lie to his daughter. 'Em...'

'Where did you get it? Dan says that none of his has been touched.'

'Em, Olivia and Torquil brought me a bottle...'

Coral stood up, glaring at her father. 'For God's sake, Dad, how much have you had—you're bloody reeking of the stuff!'

Bruce hung his head in shame. 'A bottle.'

There was an ominous silence.

'A whole bloody bottle? In two days? God almighty...'

She sat back down, tears welling up in her eyes.

'You know, Simon said he thought you had a drink problem but I refused to believe it. Dad, how could you, especially with Amy here?'

'I'm sorry, Coral, I'm so, so sorry.'

He dropped his head onto his arms and started to sob.

Coral finally departed for work and Bruce went straight back to bed. He immediately dropped into a deep, dreamless sleep, finally waking up feeling considerably more refreshed. He sat up once more, stretched and looked at his watch. He jumped up in alarm; it was past ten o'clock and Simon was coming at eleven!

Agni Krasniki viewed the image from the security camera at her front door with considerable suspicion. She had received a phone call earlier that day that had aroused her curiosity, but she was a woman who trusted no-one. She pressed the intercom button.

'You have come alone?'

The rather tinny reply was immediate. 'Of course, Ms Krasniki, as you requested. As you can see, I am by myself.'

His accent was heavy, almost too heavy. She frowned; she didn't know this man, yet he seemed to know exactly who she was and how to contact her. Should she take the chance?

'One minute.'

She returned to the lounge and crossed to the dummy radiator, unscrewing the valves and lowering the cover. She removed one of the handguns, checked that it was fully loaded then, ensuring that the safety catch was on, she pushed it into the waistband at the rear of her tight jeans. Returning to the entry system, she pressed the intercom.

'I will be right there. Stand ten feet away from the door before I open it.'

He was not what she had expected but he had an imposing presence. She had the impression that he was ex-military; he had a superb physique, narrow waist, broad-shouldered, muscular... she felt a vague tingling in her loins. Where Dzhokhar Meta had been a lecherous slob, a man whose power had its source in evil, this specimen emanated sheer, raw masculinity; it attracted her strongly but she knew she must tread carefully. Her hand resting on the butt of the pistol, she scrutinised him.

'Turn round. Take off your jacket.'

Without a word, the man obeyed her. She could see his biceps bulging beneath the black T-shirt; this was a proper man...with no weapon concealed. At least, not under his T-shirt, she thought, a faint smile on her lips.

'Very well, come in. Place your hands on your head and keep them there.'

Still carrying his jacket, he obeyed and walked past her. He had greeted her in her own tongue at first before lapsing back into his heavily accented English, but he had made no objection to her requests. A good start, she thought. She closed the door, her own hand still behind her back. Although he didn't appear to be carrying a weapon, you never knew...

'To the left—into the lounge. Keep your hands on your head.'

She closed the lounge door behind her and pointed to one of the armchairs.

'Sit. Keep your hands where I can see them.'

He sat down, placing his jacket on the arm of the chair before joining his hands across his flat stomach. He smiled up at her.

'Thank you, Ms Krasniki. I can assure you that I come in good faith and that I am not carrying any weapon.'

'We will see. How did you get my phone number?'

'I was given it by Mister Meta. I presume you know what has happened?'

She nodded. 'You worked for Meta?'

'Yes.'

'And how did you escape?'

'It was misty. When I saw that Mister Meta had been killed, I decided that there was no point in remaining.'

'So why have you contacted me?' asked Krasniki. She was suspicious; did this man have an agenda, was he simply looking for a new employer? She would take no chances. The man let out a long sigh; he looked weary, she thought, a look of sadness casting a fleeting shadow on his face.

'Ms Krasniki, I will be totally honest with you. One of those pigs who took Mister Meta also escaped and I followed him. He was careless and I managed to capture him. With a little persuasion, I managed to find out who is behind these killings and where they operate from. They killed Mister Meta; I believe they also killed your brother, Aleksander.'

Agni Krasniki felt a chill run down her spine. 'How do I know you are telling me the truth? And why did you not bring this man to me—I would very much have liked to interrogate him myself?'

The man shook his head. 'It was too big a risk, Ms Krasniki. As you know, there is an extensive manhunt ongoing. It was difficult enough to come here by myself without being seen; to bring a captive would have been foolish in the extreme.'

She glared across at the stranger, still unsure whether to believe him or not. 'Then you could have taken me to *him*—surely you could have kept him securely for a few hours. How do I know you are not telling me a pack of lies?'

In a single movement she reached behind her and pulled out her handgun, pointing it at the stranger's chest; he didn't flinch.

'You are quite correct, Ms Krasniki, and I would have been happy to...'

He favoured her with an evil smile. '...but, unfortunately, the captive did not survive my interrogation.'

She continued to point the gun at him.

'Can you prove that?'

'I have photographs on my phone.'

'Show me...slowly.'

He removed the phone from his jacket, scrolling with one thumb. She stood up, still pointing the gun, and looked at the gruesome images. Seemingly satisfied, she put on the safety-catch and returned the gun to her waistband. He returned the phone to his jacket as he spoke.

'Other than that, I have only my word.'

She frowned; although she tended to believe his story, she had a suspicion what this stranger wanted.

Money.

'And I suppose you want paid for this information?'

The man shook his head again. 'No. Like you, I want revenge. Dzhokhar Meta was like a father to me. I want to find the people responsible for his death but I cannot do this alone. I know that you, too, seek revenge. I do not want money, Ms Krasniki; what I *do* want is to work with someone to find the killers and, after that...'

He shrugged '...well, who knows what could be accomplished...'

He looked straight into her eyes and smiled. She felt that tingling again...and despite any issue with the language, she was certain that he had chosen 'work *with*' rather than 'work *for*.'

Agni Krasniki liked that.

Bruce was still towelling his hair dry when he heard the roar of a powerful car engine. A surreptitious glance from behind the bedroom curtain confirmed that Simon Fox's Porsche was sitting in the driveway, fifteen minutes early. Dropping the towel on the floor, he quickly pulled on some clothes, but his friend had rung the doorbell twice by the time Bruce descended the stairway and opened the door. As always, Simon was immaculately dressed in a crisp white shirt, perfectly-knotted dark tie and a beautifully tailored blue pinstripe suit.

'Simon, nice to see you, come—'

Without a word, Simon Fox had already barged into the hallway, a thunderous expression on his handsome features.

'...em, is everything okay?'

'You tell me, Bruce.'

Simon handed Bruce a sheet of A4 paper.

'Read it,' commanded the QC 'Hot off the fucking press.' Bruce obeyed, his heart sinking even as he scanned the opening line.

'Bonnar's Byte.

By

Miriam Bonnar'

'You heard it here first, folks...'

My dear readers, I am well-aware that there are those among you who refer to me as the 'Queen of the Conspiracy Theory'. I am thick-skinned, the taunts run off me like water off a duck's back.

I am equally certain that there are also those among you who have doubted my claims of the existence of a group that I have christened the 'Civil Guard'.

Well, I now have all the proof that I need—a recorded interview, no less, with a certain divorce attorney who claims that not only has he been interviewed by the 'Guard', but he has also actively been asked to join their ranks.

The only qualification, as far as I am aware, is that members of the 'Guard' must have suffered the loss of a friend or family member at the hands of a criminal. To be more specific, a criminal who has gone unpunished.

Hence the recent spate of killings, in the name of Justice.

But is this right, or wrong, I ask?

Now, dear readers, you will recall that I previously spoke of the murder of that particularly odious young man by the name of Darren Beagan. A convicted felon, Beagan had hovered on the fringes of the criminal fraternity for years.

He is, or was, a decidedly 'bad lot'.

As you will recall, Beagan was (allegedly, I must add) responsible for the death of the wife of the previously-mentioned divorce attorney, a crime for which he was never convicted. A crime which saw him walk away from a car fire, caused by his own drink-and-drug-induced reckless driving, a fire in which the woman burned to death, trapped and terrified.

Can you imagine what it must be like; to lose your beloved wife, the mother of your children, in those most dreadful of circumstances, then to watch the perpetrator of this heinous crime, the instrument of your worst nightmare, walk free? Although he was convicted of lesser charges, this particular example of the dregs of humanity exited the courtroom with a jeer and a gesture, leaving a family bereft of their matriarch.

What would you do, given the opportunity for revenge?

Now, I am not for one minute claiming that Beagan's death was part of an initiation ceremony. I have no evidence to support that. I cannot tell you, one way or another, if the Civil Guard have welcomed a new recruit to their ranks.

It will be up to Scotland's Finest to decide if Bruce Redpath is, indeed, an innocent party.

Or was Beagan's death really a 'rite of passage'?

Dear readers, you may ask yourself if this is pure conjecture on my part. The answer is a resounding 'no'. What I have told you is straight from the horse's mouth. A horse by the name of...

Watch this space...time will tell!

Bruce continued to stare at the page, his hands shaking. He couldn't believe it. Finally, he met Simon's cold, hard stare.

'What the fuck were you thinking? We *agreed* not to tell the police, I presumed that you would have the good sense to keep your story to yourself. But no, not only do you decide to tell a third party, but that third party just happens to be the worst source of malicious gossip and false news this side of the bloody Kremlin, from what I can gather. Why, in the name of God, did you tell her all this? *Why*, Bruce?'

He couldn't answer. Miriam Bonnar had sounded so kind, so sympathetic, so understanding...

What a bloody fool he had been!

'She...she...'

'She fucking what?'

'She believed me, Simon. She bloody *believed* me, when nobody else seemed to.'

'Oh, for fuck sake, that's pathetic, and you know it! I *never* said that I didn't believe you.'

'Well, you inferred that you didn't when you refused to allow me to tell the police.'

Simon Fox raised his voice. 'Yes, because I knew that *they* wouldn't believe you. I never once said that *I* didn't believe you.'

'Coral doesn't believe me either.'

'Look, the issue of who does or doesn't believe you is entirely irrelevant. You're now on record as having stated that you met with this so-called 'Civil Guard'. Not only that, but that they tried to recruit you!'

He shook his head in exasperation. 'It's only a matter of time before DCI-bloody-Mazzoni gets wind of this, not to mention what's-her-name...DCI Jarvis, she who's in charge up in town. God Almighty, you've brought a ton of shit down on your head, Bruce and, to be quite frank, I don't know if I can help you now.'

'But—'

'NO, Bruce, there's no 'but' any more. You've gone from having an alibi of sorts to having probable cause, at the very least. If they pay any credence to Bonnar's assertion that Beagan's death was some form of 'rite of passage', as she ever-so-succinctly puts it, then you're in very serious trouble. Especially if, as she claims, she has a recording of it. Has she?'

Bruce shook his head and let out a groan of dismay. 'I don't know, Simon, I just don't know. I'm so, so sorry...'

'So am I, Bruce, believe me.'

Finally, Simon Fox ran out of steam. 'Listen, any chance of a coffee—I left in a bit of a hurry, as you might imagine.'

It was nearly one o'clock before Simon departed. The coffee had calmed him somewhat and, by the time he left, he was making a concerted effort once more to boost Bruce's spirits. To no avail; once his partner—his defence counsel—had left, Bruce collapsed on the couch in a mood that was verging on suicidal. He felt even worse that he had during his night spent in the cells, if that were possible. He replayed the conversation with Miriam Bonnar over and over in his mind, each remembered word eliciting toe-curling embarrassment. He now realised that she hadn't the slightest intention of contacting Chief Superintendent Paula Noone; she had lied and he had fallen for it, hook, line and sinker. Miriam Bonnar had been sympathetic, understanding and in complete agreement with his personal feelings.

And she had well and truly got her revenge.

In an effort to distract himself, and in the absence of any further personal supplies of whisky, he switched on the lunchtime news; with a sense of dread, he watched as the female announcer looked at the camera and said 'Good afternoon.' Her expression was grim.

'The body of a man has been discovered near Bathgate in central Scotland. Police have not yet released the victim's name but it is understood that he died of gunshot wounds. It is thought that he may have been one of the suspects being sought by Police Scotland following the recent gang-related shootings that left three men dead and a police officer in hospital with serious gunshot wounds. One other suspect is still believed to be at large, with a widespread manhunt still ongoing. The public are reminded not to approach anyone...'

Bruce switched the television off and closed his eyes. He felt numb.

Five figures sat in the smoke-filled room; despite it being mid-afternoon, the curtains were drawn tight, the only illumination provided by two heavily shaded table-lamps.

Agni Krasniki sat in a large and comfortable easy-chair, leaning forwards with her elbows resting on her denim-clad knees, the ubiquitous Turkish cigarette in her hand. Her dark, curly hair was tied back in a severe ponytail. Across from her, on the couch, sat three swarthy, hard-faced men. She had known these men for years; they were her closest and most-trusted henchmen. In the remaining easy-chair sat the man who had brought her the information; the very reason for the assembly.

The three men seated on the couch gave him an occasional, suspicious glance. He had greeted them in their native tongue and, on the occasions that they had made a comment in their own language, he had responded in kind. However, for the most part he spoke in heavily accented English. He looked confident, aloof and unafraid, despite being the stranger in their midst. Agni Krasniki's reluctant admiration for this rugged, attractive man was growing, despite her caution. She took a deep draw on her cigarette before addressing the intimate assembly.

'So, we know what is to be done. Kill if necessary but I want the ringleader, if such a person there is, brought to me. If these people are responsible for the death of Aleks, then I will be the one to repay the debt, Is that clear?'

There was a mumble of assent, a nodding of heads.

'Good. We will set off when it gets dark.'

She addressed the three men on the couch. 'You will travel together in one vehicle...'

She nodded at the stranger. '...and you will come with me. That way I will be able to keep an eye on you.'

Chapter 20

Thursday 4th December, afternoon.

Paul Maguire was becoming desperate. Since he and his rather unwelcome lodger had heard the news of Dzhokhar Meta's death, David Doyle had lapsed into a foul, uncommunicative mood, spending most of his day slumped in Maguire's favourite armchair, with a beer or, preferably, a whisky clutched in one hand and a cigarette in the other. He barely spoke, mostly responding to Maguire's attempts at conversation with an undecipherable grunt.

Maguire had spent the last few days making a number of increasingly frustrating phone calls to all his underworld contacts, trying to glean even the slightest morsel of information in relation to the murders of Suzi Flint and the other victims. To no avail; hence his desperation. He could see the days turning to weeks, the weeks to months...

His own bleak reverie was broken by the ringing of one of his burner phones. He looked at the screen and answered the call.

'Hello.'

'Awright, Paul?'

'No, I'm fucking not all right, he's doing my fucking nut in.'

The caller let out a guttural laugh. 'Ha! Aye, Ah can imagine. Well, Ah might have somethin' for ye.'

Fifteen minutes later, Paul Maguire was sitting at his laptop, reading *Bonnar's Byte*. Not only that, following the transfer of a four-figure sum to his bank account, Higgins had forwarded Miriam Bonnar's home address. Maguire smiled and folded down the screen. Time for a chat with Davie.

Bruce was staring despondently out of the lounge window, across a rainswept River Clyde. It was a different view than the one from his own home, the river was narrower here and the elevated position

232

of Dan and Coral's house afforded a splendid view of Dumbarton Rock. He couldn't have cared less.

Coral would be home soon, followed by Dan and Amy. Normally he looked forward to the return of the happy little family group but, today, he dreaded their arrival, knowing that he'd have to explain his foolish actions. There wasn't even the prospect of a drink to look forward to—alcohol was now officially off limits, apparently.

He had tried to contact Miriam Bonnar, at the very least to give her a piece of his mind but, as he had expected, she had failed to respond. He had also phoned Cal Gibson but he, too, hadn't picked up. Again, he wasn't in the least surprised; Gibson would undoubtedly be having a good laugh at Bruce's expense as, no doubt, he had been in on the deception.

He leaned his head back and closed his eyes, jumping at the sudden, strident ringing of the phone. He looked at the screen in surprise.

Cal Gibson.

He stared at the phone for a few moments until it rang off. Gibson could go to hell. It rang again...shaking his head, he answered the call.

'What do you want, Gibson? I've had enough of your lies...'

'Mr Redpath, please, I need to talk to you.'

'Well, I needed to talk to you earlier, but you weren't answering, so I'm buggered if I should let you talk to me.'

'Please, Mr R, I *have* to speak to you, it's a matter of life and death.'

At least there were no quotations forthcoming.

'What is?'

There was a pause. 'I can't say over the phone.'

'What? Why the hell not?'

Gibson paused again. 'Em, well, you just never know who might be listening.'

'Oh, stop being so bloody melodramatic, Gibson, say whatever you have to.'

'No—look, can you come down to Langbank Station? Please, Mr Redpath, I wouldn't ask unless it was vitally important. Please?'

Bruce was about to ask why Gibson didn't just come up to the house when he remembered that the investigator didn't actually know where Coral lived. He decided that it was best to keep it that way. There was also an unfamiliar tone in Gibson's voice that hinted at trouble and the man had certainly aroused Bruce's curiosity. Anyway, maybe the walk down the hill would do him good. At least it would take his mind off his own predicament and might allow him to vent his spleen!

'Okay, fine, it'll take me about fifteen minutes. This had better be worth my while, Gibson.'

The rain was getting heavier as he walked under the railway bridge. He had had the foresight to rummage about in the coat-cupboard and borrow an old Berghaus jacket belonging to his son-in-law, as well as a hat and a pair of walking boots, which were a bit on the small side. He turned into the small dead-end road that ran up to Langbank station entrance, the flashing of headlights indicating Cal Gibson's black Range Rover. He walked across and opened the passenger door, then stepped into the warm, plush interior. It smelled strongly of aftershave. He looked at Gibson; the man was clearly worried—or scared.

'Well, I'm here, although after the way you and Miriam Bonnar behaved, I sincerely hope that I'm about to receive an apology.'

Gibson looked stricken. 'She's gone.'

'What? Who's gone?

'Miriam. She's gone and I think she's been abducted.'

Bruce opened his mouth in surprise, then shook his head.

'Oh, for God's sake, what's this all about? Is this some other bloody trick the two of you are trying to pull?'

Bruce reached for the door handle but Gibson put his hand firmly on his arm, shaking his head fervently. 'No, Mr R, honestly. She's not where she's meant to be.'

Bruce suddenly realised that Cal Gibson was on the verge of panic. This was no ruse, he concluded; he turned in his seat.

'Okay Cal, just try and calm down, will you...that's better...now, where was she meant to be, exactly?'

Gibson took a deep breath, although his hands were shaking as he squeezed Bruce's arm. 'Well, you know that nice wee hotel up in Blytheswood Square—just along from your office?'

Bruce nodded. 'Yes, of course I do.'

'Well, I was supposed to be meeting Miriam there at four o'clock, but she didn't arrive. I checked at reception...'

Bruce looked at the clock on the dashboard. It showed just after five-fifteen. He frowned. 'But wait—that's only just over an hour ago and you've already driven down here! For God's sake, she's probably just been held up in traffic or something.'

Gibson was shaking his head again. 'No, Mr Redpath, she's not. You see, I saw her car and I parked just along from it; I thought she must have got there early, but she hadn't checked in.'

'Well, she's probably just gone shopping or something.'

Gibson shook his head furiously.

'No, no, you see...'

The man was almost frantic now. 'I found her suitcase—it had been dropped over the railings into that wee park bit in the middle.'

Bruce's eyes widened. 'Her suitcase? You're *sure* it was hers?'

'Yes, absolutely. I recognised it right away.'

Bruce frowned. 'Wait, how did you...?'

Gibson gave a rather maniacal half-smile. 'You see, Mr R, Miriam and I...we're...well, we're close.'

The penny dropped.

'What? You mean you and Miriam Bonnar...you're an item?'

Gibson nodded.

'It's a lonely life doing what I do, Mr Redpath. Miriam was lonely too and, well, we just kind of got together, you know. We're very fond of each other, she comes through and stays in the hotel every few weeks, we...'

Tears were welling up in his eyes now; Bruce felt vaguely sympathetic.

Vaguely.

'Well, I understand your concern but who on earth would abduct her? I mean...wait, has this something to do with that rubbish she printed about me?'

'I think so. She was upset—she called me on the way through, said she thought she was being followed. She can be a bit paranoid at times so I told her not to worry. I tried to get there earlier but I got delayed then, when I arrived, her car...well, like I told you.'

Bruce stared at the rain streaming down the window. Was this just another fabrication?

'Have you called the police?'

Gibson shook his head once more. 'Em, I'm not really in a position...the police and I don't really get along, if you know what I mean...that's why I wanted to see you, Mr R. You've got a contact, haven't you? Your friend—what's his name?'

'Rob? For God's sake, I can't call him, not after what's happened.'

'Please, Mr R, just a quick call—look, you make the call and I'll talk to him. We've got to do something.'

'But how would you even know where she's been taken—always assuming she *has* been taken? How can the police possibly hope to find her?'

Gibson sighed. 'She wears a tracking device when she goes out.'

'What? You're bloody joking! God, the woman *is* paranoid!'

'Aye, and rightly so. Miriam has a lot of enemies. I mean, look what's happened today!'

Bruce wasn't surprised; after all, he counted himself among them! Anyway, the man had a point.

'Okay, let's assume she *has* been taken, won't they find the tracking device?'

Gibson gave a sly smile and Bruce shook his head. 'Oh God! So where does she wear it, Cal?'

'Best not to ask, Mr R, best not to ask...'

After a few more minutes of Cal Gibson's pleading and cajoling, Bruce finally relented and agreed to call his friend, DCI Rob Connor, although he didn't hold out much hope. Still, it would be nice just to hear his Rob's voice for a few minutes. Maybe he'd even get a quick word with Mel; if ever he needed her arms around him, comforting him, it was now. Fortunately, Rob Connor's number was among those entered on his contacts list by Torquil Carnegie. He dialled and the policeman answered on the fourth ring; he sounded weary, Bruce thought.

'DCI Connor. Who's this?'

Bruce took a deep breath. 'Rob, it's Bruce...'

'WHAT!'

Rob lowered his voice suddenly. 'Jesus Christ, Bruce, you can't be phoning me, not now...for fuck sake...'

'Rob, it won't take a minute, it's really important...'

'*No*,' hissed Rob. 'I can't speak to you, I'm really sorry, don't call me again.'

The line went dead. Gibson was looking at Bruce, an expression of horror on his face. Bruce shook his head.

'Sorry, as you probably gathered, he won't talk to me. He sounded in a hell of a state. I suppose it just wouldn't be right when I'm still a suspect...here, what are you doing? STOP!—stop the car right now!'

Cal Gibson had driven off, pulling quickly onto the old A8 that ran parallel to the main Greenock-Glasgow dual carriageway.

'We need to go and rescue her, Mr Redpath. I'm sorry, but I can't just abandon her.'

'NO, Gibson, stop the car—let me out, you fucking idiot!'

Gibson gunned the accelerator as he pulled on to the main road. He reached forward and switched on a little tablet that was clipped to the dashboard. A map of the area appeared and Gibson touched the screen, zooming out to a wider spread. A tiny flashing light appeared.

'There—got her! Right, it looks as if they're heading out towards the south side of Glasgow.'

Bruce gave a snort of disgust, lifted his phone and accessed his contacts.

'That's it, I've had enough of this nonsense, you're off your bloody head. I'm going to call...'

Who was he going to call? He hadn't a clue. As he stared at the screen, his phone rang, the display showing that it was Coral. He answered.

'Coral, thank goodness...'

She sounded distraught. 'Dad? Where in God's name are you? You need to come home. NOW, Dad...'

'Coral, what the hell's wrong? Listen, I need you to—'

He heard voices in the background. Coral seemed to be objecting to something, then a familiar voice rang in his ear, sending his stomach plummeting down to his too-tight boots.

'Mr Redpath. This is DCI Mazzoni. I need you to come back to your daughter's house right away. Do you understand, Mr Redpath? Wherever you are, I need you to come home. Now!'

They had reached the M8 and Bruce stared out of the windscreen at the dark ribbon of motorway stretching ahead of them. Bruce ended the call; his heart was pounding; what the hell was Mazzoni wanting him for this time? They sat in silence for a few minutes, then his phone rang again. His heart started to race and he looked down at it in dismay, but this time it was Simon Fox. Breathing a sigh of relief, he lifted the handset to his ear.

'Simon, thank God.'

'Bruce, where the fuck are you?'

'Em, we're just...'

He paused; he had a feeling that it might be best not to divulge his location. 'What's wrong? I've just had DCI—'

'Yes, so have I. She's turned up at your daughter's house with a warrant for your arrest for the murder of Darren Beagan.'

Bruce froze.

'Bruce, did you hear me? Wherever the hell you are, you need to turn round and go home, right now. Otherwise you'll be in even bigger trouble. Do you hear me?'

'But...but, how...?'

'They've managed to dig up several pieces of CCTV footage from various security cameras that allegedly show you walking from the scene of the crime to your house. They've hinted that there's additional evidence although they're not telling me what it is. However, they've obviously got enough for a warrant. I'm sorry—'

Bruce swiped the screen and ended the call. Gibson looked at him, a wry smile on his thin lips. 'Looks like I've got myself a fugitive, Mr Redpath. So what's it to be—turn back and go to jail or come with me and see if we can sort this whole bloody mess out?'

Bruce switched off his phone; they could all go to hell! Suddenly, he started to laugh. A slightly unnatural laugh, verging on the hysterical, but a laugh nonetheless. Gibson glanced at him with a look of alarm.

'You all right, Mr R?'

The tears were now streaming down Bruce's face. 'Yes; yes, actually I think I am. But the irony of it all—after all these fucking years of upholding my precious 'law', of adhering to 'due process' I suddenly find myself charged with a murder I didn't commit and on the run from the bloody police!'

The laughing stopped and he shook his head, a smile still on his face. 'You know, Gibson, sometimes the law really *is* a ass!'

Chapter 21

Thursday 4th December, evening.

'Okay, we are approaching the location now—it should be just around this bend. I suggest we do not stop, or even slow down. I do not know if there are cameras at the gate.'

Agni Krasniki glanced at the man seated beside her as she gently eased the powerful black Mitsubishi pick-up round the long, right-hand bend. The road was quiet and the rain had eased considerably, the moon now making a fitful appearance between the banks of dark clouds that still scudded across the sky. The road straightened and, in the sweep of the pick-up's bright headlights, they could see a small lodge on the right-hand side of the road.

'There!' said the man, pointing.

They passed the entrance; curved, whitewashed walls led to two tall stone pillars, each of which supported an ornate cast-iron gate. These were currently standing open, guarded only by the cosy-looking little lodge house, a wisp of smoke emanating from its tall, gothic chimney; there was a smell of woodsmoke in the air. A light showed in one of the rooms and, above the purr of the engine, they could hear a dog barking. As they passed, slowing almost imperceptibly, they both turned their heads, taking in as much information as they could. One of the pillars bore a neat sign, proclaiming the entrance to Glenbreakerie Estate, while the notice on the opposite pillar merely stated 'Private Property'.

'Hm,' grunted Krasniki. 'I do not think we should enter by the main gate.'

'No,' replied her companion, raising his head to look at her. 'But, according to this map, if we drive for about half a mile, there is another road that runs around the perimeter of the estate. A short way along there is an old farm track leading to the rear of the house; I think that will be the best way.'

A few minutes later, Krasniki indicated and turned right on to the narrow B road. Another few minutes and her companion said, 'Stop; look, there, the track is inside that gate.'

She braked violently, the vehicle driving behind her screeching to a halt and narrowly avoiding hitting the back of the pick-up. She glanced in the mirror, uttering an oath in her own language. The man beside her grinned and gave a response; Agni Krasniki smiled in the darkness.

The man jumped out and, after unwinding the wire that was securing the gate, he pulled it open. Agni Krasniki eased the pick-up inside and drove through the entrance, the vehicle behind following her. He closed the gate behind them and clambered back in to the warmth of the pick-up, but she turned and looked at him, a frown on her face.

'What the fuck are you doing?'

'What do you mean?'

'We may have to leave quickly; why have you shut the fucking gate?'

He swore inwardly; of course, he should have left it open.

'Of course, Ms Krasniki, you are right, I am sorry. I will open it.' As he got back out, she called after him

'And you can drop the 'Ms Krasniki'. You may call me Agni.'

He smiled to himself as he pulled the gate back open.

The track was rutted and uneven and they bumped their way slowly uphill for a few minutes until they crested the rise, then she stopped and switched off the engine. The vehicle behind, now travelling at a slightly safer distance, did the same. They sat in silence for a moment, surveying the scene.

To their right, partly hidden by a copse of trees, lay some old farm outbuildings, in a rather dilapidated state. There was an ancient, corrugated-roofed barn, one of whose walls had partially collapsed, leaving bricks strewn across the ground. The surrounding land was neglected, the grass long and studded with unkempt bushes and tussocks of straggly foliage. It looked as if it hadn't been cultivated for many years.

Ahead of them, at the bottom of the small hill, sat an imposing edifice, built in traditional Scots Baronial style and complete with an imposing corner turret.

Glenbreakerie House.

To the right of the house lay what looked like a stable block, to the rear, at the foot of the slope, was a small walled garden, with stone-built outhouses attached. There was no perimeter wall, no security fence. Agni Krasniki furrowed her brows.

'You are certain that this is the place?'

'Yes. It is exactly as he told me.'

'And you are sure he wasn't lying? It seems...well, very vulnerable, unprotected.'

The man smiled, his white teeth gleaming in the glow of the dashboard lights. It was a cruel smile, she thought.

'Yes. I am sure. Absolutely sure—trust me.'

Krasniki also smiled. She *was* beginning to trust this man, albeit only very slightly; time would tell. However, she lowered her right hand slowly and gently towards the pocket in the door, placing her palm around her handgun. Best to be safe...

'Good. Right, it is time.'

She opened the door, as did the man, and they exited.

'Agni?'

'Yes?'

'I do not have a weapon.'

She grinned at him. 'Then you will just have to improvise, my friend, I am sure that you will manage.'

Trust had to be fully earned, after all.

They were ready; the three men from the other vehicle had removed their weapons from the false base of their vehicle's luggage compartment, and they had donned their ski-masks, as had Agni and her companion. They assembled just in front of the pick-up.

'Right, we know the plan but let us go through it once more time.'

She placed a hand on her companion's shoulder; he wondered if it was a gesture of affection.

'We will go round to the front...'

Her companion watched as one of the tussocks started to rise, almost imperceptibly. Then another, another...a voice called out, commanding, incisive...

'Drop your weapons, you are surrounded. Put your hands on the vehicles. NOW!'

They *were* surrounded. Four figures, adorned in full military camouflage, were pointing an assortment of weapons in their direction. Agni Krasniki raised her handgun very slowly, but the voice called out again.

'Drop the weapon, Krasniki. I won't fucking hesitate.'

With a snort of disgust, she dropped the handgun on to the grass at her feet and placed her hands on the bonnet of the pick-up. The three men did the same but, to her surprise, her companion stepped slowly away.

What the fuck was he doing? Was the idiot trying to impress her? What could he possibly hope to accomplish against...

Her erstwhile companion removed his balaclava; the man who had spoken the command smiled at him, his rifle still raised.

'You okay?'

'Aye, just aboot.'

'Heard you had a bit of a shocking time.'

The man grinned. 'Don't fuckin' start—just as bloody well your lot turned up when you did, another few minutes o' that an' I'd have sold ma fuckin' granny, eh.'

Agni Krasniki spun round. 'You fucking bastard. I will rip your fucking throat out, you piece of shit!'

The man with the gun shouted. 'Shut your mouth, bitch, or I'll fucking shut it for you.'

As he spoke, one of the other three captives had reached into the front of his jeans, pulling something out. In an instant, Agni Krasniki's former travelling companion had grabbed the rifle from his friend. As the man turned, raising a small handgun, the rifle fired, hitting the captive in the neck. He collapsed, his death-cry gurgling out of his shattered throat as a spray of blood splattered across his companions and the vehicle behind him.

'Fuck sake—nice shot, sunshine!'

'Aye, well, got tae keep my hand in. Right, let's get this bunch o' fuckers down the hill.'

He handed the rifle back to his friend then walked across to the still-mumbling Krasniki. He bent down to retrieve her gun then, as he stood up, he placed his hand on her leg, running it up her denim-clad thigh and squeezing her buttock. She squirmed at his touch but he groped her more firmly as he bent forward and hissed in her ear.

'Nice arse, Agni! Shame we never got together, might have been fun...still, you never know what'll happen later.'

As he stood up and removed his hand, she turned quickly and slapped him hard across the face. Laughing, he grabbed her wrist savagely before she could inflict any further damage. She brought her face close to his; he could smell cigarettes from her breath as she hissed

'In your fucking dreams, you prick. You will live to regret this.'

He let go of her wrist then turned and walked away as the other man commanded. 'Right, let's get that body up in the old barn for now, then it's time for you bunch of bastards to face the music.'

Bruce's somewhat maniacal euphoria had dissipated as Cal Gibson continued to follow the little dot on the tracker screen. They had been delayed for some time in a traffic jam, caused by temporary roadworks, but the dot had now been static for about fifteen minutes. Whoever they were following appeared to have reached their destination. Gibson had spent most of the journey mumbling to himself and, from the few words that Bruce could decipher, he was frantic about Miriam Bonnar's fate. Bruce had remained silent; there was little he could say that would comfort the man and he was now wondering just what the hell Gibson planned to do once they reached the location of the little red dot. He was tempted to turn his phone back on but had decided against it; after all, it would only hasten his own arrest.

They had passed over the River Clyde and were heading towards the Glasgow borough of Rutherglen. Suddenly, Gibson pulled in at the side of the road.

'Right, Mr R, we're nearly there, it's just through this next set of lights.'

'Hm. What do you intend to do once we get there?'

Gibson shook his head. 'Not sure; we'll just have to wing it.'

'Wing it! For God's sake, man, you have no idea how many people there are and, for all you know, they might well be armed! We can't exactly just walk in and demand Miriam's return.'

Gibson winced at the mention of her name; he indicated and pulled the car back on to the carriageway.

'We'll see...'

They stopped briefly at the traffic lights then drove on for a few hundred yards, Gibson slowing the Range Rover, scanning the side of the road. They approached what looked like a disused garage, behind which a row of lock-ups ran at right-angles along a litter-strewn lane. There were no street lights but Bruce could see the looming bulk of a derelict warehouse at the end of the lane; the whole area appeared deserted. Gibson pulled in to the dilapidated forecourt, stopped the car and let out a sigh.

'Thank fuck, there's no cars about. She must be in one of those garages.'

Bruce looked about; Gibson was correct, the place was deserted. With a strong feeling of unease, he opened the door and stepped out. Gibson was carrying the small tablet as they walked along the rutted lane, scanning the derelict-looking garages. The doors to most of them were caved in but, at the end of the row, one of them was closed and locked. Gibson trotted over and banged on it.

'Miriam, Miriam, are you in there?'

They could hear a moaning sound from within.

'Jesus,' muttered Gibson. He crashed his shoulder against the half-rotten wood.

'I'm coming, babe, it's okay, it's Cal.'

He turned to Bruce. 'For God's sake, Mr R, give me a hand.'

Bruce joined in and, with a bit of effort, the lock finally gave way and the door crashed inwards. The interior was pitch black but Gibson took out his phone, switching on the torch. Bruce blinked for a moment then let out a gasp.

At the back of the garage, a heavy woman was tied by her hands and feet to an old office chair. She was wearing dark-coloured trousers but her top half was naked, her large, pendulous breasts showing numerous angry red marks. She was gagged with what looked like the sleeve of her blouse and the expression in her eyes was one of both pain and fear. Gibson ran over.

'Fuck, Miriam, are you okay? Oh, dear God, what have they done?'

He loosened the gag and she started to moan.

'Cal, Cal, I thought they were going to kill me.'

As Bruce approached, he could feel the nausea rise in his throat as the extent of Miriam Bonnar's ghastly injuries became more apparent.

'He used a lighter, Cal, one of those old fashioned petrol ones.'

'A Zippo,' Gibson hissed angrily. 'The fucking bastard. Don't worry, Miriam, I've got you, you're going to be okay...'

He looked round at Bruce. 'We need to phone an ambulance, Mr R.'

Bruce pulled out his phone and stared at it, dreading what he might see if he switched it on. Gibson saw his expression and handed Bruce his own phone. Miriam Bonnar screwed up her eyes as the torch shone in her face and Bruce could see that her lips were swollen and her cheek was starting to bruise; he felt the bile rise even further and he turned away as Gibson spoke.

'I'll untie Miriam, you call the...what, Miriam, what is it?'

Miriam Bonnar was mumbling something; with considerable effort, she raised her voice a little.

'I told them, Cal, they know where it is.'

'Shit!'

Bruce turned and looked back over at them. 'Know where *what* is, Gibson? What do they know, whoever the hell *they* are?'

Cal Gibson averted his eyes. 'They know where the Civil Guard are based.'

Bruce could feel his hackles rise and Gibson obviously sensed it. He stood up as Bruce responded.

'And just how the fuck do they know that?'

Gibson moved behind Miriam Bonnar's chair as the terrified woman stared up at him with puffy, tear-filled eyes. His voice was hoarse as he spoke. 'Em, the thing is Mr R, you see...actually, I followed you that night; I know where they took you.'

The gloomy interior of the garage began to spin; Bruce was using every ounce of self-control that he possessed to stop himself from grabbing Gibson and wringing the man's neck. He had known all along—all of Bruce's trauma, his grief, his imprisonment, could have been averted if Cal Gibson had been open and honest in the first place. He leaned on the oil-stained workbench beside him, worried that he might actually collapse. His hand landed on something cold and hard and he looked down; it was a large, rusty spanner. Almost in a daze, he picked it up, regarding it as if he had never set eyes upon such a tool.

'Mr Redpath, please, you've got to understand...'

Bruce took a step towards Gibson. 'Understand what, you lying, conniving little fuckwit? That I was thrown in prison, that I've been charged with murder, all because you didn't tell the fucking truth?'

'I *did*, Mr Redpath; well, just not all of it. And I *would* have told the rest if it had gone to court...Mr Redpath, please...'

Bruce had raised the spanner threateningly. Miriam Bonnar looked up at him with her puffy eyes, her speech slurred as she spoke.

'Bruce, please, it was all my fault. I told Cal not to reveal the whole story, I wanted an exclusive...I wanted revenge...please. Don't blame him. It was all me. I'm so sorry...'

She started to cry; he looked down at the pathetic, sobbing woman, trying not to look at her defiled body. His temper subsided as quickly as it had risen and he placed the spanner back on the workbench. He shook his head, mumbling half to himself..

'She needs medical attention; we need to get her to a hospital.'

Gibson remained silent, staring at the woman as if in a trance. Bruce grabbed the man by his shoulders and shook him; he was sorely tempted to raise his hands and strangle the detective.

'Gibson—for God's sake, we need to help her.'

'No!'

Bruce and Cal Gibson turned as one to stare at Miriam Bonnar. Despite her injuries, her voice was emphatic. Bruce tried to object.

'Miriam, you need—'

'I said no!'

Gibson finally came to his senses. 'But Miriam, love, you're hurt.'

'I don't bloody care, Cal. Just phone an ambulance, but get after these bastards, find out who the hell they are. I'll survive'

Bruce could see a look of cold fury spread across Gibson's face as he gently stroked Miriam Bonnar's thick hair. The woman looked as of she was on the verge of passing out; Bruce knew how she felt, albeit for different reasons.

'Are you sure, love?' asked Gibson.

With a great effort of will, Miriam managed a weak smile.

'I'm sure. Now just bloody go, before you lose them.'

Gibson straightened up and looked at Bruce. 'We can phone an ambulance on the way.'

'On the way where?'

'Look, Mr R, there's no way we're letting those bastards get away with this, we're going after them.'

'We?' He shook his head. 'No, I've had enough, I'm done. I'm not going anywhere.'

Gibson regarded him shrewdly as Miriam Bonnar finally closed her eyes, her head slumping forward.

'So are you telling me you're not curious? You just want to stay here and get lifted for a crime you didn't commit?'

He took a hesitant step from behind Miriam Bonnar's chair and approached Bruce, his voice low, his tone coaxing, enticing. 'You *really* don't want to know who took you, where they took you? You don't want to go to the place that 'the very stones prate of my whereabouts'?'

Bruce let out a groan of despair; he would go, even if it was only to put a stop to Gibson's incessant and infuriating quotations.

Chapter 22

Thursday 4th December, evening.

'So are you planning to tell me exactly where we *are* we going?'

Bruce had barely spoken a word to Cal Gibson since they had left Miriam Bonnar, lying on the floor of the lockup, semi-conscious and wrapped in a blanket that Gibson had taken from his Range Rover. Gibson had found her jacket discarded in a corner, her mobile phone fortunately still in the inside pocket and, just before they left Rutherglen, he had used it to call the emergency services to summon an ambulance. To Bruce's relief, Bonnar's condition seemed to be reasonably stable, although he knew that the emotional scars would, undoubtedly, take a lot longer to heal. Gibson turned and looked at him, obviously lost in his own thoughts.

'Sorry, Mr R, what was that?'

'I asked where we were going.'

'Oh aye, right; well, it's down the A73, past Lanark. Quite near Biggar...'

The inevitable shutters started to close in Bruce's mind, but he forced them back up, remembering a happy Easter break spent with his wife, Dorothy, and his two daughters, exploring the South Lanarkshire countryside. They had stayed in a nice bed and breakfast in the little market town of Biggar; it had been a happy time and the thought of it cheered him somehow. He briefly wondered why he had suppressed all these joyous memories but Gibson was still speaking.

'...called Glenbreakerie House. Fancy big place, turrets and everything.'

'Do you know who owns it?'

Gibson shook his head. 'Nope, not a clue. I tried to find out but it's one of these places that seems to be held in trust, or something. Very hard to get to the bottom of it. I dare say we'll find out tonight, though.'

This was what had been worrying Bruce since they had joined the M74, the main artery to the North of England. Given the scant information they held about the occupants of Glenbreakerie house, plus the fact that an apparently violent gang appeared to also be en route, Bruce was at a loss to think what they would be able to accomplish. He decided to voice his concern.

'Look, would we not be better to involve the police? I mean, what the hell are we going to be able to do?'

'Knock yourself out, Mr R. It's your call.'

It was, but there were implications. Suddenly, an idea flashed through his mind.

'Actually, I *do* know someone...'

Gibson shot him a glance.

'Aye, and look where that got us last time!'

'No, there's someone else that might be able to help.'

'Might' being the operative word, he thought.

He pulled out his phone and, without thinking, switched it on. When it finally booted up, the list of missed calls and texts seemed endless. Ignoring them, he accessed his contacts.

'Shit! Shit, shit, shit! It's not there...'

And why would it be? He had never mentioned Finlay Whyte to Torquil, or to anyone else at the office, for that matter. He racked his brains but he just couldn't recall Finlay's number; but he knew someone who could give it to him.

'Gibson, I need you to call someone for me.'

Gibson favoured him with another sly glance. 'Can't you call them yourself?'

Bruce shook his head; there was no way Mel Connor would speak to him, she would have been well warned off by Rob.

'No, it'll need to be you. I need you to phone Mel Connor and ask for Finlay Whyte's mobile.'

'Who's he, when he's at home?'

'He has a contact in the police through in Edinburgh. He might be able to get a message to her.'

But, as he said it, he realised that it was highly unlikely; presumably Finlay Whyte would, by now, know of the accusations against him. Still, it was worth a try...anything was worth a try.

Gibson considered this for a minute then, pulling his mobile from his jacket pocket, he handed it to Bruce.

'Right, put it on hands-free and make the call.'

It seemed to ring for an eternity but, eventually, Mel's voice answered. Bruce felt a lump rise in his throat.

'Hello, who's calling?'

'Is that Mel Connor?' said Gibson.

'I asked first, if you don't mind. Who's calling?'

Bruce nodded and mouthed 'It's her.'

'Mrs Connor, I'm a friend of Bruce's—'

'WHAT! Oh my God, is he okay?'

'He's as well as can be expected, but we're in...well, a bit of fix. Look he's asked you to give me the phone number for a chap called Finlay Whyte.'

There was a pause. 'I'm not sure...what do you want Fin's number for?'

'Bruce says we need it...'

'And why can't he ask me himself?'

Gibson turned to Bruce; he couldn't help himself.

'Mel, it's me, it's Bruce. Listen, I'm okay but I need Finlay's number, it's really urgent...Mel, Mel, are you all right?'

At the sound of Bruce's voice, Mel had started to cry but, between sobs, she managed to speak. 'Oh Bruce, what the hell's going on? Rob says they've issued a warrant...and that you're on the run...'

'Mel, please listen to me—I didn't kill Beagan, I swear...'

'Well, of *course* you bloody didn't, I know that...'

Suddenly, Rob Connor's voice sounded in the background.

'Mel, who's that on the phone?'

Mel replied instantly. 'Oh, just one of the girls.'

'Are you okay, love? Has something happened?'

Her voice lowered. 'I'll text it to this number. Bruce, for God's sake, please just come home, *please*!'

'I will, Mel. Got stuff to do first though.'

Another pause. 'Take care of yourself, Bruce Redpath. I love you, you stupid bugger.'

She was gone before he could reply. Thirty seconds later the phone pinged as Finlay Whyte's number arrived.

'Hello, who's this please?'

Again, the sound of Finlay's voice caused Bruce's emotions to almost spiral out of control, but he managed to calm himself.

'Fin, it's Bruce.'

'Bruce! Good God, I wasn't exactly expecting to hear from you, you old renegade.'

Although this brought a smile to Bruce's face, he felt his own tears welling up. He had been prepared for Finlay Whyte to hang up on him but the pathologist's light-hearted tone immediately lifted his spirits.

'Listen, I need to run something past you. I don't have much time so, please, just bear with me, I'll try and keep it as brief as possible.'

Despite his assurance, his narrative took well over five minutes; when Bruce finally stopped speaking, there was a long silence. Fin let his breath out slowly then spoke.

'Wow! Okay, fair enough, I'll call Paula and pass this on. It's one hell of a story, mind you, but I'll plead your case as best I can and hopefully she'll buy it. Will I get her to call you?'

'No, the phone'll be off; just tell her what I've told you. It's the truth, Fin, every word. Oh, and I wouldn't be surprised if there are firearms involved, might be worth telling her that too—just in case.'

'Dear God—right, will do. Listen, will this Bonnar woman be okay, do you think?'

'I hope so. She wasn't in great shape but the ambulance should have got to her by now. She'll survive, although I don't doubt that there'll be emotional scars.'

He cast a glance sideways at Cal Gibson, who appeared to be chewing the inside of his cheeks; it didn't bode well for what lay ahead. Fin was speaking again.

'So where are you just now?'

He didn't reply.

'Bruce?'

'Em, I can't really say...listen, thanks, Fin, I really owe you...'

Finlay Whyte chuckled. 'You already owe me, and I'll hold you to both. Listen, let me get off now and call Paula Noone; by the sounds of it, the sooner the better!'

'Absolutely. I really don't know how to thank you...not least for believing me.'

Finlay laughed. 'I'm sure we'll think of something! You're one of the most honest men I've met, Bruce Redpath, of course I bloody believe you, let's just hope I can convince Paula. Listen, you take good care of yourself, my friend, and for God's sake don't be doing anything bloody stupid...'

A bit too late for that, Bruce mused.

'Can ye no' go any fuckin' faster?'

Paul Maguire bit back a sarcastic response. David Doyle's mood was what could best be described as volatile and the man had already had a rant when the BMW had required refuelling.

'Last thing we want's a ticket, Davie. Anyway, if the cops *did* pull us over, a ticket might be the least of our worries.'

Doyle seemed to accept this wisdom, given the contents of the boot. A speeding ticket *was* certainly the least of Paul Maguire's concerns.

He had never been a violent man; his physical attributes were meagre and, on the one occasion that his father had urged him to stand up to the school bullies, he had ended up in hospital with a fractured femur, a broken nose and missing two teeth. He was well aware of David Doyle's reputation and, if he was being totally honest with himself, he had enjoyed the protection, not to mention the remuneration. it had afforded him over the years. By implication, he had been pretty much untouchable, at least in a physical sense. But the brutal treatment of Miriam Bonnar had left him sick to his stomach; he could still hear her screams ringing in his ears and he dreaded to think of the images that would undoubtedly materialise and haunt him in the depths of the night. But what was worrying him more was how the course of events over the next few hours would run. Would he be expected to participate? Until they had set out, he had thought of himself merely as the driver but, along with Doyle and the three thugs seated in the back of his car, it seemed that he was now considered to be a member of Doyle's 'assault team.' The boot of the car contained baseball bats and three sawn-off shotguns but Paul Maguire had never fired a gun in anger and he certainly didn't want that to change tonight.

'So, Paul, ye up for this, eh?'

It was as if Doyle had read his mind. He reached a decision.

'Might be best if I stayed with the car, just in case we need to get away quickly. I'll leave the heavy stuff to you.'

'Like fuck ye will. Ye're in it now, whether ye like it or no'. There's only the five o' us, Ah'm countin' on you so dinn'ae let me doon.'

Paul Maguire felt that there had been an implied 'or else' at the end of Doyle's statement. He nodded.

'I won't, Davie, don't worry.'

Just leave the fucking worrying to me, he thought.

Bruce woke with a start; he hadn't meant to doze off but the emotional stress had taken its toll. They appeared to be on a narrow back road twisting through the moonlit countryside.

'Where are we, Cal? This isn't the man road.'

'Of course it's not, Mr R. We can't exactly just turn up at the front gate, can we? I found this when I...'

Bruce knew what Gibson had been about to say and briefly felt his hackles rise.

'...em, last time I was here. This road runs along the back of the estate and there's an old farm-track that'll take us up behind the big house.'

Bruce sighed; he was exhausted, thirsty and hungry and he also needed to relieve himself; he had the feeling it was going to be a very long night. He lapsed back into silence but, after a few more minutes, Gibson spoke again. 'Right, this is it, there's the gate... fuck!'

'What? What's wrong?'

'It's open, that's what's wrong. It was shut the last time.'

Gibson stopped the car.

'I'll need to get out and have a wee look.'

'A wee look? A 'look' where? You can see there's nothing there. Anyway, it's just an old gate to a farm track.'

'Might look like that to you, Mr R, but this is no ordinary farm track, I can assure you. There's sensors on the gate to alert the house if anyone unexpectedly tries to come in this way.'

Bruce experienced a twinge of near-panic. 'So do they have security cameras and such like as well?'

Gibson gave him a disparaging look. 'Of course they do. Cameras...and more. As I said, there's an infrared alarm sensor on the gate but, if it's already open, then it must be disabled. Either that or someone's forgotten to reset it. Careless...look, you stay here a minute.'

'How do you know all this—?'

But Gibson had jumped, leaving Bruce alone in the car, the engine still running. For a moment he was tempted to jump into the driver's seat and speed off, but Gibson returned after a few seconds.

'Right, it seems to be deactivated right enough. There's a wee hill, there might still be someone up the top. Look, if you can just walk up, I'll pull the car inside the gate. If it's clear, give me a wave and I'll come up.'

'And if it's not? What then—do you expect me to take on...well, God only knows. Look, this is getting bloody ridiculous...wait, where are you going?'

'Oh, for fuck sake, if you won't do it, then I will. I'm not taking any chances. You drive the car, wait at the bottom of the hill. I'll wave if it's okay then, once you're up, there's an old barn over to the right, Turn the car and reverse in to it, just in case we need to get away fast.'

Gibson walked inside the gate and stopped, looking down at the moonlit ground. He came back over as Bruce was getting in to the driver's seat.

'I was right—there's fresh tyre tracks in the mud so somebody's definitely been up this way. Bring the car in and kill the lights and the engine, we don't want anyone to know we're here.'

He sprinted off up the hill as Bruce edged the Range Rover through the narrow gate and on to the soft, uneven surface. A few minutes later, he saw Gibson waving, beckoning for him to proceed. He drove carefully, with only the sidelights on, soon reaching where Gibson was standing. He wound down the window.

'Right, were all good. There's a few more tracks up here but there's no-one about. Turn the car and reverse it over there, just behind those trees. Watch out, there's a lot of old bricks and junk lying about, last thing we need is a puncture. There's infrared cameras further down, nearer the house, but I know where they are, I can avoid them.'

Bruce looked over to where the skeletal remains of the old barn stood, partially obscured by the bare branches of the copse; a few sheets of rusted corrugated iron clung on grimly to its roof. A few minutes later the car was safely out of sight and Bruce had joined Cal Gibson at the top of the hill.

Glenbreakerie house appeared idyllic, almost like a fairytale castle. A few lights shone in the downstairs windows and there were a number of external lights that resembled old-fashioned streetlamps. These cast a warm glow over the immediate perimeter of the house and the surrounding grounds appeared neat and well kept, as did the outbuildings. Bruce turned to Cal Gibson.

'Are you absolutely sure that this is the place?'

'Certain. They took you in the front door, they took you back out the front door.'

'But you can't see the front from here—surely this is the back we're looking at?'

'Aye, but I sneaked down and waited.'

Bruce could feel his temper rise once again but now was not the time for recrimination. 'So what do we do now?'

Gibson shrugged. 'Not sure; I'm having a wee...fuck, what the hell's that?'

The peace of the evening had been broken by the sound of a vehicle slowing down and they could see lights reflecting on the bare branches of the trees that lined the road behind them. Crouching down, Gibson trotted over to the summit of the hill, returning a few seconds later.

'Quick, get round the back of the bloody barn; there's a car coming up the track!'

They scrambled round the perimeter of the dilapidated outbuilding, Bruce stumbling several times over the strewn rubble. They heard the car labouring up the hill as its wheels slipped on the muddy surface but, a few minutes later, the vehicle crested the rise and came to a halt. Five figures stepped out, surveying the tranquil scene that was Glenbreakerie House; Bruce felt Gibson's body tense as he whispered.

'Christ, that's Paul Maguire—see, the skinny one with the dark hair.'

Bruce squinted; he vaguely recognised him from the footage following Suzannah Flint's trial.

'Do you know him?'

'A bit. Had a few dealings with him, he's a slimy so-and-so, wouldn't trust him a bloody inch.'

Bruce suddenly remembered the conversation with Peter Caira at a Monday morning partners' meeting a few weeks previously;

it seemed a very long time ago. He whispered in Gibson's ear, 'So is that guy beside him David Doyle—you know, they were both involved with Hooley Transport?'

Gibson nodded. 'Aye, likely he is.'

As he spoke, Doyle put a hand in his pocket and removed a packet of cigarettes, placing one in his mouth. He delved into his other pocket and removed a small object that glinted silver in the moonlight. Lifting it, he it flicked back the lid, the blueish flame of the burning petrol illuminating his face for a second. Bruce was aware of Gibson getting to his feet, his teeth clenched as he hissed.

'Bastard—you fucking bastard! It must've been him that tortured Miriam, he's got a bloody Zippo lighter...'

Bruce put his hand on his companion's arm. 'Leave it, Cal, Not now, there's five of them.'

Gibson subsided but continued to mutter to himself. Doyle and his associates stood for a minute more then returned to the car, opening the boot. A few minutes later, armed with the three sawn-off shotguns and baseball bats, the five dark-clad figures headed stealthily down the hill. Gibson got to his feet.

'Right, I'm going after them. What about you, Mr R?'

Bruce shook his head. 'I'll stay here. I'm in enough trouble as it is.'

'Fair enough; watch out for me, get ready to make a quick exit if you see me coming up the hill. Good luck.'

'You too. And be careful, they're armed.'

Gibson flashed a smile—well, more of a sneer—his teeth glinting in the moonlight. 'So am I, Mr Redpath. You don't need a fucking gun to be dangerous..'

Crouching behind the crumbling wall, Bruce watched Gibson make his way surreptitiously down the slope until, finally, he disappeared behind the stable block. He was cold and he was now desperate for the toilet. He stood up but, despite the silence of the night, he felt vulnerable and exposed. He decided to take cover further inside the ruinous building, where he would be able to relieve himself then wait in the comfort of the Range Rover. Scrambling over a pile of rubble he approached the rear wall, unzipping his trousers as he did so. Suddenly, his foot struck something and he fell forward, involuntarily putting his hands out in front of him. Bracing himself, he was surprised to find that he had landed on something soft; he felt his right hand touch something wet and, at first, he suspected that it was probably cow-dung. He pulled back to a crouching position but, as his eyes adjusted to the near-impenetrable darkness inside the ruin, he stared down in horror at the inert body, the ragged wound where the man's throat had been just visible in the faint glimmer of moonlight. He lifted his hand…

Stifling a scream, he stood up and retched violently, although his stomach was almost empty. He staggered back towards the Range Rover, desperately wiping his hand against his trousers in an attempt to remove the blood.

He stood for a few moments, his arm leaning against the comforting bulk of Gibson's vehicle. The nausea was subsiding but he was aware that his bladder was now at capacity. Quickly, he relieved himself next to the vehicle, noticing that his hands were shaking almost uncontrollably. In the harsh light of the moon he could see the bright red blood stains; another wave of nausea threatened to engulf him but he took a deep breath and fought it back.

He desperately tried to marshal his thoughts; who was the dead man? Should he just drive off and leave Gibson to his fate? He opened the driver's door, relieved to see the key still sitting in the ignition. He was tempted—after all, what had Gibson done for him? If the private investigator had told the truth in the first place, Bruce would never have spent a night in a cell, he wouldn't now stand accused of a murder that he didn't commit. He shook his head, he could barely think coherently; should he allow Gibson a further ten minutes? He looked at his watch and was surprised to see that it was just past nine-thirty, it felt like an age since he had left Coral's house. His heart skipped a beat; his daughter would be worried sick, as would all the others. His younger daughter, Fliss; Mel, Rob, Simon—he had brought untold upset and trouble into all their lives on account of his stupid fixation with these bloody killings. He reached a decision; it was time to go home and face the music, once and for all. He was about to step into the car when he stopped; the distant sound of a police siren carried across the still of the night.

Help was on its way.

The sirens were closer now and Bruce, having had a temporary change of heart, carefully made his way back around the ruined barn, making sure he gave the darkness where the body lay a wide berth. Crouching low, he clambered over the pile of rubble and looked down over the peaceful grounds of Glenbreakerie House. All was still, the lights were still burning in the windows, it looked the picture of rural innocence. The aged BMW saloon remained at the top of the hill, pointing down the slope towards the rear of the house and ticking occasionally as the engine cooled. There were more sirens now, closer, urgent...he realised that he was holding his breath and he let out a long sigh. If Gibson didn't come back up the slope in the next few minutes, he would leave. Best not to get caught at the locus.

He could now see the blue lights reflecting on the trees as the police convoy made its way up the main drive, approaching the front of the property. Suddenly, the peace was shattered; doors opened, officers clad in skip-caps and body armour jumped out, some of them obviously armed and running in an organised manner towards the house. There was shouting, the sound of breaking glass and he crouched lower, afraid he might be seen. He realised that he really should leave but his curiosity had now got the better of him, as had a vague and slightly inexplicable loyalty to Cal Gibson.

As he peered through the darkness at the scene below, he noticed a gaunt figure sprinting up the hill and, as it drew near, he recognised Paul Maguire. Without a backward glance, Maguire opened the door of the BMW, started the engine and attempted a quick U-turn on the wet, slippery grass. The wheels spun for a moment before the car catapulted backwards, narrowly missing Bruce and crashing into the remains of the brick wall. There was a tinkle as one of the rear lights shattered, then Maguire revved the engine alarmingly and careered off down the slope towards the road. Bruce turned and looked back down the hill, where a second figure was now labouring up the slope, slithering on the wet surface. It was the man that Gibson had identified as David Doyle. With a great effort, and considerably out of breath, Doyle reached the top, shouting between his gasps for breath as he futilely punched the air in front of him.

'Ya fuckin' bastard, Maguire, Ah'll fuckin' have you fur this...'

Doyle bent over, his hands on his knees as he continued to catch his breath, glaring furiously at the single disappearing tail-light of the BMW. Bruce suddenly became aware of yet another dark shape running diagonally up the slope from the far right-hand side of the stables. As this new participant in the unfolding drama drew nearer, Bruce realised that it was Cal Gibson, his features set in an expression of pure hatred. Doyle obviously heard Gibson's approach and turned; too late, Gibson's fist caught the man on the side of the head, knocking him to the ground. Before Doyle could move, Gibson had jumped astride him, grasping Doyle by the throat and banging his head up and down on the ground.

'Cal!' shouted Bruce. 'Cal, for fuck sake stop...'

A noise made him turn; yet another dark-clad figure was approaching, a sawn-off shotgun raised and pointing directly at Gibson's head. Bruce recognised the man as one of the other occupants of Maguire's recently-departed BMW.

'Cal,' he hissed, but Gibson was oblivious, his attention apparently focused exclusively on squeezing the life out of Doyle. The man with the gun crept closer; he couldn't possibly miss, but Bruce daren't shout any louder in case the weapon was turned on him...in desperation, he fumbled about, his hand finding a loose brick; without hesitating, he grasped it, stood up and threw it with all the energy he possessed at the armed man. It struck him on the side of his head just as he turned, the shotgun firing with a loud crack. Gibson screamed and fell to one side as the shooter collapsed on the ground. Even in the dull light of the moon, Bruce could see the bloody wound on the side of his victim's head. He ran over to where Gibson was lying, clutching his arm and moaning. Blood was already soaking through his jacket.

'Cal! Cal! God almighty, are you okay?'

The man looked up at Bruce, his face contorted in pain.

'You get out of here, Mr R. Leave—go on.'

'No, I can't leave you, Cal, you've been shot...'

'It's only my arm...I'll be all right. *Please*, Mr R, there's nothing more you can do, you don't want to be caught here.'

The night was rent with further shouting, loud and authoritative. This was closely followed by the sound of more shots being fired, then a scream. Bruce stood up in alarm.

'For fuck sake, GO!' shouted Cal. 'NOW!'

Without a backward glance, Bruce ran over to where the Range Rover was concealed and yanked the door open. He was about to enter when a shape materialised from the darkness and pulled him back.

'What the hell...?'

The night seemed to explode in a shower of stars, then Bruce Redpath collapsed in a heap on the filthy, hard concrete floor of the barn.

Chapter 23

Thursday 4th December, night.

It was as if someone was hitting the back of his skull with a hammer. Relentless, debilitating...he groaned in pain and opened his eyes but could see nothing. He couldn't remember what had happened and briefly wondered if he had lost his vision. The throbbing seemed to be getting worse, now almost a tangible entity. Very gradually, he managed to drag himself up to a kneeling position, the feeling of nausea once again rising in his chest. His mouth felt as if it was lined with sandpaper and it was so dry that he was unable to swallow. He reached round to the back of his head, where there appeared to be a large lump; did it feel wet? As he brought his hand round, holding it up to his face, his nostrils were assailed by the sharp, metallic tang of blood. He frowned; was the wound really that bad? How much blood had he lost? Then suddenly, he remembered...

Everything.

The jolt of adrenaline brought him to his senses, although the loud throbbing persisted. His vision regained, he turned and looked around him but the derelict barn was empty, the Range Rover gone and he felt a wave of dark despair engulf him. The throbbing seemed to be overhead now and he looked up, screaming out in pain as a bright light suddenly shone excruciatingly into his dark-adapted eyes. Someone had started shouting, they were nearby. Were they shouting at him?

'DOWN! GET DOWN, ON THE FLOOR! NOW! HANDS BEHIND YOUR HEAD!'

He looked towards the source of the command, although a second voice, to his left, seemed to be repeating the words. The light was dazzling him and he narrowed his eyes, the images resolving as his pupils adapted to the bright light. The throbbing was almost intolerable now, it seemed to be all around him, he could feel it...the owner of the voice continued to scream at Bruce to get down and place his hands behind his head. The man was pointing something at him.

It was a gun.

With a feeling akin to relief, Bruce complied, placing his hands behind his head and lying face down on the ground once again. He closed his eyes, resting his cheek on the cold, harsh concrete. Maybe it was all just a bad dream, maybe everything would just go away.

It didn't.

Within seconds, strong hands had wrenched his arms mercilessly downwards and he was aware of something cold and unyielding being placed around his wrists. The throbbing sound and the light moved away, the lights of the helicopter flashing as it headed off to carry out a further sweep of the policies of Glenbreakerie House. Bruce felt himself being pulled roughly to his feet by a Kevlar-vested policeman, his skip-cap pulled low over his dark brows. Finally, he managed to find his voice, although it sounded weak and hoarse.

'Listen, you don't understand, I'm—'

The cop half-turned as he continued to drag Bruce across the grass to where a marked police vehicle was parked, its blue lights flashing.

'Can it, matey. There'll be plenty o' time for confessions, don't you worry!'

'No, my name's Bruce Redpath, I'm a lawyer. Look, you don't understand...'

The policeman stopped and turned towards Bruce, a cynical, animal-like sneer on his face. 'Naw, you're right, pal, I *don't* understand. I don't understand why you've been found at the scene of a major incident, twenty feet away from a dead body and wi' your hands covered in blood. So why don't you just shut the fuck up, get yer sorry arse in the van, then we can all get home tae our fucking kip. Move it!'

The police vehicle bumped its way down the rough track then picked up speed as it turned onto the road. Bruce sat on the hard seat, his hands still securely cuffed behind his back. He had no idea of the time, no clue as to his destination. The same policeman sat across from him, now staring intently at his mobile phone and completely ignoring Bruce. There was one other occupant; a man in his mid-fifties, Bruce reckoned, his hands also secured behind his back. Dressed in brown corduroy trousers above well-polished brogues and a heavy, beige cable-knit pullover, he had the appearance of a stereotypical country vicar. Bald, with a thick band of greying hair around the rear of his cranium and a neat, grey goatee beard, the man was staring morosely at the floor. Bruce looked over but the man ignored him, his expression one of abject misery.

Bruce turned away, realising that his own expression was probably much the same.

He must have dozed off; he was wakened when the vehicle came to an abrupt halt. There were voices outside, there was a clanking sound as if something large and heavy had been moved. The cop seated across from his was now on the alert and glaring over at Bruce; his hand was resting on the butt of his pistol, as if he was expecting further trouble. He certainly wasn't going to get it from Bruce; he was cold and sore, his arms ached, he felt sick...

The rear door opened, words were exchanged, Bruce recognising the camaraderie, the banter, the dark humour. He was unceremoniously assisted out of the van and, with considerable effort, he mumbled, 'Where are we?'

The cop who had escorted him laughed; it sounded cruel, somehow. 'Ye're at the fuckin' Govan Hilton, matey! Right, come on, let's get ye booked in; single room, en-suite.'

A few minutes later, Bruce had been informed that he was at Govan's Helen Street detention centre, or 'suite,' as it was somewhat euphemistically termed. He was relieved of his phone, his watch, his belt, his shoelaces...

What upset him most was the fact that it had been less than a week since he had been subjected to exactly the same humiliating procedure in Greenock Police Station.

Fifteen minutes later, he found himself in another bleak and comfortless cell, with only his despair for company; it was no bloody wonder they had taken his belt and his shoelaces, he thought. He lay on the bed and started to sob, alone, afraid and hopeless.

◈

He had fallen into a restless, nightmare-ridden sleep, tossing and turning on the hard bed. He was wakened as the cell door opened, a voice calling out, 'Bruce Redpath? Right, come on, get yourself up.'

He felt dreadful; his head ached—should he not have seen a doctor about his head wound? He stood up, swaying slightly; the officer at the door gave him a cynical look.

'Don't bloody act it, sunshine. You'll get little sympathy here. Right, look sharp.'

Bruce followed the man from the cell. A uniformed officer was standing outside, ready to escort him to wherever he was headed. It was, of course, an interview room. He sat down at the now-familiar metal table and waited, the uniformed cop standing at the doorway; a minute or so later, the door opened and two people entered, walking round the table and sitting across from him. A tall, careworn woman with short greying hair and a younger, attractive blonde officer, their expressions suitably grim. The older woman regarded him with her red-rimmed, watery blue eyes for a few moments.

'Right. Bruce Redpath, isn't it?'

Bruce nodded. 'Yes.'

'Good. Do you have legal representation, or do you need a duty solicitor?'

Bruce looked at her with his own red-rimmed eyes. 'Actually, I *am* a solicitor.'

The two officers exchanged a look, then the older woman spoke again. She sounded exhausted.

'Fine. Right then, Inspector Kerrigan, start the recording.'

The younger woman reached across to the video recorder and switched it on. They waited a few seconds, then the older woman spoke. 'Okay, interview started at seven forty-six a.m. We are in interview room two at Helen Street detention centre. Present are Chief Superintendent Norah Jarvis...'

Bruce recognised the name—she had been leading the investigation into the recent murders.

'... Detective Inspector Karen Kerrigan and Bruce Redpath...'

She paused, consulting her notes, then continued. 'Mr Redpath states that he is a solicitor and has waived his right to legal representation...'

'Wait—that's not what I said!'

Jarvis glared across at him. 'I asked if you wanted a solicitor, Mr Redpath, then you stated that you *were* a solicitor.'

'Yes, but I'm a divorce lawyer, not a criminal one. Look, you need to contact Simon Fox, he's my partner—actually, he's also my counsel. He needs to be here...his number's on my mobile.'

The officers exchanged another glance.

'Simon Fox?' exclaimed Karen Kerrigan, looking at her superior officer with a sneer. 'Isn't he the bugger who gets all the bad guys off the hook?'

Norah Jarvis gave a grim smile and nodded. 'Aye, one and the same, Inspector. Okay, Mr Redpath, is that who you are requesting to represent you?'

Bruce looked at the two officers, realising that sympathy and understanding were most definitely not on offer.

'Yes. I'm saying nothing until Simon Fox gets here.'

Norah Jarvis scowled at him. 'Fine. Interview terminated at seven forty-nine a.m.'

He was brought a plastic mug of tea and a couple of slices of toast. Despite his pervading feeling of despair, he ate and drank with gusto, realising that the was starving. His head was still pounding but the bump seemed to have subsided somewhat. He was sitting on the bed, staring at the wall, when he heard the cell door open.

'Right, sunshine, come wi' me.'

He stood up and exited the cell and was taken to the same interview room, expecting to be greeted by the comforting and familiar face of Simon Fox, QC. As he entered he halted in surprise as, seated on the other side of the bare metal table, was DCI Paula Noone. She looked across at him, giving him what looked like a rather forced smile.

'Good morning, Bruce.'

'Paula! What the hell are you doing here?'

She gave him a questioning look. 'I might ask you the same thing, Bruce. What, in God's name, were you doing at Glenbreakerie House? Oh, for goodness sake, sit down before you fall down.'

A look of concern now appeared on her face. 'Wait—are you okay?'

He sat down across from her.

'No, not really, my head's bloody splitting; someone hit me and knocked me out.'

She stood up, vaguely muttering something about incompetence. She opened the door and barked, 'Get some paracetamol for this man—he should bloody well have been attended to last night! And bring us a couple of coffees; and biscuits.'

There was a brief remonstration, to which she responded, 'Don't bloody argue with me—just get on with it! This man had been assaulted and injured, he should have been treated when he was booked in. If he's suffering from concussion, or worse, then someone's going to get their bloody arse booted, so I suggest you do what I bloody well tell you.'

She came back in to the room, an angry expression on her face. As she closed the door, Bruce spoke.

'Look, to be fair, I didn't mention it at the time, the policeman wasn't exactly...well...'

Paula Noone interrupted. 'Makes no difference, someone should have noticed, or asked if you had been injured. It's standard procedure—or should be...'

She sat down, sighing heavily. 'But I suppose it's been a hell of a long night for all of us.'

She sat in silence for a moment, staring at the scored surface of the desk as if struggling with some personal dilemma until, finally, she looked across at Bruce.

'Okay, I'm going out on a bit of a limb here and, at the moment, this conversation is going to be strictly off the record. You'll need to make a formal statement later, of course.'

She paused again, a further look of doubt on her drawn, weary features, then leaned forward and regarded him with her piercing hazel eyes. He felt that he was being assessed, somehow.

'Look, I'll be straight with you. I'm a pretty good judge of character and I also trust Finlay Whyte's judgement—in fact, to be absolutely honest, if it wasn't for him, I wouldn't be here in the first place. This whole incident...well, it's going to have massive repercussions...'

She paused once more, then took a deep breath. 'It'll be public knowledge in a day or so anyway, but I must insist that you don't say a bloody word until it all comes out. First of all, I need you to tell me just what the hell's been going on—right from the very beginning. And don't bloody miss anything out—d'you understand?'

Bruce finished relating the bizarre sequence of events; Paula Noone rubbed her hands over her face. He felt as if an enormous weight had been lifted, although the Chief Superintendent hadn't yet responded to his narrative. Finally, she placed her hands on the table, staring straight into his eyes.

'Jesus! That's one hell of a story, but I have to say it pretty much ties in with what we've uncovered so far. Okay, I'll accept all that at face value. Now, I'm sure you have plenty of questions yourself—I'll answer those that I can but, again, you have to keep this to yourself in the meantime.'

She gave him a grim smile. 'Anyway, I gather you're not a great fan of the press, are you?'

He shook his head. 'No, I most certainly am not; by the way, how *is* Miriam Bonnar?'

'Well, physically she'll heal, but mentally? I'm not really sure; after what happened to her she's bound to take a while to recover. It was bloody inhumane...'

There was a silence; Bruce unsuccessfully tried to shut the disturbing images from his mind.

'And Gibson—is he okay?'

'Well, he took a bad gunshot wound to his upper arm but he'll survive. That's the least of his worries, however. Unfortunately, it's pretty certain that we'll be charging him with the murder of David Doyle.'

Bruce closed his eyes; there had been too many deaths...he opened them again and looked over at her. 'But surely there were mitigating circumstances? I mean, it was Doyle who tortured Miriam Bonnar—we saw him light a cigarette with a Zippo lighter, Bonnar said that was what they used when...anyway, after what they did to her, no wonder Gibson lost his head.'

Paula Noone arched an eyebrow. 'And isn't that exactly what the Civil Guard were doing? Taking their own form of retribution? I gather you had an objection to *that*, didn't you?'

He nodded his assent. 'Yes, fair point, you're absolutely correct...'

Another disturbing image flashed into his mind.

'...em, what about the body...'

'The one in the ruined barn? Yes, that *is* a bit of a strange one. Right, here's a few things that you won't know yet. The so called 'Guard' held their kangaroo courts in the basement of Glenbreakerie House—presumably that's where they took you—and, when we finally gained entry, it appears that one of their 'trials' was actually in progress.'

'What? Good God, so you caught them in the act?'

'Yes, we did. A woman by the name of Krasniki—remember, her brother was murdered a few weeks ago?'

Bruce was unlikely to forget; he simply nodded.

'Well, we already knew a fair bit about Agni Krasniki's operations, although up until now we didn't know her identity. In fact, we didn't even know that Aleksander Krasniki *had* a sister, shows you how efficient she's been at keeping herself under our radar. What we *did* know was that someone was running a prostitution racket, using underage girls, in Edinburgh and also up in Aberdeen. But that's not all; she would advise the 'clients' that the girls were of legal age then once they had used their 'services' a few times, she'd show the clients the birth certificates and start blackmailing them. All very neat, the victims were hardly going to come to us, were they? Seems she also dabbled in drug supply, mainly to her girls. A right nasty piece of work. We also came across two of her cronies, they were being held in one of the side rooms off the basement, presumably where you were given the opportunity to shoot Beagan. We think that the body that you had the misfortune to discover may have been a third member of her team. At the moment, we're working on the theory that Krasniki and her thugs had also come to Glenbreakerie with the intention of taking revenge for her brother's killing, but we suspect that, somehow, her plan backfired and she ended up being caught by the...well, the foot-soldiers of the 'Guard', I suppose you'd call them. Of course, it might have been some kind of double bluff but, as you might imagine, she's not saying anything at the moment, she's simply claiming she was abducted for no apparent reason. You were just unlucky to stumble over the body, so to speak.'

'Mm, just one of many unlucky sets of circumstances I found myself in, I'm afraid.'

'Quite.'

She nodded and he could feel a rising sense of excitement as he asked. 'So, you were saying, you've caught the members of this Civil Guard?'

She nodded; somehow she didn't look particularly happy about it. 'We have—at least, most of them. From what you've told me, there should have been eight but at the moment we can only account for seven. We also suspect that some of their 'foot-soldiers' may have escaped but, unfortunately, we don't know how many. That's probably who knocked you out and stole Gibson's Range Rover. By the way, we found it abandoned in Lanark and we suspect that they may have had another vehicle parked there. There's a massive manhunt ongoing as we speak, it's only a matter of time before we pick them up. Well, hopefully.'

'Can you tell me who they are?' Bruce asked, leaning forward in his chair.

She paused and steepled her fingers as she considered how much information she could divulge.

'Hm, well, as I said, it'll be in the papers very soon...most of them are probably unfamiliar to you, just wealthy, private individuals

273

who have experienced the loss of someone close to them as a result of criminal activity. Two of them you might know, however...'

He waited expectantly.

'Are you familiar with a retired Professor of Law, Donald Lauchlin?'

Bruce's jaw dropped in astonishment. 'What? Good God...surely not? I mean, he was one of *our* professors...no, surely you must be mistaken.'

She nodded, a sympathetic expression on her austere features.

'I'm afraid so, Bruce. He was the main man, so to speak, the mastermind behind the whole thing.'

His mind returned to the night he had been taken in front of the Civil Guard, the certainty that the man who had addressed him was a lawyer. Had there been something vaguely familiar in his tone?

Bruce shook his head in denial. 'No, it can't be...there *must* be some mistake.'

'No, there's no mistake. Glenbreakerie House is his family home, although it's held in a trust of some sort. He's behind the whole Civil Guard affair, I'm afraid.'

Bruce was stunned. This man was a paragon of virtue, he represented everything that Bruce held dear.

'But *why*? Why on earth would a man like Lauchlin resort to violence of this sort?'

'He had his reasons; about ten years ago, his wife's car was rear-ended by a lorry driver at a set of traffic lights. The poor woman was killed instantly but the lorry driver managed to avoid conviction on the strength of a so-called expert witness who claimed the accused was suffering from some vague, rare sleep disorder. The investigating officers suspected that he'd driven for considerably more than his scheduled hours, quite probably he—or his employer, for that matter—had interfered with the tachometer. We also discovered that he was a habitual gambler and we were pretty certain that he'd been at an illicit poker game the night before, although no-one was prepared to give evidence. Basically, he was unfit to drive but, with the bloody expert-witness's testimony, there was bugger all we could do about it and the bastard got off. Unfortunately, it seems that Lauchlin never really got over it. I'm surprised that you don't remember the case; it was quite high-profile at the time. The lorry driver mysteriously disappeared a few years later, it was assumed back then that he committed suicide but we might be reopening that case in light of what we've subsequently discovered.'

Ten years ago; Bruce had been dealing with his own personal hell at that time, he would have been unlikely to notice. Paula Noone sighed and shook her head, staring down at the table.

'The next one is by far the worst, I'm afraid. The repercussions are going to echo about for a long time.'

She looked back up at him.' Lauchlan's second-in-command in the so-called Civil Guard was none other than Amelia Khan, deputy Chief Constable of Scotland's police.'

Chapter 24

Friday 5th December.

It was over.

Bruce had made his formal statement, in the company of Chief Superintendent Paula Noone and a rather disgruntled-looking Chief Superintendent Norah Jarvis, the latter seemingly still convinced of his criminality. The recording was finally stopped and Jarvis made a somewhat hasty exit. Paula Noone leaned back in her chair and regarded Bruce.

'Well done, Bruce. I know that couldn't have been easy for you, the whole thing must have been a bloody nightmare.'

He sighed. 'Yes, well, that's putting it mildly. Em, do you think she believes me?'

'Norah? Och, she'll come round, basically she doesn't trust anyone. Don't worry.'

'So is that it? Is that me...well, off the hook?'

She nodded. 'Yes. Gibson has recovered enough to give us a statement and he's corroborated what you've told us about your abduction by the so-called Civil Guard. Given the timescale involved, there's no way you could have carried out Beagan's murder. I'll have a word with DCI Mazzoni but it'll just be a formality, keeping her in the loop. I dare say the truth will come out in due course anyway once we interview everyone, but it's going to be a bloody nightmare, especially once the Press get hold of it...'

The same pained expression crossed her face. 'Listen—do you remember that day we met for lunch, with Finlay?'

'Yes, as I recall you seemed very reluctant to talk about the killings.'

'I was; you see, I'd been investigating the Krasniki murder and I'd been...well, not exactly warned off, but certainly told not to try *too* hard, if you get my meaning. This was all very much 'off the record' and low key, of course, just a quiet word here and there. But I got the feeling that it was coming from a higher lever, although I had no idea just quite how high that was. No bloody wonder, if Khan was involved. It really went against the grain, I can tell you.'

'But why?' asked Bruce. 'I mean, one of Scotland's most senior officers, how on earth did she get involved?'

'I don't know Bruce. It seems that everyone involved had experienced some form of tragedy, I don't know what Khan's story was, although I'm determined to find out.'

Bruce frowned, recalling an earlier conversation . 'You know, a few weeks back, my friend, Rob Connor—he's a DCI down in

Greenock—well, he said pretty much the same thing when he was investigating the case with Doyle and that woman who died, Flint, I think her name was. He was pretty upset about it too.'

'Really? That's very interesting! I wonder just how many lower-ranking cops were getting the same message—I suspect this is going to open up an enormous can of worms, Bruce. Still, that's our problem, not yours.'

She made to stand up but he spoke again. 'What's really bothering *me* is the fact that I could have ended up in court, charged with a murder that I didn't commit. In fact, I could have ended up in bloody jail.'

She shook her head. 'Honestly, I don't think it would have come to that. Gibson would have told us the full story eventually. Anyway, you had the 'Fantastic Mister Fox' on your side...'

He looked up in surprise. 'Who?'

She laughed. 'The Fantastic Mister Fox—that's what he's known as in police circles; he's not the most popular member of the legal profession, as you may have gathered.'

'You know, it's funny, I never really though about it that way but I suppose I can see your point. The thing is, Simon's always maintained that it wasn't about 'getting people off' as such, it was just about making sure that any conviction was absolutely safe.'

'Well, he *would* say that, but, let's face it, from our point of view it's one and the same thing. You've seen a major incident at first hand now, you must know the pressures our officers come under. A couple of words out of place in the heat of the moment, a simple error reading rights in the middle of a dangerous situation, then along comes Mr Fox and, suddenly, all their efforts, the danger they placed themselves in, possibly months of gruelling work, it all goes out the window on a technicality and some evil bastard walks free. It's bloody hard to swallow, let me tell you.'

She gave him a strange look. 'The thing is, I'm now investigating this bloody case, yet there's a very small part of me that wonders if the Civil Guard actually weren't too far off the mark...'

He looked at her in alarm.

'...but just a *very* small part, Bruce, don't worry.'

She rose and moved towards the door and smiled.

'Are you coming? Or would you rather stay?'

It was only as they passed through the final security door that the reality of his situation struck him.

'Paula?'

'Yes?'

'What now? I mean, what happens, how do I get home?'

'Oh, don't worry, we've got that all in hand. As to what happens—nothing! You're a free man once more. Of course, you'll be called as a witness when it all comes to court but, as far as we're concerned, you're now an innocent party. A victim, even...right, come on...'

They entered the public area of the detention centre; a couple of uniformed officers were standing chatting and several smartly dressed women were having a rather heated discussion; whether they were detectives or solicitors, Bruce couldn't tell—and he didn't care. He looked about, expecting to see Coral, or maybe 'The Fantastic Mister Fox' waiting for him but instead, and much to his surprise, Finlay Whyte stood up and walked towards him, a wide smile on his handsome face.

'Bruce! Thank God!'

Bruce smiled in surprise back and extended his hand, but Finlay ignored it, pulling him instead into a fierce embrace. As the pathologist's muscular arms enfolded him, Bruce relaxed and buried his face in Finlay's shoulder; he had never before felt so grateful for this most basic form of human contact.

They bade Paula Noone farewell and sat in the comfort of Finlay's Audi. Bruce felt in his jacket pocket for his phone, which had been returned to him along with the other items removed when he was taken into custody. He frowned at the dark screen as Finlay started the engine.

'Just turn it on, Bruce, you've nothing to worry about now.'

He pressed the button and waited. As the screen filled up with all his missed messages and calls, the phone started to ring. He swiped it immediately.

'Simon.'

'Bruce—are you okay?'

He considered the question for a moment. 'Yes, I think I am. Did they try to contact you?'

'The police? Yes, I spoke to Paula Noone earlier, she's filled me in. I take it you've been released?'

'Yes, just a few minutes ago. I've made my statement—'

'You've WHAT?'

'Simon, it's fine, really. Paula believes everything I've told her. Cal Gibson has backed up my story and she's going to speak to DCI Mazzoni, she says the charges will be dropped. I'm a free man, apparently.'

'Well, I hope to God she keeps her word. Look, I'm just about to leave and come over...'

'You don't have to, I'm out and I've got a lift...' He turned and smiled at Finlay.

'Are you sure? I can be there in half an hour.'

'No, thanks, Simon, I just want to get home as soon as I can, get a bath and leave it all behind me.'

'Okay, fair enough.'

He sounded very slightly relieved, Bruce thought.

'I'll instruct Mrs Aherne to clear your diary for the week, then we'll just take it from there.'

Bruce was very slightly disappointed in Simon but he realised that he had missed his charismatic partner. In fact, he missed everyone at the office! Still, it had all worked out okay in the end, he supposed; time would tell, however.

'I'll let you get on then, Bruce. I'll come over and see you at some point during the week, I've got a pretty full diary but I'll make the time.'

'Em, what about my bill?' asked Bruce, a smile forming on his lips. Simon let out a guffaw of laughter.

'Hah! You couldn't afford me, Mr Redpath. Don't worry, this one's on the house!'

He fell asleep almost as soon as Finlay had pulled on the M8 and was only roused by his friend's loud cursing.

'For fuck sake, you moron!'

A long blast in the horn followed as Bruce blinked himself awake. 'What...what's happened?'

'Oh sorry, I didn't mean to waken you, that bloody van just pulled in right in front of me.'

Finlay turned and smiled at him. 'You went out like a bloody light, you know—you've been snoring like a pig all the way down the road.'

Bruce grinned back. 'I'm terribly sorry, I was absolutely exhausted. The room last night wasn't up to much. As for room service...'

Finlay laughed. 'I hope you queried your bill... and, anyway, your snoring doesn't bother me in the slightest!'

'Finlay, where are we going—we're in Port Glasgow, you must have missed the turn-off for Langbank.'

Finlay Whyte gave him a knowing wink. 'We're not going to Coral's house, Bruce. Trust me.'

Half an hour later, they pulled up in front of the Connor's house, high above the village of Inverkip; Mel was at the door even before Bruce had opened it and as he got out, he fell into her arms. If anything her embrace was even fiercer than Finlay's; and considerably more perfumed...

'Oh Bruce, my darling, are you okay? I was so worried!'

She squeezed him even harder; behind her, Rob was standing, a strange, almost pained look on his face. Finally, Bruce extricated himself from Mel's embrace and took his friend's hand. Rob gave him a rather forced smile.

'Bruce. Look, I'm so, so sorry, it was just...'

Bruce smiled back at his friend. 'Rob, it's fine, really. I totally understand, obviously at that point I didn't know what was happening. Of course, I know now that you couldn't speak to me at that point. Please, forget all about it...'

Mel was ushering them all inside, aware of the twitching of a few sets of curtains. As she closed the door behind her, she turned to Bruce. 'Right, my darling, I've run you a bath and I've got you a few things—including a razor— they're on one of the beds in the spare room. You're going to stay here until Sunday then we're all coming over to help you get your house back into shape. Been a wee while since you've been there, I dread to think what kind of mess you've left it in.'

Bruce had a fair idea but he didn't comment. It was, undoubtedly, worse than she anticipated.

'But what about Coral—isn't *she* expecting me?'

Mel smiled, warmly, sweetly. 'Don't you worry, it's all arranged, Bruce. They're coming over after work, as are Fliss and Nat.'

As she led him up the stairs, she spoke over her shoulder.

'Oh, and Fin's staying too, I hope you won't mind sharing the spare room with him...'

The weekend passed all too quickly. Mel seemed to be of the impression that the road to Bruce's recovery lay in copious quantities of food and excessive pampering and he certainly wasn't going to complain. The family had come and gone, there had been tears and laughter, there had been long, intense conversations. He had done his best not to divulge too much of what Paula Noone had told him but he had gathered from Rob that a fair amount of it had already been passed along the inevitable police grapevine.

It was seven o'clock on Sunday evening and he was standing at the door of his own home, reluctant to say goodbye to Mel and Rob. She had a tear in her eye as she embraced him for the umpteenth time.

'You're sure you'll be okay? You're welcome to come back down.'

He smiled at her. 'I'll be fine, Mel. I need to get back into the routine at some point. Thanks for all your help, I don't know how I'd have managed without you.'

'Och, it was nothing; anyway, just call if you need anything, even if it's just to talk.'

She turned away and reached down, picking up a brown paper package that she had left lying beside the front door. She handed it to him. 'Em, look, I hope you don't mind, I took the liberty...'

She started to cry.

'Mel, what on earth's the matter?'

Rob put his arm around his sobbing wife and gave Bruce a smile. 'Best open it, mate.'

Bruce pulled away the paper; it was a framed photograph, taken some twelve years ago. It showed a considerably younger Mel, Rob, Bruce and Dorothy, as well as his children, Coral and Felicity. They were all grinning happily, the kids pulling silly faces as they clutched some newly-acquired cuddly toys. He stared at it, feeling a lump rise in his throat. Mel looked up at him.

'It was the day we were down at Culzean Castle; I don't know if you remember...'

He nodded slowly; he remembered every single moment, every single detail; the daffodils, the ducks that his daughters were desperate to pet, the picnic...it seemed like only yesterday.

'Thank you Mel, thank you so very much.'

He didn't trust himself to say anything more; Rob ushered his wife out and Bruce closed the door behind them. Clutching the little rectangle that was bursting with so many memories, he went in to the lounge and crossed to the large cupboard. Placing the photo carefully on the floor, he opened the door and removed a number of bubble-wrapped packages; they were dusty but intact. He started to pull away the wrapping, removing the various frames and wiping the glass.

Half an hour later, Dorothy Redpath was, once again, resident in the house on the Esplanade.

Chapter 25

Wednesday 10th December

It felt strange, being by himself and back in his own home. Bruce realised that it had been just short of two weeks since he had spent a night alone, whether it had been with his daughter, Coral, and her family, with the Connors—or in a cell! He smiled; he had received a phone call that morning from Simon, saying that he was coming to visit him that afternoon. It would be nice to have the company.

Mel and Rob had been a great help, the former cleaning and tidying without a single word of complaint, although he had observed the occasional raised eyebrow. The house was sparkling, the fridge was well stocked and his laundry was up to date. The only item conspicuous by its absence was alcohol.

He looked at his watch; Simon would be arriving soon and he switched on the kettle, removed the decent coffee from the fridge and looked out the cafetiere. A few minutes later, he heard the characteristic roar of the Porsche's powerful engine as it pulled into his driveway.

He opened the door as Simon climbed the steps, dressed, as always, in an immaculately tailored suit and a crisp white shirt (although today unusually open at the neck) With a slight smile of relief, Bruce supposed he was no longer a client.

'Come in, Simon—good to see you.'

They shook hands; Simon favoured him with a smile but he appeared weary. He handed Bruce a white carrier bag.

'A wee gift, to celebrate your freedom.'

Bruce removed the box from the bag—it contained a bottle of twenty-five-year-old Macallan malt whisky.

'Wow! Thank you very much, that looks very appetising; I can't wait to open it.'

'Yes, well, not all at one sitting, please; right, I could murder a coffee...'

Half an hour later, they were seated in the bright, tidy lounge, talking mostly about the affairs of the office, about the business of the other partners. Finally, Simon placed his mug on the table and took a deep breath.

'So, how up-to-date are you with everything?'

Bruce shrugged. 'Well, just what I've seen on the news and in the papers, I suppose. I've not been carrying out any further investigations, if that's what you mean; that's well behind me.'

'I'm very glad to hear it. The big shock, of course, was Amelia Khan. Scotland's police are in bloody disarray, by the sounds of it.'

'Yes, Paula Noone did say that the repercussions would go on for some time. Have you any idea why she was involved?'

Simon nodded. It transpired that, while a student at Leeds University, Amelia Khan's younger sister had been brutally raped and murdered. Once again, the accused had managed to evade conviction.

'So she's been carrying this grudge around with her ever since?' asked Bruce, in astonishment.

'Seems so; in fact, it appears that was what prompted her to join the police once she attained her degree. There followed the inevitable years of disillusionment, failed convictions, all the usual crap that officers have to face...took its toll, by all accounts.'

Bruce shook his head. 'It must, I suppose. Still, it's back to the old chestnut about due process, isn't it? No-one can be above the law, no matter how unfair it all seems. Speaking of which, it was also a hell of a shock about Professor Lauchlin.'

Simon pulled a face. 'I know—I can still hardly believe it myself.'

'Will he plead his own defence, do you think?'

'I don't know. He might never make it to trial.'

'What? Why on earth not?'

'Poor old bugger's got cancer, apparently. Advanced, pancreatic; from what I can gather he's only got a few months left.'

They sat in silence for a few moments, remembering their old professor. While they had been at Glasgow University, Bruce had almost felt that Professor Donald Lauchlin *was* the law. It seemed unbelievable...unbidden, a stray thought entered his mind.

'Simon?'

'Yes?'

'You *did* believe me didn't you?'

Simon flashed his smile. 'Don't be so bloody ridiculous, Bruce, of *course* I believed you!'

'It's just...I like to think that I'd never be capable of...well, you know what I mean?'

Simon nodded but remained silent.

'...but in that room, with the gun in my hand, I was tempted—just for a moment...'

'And what happened?'

'I actually pointed the gun at Beagan—by then he was just a, terrified, pathetic...bastard!'

There was a tone of hate in Bruce's voice

'And?'

Bruce's head slumped and he started at the floor. 'I couldn't...I fired the gun into the ground. The sound of the shot brought my captors back, of course. I don't really remember much after that, but I realised later that my prints would be all over the gun.'

'He wasn't shot!'

Bruce looked up in surprise.

'He wasn't shot, the post-mortem determined that.'

'But...wh...how...?'

'Think about it, Bruce. How would the police manage to explain you shooting Beagan? Where would an honest, upstanding lawyer like yourself get access to a handgun—and would you actually have had the nerve to look someone in the eye and shoot them in cold blood? No, they simply dumped Beagan in the car boot then torched it. It had to look like retribution, after all and you'd have been well-clear of the scene before...'

His voice tailed off; Bruce could feel beads of perspiration break out on his forehead; Simon sighed. 'Yes, the brutal irony of it; just the same as...'

'Don't, Simon, please!'

They sat in a rather sombre silence for a few moments; Simon was fidgeting with his cufflinks, appearing uneasy.

'What is it, what's bothering you? Look, I've known you for over thirty years, I know when something's on your mind.'

Simon gave him a weak smile and let out a long sigh. 'You remember the woman in the pub—Joanna Hume?'

Bruce felt the back of his neck tingle; this wasn't what he had been expecting. 'Yes, of course, although you reckoned that wasn't her real name.'

'Hm. Well, anyway, the police tracked her down; or, rather, she tracked down the police...'

Bruce stared at his friend.

'...so, it seems her name *is* Joanna Hume, she's a GP at a surgery in Gourock. Everything she told you was true. She's just recently moved to the area, she *was* visiting her sister in Kent last week; your first arrest didn't make the national newspapers but the incident at the weekend has been plastered across the media. As soon as she saw your name, she came forward. Oh, and her bloody dog *is* called Bruce, by the way!'

Bruce finally found his voice. 'Em...so, are you saying that it *wasn't* her who spiked my drink?'

Simon shook his head, an expression akin to grief on his handsome features.

'No.'

'But...but then, who...?'

Simon looked his friend straight in the eye.

'There's no easy way to say this, Bruce. The police are certain it was Rob Connor. He's been taken in for questioning, apparently.'

The room started to spin; Simon was still talking but Bruce couldn't hear what he was saying, he couldn't speak...Simon was standing in front of him now, shaking him, shouting at him...

'Bruce! Bruce—for God's sake, are you okay?'

He managed to control the wave of debilitating panic that threatened to overwhelm him, forcing himself to stand up.

'Sorry...I need to check my phone...'

He stumbled out of the lounge as Simon continued to shout after him. His phone wasn't in the kitchen, he must have left it in the bedroom. Clumsily, he mounted the stairs and retrieved the missing handset; the screen was filled with notifications of missed calls from Mel, nine in total. He accessed his messages then, with some difficulty, managed to send a text

'I'm on my way xx'

Simon tried in vain to dissuade him from driving but, finally, he gave up, urging his friend to be careful. Forty minutes later, he arrived outside the Connors' house, where an unfamiliar car was already parked in the drive. He rang the bell and Mel's mother answered, her eyes tearful.

'Bruce, thanks for coming down.'

'How is she?'

The woman shook her head. 'How the hell do you think she is?—her world's just collapsed around her. We're just waiting to take the kids when they get home. The police came over an hour ago and took him away. From what we can gather, he's likely to be remanded in custody...'

The woman started to cry and Bruce walked past her, entering the lounge. Although the day was darkening, the room was lit by a single small side-lamp that illuminated the normally bright and welcoming space with a dull, melancholy glow. Mel Connor was lying on the couch, curled foetus-like as she clutched a cushion. He sat down beside her and stroked her curly blonde hair.

'Mel, Mel, it's me, it's Bruce.'

She turned round and looked up at him; he was aghast. Her eyes were red, her face puffy and swollen, dark mascara trails ran down her ruddy cheeks. She had been his rock, she had been his saviour; now her own life was in ruins. She turned and silently put her arms around him and he could feel her fragile body racked with sobs. He continued to stroke her hair; there was nothing useful that he could say.

Bruce stayed overnight; the decision had been taken to allow Ailie and Fraser to remain at home, rather than leave with their grandparents; after all, they would have to come to terms with the sudden absence of their father sooner or later. As he lay in the single bed, with sleep inevitably evading him, he tried to make sense of the situation. He had had a long conversation with Simon, who had driven down that afternoon and, after some considerable persuasion, the QC had agreed, in principle at least, to defend Rob. Mel had remained in her bedroom, refusing to join the discussion and Bruce didn't really blame her. It was a discussion he would have given almost anything not to be having. Simon had also given Bruce an explanation of what had actually happened.

When Bruce had arrived at 'The Bay' Rob had already ordered him a pint, which was sitting on table; what better way to administer a dose of Rohypnol? Rob's apparent concerns regarding his superiors were simply an extremely convincing smokescreen to ensure that Bruce believed him and it had worked admirably. According to Simon, it seemed that there was a network of police officers who believed that the actions of the Civil Guard were not only acceptable but represented 'real' justice. No doubt many of them had seen cases dismissed, charges dropped and seemingly guilty parties walk free, but it didn't make it right and it certainly wasn't justice as far as Bruce was concerned. However, none of this changed the reality that his oldest friend, DCI Rob Connor, was now in some very serious trouble. The implications for Mel were, without a doubt, catastrophic. Finally, Bruce had asked the question that he had been dreading.

'Simon, why would Rob betray me?'

Simon gave him a long look. 'Basically, because you trusted him. He already knew how you felt about the so-called Civil Guard but they obviously wanted to try and recruit you. You were a natural candidate, after what you'd been through. You matched all their criteria— you're a good lawyer, you'd lost someone close, you'd seen the guilty party walk free. The more 'good and honest' people they had on their books, the stronger they would have become. Rob was at the trial, he also saw that piece of human trash, Beagan, get off with manslaughter. How do you think that must have made him feel, how angry must he have been? But they could hardly just send you an invitation, could they?'

Bruce shook his head. 'But why on earth would he have become involved with them in the first place? He's...he was a policeman, a bloody good policeman...'

Simon shrugged. 'Who knows? Probably just the culmination of years of disillusionment, years of watching people that he knew were guilty as hell getting off scot free. No doubt he was approached by a senior officer of a similar opinion, maybe he was 'interviewed' just as you were. After all...'

As Simon hesitated, Bruce continued, knowing what his friend was about to say. To his surprise, he found himself able to mention it without the customary shutters descending. He supposed that was progress...of a sort.

'Yes, I suppose after Dorothy's death, Rob had a bit of an axe to grind himself, didn't he?'

Simon nodded. 'Exactly. Dorothy was Mel's cousin, they were extremely close. The poor girl was devastated, but she felt she had to be strong for you. Rob would have had to deal with that first hand.'

Bruce had felt a wave of guilt wash over him, remembering Mel's strength in comparison to his own emotional collapse. Simon wasn't finished, however.

'And don't forget that Rob was one of the first officers on the scene. Think how he must have felt, seeing the vehicle registration, knowing who was inside...'

Bruce had raised his hand, indicating for Simon to stop; there were still memories that he daren't face.

'Sorry—but you must see that Rob was perfectly placed to incapacitate you, otherwise you'd never have had that meeting with the Guard. He shared their views, although he hadn't personally lost anyone. But Mel had—you had, and that was enough. Anyway, as it turned out, it was all to no avail, as you turned them down.'

'I could have been charged with murder, though!'

Simon had flashed the trademark grin. 'And I'd have ensured that you weren't convicted.'

'But...but how could you be so sure?'

The QC had chuckled. 'This is me you're talking to, Bruce, The Fantastic Mr Fox!'

Bruce managed a smile. 'You know about the epithet, then?'

'Of course I do—I don't mind it actually, it could be worse. A lot worse..!'

Bruce turned on his side, his eyes staring in the darkness as he tried in vain to shut out Mel Connor's incessant sobbing from across the upstairs hallway. Sleep was a long way off.

He went home on Thursday afternoon, leaving Mel silent and uncommunicative. Her parents had remained, prepared to stay for as long as necessary, and they had given the distinct impression that he was now 'in the way'. Somehow, he had the feeling that they held him responsible.

He had eaten a meagre dinner, having little appetite. He avoided switching on the television, afraid that he would hear his friend's name mentioned. At nine o'clock, he was seated in the kitchen, staring at the bottle of whisky Simon had brought. It was meant to be for a celebration, but surely an emergency was of equal importance?

He knew that the nightmares would come, sooner or later; he woke up in a sweat, imagining that the was back in prison, tied to the bed and about to be tortured by a group of faceless individuals. He had no clear impression of what would happen to him, but the screams of torment from the other occupants indicated unthinkable agonies...

His heart was pounding; he got up, went to the en-suite and splashed cold water on his face; surely he hadn't drunk that much? He stumbled back to bed, pulled up the covers and, for the first time in years, he prayed.

Another nightmare ensued; the shouting had started again, the threatening commands, issued by masked figures who emanated unseen menace. He was being told to get down, they had guns, they were pointing at him...

He sat up again, blinking himself into wakefulness; this time, the shouting continued...

His heart now hammering in his chest, he jumped out of bed, crossed to the window and pulled the curtains open very slightly. Outside, in the light of the Greenock Esplanade's new LED street lighting, he saw a group of figures. Someone was lying face-down on the pavement, their hands behind their head, just as he had been commanded to do a week ago. Several other figures were pointing what looked like handguns at the prone figure. Two marked police cars blocked the road, their blue lights flashing.

Now, someone was walking up his driveway; they looked vaguely familiar. He pulled the curtains shut, retrieved his slippers and pulled on his dressing gown as the doorbell rang.

As soon as he opened the door, he recognised her: DCI Mazzoni. Her demeanour wasn't much improved but he realised that the malice of her glare was no longer directed at him.

'Mr Redpath, sorry to disturb...can I come in?'

Without a word, he held the door open and ushered her into the lounge, switching on the light. They stood blinking in its glare for a few moments until, finally, he managed to speak.

'Um...what's going on?'

It sounded lame and feeble, but he couldn't think of any more suitable words.

'Mr Redpath, I have to inform you that we've arrested a man on suspicion of attempting to enter your house, possibly with intent to harm you.'

He looked at her in astonishment. 'What? To harm me...but who—?'

She shook her head. 'At this stage I don't know, honestly. Look, we were given information from Chief Superintendent Jarvis, in Glasgow. She was concerned that one of this so-called Civil Guard crowd, one of the ones who got away, might try and...'

She looked away briefly '...well, they might try and make contact with you, let's just say.'

'What? Why on earth would they do that?'

He sat down and DCI Mazzoni, uninvited, did the same. She looked across at him and raised an eyebrow.

'Mr Redpath, you're an intelligent man, you're going to be one of the key witnesses in this case. Why do you think? The man was armed...'

He suddenly felt physically sick. 'Y-you mean he was planning to kill me?'

She shrugged. 'I can't say for sure. But we've apprehended him now, so you're safe.'

As the shock subsided, it was replaced with a rising anger.

'Wait—are you telling me that you suspected that this might happen and you didn't say anything? You were using me as bait?'

'Well, that's being a bit extreme...'

'No it bloody isn't! You were obviously watching my house, by your own admission suspecting that someone would come after me to silence me. God-all-bloody-mighty, this is an absolute disgrace!'

'Mr Redpath, calm down, please. We had the situation completely under—'

Bruce jumped to his feet, glaring down at the officer. 'CALM DOWN! Don't you fucking tell me to calm down, DCI Mazzoni! First of all, you arrest me for something I didn't do, you were about to charge me for a murder I didn't commit, on the strength of evidence that was clearly fabricated, and now I'm nearly killed in my bloody bed! And you have the nerve to tell *me* to calm down!'

'Mr Redpath, please...'

'NO, DCI Mazzoni. I'll thank you to get out of my house. NOW. Oh, and if you *do* happen to suspect that anyone else is thinking of making an attempt on my life, it might be common courtesy for you to inform me beforehand!'

◆◆◆◆◆◆◆◆◆◆◆◆

Simon returned on Friday afternoon, his mood suitably sombre. Bruce had lain in bed until nearly twelve, after having drifted into a deep, dreamless sleep about six a.m. They sat in the lounge, each clutching a mug of instant coffee. Finally, Simon spoke.

'Look, this was all complete news to me, I had no idea—'

'I didn't think that you would have, I just can't bloody believe that the police were prepared to take the risk of someone killing me.'

'Mazzoni has assured me that they were keeping you under careful surveillance.'

Bruce was still furious. 'Yes, but what about the night before? I stayed at Mel's—what if this bloody killer had come sneaking about down there? A lot of good their bloody surveillance would have done in Inverkip! The kids were in the house too, it doesn't bear thinking about!'

'Point taken. Look I don't think that there's a great deal we can do about it, but I *will* make a formal complaint to Norah Jarvis.'

Bruce took a deep breath, trying to calm himself. 'Have they any idea who he is?'

Simon nodded. 'Yes, he's an ex-Royal Marine by the name of Andy Moore.'

Bruce's eyes opened wide in surprise. 'What—wait, wasn't his sister killed by...'

'...Rik Shearer? Yes, one of my former clients and the first victim of the Civil Guard—well, the first *official* victim, I suppose! Looks like he's been planning revenge ever since he left the forces. They think he was one of the two who escaped from Glenbreakerie House, quite probably the guy who whacked you and stole Gibson's Range Rover.'

Bruce sat in a shocked silence for a few moments as Simon continued. 'They don't seem to think he was actually one of, well, the 'Jury', I suppose you'd call them. He was in command of the team who carried out the abductions and, ultimately, the brutal punishments. A true psychopath, by the sounds of it, completely devoid of empathy, it seems, and driven purely by revenge. They've already got the other so-called 'soldiers' in custody. Fortunately they were all arrested when they raided the House.'

'So who was the other one who managed to get away? Do they have any idea?'

Simon shook his head. 'No, they don't.'

The conversation moved on to discussing Bruce's return to work. He was insistent that he was coming back after the weekend and, with some reluctance, Simon had finally agreed, with the proviso that he could move the date back if he didn't feel up to it. Eventually, the conversation stalled slightly and Simon stood up.

'Right, I need to get on, got a lot to do—as always! Look, try not to worry, Bruce, you should be fine now.'

Bruce wasn't entirely convinced; as he opened the door, Simon continued, trying to lighten the tone. 'Looks like it's going to be a decent enough weekend—are you golfing tomorrow?'

The look of horror on Bruce's face elicited a slight gasp from Simon Fox. 'Oh shit, I'm so sorry, Bruce, I never...well, have you anything else planned for the weekend?'

Bruce shrugged. 'Actually, I had; something I haven't done for years, although I'm not sure that I really feel like it now.'

Simon gave him a weak smile. 'Life goes on, Bruce, life goes on. What was it anyway?'

Bruce managed a smile in return. 'Well, if you must know, I was going through to Edinburgh Zoo.'

'The Zoo? God, I've not been there for years!'

'Me neither. Then an early dinner and a visit to the theatre. Well, that *was* the plan.'

'Don't be silly, Bruce; go, you need a bloody break. I take it you're not going on your own?'

Bruce smiled again; a slightly broader smile this time. 'No, I'm not.'

Simon slapped his friend's shoulder. 'Good for you—so who's the lucky lady?'

'That *would* be telling, Simon.'

Simon Fox frowned. 'Wait—I hope it's not bloody Miriam Bonnar?'

This time Bruce laughed. 'Bugger off, Simon—I'll see you on Monday!'

Chapter 26

Monday 15th December

It felt like an age since he had walked up the worn stone steps that led to the Blytheswood Square offices of Redpath, Fox, Carnegie, yet it had only been just over two weeks. The period he would normally take as a summer holiday, he realised.

As he opened the door, Rayna Aherne was already half way along the hallway, arms stretched wide as she clutched him to her not inconsiderable bosom. She stroked the back of his head, murmuring in her soft, Irish brogue, 'Oh Bruce, it's just wonderful to have you back.'

She smelt of fresh laundry; he mumbled into her shoulder. 'And it's wonderful to be back, Rayna. I've really missed you.'

He opened his eyes; a grinning Torquil Carnegie was standing behind Mrs Aherne, his hand outstretched; extricating himself from the warmth of her embrace, he took the young man's hand, returning the fierce grip.

'Great to have you back, Boss. Y'okay? Seems like you've developed a bit of a rep!'

Bruce couldn't help but return the enthusiastic grin. 'Really? We'll see...good to see you, Torquil.'

Mrs Aherne fussed for a few moments more, then announced.

'They're ready for you in the boardroom, Mr Redpath, coffee'll be along in a jiffy; I've got your favourites, dark chocolate gingers.'

He briefly wondered just *how* much she actually knew about him.

He had been very slightly nervous but the Partners' meeting had been a balm to his still-troubled psyche. After asking about his well-being, he had been brought up to date with the more mundane matters of office life. It seemed that Torquil had been correct; apparently there had been considerable demand for his services following the coverage of the case that was now officially known in the media as 'The Civil Guard.'

'Maybe need to put your fees up, Bruce,' Simon had quipped.

Bruce smiled; it was good to be back.

As the meeting had ended, Olivia Carnegie had reached into her briefcase, handing Bruce a sheet of paper.

'Thought you might like a read at this; she's bloody irrepressible, the woman! I've just printed it off the website.'

Bruce took the sheet and started to read.

'Bonnar's Byte
By Miriam Bonnar.'

'...you heard it here first, folks...!'

'The man who lived...(apologies, Ms Rowling!). I hate to say I told you so, dear readers...but I told you so...'

Bruce smiled and folded the sheet, placing it in his pocket.

'Thanks, Olivia, I'll read it later. I'm not quite in the mood for further revelations about myself. I'm surprised to see her back in the bit so soon, though.'

Olivia gave him a strange look. 'Well, *you* are!'

'Yes, but I wasn't...'

The smile faded, his voice tailed off; he wasn't sure how much Olivia knew about the brutal treatment of Miriam Bonnar and now certainly wasn't the time to tell her. Aware of a slight tension, Simon closed his briefcase and looked over at him.

'Right, that seems to be us then. Bruce, great to have you back with us...'

There was a mumble of assent.

'...I've just got a quick call to make, then I'll come through and have a chat, okay?'

◈

Bruce placed the piece of paper back on the desk just as Simon knocked on his door.

'Come in.'

His friend entered and sat down, unbuttoning his jacket and hitching up his well-pressed suit trousers. He nodded across.

'You've read it, then?'

'Yes. Actually, it paints me in not too bad a light, which makes a pleasant change.'

'Won't do your 'rep,' as Torquil succinctly puts it, any harm, then?'

Bruce smiled. 'No, I don't suppose it will.'

Simon gave him a scrutinising look. 'You're *sure* you're okay? You don't need to come back, we can easily move—'

'No, I'm absolutely fine, thanks, Simon. This is exactly what I need, to get back into the routine. To be honest, I was running out of things to do in the house.'

'Em, I noticed that you had Dorothy's picture back on display; are you okay with that?'

'Yes, I am, and I've put more photos out since. It was high time... the great irony is that, for all those years, I suppressed any thoughts of her when, in fact, I should have been celebrating her life, the wonderful years that we had together. I wish I had just let time do the healing—so much for the expensive therapy, eh?'

A serious look suddenly crossed Simon's handsome face.

'How's Mel bearing up?'

Bruce didn't reply immediately. The truth was, she wasn't bearing up at all and he was worried that she was having a breakdown of some sort. The Connors' had a not-inconsiderable mortgage, two nice cars, two young kids; it didn't bear thinking about, although he had thought of little else for the last few days. His own mortgage was long since paid off; he was comfortably prosperous and he had decided that, one way or another, he would make sure that Mel was looked after. Simon broke into his reverie.

'I had a chat with Rob; he doesn't want me to defend him.'

'What? Why not, for God's sake?'

'Says it wouldn't look good; apart from the fact that you're my partner, it seems that retention of my services is pretty much seen an admission of guilt.'

Bruce shook his head angrily, he would have happily covered Simon's fees for his friend. His mind paused mid-thought; a friend who had put Rohypnol in his drink, a friend who had been complicit in his abduction and subsequent arrest. But a friend he had known since his school-days, a friend whose wife was Mel Connor...

Simon continued. 'I've spoken to his representation though, in an unofficial capacity. They've advised him to plead guilty, he's been told that it'll go better for him; I also suspect there's a bit of a deal been made, he may be providing the authorities with additional information. It's out of my hands now anyway, I'm afraid.'

They sat in a contemplative silence for a few moments, then Simon smiled.

'So how was your day out in Edinburgh?'

'What? Oh, yes, it was really nice, thanks. The Zoo was amazing—it's changed a lot since I was last there, it's greatly improved. Lovely dinner too, a nice wee place at the top of the Royal Mile.'

'And did you have a sleep-over?'

Bruce chuckled. 'None of your business, Mr Fox!'

'No, I don't suppose it is!'

The phone on his desk rang; as Bruce lifted the receiver, Simon took his expensive Cross pen from his pocket and scribbled something on the notepad that lay on the desk. He tore off the sheet and folded it, placing it front of his friend.

'I'm not sure if you're aware...'

Bruce held his hand up as he placed the receiver against his ear.

'Just a minute...Hello...Mrs Aherne...Mrs Aherne...!'

'...but the police are still searching for the final member of the Civil Guard...'

'...Mrs Aherne...what on earth's the matter...calm down, please...'

Simon got to his feet, buttoning the jacket of his suit.

'...Mrs Ah...WHAT?'

Bruce looked up at Simon Fox as the door to his office burst open. Two figures entered; one, a tall, well-built man with a shaved head and a neatly-trimmed beard, was closely followed by a woman who Bruce recognised immediately as Norah Jarvis, the officer who had interviewed him in Helen Street following his most recent arrest. He shuddered at the memory. She gave Bruce a curt nod then addressed Simon.

'You are Mr Simon Fox?'

'Yes.'

She held up her warrant card. 'I am Detective Chief Superintendent Norah Jarvis, this is Detective Sergeant Gordon Mills.'

Simon simply nodded as Bruce continued to stare, mouth agape; in the background, Rayna Aherne's near-hysterical voice continued to sound from the telephone.

'Mr Fox, I must ask you to accompany us. I must also warn you that anything...'

As the Chief Superintendent proceeded to caution him, Simon appeared to hang on her every word, as if hearing them for the first time. Bruce looked down at the folded piece of paper, opening it slowly. Two words were written in Simon's flamboyant script.

I'm sorry.

As Sergeant Mills firmly placed his hand on Fox's shoulder and proceeded to usher him from Bruce's office, Simon turned and, for one last time, briefly flashed the familiar Cheshire Cat grin at his friend.

'Remember Bruce... Justice and the law...two *entirely* different creatures..."